Crestwood Lake

AMY +
DAWN -

HOW WONDERFULLY
EVIL !

Crestwood Lake

Mark R. Vogel

ISBN: 1508863504
ISBN 13: 9781508863502
Library of Congress Control Number: 2015904210
CreateSpace Independent Publishing Platform
North Charleston, South Carolina

To my dearest Yang...
The best part of my life.

ACKNOWLEDGEMENTS

First and foremost I want to thank my wife, Yang. She is consistently supportive, and proud of all of my writing endeavors. She always provides her undivided attention whether I'm reading her my latest chapter, thinking out loud, or agonizing over innumerable decisions and details. Along with her trusted input, she has repeatedly helped me to crystallize my thinking. Thank you for everything my love.

I am indebted to my writing group, the HighlandScribes, for their invaluable feedback. They have been absolutely essential to improving my writing, and expanding my awareness of multifarious issues. Thank you to Lauren Cerruto, Joan Lisi, Terry Mullaney, Rob Palmer, Debbie Patrucker, Mira Peck, Wendy Vandame, and Nicole Yori.

I want to express a special thank you to fellow HighlandScribe Rob Palmer who, shortly after meeting me, masochistically offered to read my entire manuscript, and furnished a most helpful critique. Moreover, Rob has gone above and beyond the call of duty, (clichés are allowed in Vogelville), ceaselessly making himself available to offer his knowledge and sound guidance.

I must also extend my appreciation to one of my biggest fans: my mom. She voraciously read every chapter, hot off the press. And while she vehemently denies harboring any bias, she sings my highest praises (except when my characters are cursing or engaging in uncensored sexual activity).

Last, but certainly not least, I am deeply grateful to my good friends, Dr. Michael Esposito, and Dr. Scott Guerin, who served as my think tanks, consultants, reality checks, and tech support. Multi-talented and polymathic, they provided ideas and objective feedback on an array of subjects related to formulating this novel.

THE LAKE HOUSE

I don't know why I bought a lake house. Or actually I should say…I don't know why I bought *this* lake house. I always wanted to live on the water. I've always marveled at homes that were perched upon the shores of secluded, idyllic lakes. I mused about how lucky these people were, tucked away from society's commotion: the scenery, the tranquility, the splendor of nature unfurling itself at their threshold.

This lake house—with its glorious panorama of its gentle tarn, nestled into the undulating hills. Even the trees reveled at their fortunate purlieu. *This* lake house—which cost me more than my limited means should have permitted. I had no luxuries: no frivolous escapades to grant my mind an occasional, albeit ephemeral, respite. I had few comforts. I simply had the house. I simply had the view. I simply had…the memories of *her*.

This lake house—the one my wife, if she were still alive, would have never even considered. She would have balked at the price. She would have recoiled at the overgrown thicket of vines and brush that blanketed the steep incline to the water's edge. She would have hated how old the dwelling was. She would have been disgusted by all the bugs, the mice and other wildlife the woodland harbored. And if she knew, she would have been repulsed by the rumor that a previous owner, sixty years ago, killed his wife and himself in the master bedroom.

Old Gil Pearson who sold me the house denied the hearsay. He attributed it to peoples' fascination with the macabre, and the alcohol-laden gossip that was so recklessly dispensed at the local tavern. But what else could he say?

Yes, sir, I remember when I was still a youth. Walt Lorimer took his shot-gun, unloaded one barrel in his wife's head, and the other one in his. I heard it took days for them to clean up all the dried blood. Took a lot longer than that to get the smell outta the place. They didn't find the bodies for two months. So you ready to close the deal or what?

No, Gil had no choice but to deny it, whether it was true or not. I don't think he truly believed it and strangely, for some inexplicable reason, I didn't care one way or another. I never believed in ghosts, clairvoyance, God, or any of that psychic or spiritual mumbo jumbo. As my father always said, it was the living you had to fear, not the dead. And besides, I was already dead. There wasn't much more the living or the dead could take from me now. I had nothing but the house. Nothing but the vista. Nothing but my memories. Nothing but the realization that I was living in the kind of home that I had always dreamed of; that my wife would have despised. That in order to fulfill this dream, all of my others had to be shattered. If I believed in fate, I would curse its ironic sadism and twisted sense of humor.

It was summertime. Everything was in bloom, including the weeds and the bugs; especially those long, hairy centipedes that made my skin crawl on sight. "Thousand-leggers," Gil called them. They scurried across my floor like distorted little demons. I'd stomp them with all my might and still their dismembered legs would twitch.

But it was summer. It was warm and sunny and that eased, but did not eliminate my pain. The mere fact that my wife never set foot on the property assuaged some grief. The house was plagued by folklore, creatures and crepitations, but not reminders of her.

The town of Crestwood Lake (denominated by the three hundred acre lake that my property overlooked), was a picturesque Vermont community with a population under three thousand. The woods that surrounded Crestwood Lake were part of a state forest, about fifty square miles in area.

I don't know the details of the colonial period, but apparently the town was established in the 1690's. At some point it was abandoned and the government arrogated the land. In the late nineteenth century the state, in need of money, began selling plots. People built lakeside cabins and hunters, anglers, and summer vacationers rented them. A handful of individuals lived in them year round. Then, an out-of-state realty firm began buying up lakefront property. They tore down the cabins, built one-family homes, and sold them. They made millions. This development continued and became the Town of Crestwood Lake in the early twentieth century.

Gil lived about a mile down the road. My house had passed from one owner to another over the years. Lorimer, the alleged madman, had purchased it brand new from the developer who built it. After the Lorimers (whatever their demise), the property passed to their children who promptly sold it. Facilitated by an unusual number of deaths and a divorce or two, it eventually landed in Gil's father's hands. After his father died, Gil rented it intermittently for many years to numerous tenants. No one seemed to stay long. More than a few had died there. And Gil never chose to live in it. When asked why, he was oddly evasive. Now in his early seventies Gil simply wished to rid himself of the property and use the money for whatever amount of time he had left.

I never reached out to my neighbors, or should I say, the people who lived within sight of my corner of the lake. My mind was not conducive to socializing. I had no close friends. I was at an age where death and retirement to warmer states had depleted any proximate social ties. And I was so weary of being asked how I was doing, or being inundated with platitudes, that I allowed the few connections I had to wither. I didn't have the energy. It took all my might just to overcome my languor for a few hours each morning to accomplish household chores. More time than not I wallowed in my lassitude with soft music, fragrant candles, Russian vodka and tobacco. I needed every sense to be soothed; every portal to my brain to be pacified.

I felt but one breath away from an overwhelming, yet indescribable sense of doom. It was as if my vices, the feeble pleasures I had left, barely kept me from the precipice of something...something aching to consume me.

I absolutely hated my basement. It was dark, dank, and musty, and although I couldn't see them, I could sense the legions of vermin creeping behind the walls. One day, while venturing into the house's netherworld for a tool, an odor immediately assaulted me. Sure enough, another dead mouse was splayed out in one of my sundry traps. The metal bar always caught them right on the neck, leaving them with this wide-eyed, shocked stare—a dead stare. Yet somehow alive enough to peer right through your brain to the back of your skull. Strangely, I pondered what they had felt.

Then there was the ritual of disposing of the carcass. I would lean over the railing of my deck, hold the trap with the fingertips of one hand, and with the fingertips of the other, endeavor to unhinge the snare and shake loose its dead captive. I held my breath, grimaced, and tried not to let the vile, disease-ridden cadaver touch my skin. I always tossed them into the jungle of my backyard and never into my trash bin. They had already befouled my home enough. I didn't need their necrotic fetor infecting the air that I breathed any further.

And the house creaked at night. Of course, all houses creak at night. But these were strange creaks—unnerving creaks—piercing creaks. Creaks that on occasion compelled me to grab my pistol and reconnoiter the entire domicile. I could almost hear the mice and centipedes snickering at me as I skulked my way through the darkness, feebly stabbing the air with my weapon.

Before long it was fall. The lake was beautiful: spectacularly encompassed by the dizzying array of vibrantly colored trees. The air was never so clean and pure. I often resolved to meander down to the water and simply bask in autumn's palette. I chastised myself for not taking full advantage of my lakeside home. But then a few drinks later I could relinquish those thoughts, and any other pangs my psyche was repressing. But never the thoughts of her. Never the void in the pit of my stomach that would never be fulfilled again.

One night I was preparing my supper. I used to love to cook, especially for the both of us. Now, what was the point? Food was just a means of avoiding hunger. But every so often I would have a better day; a day where my languidness would temporarily abandon me. These were the times, few and far between, when I could relive a modicum of the joy that I used to glean from the kitchen.

I was making a beef stew. I needed comfort food, something hearty and rich. It was one more way of shoveling sand against the emotional tide. While chopping the onions, I caught a whiff of something fetid. Where was it coming from? I hadn't burned a candle in days and always smoked outside. I sniffed each one of my ingredients: the meat, the onions, the potatoes, the carrots, and the pot of beef broth. They all smelled normal. It seemed to pass so I ignored it and continued to work. Moments later it returned. I started sniffing my knife, the cutting board, and the counter. Anyone watching me would have thought I was losing my mind. Where the hell was that smell coming from? And then it dawned on me...the mousetraps. I scrambled into the basement, dashing from trap to trap, but didn't find a single mouse. They were all set, with untouched bait, just waiting for the moment to snap a hapless rodent's neck. I returned to the kitchen, just in time to catch a fiendish centipede darting across the floor. I stomped it so hard that I felt a jolt in my ankle. Heinous creatures. I wondered whether they carried the souls of evil spirits or dead murderers. Then I became enraged with myself. It infuriated me that this odious little bug could cause my normal, rational mind to ponder such absurdities. The one thing I always had, probably the only thing I had left, was my reason. And yet these wretched little monsters had the power to cause preternatural fantasies to invade my mind. I drank a large glass of vodka and had a smoke. I finished making my stew, ate, took a handful of pills, and went to bed.

A week or so later I was sitting in my favorite chair: a large, plush, amber-colored recliner, positioned next to my picture window overlooking the lake. When not inebriated or forlorn I would turn on my elevator music, light a candle, plop in my chair, read, and lazily glance at the water. It was a peaceful escape. I kept reminding myself that it was healthier than most of my other urges. If only I could sate my soul as well as my senses.

I was reading an old book about the French and Indian War when an odor caught my attention, that same odor, the same odor that fouled my stew, the smell of decomposition...*the smell of death.* I erupted with a torrent of obscenities. I bolted into the basement and checked the traps, once again finding nothing. I ran back upstairs, moving every piece of furniture on the ground floor. Perhaps one of those little devils died under my couch. Nothing. I went outside and surveyed the entire perimeter. The woods were home to countless other animals, any one of which could have expired within wafting distance of my windows. Still nothing. I went back inside. The scent, although not intense, seemed to permeate every room. The upstairs. I didn't inspect the upstairs. I practically flew up the stairs and searched everywhere, probing under the bed, sliding my armoire from its resting place, moving bookshelves, scouring closets, even lifting up the rug. I found nothing but two old, desiccated, centipede corpses. As obnoxious as they may be, their moldering carcasses couldn't explain the smell. Finally giving up, I lit a bunch of candles and a cigarette, this time in the house.

Days later and the smell continued. It assaulted me throughout the house. How could this be? It was near freezing outside but I had no choice. I flung open every window. I lit my wood-burning stove in the bedroom and my fireplace in the living room. I fed the fireplace until the flames roared. The wind blew through my windows with a fearsome chill. But I sat next to the fire with my bottle and my cigarettes, and kept warm. Hours passed. I eventually nodded off. When I awoke the flames were dying and the house was bitterly cold. I closed the windows, stoked the fireplace, and drank more vodka, eventually falling asleep on the floor.

I awoke late in the morning to the most horrible stench I've ever encountered. An absolutely putrefying miasma that reeked beyond description. I was about to scream, but heard a knock on my door. It was Gil, holding a small box.

"Sorry to bother you Mr. Burke, but I found some important papers I thought you should have."

I ushered him in, trying to think of how to explain the smell. I was so embarrassed that I didn't say anything at first. Gil seemed not to notice.

"I was cleaning out my attic when I came across this box I'd forgotten about. There's an old survey of the property, a certificate of easement, some old tax papers, the paperwork from when the roof was redone, and some other stuff. Never know if you'll need it."

"Thanks, I appreciate it. I'm so sorry about the smell. I know it's terrible. Something died somewhere. I canvassed the entire house and property and couldn't find anything. I opened all my windows for hours last night, but to no avail. I don't know what else to do."

"Ya know," said Gil, "sometimes critters get in through the attic. They get up in the rafters or more often than not, inside the walls. I suppose if one expired in there that might explain it."

"Yeah," I said. "That must be it. I checked everything else."

I started to offer Gil some coffee, but he promptly told me he had to be on his way. I imagined he didn't want to spend one more nauseating moment in my house. Gil wished me luck with my "critter problem" and left. He looked at me a little different than usual. I didn't think too much of it at first. Then I wondered what he must have been wondering about me. Did he think I caused the smell? Did he think I killed something? Someone? That I committed murder and hid the body in the walls? Stop. Stop, I told myself. I was doing it again: allowing my orderly mind to run amok.

I turned my attention to the prevailing matter. How could I get a dead animal out of the walls? Even if I knew its location, a large section of the room would still have to be gutted. No, that wasn't practical. I had to wait it out. It had to subside at some point.

But the smell persisted, day after day. I would open all the windows and maintain a raging fire. I was going through my wood supply rapidly. Worse yet, I had not the energy or the inclination to chop more. I had a full tank of oil so I cranked up the heat. Thank God for my vodka and pills. I benumbed myself into a narcosis each night, not solely to sleep, but to escape the omnipresent rancidity.

One night I couldn't sleep. Even after drinking and taking two pills, the smell, which was getting worse, was devouring me. The windows in the bedroom were already wide open. I felt as if I was going crazy. Sleep was my only real solace: the only time when my brain was comatose enough to block out the smell, the loneliness, and the memories of *her*. I went downstairs and retrieved a new bottle of vodka. I took a few more pills. I drank some more. I lit a cigarette. I took a swig. I took a pill. I took a puff. *I took an axe.*

That was it! I had no more forbearance. This was my home. It was supposed to be my refuge. Hadn't I agonized enough? Her death had already ravaged my life. Now I had to suffer at the hands of some filthy animal's death? I would find the merciless beast that infested my home and by God I would kill him again!

I swung the axe into the wall. I took one more gulp of vodka. I swung it again, and again. I ran to the next room and I swung it into the walls there. I furiously ran up the stairs like a raving lunatic and started swinging at the walls of my bedroom, creating gaping, ragged holes. The odor intensified, hitting me like a wave of death. At last I had found the scoundrel's final resting place! I swung the axe with all of the insanity I could muster. I swung it for every noxious breath I had taken. I swung it for every sleepless night. I swung it for every goddamn centipede I had to kill. I swung it for every moment I cried over her loss. I swung it again, and again, and again, and again, and...

• • •

The red and blue lights flashed in a steady rotation, tinting the darkness with an eerie flicker. A dark-blue Chevy pickup truck pulled up behind the ambulance and the two police cruisers blocking the road. A burly officer emerged, spit, and walked down the driveway. "Who called this in?" barked Captain Butch Morgan.

"Gil Pearson," responded one of the patrolmen. "He's over there by the front door."

Morgan walked directly over to Gil, almost as if he was going to walk through him. "What happened here, Gil?"

"Good evening to you too, Butch."

Morgan just glared at him.

"Well, I hadn't seen or heard from Mr. Burke in a while. Last time we talked was maybe three weeks ago when I dropped off some documents. I happened to pass by tonight and saw his newspapers had piled up. Thought I'd check in on him. The lights in the upstairs bedroom were on. I rang his bell a couple of times, but no one answered. Then I noticed a lot of his windows were wide open. Thought that was fairly strange for this time of year. The door was unlocked so I let myself in. The heat was turned up yet most of the windows were open. Then I smelled something—something awful. That's when I got a really bad feeling. I called for him but there was no answer. I went through the house. There were holes all over the walls. The smell was horrific. Then I found him in the bedroom. Lying there dead, decomposing, with an axe in his hand. Room looked like a dozen maniacs went berserk. All the walls were smashed. That's when I called the police."

"All right," said Morgan. "We'll take it from here. But I'll need you to come down the station tomorrow to make an official report."

"No problem," said Gil.

Later that night Gil's doorbell rang. It was Morgan. "What's up, Butch? Thought I was supposed to see you tomorrow?"

"I need to talk to you now, and alone."

"Sure, c'mon in."

Morgan strode into Gil's living room and took a seat on the brown leather couch. A small fire burned in the fireplace. Above the mantel was a framed reproduction of the Declaration of Independence. Gil's hoary terrier, Betsy, rested on her doggie bed in the corner.

"Wanna drink?" asked Gil.

Morgan nodded.

"I haven't replaced the bottle of bourbon you finished. I trust rye will do?"

"That's fine," said Morgan.

Gil brought out a bottle of rye and two snifters and placed them on the rectangular glass coffee table. He gave them each a generous pour. Gil sat in the matching loveseat perpendicular to the couch.

Morgan looked Gil right in the eyes and said, "Gil…you and I go way back. I need you to be straight with me." Morgan took a gulp of his rye. "This isn't the first body I've had to pull outta that house of yours."

"It's *not* my house anymore."

"Gil I'm in no fucking mood. I don't give a shit about the particulars. I want some answers and I want them now. I'm sick of pulling bodies out of that house. I've known you for a long time and I've done you more than a few favors over the years. Don't make me remind you of the things I made go away for you. Things that could still come back and bite you on the ass. Now this is all just between you and me, off the record. But I'm not leaving here until I get some fucking answers."

Gil drank all his rye in one long swig, poured himself another and took a deep breath. He gazed around the room aimlessly, almost as if in a daze. Finally he said, "The house is haunted."

"What?" said Morgan squinting. "Haunted how? You mean like ghosts?"

"No, not ghosts. Well maybe, but that's not the issue."

"Then what the hell are you talking about?"

Gil drank down his second serving of rye. "Haunted doesn't always mean ghosts. Whoever lives there gets premonitions about their own death. Funny thing is, they don't know that it's their death that's being conveyed."

"When you say premonition," asked Morgan, "you mean like a vision?"

"No not necessarily. People always think premonitions are visions, dreams, or vague feelings. Sometimes they are, but premonitions can take many forms. In fact, they can come to you through any of your senses. Or at least that's the way it worked at this house."

Morgan finished his rye and poured himself another. "Go on," he said.

"Well, remember the guy, I can't recollect his name, Murphy I think, who died there two years ago?"

"Yeah," said Morgan.

"He heard screams for months. People thought he was crazy, that he was hearing voices. Damn near got committed one time."

"He died of a heart attack," said Morgan.

"Yes, but if you recall, he phoned 911 screaming in pain. Had kidney stones real bad. Even the neighbors heard him. The pain, his screaming, his anxiety…gave him a heart attack while he was waiting for the ambulance. He had heard his own death screams for months. Then that woman about twenty years ago: the flamboyant blonde who cheated on her husband. Kept going to the doctor because she had this strange, bitter taste in her mouth. I know because I used to fool around with the doctor's nurse. Anyway, her husband ended up poisoning her with cyanide. Slipped it in her drink"

"And cyanide supposedly tastes like bitter almonds," said Morgan.

"That's right," said Gil.

"What about Lorimer, the guy who shot his wife and himself. What was his premonition?"

"Can't say," replied Gil. "I was just a little boy. I suspect this stuff started after that incident, but who knows?"

"So what happened to Burke?"

"He *smelled* his own death."

Morgan thought for a moment and said, "You smelled his decaying body when you stopped by tonight."

"I did," said Gil.

"But how do you know *he* smelled it before he died?"

"Like I told you, I stopped in to see him three weeks ago. He was going on and on about this death-like stench in the house. How it was driving him crazy. How he searched the whole damn place inside out and couldn't find anything."

"And…"

"Well that's just it," said Gil. "I didn't smell anything."

THE INTRUDER

My divorce was finally behind me. It was a typical divorce: enmity, screaming, finger-pointing, lawyers, fighting over property and money. Thank God we didn't have kids. We ultimately agreed on selling our house, paying off the mortgage, and splitting what was left over. I used my share toward a down payment on my new digs: a quaint colonial in a remote section of the county, in the town of Crestwood Lake. It was bigger than what I needed, but the best thing about it was how secluded it was. My property abutted protected woodland: thousands of acres of peace and quiet, just like my childhood home. I had only two neighbors within sight, the Carltons across the street, and Betty, an elderly woman who lived next door.

The house had two main floors, an attic, and a basement. The upstairs had four bedrooms. The master bedroom is where I slept. I turned the smallest one into a laundry room. Another I used for storage. The last one became my office. It was on the front side of the structure and had a broad window facing the street. The basement was gross and damp, and I didn't use it. Half of it still had a dirt floor. It was replete with bugs, and dark, cobwebbed crawlspaces, and had only a few small windows. My garden tools I kept in an outdoor shed.

The house was old. Well before me, the Millers lived there, raising a son and a daughter. Mr. Miller's declining health eventually necessitated confinement to a nursing home. Sometime after his admission Mrs. Miller went to live with her daughter. The son stayed there for a while and then moved out of state. The property languished for years. Finally I purchased it from the daughter Margaret. Her parents had both passed on by then.

The house was airy with plenty of large windows, which I liked to keep open when the weather permitted. I cherished the smell of the clean, pure air as it swept through the rooms. I felt renewed by the invigorating, sylvan breezes. Whenever I felt a little anxious, I'd stand by one of my windows, deeply inhale the forest air, and envision my body and soul regenerating.

I also relished drenching my house with light. It seemed to mitigate the dysphoria that burgeoned if I thought too much about the past. So my windows were open and my shades were up. I had fresh air, light, and the beautiful arboreal scenery. Yes, outsiders could see in, but being at the end of a cul-de-sac, rarely did anyone get close enough. I kept the bedroom shades down for a modicum of privacy. Otherwise I strolled through the dwelling like the last person on earth. And if someone did get a peek of me in my bra and panties, oh well. The thought kind of titillated me a bit, truth be told.

But the deeper truth was that I was by no means ready for a new relationship. I desperately needed freedom to just be me, and to just be with me. I socialized occasionally with a few close girlfriends, but more than anything else, I needed time alone. My new home and its setting were perfect for the solitude I desired. Whatever unfulfilled need that begot my exhibitionistic whimsies would just have to wait.

If only I didn't have to work. If only I could just stay home, plant flowers, read, and imbibe the crisp air. But I wasn't rich and the brunt of my income went toward living expenses. So five days a week I dragged myself back to civilization. Five days a week I dealt with paperwork, meetings, and jerks: the guys who thought a divorce decree was a license to copulate indiscriminately. I wouldn't admit this, not even to my girlfriends, but I used it to my advantage. Men are so easy to manipulate. Actually, they manipulate themselves. It's just like dangling a steak in front of a dog. He'll perform all kinds of tricks just in the hope of getting it. I didn't sleep with any of them mind you. Didn't have to. In fact, I really didn't have to do all that much. I dressed femininely and attractively, but not overtly sexy. If you go too far the balance of power starts to shift. I smiled, I complimented, and I schmoozed, always in a nice pair of heels. It was so uncanny what a simple pair of heels could do. I could be completely covered in a pants suit, but add a pair of high heels and Ryan would take the extra service call, Mike would give me the last doughnut, and even my boss would act more pleasant. Dogs and steaks.

My driveway was next to the right side of the house, as viewed from the street. To the right of the driveway began the woods. One morning, leaving for work, I drove down its length and then made my usual right turn, passing the front of my house to continue along the meandering road. I glanced up at my home and suddenly gasped. Someone was standing in the window! I did a double take. It was gone. That was weird. I looked a third time. Still nothing. I thought no more about it and went to work.

However, it popped into my head later that day. The thought was creepy. What would I do, a single woman all alone, if some whacko *did* break in? I did own a gun. My father was a marine and served in the military police. After the service he worked as a bouncer, a private investigator, and even a bounty hunter. When I was a little girl he would take me into the woods beyond our backyard and teach me how to shoot. My father had an arsenal of pistols and he made sure I knew how to load and fire all of them. He always talked about knowing how to protect yourself. He knew the evil that men could do, and felt I would be safer if I knew how to use a weapon. My mother utterly hated it, but I thought it was cool. That was until I turned fifteen and discovered pot, boys, and sex.

When I got my first apartment, while I was still single, my father bought me a .25 automatic pistol. "A ladies' gun," he called it. Indeed, it was small, light, and easily fit in my hand. I sarcastically said, "Thanks for the housewarming gift Dad," and put the gun and bullets in a box in my closet. Now that box was in my attic. I still would have rather had some pretty dishes.

I loved my weekends, even though they went so fast. I didn't have to think about work and I didn't want to think about my ex. Nevertheless, he would intermittently call. I guess a divorce is never completely over. There's always something that comes back to haunt you. Or maybe he *chose* to haunt me. I don't know. The phone would ring and I'd cringe, waiting for the voice mail recording to finish:

"Hey Trish," he would say in his typical impassive voice. "It's Don. Just want you to know I found your birth certificate in one of our old boxes. I'll put it in the mail. See ya."

How was I to interpret that? Of course I need my birth certificate. But he didn't *need* to call and tell me. He could have just mailed it to me with a note. Maybe he was just being nice. Maybe I was reading too much in to it.

Or maybe the prick couldn't accept our divorce. Maybe this was his way of harassing me: veiling his petty spitefulness in facades of courtesy. He'd call other times too. Always with something seemingly important that didn't categorically require contact, yet important enough that if I challenged it, he could twist it around and make me look like the asshole. Don was quite talented at that. He also didn't take criticism or rejection well. Don had a fragile male ego and any affront incited a response. An acquaintance once told me about a woman Don had terrorized after their breakup. I asked him about it once. He summarily downplayed it and recriminated the acquaintance by claiming she was friends with the woman and therefore biased. Still, I didn't like the look in his eyes when I brought it up.

Finally I forced myself to stop thinking about him. I had wasted enough of my weekend processing all the permutations in my head. The next day, Sunday, was an unusually warm fall day. I resolved to get some serious yard work done before the cold weather arrived. After about three hours of toiling on my property I decided to take a break. I walked up my yard toward the front door to get some water. I looked up and there it was again! A tall dark figure standing in my upstairs office window! This time looking right at me! I couldn't make out the face, but clearly it was glaring straight at me. I gasped. I didn't know what to do. I ran across the street to the Carltons. I charged up to their front door and began ringing the doorbell furiously. Eve Carlton opened her door.

"Call the police! Call the police! Someone's in my house!"

Eve got on the phone. Meanwhile her husband Jim came downstairs to see what all the commotion was about. I told him what was happening. Jim got his shotgun and headed toward my house. Eve tried to stop him but he said, "I'm not going inside. I'm just gonna wait outside in case he tries to get away." I looked at my window again and didn't see anything.

Two squad cars pulled into the cul-de-sac. As the officers got out I quickly told them who I was and that I saw someone in my window. They drew their weapons and double-timed it up my driveway. Eve alerted them that the tall guy with light red hair and the shotgun was her husband. When Jim saw the police he put his gun down and told them he didn't see anybody leave. The officers went through my house from top to bottom and found nothing. They opened every closet. They inspected the attic. They shined their flashlights into every spooky crawlspace in the basement. They found nothing. They even searched the neighboring woods.

When the officers finished Jim waved us over. Eve and I walked up my driveway and met them by my front door.

"Don't know what to tell you, ma'am," drawled one of the officers. "We looked in every place someone could be in. We didn't find anyone. Didn't see or hear anything in the woods either."

Jim picked up his shotgun and unloaded it. "I didn't see or hear anything either. First thing I did was walk around the house and check out the woods."

"Is it possible you saw something else that looked like a person?" asked one of the officers.

They had me doubting myself. They reminded me to keep my doors locked and call them immediately if I saw anything. As if I didn't know that. They said they'd alert the rest of the squad and tell them to make some extra patrols during the next few days. I felt like a fool.

Jim and Eve came in, I made some tea, and they stayed with me a while to ensure I was OK. We had already met before and chatted on a few occasions. Like me, they were in their late thirties. Jim was a carpenter and a mason. Eve, a cute, short-haired brunette, was a clerk at the high school. As we were talking someone gently knocked on my door. It was Betty. We had already met as well. When I first moved in she welcomed me with a homemade pie and a long, pleasant chat.

"Hi, honey," said Betty. She kissed me on the cheek and rubbed my arm. "I saw the police come over here; I wanted to make sure you were all right."

Betty was a sweet lady. Most people would have called her a rube and I guess in a way she was. She was well into her seventies, old-fashioned, and not known for her intellect. But she exuded a genuine kindness and concern for others, something you don't see very much of these days. She was short, thin, had soulful brown eyes, and always wore her gray hair in a bun.

Betty joined us for tea and I filled her in on the latest drama in my life. I tried to explain away my perceptions. "What bothers me," I told the group, "is there's nothing in that room that would look like a person." I then went on to share my fears that maybe my ex was harassing me.

"Well," said Jim, "it'd be pretty hard to explain how he got out of here without being spotted, at least by me, before the cops got here. I mean…I guess if he ran full speed into the woods as you came over here, he might have been out of sight before I got there, but that's still a stretch."

We talked more about my ex and his character. Eve and Jim asked a slew of questions about him, almost as if they were detectives endeavoring to determine if he was a viable suspect. Eve assured me that our neighborhood was safe and rarely had any crime or shady figures. She went on to say how I was going through a difficult period and that stress and anxiety can have all sorts of effects on our minds.

Finally Betty spoke up: "You ain't going crazy, honey. People don't just see things…unless they're totally frickin' out of their minds and you ain't. You saw something, but it wasn't your ex. In fact, it wasn't even a person. Damn…everybody knows your house is haunted."

"What?" My eyes and mouth were wide open.

Jim raised his hand and quickly jumped in: "Now c'mon, Betty, don't go in to that malarkey. Trish has been scared enough today. What's wrong with you? You want her to start worrying about ghosts now too?"

"All I'm doing is telling her the truth. She oughta know."

Eve rolled her eyes. Jim sneered. Betty started talking about the Millers and their son.

"Their son didn't move away," said Betty. She took a sip of her tea. "He was murdered. He was murdered by his own father. Their son was a nut case. Was in and out of loony bins God knows how many times. Apparently one night he attacked the mother. The father had to shoot him to stop him. They buried him in the woods. Told everyone he was sent away to some funny farm in another state. Ever since then his spirit has haunted this place. I'm telling ya, honey, you ain't crazy, 'cause you ain't the first person to see things in this house."

Finally Eve couldn't tolerate any more. "Betty, those are all rumors. You didn't even live here until after the Millers and their son were gone."

"Same as you," said Betty jutting her jaw forward.

"That's right," responded Eve. "But that doesn't make what you're saying true. Mr. Miller went to a nursing home, Mrs. Miller went to her daughter's, the son was here for a while, and then he moved away."

"That ain't like how I heard it. I was told by more than one person in this town that old man Miller killed his son. And ever since then weird things have been happening here."

"Of course you heard it from more than one person," said Jim. "That's what a rumor mill is. One person tells another, who tells another, and so on. Next thing you know you have a whole bunch of people reciting the same story. Makes it seem valid because there's so many people saying it. But the truth is everybody is just spitting out the same hogwash."

They went back and forth for a few more rounds. Personally I had heard enough, so that when everybody started to leave, I felt more relieved than alone and frightened. Jim and Eve told me to contact them if I needed anything. I could see the concern in their eyes.

Betty was the last one out. She hung back and let Jim and Eve get halfway down my driveway. Then she looked at me and said, "Honey, I don't mean to scare you. I'm trying to reassure you. You ain't crazy 'cause I've seen his ghost myself a time or two. He peers out the windows and then disappears. I wouldn't worry about it though. Spirits don't harm the ones who did them no wrong. Most are just lost souls still connected to the places that were meaningful to them in life. You ever get the willies or just need some company, you come over and see me ya hear?"

Betty's remarks struck me as odd. On one hand she was trying to soothe me, but on the other, she blithely informed me that I have a ghost and not to worry about it. As if this shit happens every day. Now I was starting to get the creeps. I never believed in such things and even if it wasn't true, it still made me nervous. I slept terribly that night. I lay in bed for hours listening to every little creak, picturing ghosts. Damn you Betty. Why did you have to tell me that story? I actually started wishing it was just my ex being a jerk.

The next day when I came home from work I walked in the door and got the strangest sensation. *As if someone had been in my house.* I dismissed my feelings and chalked them up to yesterday's ghost stories. *And then I noticed things had been moved.* One of my chairs that I always kept tucked under its accompanying table was halfway pulled out. Well…maybe I left it there and forgot about it. But then one of my upstairs windows, which I could have sworn I closed, was partially open. The placement of various items on my dresser seemed different but I wasn't sure. It was as if they had been moved just slightly. As if someone had picked them up, examined them, and set them back down. Then I found my panty drawer was ajar. That's when I freaked out.

I called Jim. He came right over, shotgun in hand. He searched the entire house and found nothing. We checked all the doors and windows. Everything was closed and locked except the one window that was partially open. But it was a second floor window and a ladder would have been needed to reach it. Moreover, the screen and the surrounding dust were undisturbed. No one had come in through that window. Jim strode around the house's perimeter, but found it equally barren of clues.

Jim said he'd keep an eye out, and if he was home during the day, he'd take sporadic walks around my property. But I could tell from his voice that he was starting to have doubts about my emotional stability. Eve called a little bit later and asked if I wanted to spend the night at their place, but I politely declined. I hung up the phone, but it rang again a few seconds later. I didn't check the caller ID; I assumed Eve had forgotten to tell me something.

"Hello," I said.

"Oh, Trish…uh…I didn't expect you to answer."

It was my ex. Goddamnit! He was the absolute last person I wanted to talk to. "What do you want, Don?" I said curtly.

"Uh, well I have a box with a bunch of your things, or things that I guess were ours, but I thought you might want. I've been going through stuff with the move and my new apartment. If you want I'll drop it off."

"No! I do not want you coming by or dropping off anything. Whatever it is just throw it out."

"Geeesh, you don't have to bite my head off. Ya know, I could have just thrown this stuff out and you would have never known. But I thought you might want it. I'm sorry; I was just trying to be considerate."

There it was: the old twist-the-situation-around-and-make-me-look-like-the-bad-guy routine. Only this time he wasn't exactly twisting. I did shout at him. I felt a twinge of guilt, but then I thought: *this prick could be sneaking into my house.* So as diplomatically as I could, I said, "Look, I'm sorry for snapping at you, but I really don't want to see you, and I really don't want you coming here. I appreciate your consideration, but I need to not have any contact with you right now. We *are* divorced you know. It's over. And I need it to truly *be* over in order to work through this. OK?"

"Well screw you! I was trying to do you a favor, but you just *have* to be a bitch. This is why we're divorced. Ya know, you'll get yours someday."

"What do you mean by that?"

Don told me where to go and angrily hung up the phone. That night I rummaged through my attic, found the .25 auto my father gave me, loaded it, and placed it in the nightstand drawer.

The week passed without any further incidents. Friday finally came. What a relief. I needed the weekend so bad. It took every ounce of my strength to get through the workweek with all the anxieties on my mind. The customers, the phone calls, the deadlines, the unwanted advances from the weirdo in the warehouse…I was sick of it all. I just wanted to go home and open a bottle of wine.

I walked through the door, placed my purse on the counter, and massaged my temples for a moment. I went straight to my bedroom, changed into my comfy clothes, came downstairs, put on some music, and poured myself a big glass of Chianti. I strolled out of the kitchen and dropped the glass, wine and all, as I screamed.

My basement door was open. I never go in the basement. I know it was closed earlier in the week after Jim had ventured down there while investigating the house. I ran straight to Eve and Jim's. Scurrying across my front yard I looked back…just in time to see the dark, shadowy figure in the window! Glaring at me once again!

I didn't bother with the bell. I pounded on the door. Eve answered. I was hysterical. I kept screaming "Call the police! Call the police!"

Eve held me, trying to calm me down. Jim called 911 and once again, grabbed his shotgun. He sprinted across the street, ran around the house to see if anyone had fled, and then dashed inside.

This time three police vehicles arrived, two standard cars and one pickup truck with a flashing light. The officers from the cars jumped out with automatic pistols in hand. An older officer, tall and muscular, stepped out of the pickup, brandishing a large revolver. He was obviously in charge. I couldn't hear him clearly, but he was directing the others. They headed straight for my house. I waited, trembling in Eve's arms across the street. I could see Betty wending her way toward us. Eventually the officers and Jim emerged—only the officers and Jim—no one else.

The older officer approached us, escorted by Jim. He wore the same tan pants and shirt as the other officers, only his pants had gold stripes on the outer sides, and his shirt sported a gold badge. He wasn't wearing a jacket or a hat. He seemed impervious to the cold. He was quite imposing, with a crusty exterior and a gruff manner.

"You the owner of the house, ma'am?"

"Yes, I am."

Betty was standing next to me at this point.

"Patricia Dukowski?" said the officer.

"Yes, well, um…for now."

The officer gave me a bemused stare.

"I just got divorced and will be legally changing back to my maiden name, but yes…uh…for now I'm Trish Dukowski."

"I'm Captain Morgan, Butch Morgan, Chief of the Crestwood Lake Police. I understand this is the second time you called us about someone being in your house?"

"Uh…well…yes…actually—"

"Ma'am, we went through every inch of the building and scanned the immediate vicinity. There's no one there."

"But my basement door was open. I always keep it closed. And I thought I saw—"

"Saw what?"

His brusqueness irked me just enough to get over my fear of looking like an idiot. "I thought I saw someone in the window."

Betty started rubbing my back.

Jim said, "I went down your basement this past Monday. Maybe I left the door open."

"No, I closed it. I always keep it closed. Plus, if we hadn't closed it, I would have noticed it before now. I couldn't have gone all week without seeing it. I always keep it closed."

"Well, ma'am," said Morgan, "I don't know what else to tell you. We've scoured the house twice now. Your neighbor here canvassed it a couple times. We've had extra patrols on this street since your first call. Maybe if you got a burglar alarm or some of those motion detectors, it might make you feel safer."

"The house is haunted. You know that, Butch," said Betty.

"Don't start that shit," barked Morgan.

Betty recoiled.

"It might be my ex-husband," I said to the Captain.

"What makes you say that?"

I started explaining some things about his character and how he made me feel when the Captain impatiently interrupted me again.

"Ma'am, has he ever got physical with you, harassed you, or made any specific threats?"

"Well no," I said, looking down and away, "not a specific threat."

"He ever been arrested before?"

"No." I became aware I was wringing my hands.

"Ever need to take a restraining order out against him?"

"No."

"Then do you have any *real* reason, other than he's your ex and there's some bitterness between you, that he might be fixing to harm you? Anything that would give me the slightest legal leg to stand on to investigate him?"

"Well, no…I guess not."

The Captain and one of the patrolmen asked me a few more miscellaneous questions for their report, and then gave me the standard "call-us-if-you-need-us" dismissal. The Captain spit on the walkway as he sauntered away.

Jim and Eve invited me in. I certainly didn't feel like being alone in my house. Betty gave me a hug and a "you-know-what-I-think" look and went home. Eve opened up a bottle of wine as Jim went down to their cellar. A little while later he came up with a big box full of surveillance cameras.

"Trish, listen to me. I'm going to help you put your mind to rest once and for all."

I was thinking he wanted to cure me of my pain-in-the-assness, but I let him continue.

"At our last residence, which was located in a busier area, we had an attempted break-in and a few incidents of vandalism. It was the main reason we moved. In any event, I bought these weatherproof, outdoor cameras. They were expensive…real high-tech. I positioned them all around our old house. I never put them up here because I felt we didn't need them. The cameras watch and record everything. They transmit back to this unit (Jim held up a large metal box), which you connect to a computer. It can record a zillion hours of surveillance. You play it back on your computer. Just put it on fast forward and you can watch days of footage in no time. We got about an hour of daylight left. I'll go over to your place and attach these cameras all around. I can screw them right into the trees. You stay with us a couple of days and then we watch the video. Whaddaya say?"

I instantly agreed. I was positively afraid of staying in my house at this point. And I certainly liked the idea of confirming whether anyone, or any *thing*, went in or out of it. I went back with Jim. While I packed a bag he attached the cameras to trees on both sides of the house, and the back, as well as the telephone pole in front. The entire circumference was now being recorded.

After packing my things I made sure each and every door and window was closed and locked. I made a rough mental survey of everything in my rooms, hoping that if something was moved, I'd notice it upon returning.

Thus began my surveillant sojourn at Jim and Eve's. For the next week I didn't set foot in my house. I went to work, came home and got my mail, and then went straight to Jim and Eve's. I checked my messages from Eve's phone. My ex never called. But most importantly, every night, Jim, Eve, and I, would watch the recordings for that day. Every night we sat mesmerized in front of the computer, examining the footage from all four cameras for the last twenty-four hours. I left all of the outside lights on so we could see everything at night as well. We did this for a full week.

Interestingly, the police came by twice and walked around the property. I didn't think the Captain took me that seriously. But except for the cops, a few raccoons, a bunch of deer, and one possum, nothing—absolutely nothing—approached or exited the house. Eve said she even kept an eye on my windows periodically during the day and saw nothing as well.

Saturday morning came. Over seven days and no culprits: no interlopers, no trespassers, no ex-husbands, and no ghosts. I'm not sure if ghosts would show up on a camera, but we didn't see any shadowy or spectral images nonetheless. Eve and Jim escorted me to my house that morning. Jim brought his gun and once more, went through my home from top to bottom. He shined a flashlight all around the attic and the basement. I followed close behind. Everything seemed in order, and in place, as best as I could remember. Once again, Eve and Jim told me not to hesitate if I needed them. They both gave me a big hug and bid me farewell. I thanked them repeatedly.

I unpacked and took a shower. I kept thinking of the shower scene from the movie *Psycho*. I barely rinsed and jumped out of the stall. As I hastily dried myself I thought, *this is nuts. I can't live like this. I can't live afraid every day. Nobody's here. Relax. Relax. Relax.*

I spent the day doing chores. It helped take my mind off things. I did laundry, cleaned the kitchen, ironed some clothes, and vacuumed the rugs. I didn't feel comfortable vacuuming. I couldn't hear what was going on around me, and kept nervously looking over my shoulder like a roadside deer. Evening came. I had some canned soup and crackers. I didn't feel like cooking and I wasn't that hungry anyway. I opened a bottle of wine and called my girlfriends. I didn't tell them what had been going on. They'd think I was losing it. When asked why they hadn't heard from me I blamed it on work. I told them I'd been staying late each night and going to bed early. We chatted for hours. When I finished the bottle of wine I got off the phone.

I wasn't drunk, but I definitely had a buzz. More than anything I felt worn out. Between my physical and emotional exertions, I was ready for bed. The phone rang. Oh no, not him…please don't let it be him. Not the ex. Or maybe it would be better if it was him. That would mean he's not in my house. I glanced at the caller ID—it was Eve.

"Just called to check on you before we turned in. I saw your lights were still on."

I told her I was fine and thanked her profusely for all she and Jim had done for me. Then we said good-night. I decided to leave some lights on downstairs. Screw the electric bill; it would help me feel a little safer. I certainly left the outside lights on. I rechecked all the doors and windows. Everything was locked and the basement door was closed. I left a small light on in my office; the room where I saw the figure in the window. I had three cordless phones. One was next to my bed. I checked the one in my kitchen and the one in my office. They were both on and in their chargers. As I checked the one in the bedroom I heard a creak behind me. I spun around—and was thrown to the ground with tremendous force! I tried to scream, but he clamped his enormous hand on my mouth so hard my teeth cut my inside lip. He sat on my stomach, clasped my hair with his other hand, and banged my head against the floor. He was gruesome! He was a monster! Long, straggly, grimy hair, shooting out in random patches from his balding, mottled scalp. He gripped my neck and growled like a wild animal. Sallow skin, sunken eyes—grimacing, as if in terrible pain. His lips were tightly closed, but I could see he was clenching his teeth. Dried blood lined the corners of his mouth. He ripped the one hand from my hair and put it around my neck as well. Now both hands were choking me. His clothes were ragged and filthy; the stench was terrible. He continued to choke me and growl. I couldn't breathe. I couldn't scream. Tears were erupting from my eyes. I had to do something. I writhed, kicked my legs, and punched his arms but he didn't flinch. He was strong and insanely determined. Then he took one hand off my neck, but squeezed all the harder with the other one. He opened his mouth and pulled out one of my panties! I don't know what was worse…my fright or my repulsion. He was missing many teeth. The ones he did have were yellow or rotted. His breath was beyond description. He squeezed the panties with his one hand and gritted his rotted teeth. I was losing my mind in terror. Thoughts whizzed through my brain. I heard my ex saying:

You'll get yours someday.

I saw the Captain looking at me as if I was a hysterical female.

And I heard Betty proclaiming: *the house is haunted.*

My thoughts, still racing: my ex, the figure in the window, the police, the ghosts—*the drawer!* I tried to poke him in the eye with my right hand but couldn't reach. But it did distract him for a moment. I flung the drawer open with my left hand. He seemed oblivious, piercing my skull with his demonic eyes. He threw my panties over his shoulder. I swept my hand across the bottom of the drawer. Finally I found it. He grabbed my neck with his free hand. Now both hands were squeezing my throat again. I grabbed the pistol and fired. The sound was tremendous. I hit his shoulder, he let go, I fired again, hitting him somewhere around his waist. Blood spurted everywhere. He screamed, momentarily repelled by the bullet. He clenched his stomach with one hand and lunged forward to grab me with the other. I fired again, hitting him in the face. Now he sprung back, blood erupting from his nose and mouth. And yet he still had the maniacal tenacity to glare at me with this unearthly rage. I fired again, right into one of his bloodshot eyes.

● ● ●

A week had passed. I was staying with Jim and Eve once more. I wasn't going back to that house ever again. The police and other officials were there almost every day. I was working out arrangements to live with one of my girlfriends for the longer term. I didn't go to work all week. My boss, normally testy, was surprisingly understanding and supportive. Even my ex called to see how I was. Strangely, I found it comforting. Maybe because I now knew he wasn't the perpetrator. Maybe because I realized that he wasn't being as manipulative and intrusive as I thought.

Captain Morgan was exemplary. He and his staff conducted an extensive investigation. Every day the captain came by to check on me and give me updates. His incredulous and coarse demeanor had significantly changed. He even helped keep the parasitic press at bay. By the end of the week, enough of the details had been compiled to appreciate the whole picture.

It was the Miller's son, Angus. As usual, the rumors were a compilation of facts and falsehoods. He was indeed psychotic. "One of the worst I've ever seen," said the state asylum director, as told to me by Captain Morgan. The Captain interviewed the asylum director, two of his psychiatrists, an administrator from a private institution he was also in, his retired high school principal, and most importantly, his sister Margaret.

The Millers knew their son was in trouble at an early age. As a child he liked to trap various animals. But unlike the other kids who would feed or play with them before setting them free, he liked to kill them. Angus drew strange and morbid pictures, had few friends, peeked at his sister in the shower, and compulsively masturbated. An unusual number of dead animals would turn up in the Millers' yard.

His teachers had a distinct reaction to him. They described him as odd, asocial, and lost in his own world. A few were afraid of him. Angus was always on the border of flunking out. Then the paranoia and rage began. He accused other students of various misdeeds against him, punched the lockers and pounded his fists into desks. He was suspected of a series of vandalistic acts. He eventually attacked a number of students and one teacher without any provocation. Finally he had to be removed from the school.

His parents brought him to countless doctors. Angus was in and out of psychiatric facilities and given all types of medications. One psychiatrist suggested a lobotomy, but Mrs. Miller wouldn't hear of it. His parents always had to fight with him to take his medication. When he did he was calmer, but not any closer to reality.

I started feeling so sorry for the Millers—the hell they went through. Angus screamed at night, urinated in the front yard, smashed things for no reason, obsessed about "beings" plotting to kill him, and glared at his parents as if they were his mortal enemies. One day Mrs. Miller found him eating a chipmunk he had captured. It was more than she could bear. She lost control—so did Angus. He attacked her, choking her as he did me. Mr. Miller grabbed a chair and swung it into the back of Angus's head, knocking him out cold. That's when Angus was placed in the state asylum for the criminally insane. Sometime after that the rumors began about Mr. Miller killing his son and burying him in the woods.

The years passed, but the toll taken on the Millers was manifesting itself. Mr. Miller developed early-onset Alzheimer's and rapidly declined. Mrs. Miller's health was failing as well. He died in a nursing home and she died shortly thereafter of a heart attack while living with her daughter. Margret still blames her brother for their parents' deaths.

Shockingly, Angus was eventually discharged from the asylum. The doctors concluded that he had been stable for a long enough span, and legally couldn't be held against his will any longer. The stupid shrinks never fully appreciated that the reason Angus was "stable," was because he was confined to an asylum and forced to take high doses of tranquilizers every day. Did they honestly think he would continue his medication regime on the outside?

The asylum contacted Margaret, Angus's only living relative. She wanted nothing to do with him and certainly wasn't going to let him stay with her. She let Angus have the old house. She figured it was worth relinquishing whatever money she could have received for it to avoid dealing with him. Angus, now almost forty, subsequently returned to his childhood home. At this point things become sketchy. We know he never followed up with his outpatient treatment. Not surprisingly he stopped his medication and deteriorated into increasing psychosis. He was there for about three years. The homeowners before the Carltons and Betty both moved away during that period. Captain Morgan was tracked down the gentleman who lived in Betty's house, a Mr. John Latimer, who confirmed that Angus was why he moved. Latimer explained that Angus screamed at night, defecated in broad daylight on the front yard, and stood in the windows staring at the neighbors. The day Latimer saw Angus eating a dead raccoon was the day he decided to move.

Just before moving, Latimer informed the police about his neighbor's behavior. Fear of retaliation prevented him from notifying the authorities sooner. He knew Angus was crazy and assumed he could be dangerous. When the police came to the house it was obvious what they were dealing with. The squalor was horrifying. Angus stank of feces and filth and was floridly psychotic. The police took him away and he was returned to the state asylum. His sister was contacted and informed of the recent events. She retained a lawyer and procured the right to be Angus's legal guardian. She then used some of her inheritance to have Angus transferred to a private institution in another state. She assumed that would keep him away for good. It was around this time that the Carltons and Betty arrived.

Little did Margaret, or the Crestwood Lake police know that Angus eventually escaped from the private institution. Nobody contacted her or the local authorities. Years had elapsed since he was sent to the facility. During that time, the staff who knew of Margaret had left, and she certainly didn't maintain contact. Moreover, private institution or not, the psychiatric system is flawed: it's littered with incompetent practitioners, in a society that just doesn't give a damn about its mentally ill. Bottom line: an inveterate, dangerous lunatic was able to flee, and nobody made the effort to inform the necessary parties. Unbeknownst to everyone at the time, Angus somehow made his way back to the house.

Margaret hadn't been to the house since her brother was transferred to the private institution. For years she did nothing; she couldn't deal with it. Eventually she got tired of paying the property taxes and decided to sell it. When she entered the house for the first time in years she vomited. Animal carcasses, desiccated feces, a pervasive, putrid stench…it was unimaginable. Margaret was unaware that her brother had returned and was living there.

Margaret had to close this chapter of her life. She had to get rid of the place. First it had to be cleaned. She was able to find a cleaning crew willing to tackle the job, but it was costly. Repairmen fixed the numerous holes in the walls and other assorted damage caused by her brother's deranged frenzies. Lastly, she had the entire place painted, and then put it up for sale. That's when I came in to the picture.

After Angus tried to kill me the police naturally scrutinized the structure again. What they found was amazing. In the back corner of my bedroom closet was a trap door, normally obscured by my rack of dresses in front of it. It fit perfectly into the grooves that held it in place, but could be slid open or closed. When closed, it was virtually seamless with the surrounding structure. Angus had left it open on that fateful night and the police found it easily.

The trap door led to an extremely narrow passageway between the walls which terminated in the basement behind the stairs. Adjacent to the stairs was a long crawlspace which enabled access to the rest of the basement. If one were to descend the basement stairs, turn, and shine a light into the crawlspace (as Jim and the police had done repeatedly), they would see nothing. If, however, one actually crawled to the end of it, then the small opening under the stairs came in to view. This portal allowed Angus to ascend upward, through the walls, and into the bedroom closet.

But there was more—much more. Another hole behind the stairs led to a tunnel. That crazy, paranoid freak, over the years, had little by little, dug out a tunnel from the basement, seventy-five yards out into the woods. No wonder the searches and the cameras came up empty. Angus was getting in and out of the house from deeper in the woods. When the police or Jim came inside (or his sister, the cleaners, repairmen, etc.), he could simply retreat into the walls or the woods, and wait until they left.

The thought of what he did in my home while I was at work made my stomach churn. They found fresh fingerprints in every room, particularly the bathroom and on my clothing drawers. I felt nauseously violated to the core of my being.

Captain Morgan also told me what the coroner had to say. Angus's ghastly appearance was due to his psychosis, multiple ailments including liver disease, and malnutrition. He had been living off whatever wildlife he could catch. In the woods surrounding the terminus of the tunnel, the police found assorted traps, and the skeletons of numerous creatures.

I decided to move in with one of my girlfriends. But first I had to get rid of all my personal items that Angus touched, or might have touched. I threw out a lot of stuff, including everything from my bathrooms and all of my underwear. Then the movers came. Half of my belongings went into storage while the rest was being delivered to my new residence. After the movers left I packed my car with a few remaining items. Jim, Eve, and Betty wished me well and demanded that I stay in touch. I pulled out of that driveway for the last time and headed down the street, all the while being watched by a dark figure in my office window.

THE DREAMS

My wife Stephanie and I had been married fourteen years. Ten years ago we moved to Crestwood Lake. Our house was situated high above the lake, on the two-mile long crest of the adjacent mountain. Well below us were the waterfront homes. I could never decide who had it better. We had this breathtaking panorama. Indeed, one could see most of the lake from our home. But they had unfettered access to the water. In the end it didn't matter. Happiness doesn't have a GPS.

We had one of the most beautiful homes in the area. It was modern and designed by some famous architect. I never heard of him, but whenever I'd mention his name to realtors their eyebrows would always rise. They called the house's design neo-eclectic. It definitely stood out, as compared to the other homes in the neighborhood, which were generally older and more traditional. My wife loved it. She called it our "little mansion in the sky." I would always snidely remark that it wasn't a mansion, but still cost me as much as one.

I was a colorectal surgeon. I worked at the medical center in Berlin, about an hour and a half away, and had a private practice. Please spare me the anal jokes; I've heard them all. Especially from my wife, who was fond of pointing out the irony of my profession when she thought I was being an asshole. She didn't fling those invectives when she was buying her fancy-schmancy shoes and bags. Or when she hired her personal trainer. Or when squandering my hard-earned money on the countless manicures, pedicures, facials, waxes and other assorted crap that females pamper themselves with.

As you've probably surmised, things weren't exactly warm and fuzzy in our mansion in the sky. I don't know why exactly—I'm sure my wife has an opinion—we had been drifting apart for a while. The sex had dwindled down and the arguments had ratcheted up. Over the last year my wife seemed to have more things to do during the evenings and weekends: the gym, yoga classes, nail appointments, dates with girlfriends, etc. I increasingly suspected that she was having an affair. Maybe she wasn't doing pushups at the gym. Maybe her trainer was doing push-ins on her.

She never cheated on me as far as I knew. And I never cheated on her. Well…uh…at least not since we got married. While we were dating I boinked her girlfriend once. One night the two of them were out drinking and her girlfriend confessed. Stephanie was absolutely livid. I've never seen her so infuriated. We separated for a while, but somehow I managed to convince her to give us another try. To this day she still throws it in my face. Women don't forget or forgive. They collect these emotional daggers and then, every so often, use them to stab you in the heart.

I looked out the window and saw her Mercedes pulling into the driveway. I could almost hear her thoughts…

As I pulled into the driveway I saw my husband's car. I wondered why he was home so early. Was he checking up on me? Hmmmph. I should be the one checking up on him. Like most men, Bill had always been emotionally distant. But over the last year or two he seemed more aloof than usual. He was always too tired to do things. Always had to work late. Always bemoaning that he couldn't do this, or couldn't do that, because of an early surgery the next day.

The hospital was rife with young nurses. I could visualize the little twenty-somethings ogling him, fantasizing about marrying a rich, handsome doctor. I could picture them with their lilting, servile voices: "Good morning, Dr. Jorgensen. Can you please refill these meds? Oh Dr. Jorgensen, here's the phone number you wanted. Here's your coffee, Dr. Jorgensen. Here's your chart, Dr. Jorgensen. Do you need anything else Doctor? Can I please lift up my little white uniform now and straddle you?"

And then the staff in his office! Every one of them, nurses and secretaries alike, were thin. How is that possible? Two thirds of the damn country is obese, yet every female in his practice is a sylph. I called him on it a couple of times, but he always gave me the same bull: that the ones with higher education or who interviewed better just happened to be thin. What a crock of shit. They were all young too. Not a gray hair among them. He probably had a little floozy at the hospital and one at his office. That's why he's "too tired" to please me on the weekends.

I've never completely trusted him since he betrayed me with my own girlfriend. My mother warned me about reuniting with him. She told me that incident would always compromise my love for him and subsequently our marriage. She was right, but I'd never admit it. And I'd never hear the end of the "I-told-you-so's."

Stephanie walked in the door and shot me a bemused look. "What are you doing home so early?" she asked.

"I had a bunch of cancellations late in the day. You wanna go out for a bite to eat?"

"No, I don't feel like it. I'm too tired."

I frowned and said, "Shopping and getting your nails done really wears you out huh?"

That was it. I had opened Pandora's Box. From there we got into a full-scale argument: shouting, swearing, blaming, the works. Her cell phone started ringing in the middle of our tirade. I threw it across the room yelling that it was probably one of her boyfriends. She accused me of "fucking one of the little size-two's in my office." We shouted obscenities at each other and then retreated to our neutral corners. I grabbed a bottle of Scotch and hibernated in my man cave, furnished with a large screen TV, a bar, and comfortable couches. My wife took a long bubble bath with her stupid candles, and her stupid New Age music.

Later that night I was getting ready for bed when my husband walked into the bedroom. He had that look on his face. It was a mixture of anger and guilt. I could tell he was still mad, but also felt bad about our fight. I hated the tension between us. It filled my chest with a tightness unlike anything I'd ever felt. More to ease my discomfort than to soothe his feelings I conciliated. "If you want to go out to dinner tomorrow night we can." I said it in an "I'm sorry" kind of voice. I couldn't actually get myself to say "I'm sorry," mostly because I felt like the fight was his fault.

"Tomorrow? I don't know, I have patients all morning, a meeting late in the day…well, OK, I can probably blow off the meeting. How about we go to Pierre's?"

"Sure," I responded. "Pierre's is good."

That was our way of apologizing to each other. We didn't actually address the underlying issues or offer contrition for our insults. Instead, one of us would just relent about the superficial issue that sparked the conflict. It was the best we could do at this stage of our marriage.

One of the benefits of being married to a doctor was the pills. We had the best sleeping pills. Some kind of barbiturate I think. Bill always warned me not to take them all the time because they were highly addictive. But damn did they work. I definitely needed one tonight. I noticed Bill took one too before getting in bed.

● ● ●

I had a hard day at the hospital, but was able to leave early. I was looking forward to dinner. Pierre's was a local French bistro. The food was good and the prices weren't too crazy. It had a genteel ambience, ideal for alleviating the day's stress. What I liked most about it though, was that it was a BYOB. One of my pleasures—of course, one that my wife could never relate to—was wine. Although I wouldn't call myself an expert, I enjoyed quality wine and had a small collection at home. I made good money and dammit, deserved to drink better stuff than the ten-dollar rotgut my wife would buy. However, restaurant prices for fine wine were ridiculous. Even though I could afford it I always felt ripped off. At a BYOB I could indulge in a top notch wine for the store-bought price.

Crestwood Lake had a small town center. Small enough that when people would say they were going "in to town" or "downtown" it almost seemed laughable. Basically, two main roads bisected each other, each with a network of side streets. Various businesses were strung along the two main thoroughfares and secondary avenues. This was Crestwood Lake's "center of town."

A new wine shop had opened up. Well it wasn't new, but the owner was. The previous owner of Crestwood Wines & Liquors, Ron Millhouse, died under very strange circumstances. They found him severed in two athwart the railroad tracks on the other side of the mountain from the lake. It certainly looked like a suicide, but nothing in Millhouse's life would have suggested that. He was apparently happily married, healthy, and had no history of psychiatric problems. His son was in college and his daughter recently gave birth to his first grandchild. Furthermore, his liquor store was financially stable and he was well liked by the townsfolk.

They did an autopsy. Nothing in his brain, body or blood could explain it. They couldn't find any evidence of foul play at the scene. The chief of police, some Neanderthal named Morgan, interrogated practically every-one in the town. He had the whole force working on the investigation at one point or another. Never turned up anything. We'll never know why Ron Millhouse trekked through the woods one night and threw himself on the tracks in front of an oncoming train.

His widow sold the store and it recently reopened as an upscale wine shop called *Grand Vin*. I thought this was quite atypical and financially perilous. How many wine connoisseurs could there be in the small village of Crestwood Lake and surrounding area? Moreover, few ads about it had been placed in the local papers. Nor did it have a website. Common sense would dictate that to establish a highbrow wine shop in a remote area, advertisement would be imperative. Crestwood Lake was not an affluent community. Sure, it was home to a few professionals like me: a handful of doctors, lawyers, financial execs, etc. But most of the residents were work-ing class: honest, decent people who worked hard for their money, but didn't make all that much.

In any event, people were talking about the new wine shop and I was aching to check it out. I needed a bottle for dinner, so here was my opportunity to visit the new store.

I parked my car and strolled over to Grand Vin. From the outside nothing had changed, except for the sign. It was a modest, wooden, seemingly handcrafted sign, with the words "Grand Vin" etched into it. It looked as if someone had painstakingly whittled the letters into the wood. They were etched in an eerie kind of font. I'm not sure what you would call it. My mind wants to say Gothic. The letters were pointy and reminiscent of some old kind of lithography you'd see on some cathedral or crest from the Middle Ages. But what do I know? I cut out cancerous lesions from peoples' bowels; I'm not a medieval historian.

The inside however, had changed dramatically. All the beer and liquor had disappeared. There were no more poster boards of bouncy little blondes holding bottles of Bud Light. No pictures of tuxedo-clad secret agents holding a martini glass and promoting some foreign vodka. No more football banners or other sports memorabilia. All of the advertising had vanished, even the little shelf talkers. No artwork or decorations of any kind remained. All the corny wine-themed knickknacks, gadgets and accessories were conspicuously absent. Also gone were the candy and cigarettes, as well as the ice and lottery machines. Even the refrigerators were removed, including the one for soda and water.

Instead it was nothing but wine. All four walls were lined with shelves from floor to ceiling, filled with bottles of wine. In the center of the room were rows of freestanding, black, iron racks, not one with an empty slot. The subtle lighting was bright enough to read the labels, but no more. The floor was now composed of a cold, gray stone. The back right corner had a small counter and cash register. Behind the counter was a doorway to the storage room.

One of the most exceptional modifications was the wines. They had entirely transformed. Rather than the former inventory of inexpensive, everyday wines, the shelves and racks were now filled with world-class specimens. All of the bottles were from Europe. It was a bounty of Old

World masterpieces: the most prestigious names or vineyards of Bordeaux, Burgundy, the Northern Rhone, German Riesling, Barolo, Tokaji, Port, Champagne, etc. The shelves were strewn with top vintages and rare bottles, many I'd never seen, but had only read about. A double magnum of the 1961 Chateau Latour stood in its own curio. In the back left corner was an entire cabinet devoted to Romanée-Conti! Six shelves' worth, starting at ten thousand dollars a bottle! How was this possible? Who was the owner? How could he afford such a treasure trove? And how could he expect to sell any of it in the bourgeois hamlet of Crestwood Lake?

Crestwood Wines & Liquors was the only liquor store in Crestwood Lake. Beer could be procured at the local supermarket, but for wine or hard liquor, the only local option was Ron Millhouse's place. Now those customers would have to travel to Concord, the nearest town with a liquor store. Why would this new merchant only cater to a minute segment of the populace?

I was the only person in the store. A slight chill seeped through the air. I turned and was confronted by a most unusual gentleman. He stood well over six feet. He looked older, maybe about seventy, but didn't seem or act the slightest bit infirm. Rather, he exuded an aura of formidability. His hair was white and flawlessly combed back. His clean-shaven face was somewhat chiseled with a strong jaw line. His eyes were imposingly dark brown, so near black that each iris and pupil practically merged into one large orb. They were fathomless and seemed to pierce whatever they peered at.

He wore an impeccable, pitch-black, three-piece suit, with a blisteringly-white shirt and blood-red tie. His breast pocket sported a matching red pocket square, meticulously folded. His black oxfords shined like mirrors. I felt in awe of his presence.

I mustered up some confidence and said, "Hello, I'm Dr. William Jorgensen." I emphasized the word "doctor." I felt the need to stress my status, as if it fortified me with some power or protection from the cachet of the merchandise, and the imperiousness of the proprietor.

"Good evening," he bellowed, in a deep, stentorian voice. "I am Luther Van Haden, the owner of Grand Vin."

He stared at me—a disconcerting stare—I'm not sure how to describe it…like I've never been stared at before. It wasn't menacing. But there was something…something unsettling and penetrating about it. Finally I had to break the silence for my own nerves' sake.

"It's nice to meet you. I've been looking forward to checking out your store. I work at Central Vermont Medical Center, my wife and I live—"

"I know who you are, Doctor."

I reeled for a moment. How could he know who I am? Maybe it was that blurb and photo of me in the local paper recently. The hospital had dedicated a new surgical wing. In any event, I felt too intimidated to challenge him.

I also felt nervous for some reason. As if it was incumbent upon me to facilitate the conversation. So I complimented his store. My plaudits were genuine, but I was dispensing them more for my benefit.

"I am astounded at your wine selections. I've never seen such an array of preeminent wines in one place. How did you amass such a stock?"

"I've been a collector for a very long time, Doctor. In fact I collect many things."

"Have you been to Europe?"

"Indeed, I have spent considerable time there."

"Have you been to any of the vineyards that these wines are from?"

"I've been to all of them."

"Been to *all* of them?" I repeated. It was almost inconceivable. This man intrigued me. My curiosity got the best of my anxiety. Who would have the time and money to visit hundreds of vineyards across the continent of Europe? "Did you work in the wine industry, or were you a wine writer?"

"No, not exactly, Doctor. But I assume you're not here to listen to my life story. I imagine you're going out to dinner with your wife tonight and need an appropriate bottle?"

"Well yes," I said perplexed, unbalanced again by his inexplicable insight. How did he know I was married? Well, I was wearing a ring. But that didn't explain dinner.

He placed his hand on my shoulder and said, "Come with me, I have just the bottle for you."

It was bizarre. When he touched me, I suddenly felt relaxed, comforted in a strange way. Seduced even. As if I'd known him all my life, like some paternal or avuncular figure providing guidance and support. He led me to one of the shelves housing fine Burgundy, pulled a bottle from the rack, and handed it to me.

"Les Amoureuses," he proclaimed with his head held high, "from the village of Chambolle-Musigny. Are you familiar?"

"I've heard of Chambolle-Musigny, but I've never heard of this specific wine."

"It's marvelous," Van Haden stated. "Simply marvelous. Elegant, feminine, it will glide along your palate like a seductress brushing her lips across your cheek."

"We're going to Pierre's, down the road, do you know it?"

"Of course," he said, as if I was an idiot to even wonder if he knew. "I recommend the ris de veau. It would be sublime with the Les Amoureuses."

"Ris de veau? That's some kind of organ meat right?"

Van Haden smiled ravenously. "Yes, it is the thymus gland of young calves, more commonly known as sweetbreads. The sooner you eat them after the calf is slaughtered the better."

I winced and said, "That's OK, I'll stick with the steak. So how much is the wine?"

"Four hundred."

"Four Hundred?" I said raising my voice and eyebrows. "That's beyond what I wanted to spend for one dinner."

"I'll tell you what…I want you to have this wine; it's *very* special. I'll let you have it for half price. Now I assure you, you're practically stealing it from me. That's a 2005. You won't find this wine—from that vintage—anywhere for that price." He looked so earnestly into my eyes. At that point I felt obligated to take it.

"Ohhhh-Kaaaay," I said. "So what's so special about it? What does the name mean?"

"Ah," exclaimed Van Haden. "I'm so glad you asked. Les Amoureuses means 'the lovers' in French. Perfect for you and your wife."

"Ha!" I said.

Van Haden instantly shot me a curious, yet somehow, still knowing look.

"Well…I…wouldn't exactly call my wife and me lovers."

"What's the matter? Is she being unfaithful?"

I was flabbergasted. Did he know something I didn't? Of all the problems a couple could be having, how did he zero in on my precise fear?

"Well…uh…ummm, well no, I mean…"

Van Haden gazed steadfastly into my eyes, his dark pupils beckoning me to divulge my heart. He placed his hand back on my shoulder, and in a most reassuring voice said, "It's OK my boy, you can confide in me."

I started to feel seduced again. I looked down demurely, nervously rubbing the neck of the bottle with my thumb and forefinger. "Well, she's been kind of distant for some time now, and I've been wondering more and more whether she has someone else. What made you ask that?"

"Dr. Jorgensen—no—Bill, may I call you Bill?"

I nodded.

"Bill, you're a surgeon. Between the hospital and your private practice I'm sure you work many hours. Often nights and weekends too I imagine, hmmm?"

I nodded again.

"Your wife, I assume, doesn't work. She has ample free time. Time that you're not available to meet her needs. Oh I'm sure you make good money and provide her with multiple comforts. But women need more than a Mercedes and manicures."

How did he know she had a Mercedes? Maybe it was a lucky guess.

"You wouldn't be the first rich doctor to have his wife stray from the marriage covenant. Here, you take this wine, Les Amoureuses, the lovers. It has magical properties. Forget the past. Forget what she might have done. Forget what *you've* done," he asserted sternly and knowingly. "You go to dinner tonight with your wife and you share this bottle. I'm telling you, things will start to change."

And with that I paid him his two hundred and headed home. I left with a mixture of emotions. I felt somehow reassured that things would be all right. Yet I was still plagued by a nagging doubt, for I couldn't seem to get past his clairvoyant inquiry into my wife's fidelity.

That night on the way to dinner I told my wife about Grand Vin and the enigmatic Luther Van Haden. Of course I omitted certain details from our conversation. Instead, I focused on the store, the wine, and the outstanding price I got for my bottle. She seemed unimpressed—until we had our first sip. It was amazing. Van Haden was right. Even my wife remarked on how good it was. Normally she doesn't care what she's drinking as long as it contains alcohol.

The whole night at dinner, all my husband talked about was that new wine shop, the weirdo owner, and his stupid wine. But I had to admit, this wine he bought was unlike anything I had ever tasted. It had a tantalizing effect on me. It didn't just taste wonderful, it made me feel different than alcohol typically does. Nothing however, not even this captivating new wine could alleviate the boredom I felt, listening to my husband drone on. Or take away the deadness I felt inside. The thought of him porking his little anorexic nurses was still making my blood boil. That son of a bitch better not be cheating on me again or I swear I'll kill him.

We came home from dinner. I was almost sorry we went. Stephanie seemed so detached—like she couldn't give a rat's ass about anything I said all night. Like her mind was elsewhere: probably thinking about blowing one of those Ken dolls at the gym. I was becoming absolutely convinced that she was interested in someone else. Even Van Haden's first thought was whether she was cheating. His words resonated in my head with increasing acuity. As mysterious as he was, there was something wise and profound about him. He had a sense about things…about life….about people…a*bout my wife.*

I couldn't fall asleep. I kept running my conversation with Van Haden through my head. Finally I took a sleeping pill. Not a great idea after the wine I consumed but I *had* to sleep. I had to be in surgery in the morning. I lay there in bed waiting for the pill to kick in. My wife had already fallen asleep. Finally I drifted off, right into one of those vivid dreams that seem so real.

My wife was getting one of her massages at her favorite spa. Only this time it wasn't a masseuse, it was a masseur: a young, callow blond with pretty-boy blue eyes. He had muscular arms. My wife was naked, lying on the table like a sacrificial oblation. Like a virgin being offered up to some lascivious deity to ravage at will.

She was on her back, her legs gently splayed. He was fondling every part of her body. She moaned rhythmically. Then his hands focused on her genitals. Her moaning increased. He kept rubbing and rubbing, working his hands in unison. My wife breathed heavier and heavier, her moaning now bordering on shrieking. He remained undaunted, rubbing and rubbing. My wife began writhing, hollering…she lurched forward and climaxed…she screamed…

I sprang up in bed, jostled out of the dream. I gasped. My God—it seemed so real. I immediately looked over at my wife. She turned her bedside lamp on. She was obviously startled, awoken by my spasmodic jolt.

"What's wrong?" she asked, extending her hands on the bed as if she was falling.

"Nothing, baby, I had a bad dream. Go back to sleep."

But I couldn't go back to sleep. The dream was too real, too disturbing. It personified my deepest fears. My mind started swirling. Was the dream some kind of omen? Was she really cheating on me? Maybe she *was* fooling around with some guy at the gym. Did she really meet her girlfriend for dinner last Friday night?

I had to sleep. I had to be at the hospital first thing in the morning. I decided to take another half a pill. I turned on my bedside light, took out the sleeping pills and broke one in two.

"You can give me the other half," said my wife with annoyance, "or I won't be able to sleep."

My husband gave me the other half of the pill. We each took our dose and turned the lights out. He couldn't settle down. I felt him fidgeting as if something was nettling him. I however, fell right back to sleep…deep into a dream.

I dreamed about my husband with my old girlfriend Gloria, the one he slept with while we were dating. They were on a couch somewhere, hugging and kissing. Oh were they kissing! It was as if they were trying to devour each other. Their lips pressed together, their tongues entwined. He was so hot for her. He never kissed me like that. They kissed and kissed and kissed. It wouldn't stop. Then he rubbed her breast. She groaned like a wanton slut. She pushed her mouth and body even harder against his. That bitch! I was betrayed by my friend and my boyfriend. I hated her! I hated him! I hated…

The alarm went off: an incessant, obnoxious buzz that sliced through my brain like a razor. My husband shot up and slammed the button with his hand. It was 6:00 a. m. I was always resentful about having to be awakened first thing in the morning. I didn't have to go to work. Why do I have to be woken up? I didn't care that he was the breadwinner and had a great paying job. I know it's selfish, but at 6:00 a. m., when your husband has been tonguing your girlfriend all night, you don't give a damn about right and wrong.

A few days later, while Bill was at work and I was home, the phone rang. The caller ID displayed "Private Caller." Someone was obviously blocking their number. I answered it. After a long pause a female voice began stuttering:

"Uh…hi…uh…is Bill, I mean, Dr. Jorgensen there?"

"*Who* is this?"

"Uh…this is Marla."

"He's not here—I'm his wife—What's this about?"

"Uh…a nurse at work gave me his number. I just wanted to ask him something about a medical issue I have that's all."

"Give me your number and I'll have him call you back."

"Uh…that's OK. I'll call him another time. Sorry to bother you," and she abruptly hung up.

Oh did my blood start to boil! I was churning inside. I knew that prick was cheating on me. I needed something to quell my nerves. I needed a drink. I went to our liquor cabinet. We were out of wine, and out of vodka. Nothing but bottles of mixers and exotic liqueurs. Ugh. I checked the bar in Bill's so-called man cave. All he had was that nasty Scotch and an old bottle of port. That's when it dawned on me. I'll go to that dumb wine shop Bill is so in love with and get more of that wine we had for dinner.

I walked, almost stormed, into Grand Vin. I thought the name alone was pretentious until I got a look at the store. No beer, no booze, no soda, just shelves and shelves of pompous wine. I don't know what the hell people see in this shit. Spending all that money for just a bottle of wine; even though the one from the other night was out of this world.

I was perusing the shelves when I sensed someone behind me. I turned and quietly gasped. Towering over me was this entrancing, distinguished, elderly gentleman. He looked like an aristocratic mortician: decked out in a black three-piece suit with a red tie and one of those showy handkerchief things in his breast pocket. Half of me felt beguiled and the other half wanted to tell him to get real.

"Good afternoon. I'm Luther Van Haden, the proprietor of Grand Vin. Who might you be?" He extended his hand.

"Hi…I'm Stephanie." I reached out and grasped his hand. An unusual feeling swept over me. He held my hand firmly—longer than a normal handshake—but it didn't bother me. It soothed me in an alluring but peculiar way.

"Ah, you must be Dr. Jorgensen's wife."

I cocked my head and said, "How do you know that?"

"Simple deduction, my dear. Your husband told me your name. I saw you pull up in your car. How many Stephanies can there be in Crestwood Lake who can afford a Mercedes and drink fine wine?"

Why would my husband mention my name? Normally he acted as if I didn't exist.

"Your husband never indicated, however, how genuinely lovely you are."

"Well thank you." I smiled coyly and tilted my head down and away. Not only did his compliment flatter me, it made sense. My husband definitely wouldn't have praised me to someone else.

"Were you pleased with the wine I sold your husband for dinner the other night?"

"Yes, I was. In fact, I'm here to get another bottle."

Van Haden's face lit up. "Well of course my dear, come with me."

He placed his arm around my waist. I felt titillated for some reason. He was twice my age and yet, I felt like a schoolgirl being embraced by some sexy celebrity. He led me to a particular shelf, removed a bottle and placed it in my hand.

"Les Amoureuses," Van Haden declared. "Did your husband tell you it means 'the lovers' in French?"

"Yeah," I mumbled indifferently, "something like that. Two hundred right?" I did remember the price.

"No, my dear. That wine is four hundred."

Normally I despised it when men called me "dear" or "honey," but when he said it, it aroused me. "Four hundred?" I repeated, losing my little girl smile. "My husband told me he paid two hundred."

"That was an introductory offer, my dear. I was endeavoring to be gracious to a new customer. But I can't continue to sell my entire stock at half price. I wouldn't be able to stay in business now, would I? You do understand now don't you?"

In reality I preferred the higher price. Let my husband pay top dollar for my wine. Serves him right after that skank Marla called. "Of course, yes, I understand. My husband can afford it," I said, waving my hand as if shooing a fly.

Van Haden instantly picked up on my tone. He looked deeply into my eyes. I suddenly realized how dark and large his eyes were.

"What's the matter, my dear, is something wrong at home?"

I hesitated. He reached out, took my hand that wasn't holding the bottle, and enclosed it in his hands.

"It's OK, my dear. I can sense that you're in pain. Please, tell me what's troubling you."

It was so weird. I felt as if I could totally trust him. As if he was my father confessor. I was still roiling inside from the phone call and was actually eager to spew it. "Look…um…don't share this with anyone, especially my husband, but…"

Van Haden interrupted—he tapped my hand with one of his, looked into my eyes, and said, "Stephanie…anything you say will stay between us. You have my vow. I know we have just met, but I would never violate any trust you consign to me."

I couldn't stop from crying. "I think my husband is cheating on me. Today some strange woman called for him. She blocked her number, initially referred to Bill by his first name, and then switched to his last. She seemed kind of nervous, as if she wasn't expecting me to answer and got caught."

Van Haden gave me one of those half-hugs, where you put your arms around the person, but don't press your body against theirs. "There, there, it will be all right. You are a breathtaking woman. Even if your husband is unfaithful, you will always be able to find a man who loves you—loves you for who you truly are. I am confident things are going to change for you."

"Thank you," I said. Somehow his words did assuage my fears.

"You take this wine now. Take it home and enjoy, it will help. And give some to your husband."

"But it's for me…and he doesn't deserve any."

"No no," he commanded. "Trust me. Give some to your husband as well. Always start with an olive branch. It will pacify him, make him less defensive. Then you can address things with him if you wish. Do as I say, all right, dear"

I smiled and said, "OK, I will. Thank you for listening to me."

"Anytime, my dear. Come by any time."

So I charged four hundred dollars to my husband's credit card and went home. The first thing I did was check the caller ID. No one had called. I opened the wine and poured myself a large glass. Mmmmmm... it was magnificent. I sat there in our big recliner, listening to soft jazz, sipping the wine, and trying to calm myself. The wine helped, but I still couldn't get Marla out of my head. I remembered Van Haden's instructions and left about a glass of wine in the bottle for my husband.

Finally Bill came home. As soon as he walked in the door I accosted him with "Marla" questions. He denied any knowledge of her whatsoever. He fervidly professed that he didn't know who she was, hadn't given any nurse his number, and had no idea what it was about. I didn't believe him, but I just didn't have the energy for a full blown fight. If I had had more incriminating evidence of his infidelity, then it would have been World War Three. He noticed the bottle of Les Amoureuses on the table.

"You bought another bottle of Les Amoureuses?"

"Yes. I needed a drink and the only booze in the house was your Scotch." I said it in a provocative tone as if I was just aching for a battle. I could tell that he sensed my potential volatility.

"OK," he said, "I'm actually glad you liked the wine."

"I saved you some if you want it."

He thanked me, poured the remainder of the bottle into a glass and took a sip. "I want to talk to you about our party Saturday," he said.

Shit! I had forgotten all about the goddamned cocktail party Saturday night. The guests were mostly other physicians and staff from the hospital. I had invited a few of my friends just so I'd have someone to talk to other than the dickhead doctors and their snooty wives. Bill invited his staff from the office: his harem of emaciated bimbos whose dress size equaled their IQs. Damn that pissed me off. Of course he had to invite his stuffy colleagues, but why did he have to invite his staff? They were employees. He didn't owe them anything. Didn't he get enough of staring at their asses all day in the office?

"What about the party?" I asked with an exasperated sigh. I knew Bill perceived that I was approaching the limit of my composure.

"I want to invite one more couple. Ted from radiology and his wife." Before I could react Bill quickly interjected, "I arranged to be off Saturday. I traded with another doctor. I'll pick up everything we need for the party and I'll help straighten up the house."

"Fine—I don't care." I grabbed my glass and headed upstairs to draw a bath.

That night when I went to bed Stephanie was already asleep. I don't know who the hell that Marla was, but she sure made a tense situation worse. Maybe my wife made it up. Maybe she concocted the story to shift any suspicions away from her. I thought about hiring a private investigator to keep tabs on her. I got in bed and continued ruminating. It took me a while to fall asleep. Then I slipped right into another dream…

My wife was at the gym—completely naked. She was lying on her back on the bench press. Above her was a barbell in the rack. She was holding on to it with both hands. Between her legs was one of the trainers, wearing nothing but a T-shirt. He was giving it to my wife with all his might. She was sweating, squirming, and moaning. Her long brown hair sprang back and forth. Behind the trainer were four more men, none of them wearing shorts. They were touching themselves…getting prepared for their turn. The first man climaxed. The second promptly took his place. Then the third. The fourth and fifth awaited. The first and second got back in the line. All the while my wife thrashed in ecstasy like a frenzied nymphomaniac. She was insatiable! I wanted to explode with rage!

I suddenly shot up in bed. I was sweating profusely. This time my paroxysm didn't wake Stephanie. I wasn't surprised; she had drunk almost the whole bottle of Les Amoureuses. Probably took a pill too. I was going out of my mind. The combination of my fears, Van Haden's insights, and these lurid dreams had to mean something. Something was going on with her. I knew it! Marla was a ruse. That was it—I decided to call a private eye. One of the doctors I knew at the hospital used one once to snoop on his wife. Found out she was boffing two other guys. I'd get the investigator's name from him. I took a pill and finally got back to sleep.

I woke up. I had to pee. My husband was fast asleep. I hated waking up in the middle of the night. It always took so long to get back to sleep. On my way back from the bathroom I noticed Bill had left his wine glass on the dresser. It still had some wine in it. What the hell. I gulped the remainder down in one swig. Maybe it would help me sleep.

Well it certainly did. Within no time I felt as if I had been given anesthesia. I plunged into unconsciousness…straight into a dream…

My husband was sitting in his big leather chair behind his desk in his office. His pants were down around his ankles. One of his petite nurse-whores, in her tight little white uniform, was kneeling between his legs. Her face was buried in his crotch. Meanwhile, one of his skinny secretary-sluts was kissing him, just like Gloria was kissing him in the other dream. He put one hand on the back of the nurse's head, and his other on the back of the secretary's. He pulled them both closer. The one kissing him started clawing his chest, like an animal in heat! With her other hand she began touching herself. My husband arched his back and came with ferocity, howling like a wild beast…

I awoke as if I had sustained an electric shock. I had to look around me to make sure where I was. It was so real! When I collected my senses my disorientation tuned into anger. This was my second dream about him with other women—too realistic to just be the vagaries of my mind. Plus that phone call from *Marla*. I always had an inkling that dreams were portentous. Now I was certain. At that instant I heard Van Haden's voice comforting me, saying how lovely I was, and how changes were forthcoming. I had to get out of this marriage. And that bastard was going to pay.

• • •

Saturday came and as I'd promised Steph, I was running errands to get ready for the party. I really wasn't in the mood, but it was far too late to call everyone and cancel. I had to go to Concord to buy liquor, but still planned to stop at Grand Vin for wine. At least that was the ostensible reason.

As I walked in a bizarre looking woman with long, wild, multicolored hair walked out. I had seen her once or twice before around town. Every community has its resident kooks.

"Bill!" said Van Haden. "It's so nice to see you again. I trust you enjoyed the Les Amoureuses?"

"It was heavenly."

Van Haden's face abruptly contorted. "I can assure you…heaven had nothing to do with it. Now what can I do for you today? Need some wine for your party?"

"How do you know I'm having a party?"

"I seem to recall your wife saying something about it when she was here."

"Oh, OK." I thought that was odd. Why would Steph disclose to Van Haden that we were throwing a party? Whatever. "Yes, I do need some wine. But please, I can't splurge on anything expensive. I need a whole case so it has to be reasonably priced. Do you even have anything like that?"

"But of course. Once again, I have just the wine for you."

He went into the back room. He returned with this "I-just-fucked-the-neighbor's-cat" grin on his face and a bottle in his hand. "Chateau Jalousie," he announced. "It's a simple, pleasant Bordeaux, with a slightly mischievous side. I can give you a whole case for $150."

"That's perfect. I'll take it." I reached for my wallet.

"How are things with the missus, if I may ask?" inquired Van Haden

I scowled. "She's up to no good. I'm sure of it."

"I'm sorry to hear that, my boy. Why don't you stay and have a drink with me?"

"That's very kind of you, but I don't have time right now. I have to go home and get prepared for the party. But maybe next week we could talk. I have an idea of what I should do."

"I'm always here. In the meantime, I'm sure you'll find this wine apropos for your current circumstances."

I thanked him, paid him, lugged the case out to my car, and went straight home.

● ● ●

The party was buzzing with activity. The house was filled with guests. Everyone was talking and drinking—especially my wife. She was doing both more than usual. I couldn't keep track exactly, but she had to be on her fourth or fifth glass of wine. To be honest, I had just as many Scotches, but I wasn't chatting up every woman at the party. Steph was decked out in one of her most revealing dresses. You know, where the neckline is almost as low, as the slit in the side is high. She was wearing her "French-whore" stockings, with the line down the back, and her highest heeled shoes. All she needed was a lamppost and a public defender.

What really irked me was how gregarious she was being with the other doctors—male doctors, that is. She seemed to be talking to them more than her own friends. Twice I saw her playfully put a hand on one of their shoulders. I started to fume. How could she have the gall to—

"Great party," blurted Dr. Rodimer.

He startled me. "Why thank you," I said. Dr. Rodimer was the head of orthopedic surgery at the hospital and was vying to replace our aging chief of staff—hence his invitation to my party. "I see you're enjoying the wine."

"It's scrumptious," said Rodimer. "I love Bordeaux. Do you speak French?"

"No, I don't."

"Ah, then you don't know what the name of this wine means, huh?"

"No. What does it mean?"

"It means jealousy. 'Jalousie' is the French word for jealousy."

I suddenly had this sinking feeling in my gut, like a dreadful epiphany. I thought Van Haden's remark about the wine being "apropos for my current circumstances" was somewhat arcane. Now I realized just how uncannily apropos it was. I must have got lost in my thoughts a little too long. Rodimer tilted his head and looked at me, as if to say, *hello, anyone home?*

"Jealousy," I said nervously, trying to think of something to say. "Well, leave it to the French to name a wine after something like that."

I then began to tell Rodimer all about the Les Amoureuses, just to make conversation. Eventually I excused myself and went to the bathroom. On my way there I stopped and refilled my Scotch. Then I headed upstairs. I needed a break from the crowd and the noise. The second floor bathroom had a window overlooking our deck. As I placed my drink on the counter I happened to peer outside. One of the deck lights was on. It wasn't that bright, but it illuminated the area just enough for me to see my wife kissing her girlfriend Judy's boyfriend! Not a peck on the cheek, mind you, but a passionate, full mouth and tongue kiss. I knew it! That conniving bitch! I punched a hole right into the wall.

I work my ass off to provide for her. I've given her a gorgeous home and expensive car. I pay for all her luxuries, take her on extravagant vacations, and this is how she repays me? I felt as if my brains were going to burst out of my skull.

I had to compose myself. I had a house full of people, mostly my colleagues. I couldn't embarrass myself in front of them—because after I got rid of this bitch, I would still have to work with them. I gulped down my Scotch and somehow found the resolve to suppress my fury. I went back downstairs, mingled, forced smiles, avoided my wife, drank more Scotch, and quietly awaited the moment when the last guest would leave. The whole time I was seething, exerting every ounce of psychic strength I had to maintain myself. I kept drinking in the hope that it would calm me. What a mistake that was.

Finally the last guests did leave. Of all people, it was Dr. Rodimer and his wife. I ushered them out, slurred "Thank you for coming," and stormed into the kitchen where my wife was finishing yet another glass of wine.

"You fucking bitch!" I shouted as I smacked her clear off her feet. She hit the floor in an instant. I stood over her, screaming. The whole side of her face was red and blood was dripping from the corner of her mouth.

"I saw you on the deck kissing Judy's boyfriend you slut!"

She threw her empty wine glass at me. "ME?" she yelled. "Who the *fuck* is Marlene?"

She tried to get up. I was incensed. I smacked her again…hard. She hit the floor once more.

"I told you I have no idea who she was. I'm not the one cheating on my spouse!" The blood vessels in my temples were pulsating.

Steph was bleeding from her nose now too. I felt a twinge of guilt. Enough to dial my rage back one notch. I turned away and headed out of the kitchen into the dining room. I needed another Scotch and the bottle was on the table. I leaned over with both my palms resting on the table. I tried to take a few deep breaths. I was still furious. I wanted to hit her again. I had to get control—I tried to think—I tried to breathe—I had to—

"I HATE YOU!" she screamed as this searing hot pain shot through the center of my body. She had plunged a large kitchen knife into my back. Blood jettisoned from my mouth, spraying all over the dining room table.

On the table was a long cheese knife. I instinctively grabbed it, twisted around and shoved it straight between her ribs into her heart. Blood spurted from her mouth and splashed my face. It was the last thing I saw as we collapsed upon one another.

Blood poured freely from both their bodies. The two streams flowed into one singular pool, gradually spreading across the hardwood floor.

He bent over and ran his finger through the commingled blood. He put his finger in his mouth and sucked it clean, smacking his lips in the process. "Marvelous!" he proclaimed. "Marvelous!"

THE WOODS

Brian Delmore eagerly lit his joint, took a long hit, closed his eyes, and held his breath with a deep sense of relief. It had been a long, stressful week at school and he couldn't wait for this moment. Like all of the teens in the area, he relied on the woods for his clandestine activities. Sundry paths crisscrossed their way through the thick growth, each with secluded spots, and Brian knew them all.

Brian spent a lot of time in the woods, more than most of his peers. He yearned to escape reality. He hated school, and the other kids, especially the boys. He was more intelligent than all of them, and smaller than most of them. The former gave them a reason to dislike him, and the latter allowed them to act on it. Brian had a few friends who also weren't part of the in-crowd. They prevented him from being completely isolated. But even they didn't know his inner world. No one knew the things that really bothered him: the things that hurt him the most.

Brian wasn't thrilled about his home life either. His parents habitually fought. His older sister, when she wasn't ignoring him, only criticized him. She criticized everybody of course, unless they flattered her. And if a boy flattered her, then she would fawn all over him. As Brian used to enjoy telling his friends, "My sister comes with serving instructions: instant whore, just add compliments."

Brian's buzz was well underway. He loved getting stoned in the woods. He felt safe in the woods, away from the bullying kids, the screaming parents, and the castrating sister. Smoking pot after being stressed was even better than just smoking pot. It was poignantly more gratifying to go from pain to pleasure, than to just go from neutral to pleasure. He took another toke and heard a twig snap. He spun around and saw nothing.

The only down side to pot was that it could make you a little paranoid. But something had to happen to spark the paranoia. It could be something trivial—but something. A sudden noise, an unexpected light, a passing cop car—any of a number of minor triggers and you became hypervigilant. He took another toke and held his breath. A twig snapped again.

He twitched his neck around like a bird. Nothing. Brian felt a little unnerved. He blew out the smoke and did a 360 degree scan of the forest. Nothing. He decided to walk away and continue down the path. He walked deliberately, watching where he was stepping. Even though pot could cause paranoia, it simultaneously provided ways to overcome it. He played the James Bond theme in his head…dum deeda-dum, dum, dum dum, dum, dum, dum, deeda-dum, dum, dum, dum, dum…He imagined he was on a secret mission, combing the woods for the enemy agent. He was Bond—James Bond. Smarter. Quicker. Indestructible. Dum deeda-dum, dum, dum dum, dum, dum, dum, deeda—two twigs snapped. *What the fuck?* He stopped and jerked his head around again, this time so hard it hurt his neck. Nothing.

He went from James Bond to Brian Delmore in an instant. His anxiety escalated. Fearful images flashed through his mind, such as running into the bullies from school, or maybe a cop combing the woods for pot-smoking kids. Holy shit! The horror of running into a cop! His parents would kill him. They were so naïve; they didn't think for a moment that their smart little boy would do something like smoke pot. They would totally freak.

Brian took a number of large hits and finished his joint. Normally he would have saved the roach, but the paranoia was getting the best of him. He stubbed it out on the ground, flicked it into the undergrowth, and decided to head home. The woods weren't working for him today. He'd grab a bag of chips, retreat to his room, and get lost in some music. Nothing on this planet was as good as listening to music high.

He walked briskly along the trail, but then heard footsteps following him. He stopped cold and turned around. The sound stopped. Nothing was there. He started walking again, this time gingerly. It started again! Almost perfect synchronicity. As he walked, it walked, if he stopped, it stopped. Once more he did a 360, intently peering between the trees. This was nuts. He had to be imagining it. It had to be the pot, or maybe his own footsteps. Like listening to music, all sounds were more acute when high. He whispered "fuck this shit," as if the feigned anger somehow made him more powerful or invincible.

He continued down the trail, it continued down the trail. He stopped, it stopped. He ran full speed, suddenly halted, and whipped around. The woods were perfectly still. He whipped around again and froze in sheer terror. It materialized. His throat closed. His heart froze. His left testicle ruptured.

Then she obliterated him.

• • •

Toby's Tavern was the local watering hole, owned by Toby Dunhill. It was a modest, subdued establishment with a small menu of simple, reasonably priced food. Toby used to work in the kitchen, but that got old fast. Eventually he hired a few cooks. Now he spent his time overseeing the day to day affairs, which basically meant sitting at the bar socializing with the townsfolk.

Toby's didn't have a pool table, jukebox, dartboard, or anything like that. The decor was austere. A fifteen-seat, U-shaped bar jutted out toward the center of the room. The solitary TV was hung from the ceiling at the open end of the U. A dozen two and four-seat tables complemented the remainder of the room. Toby's catered to the mature inhabitants of Crestwood Lake. There certainly wasn't any action for the younger crowd. If the Crestwood Lake twenty-somethings wanted a livelier place, they had to travel eighteen miles to St. Johnsbury, the nearest major town.

Vicki Larson was the primary bartender. She was there almost every day, and often nights and weekends. She'd been working for Toby for twenty-four years, beginning soon after he bought the place. Vicki was a forty-five-year-old, thin redhead, with beautiful green eyes, and the sweetest disposition you'll ever find in a woman. She normally wore her long scarlet hair up with long dangly earrings. Even though the years were starting to crease their way into her face, she was still a fine-looking woman. She was married once, to an abusive alcoholic, and never got involved again. Butch Morgan was in love with her.

Vicki had the brains to be much more than a barmaid, but she relished working in the tavern. Despite her reluctance to a new romantic attachment, she still genuinely liked people, and hence, her job. Vicki knew many people in Crestwood Lake and their business. Everybody gossiped at the bar and Vicki heard it all.

But she didn't know how Morgan felt about her. Despite being friends for two decades, she wasn't aware of how deep his adoration went. As tough as Morgan was, he still couldn't get up the nerve to bare his romantic feelings. He had come close many times, but always quailed. Over the years he had conversed with Vicki on numerous topics, even sharing intimate things about himself. But when it came to revealing his true emotions for her, he cowered like an adolescent boy struggling to ask out a schoolgirl for the first time.

Butch Morgan's real first name was Bart. When he was a kid his uncle used to playfully punch him on the arm and bellow "Hey, Butch." He did it in front of his friends a few times and the nickname stuck. Morgan grew up in a nearby town, the oldest and only boy of three children. His father was a mechanic and his mother worked various part time jobs to bring in extra money. Morgan's father was a tough-ass and demanded more from him because he was a male. He expected him to "act like a man" even when he was still a boy. He was never outright abusive, but he wasn't nurturing either. Nevertheless, his father was a good role model when it came to working hard, being honest, and taking responsibility for one's own actions. Morgan's mother was warm and loving, and without a doubt, the source of the soft spot he had under his coarse shell.

Morgan was a smart kid—not a genius—but smart enough. He went to the local state college, majored in criminal justice, graduated, became a Crestwood Lake policeman and never looked back. He was an assiduous investigator, a straight shooter, and an astute people-reader. He also didn't take any guff from anyone. He was quick to tell you what he thought, usually with colorful language. He respected his superiors (at least to their faces), and subsequently his diligence and integrity paid off. He rose through the ranks to captain/chief of police. A small town like Crestwood Lake didn't have multiple layers of management, such as deputy or assistant chiefs. The Captain was also the police chief, and answered to the mayor directly. Morgan had twenty-nine years on the job and was eligible to retire. But sitting around drinking beer and getting fatter wasn't in his blood.

Morgan was an imposing figure. His hair and moustache were fairly dark for a fifty-two-year-old. It helped him look younger than he was. He stood six feet five and weighed 270 pounds. His middle age paunch was evident, but it was part of a muscular frame and notable strength. Morgan was just as strong on the inside. He wasn't afraid of anything, and nobody—absolutely nobody—messed with him.

Morgan's personality was an incongruous mixture of diametrical forces. He had the aptitude to express himself eloquently and diplomatically, but not the constitution. He was blunt, often profane, and didn't give (to use Morgan's words), a "dog's dick hole" about what others thought about him. On the one hand was the little boy, scared of revealing his love to Vicki. Within this softer side was also the capacity for sincere compassion. If Morgan cared about you, he'd go to hell and back for you. On the other hand, if you were an evil person, if you hurt people—or God forbid—if you threatened him, then he could rip off your head and present it to your mother. I guess you could say that extremes came easier for him. They were less confusing. Maybe that's why he was timid about pursuing Vicki romantically. They had been friends for so long. But his evolving feelings for her were starting to blur the lines. Worse yet, if she turned him down, he'd be square in the middle of an emotional gray zone. What would they be then and how would it affect their friendship? Could they even go back to being friends after that?

Morgan's wife of twenty-one years had died eighteen months ago. Naturally it had hit him hard. He immersed himself even deeper in his work. Most days he'd stay in the police station well into the evening. And if an active investigation was going on, he'd work on it day and night. He never took an entire weekend off. Even on Sundays, when he was technically off duty and loved watching football, he'd still go to the station for a few hours in the morning.

Morgan missed his wife. He hated going home to an empty house. But he was slowly getting through the worst of his grief. He knew his growing affection for Vicki was evidence of that.

In the meantime, Morgan planned on having another serious talk with Gil about the town's recent incidents. Crestwood Lake had more than its share of strange occurrences, deaths, and macabre legends. Lately, however, there were even more odd or lurid deaths than usual. Every fiber of Morgan's being told him something was going on. It was beyond coincidence, even for the seemingly accursed town of Crestwood Lake.

Gil Pearson spent his entire life of seventy-two years in Crestwood Lake. His parents were also from the area. Thus, he had knowledge about the town spanning more than a century. Morgan had known Gil since his early twenties when he first became a municipal police officer. They became good friends—best friends really. At least once a week they got together to watch football or have a few whiskeys at Toby's.

Morgan confided in Gil about countless things and routinely discussed the local happenings with him. But Gil was always evasive and vague about the town's history and fables. Morgan suspected that Gil might have a few of his own sordid secrets in the mix. Whatever the issues were, he was convinced Gil knew more than he was divulging. This was partially confirmed when Morgan pressed him about the house he had sold to Burke. Morgan didn't know what to make of Gil's supernatural explanation. He was absolutely not a man to believe in such rubbish. But given the recent rash of unexplained and violent phenomena, on top of Crestwood Lake's dubious reputation, Morgan was unsure.

He also planned on stopping in Grand Vin to check out the new owner. Morgan made it a point to know as many of the citizenry as possible, especially town officials, business owners, teachers, or anyone else in the public domain. These people were invaluable for gleaning information that could assist him in his investigative work. And, being the sleuth that he was, he was particularly interested in checking out any newcomers to Crestwood Lake. He'd heard from a few people about the uniqueness of the new wine shop and more to the point, the eccentricity of its owner. Yes, Luther Van Haden was definitely on Morgan's to-do list.

• • •

It was Sunday afternoon and a broken faucet was keeping Morgan from his beloved football. The local hardware store didn't have a necessary part, so he had to schlep to St. Johnsbury where the nearest big-box hardware store was located. He was in the middle of the plumbing aisle when his cell phone rang. He looked at the phone's screen. It was the police station.

"Captain Morgan," he answered.

It was Edwards, the officer working dispatch. "Captain, sorry to bother you on your day off, but we've got an emergency."

"What is it?"

"They found a body in the woods. Bunch of teenagers were probably partying when they stumbled upon it. Don't know who it is yet, but it sounds bad. They were frantic and screaming on the phone. They didn't say who it was, just that there was a dead body. I got three units and EMTs on the way"

"Shit! I'm in fucking St. Johnsbury. I'll get there as soon as I can. Where in the woods is it?"

"North side of the lake. You know that main trail where we always find kids drinking and making fires?"

"Yeah, I know where you mean. I'll be there as soon as I can. Don't let anybody touch or move the body until I get there, you hear me?"

"Yes, sir," responded Edwards.

"Is it an accident or a murder?"

"Don't know yet, sir. All they reported was a body and a lot of blood."

"On my way," said Morgan, and he hung up.

Morgan hustled to his pickup truck, placed the flashing light on the roof and flew out of the parking lot. By the time he got to the north shore of the lake there was an ambulance, three police cars, and people all over the place. The police had cordoned off the area leading into the woods. People were encircling the scene trying to get a look. Morgan got out and was immediately accosted by onlookers bombarding him with questions. He ignored them and headed straight into the woods flanked by two officers with shotguns, walking vigorously.

The first patrolman explained what they knew so far. "It's bad, sir. A bunch of local kids were in the woods. They claimed they were just hiking, but they smelled of booze. Anyway, they found the body. It's Brian Delmore, sir. You know the Delmores right?"

"Yeah I know'em. What the hell happened?"

"He's in pieces sir."

"WHAT?"

The patrolman's voice quivered. "He's in pieces, sir."

"What do you mean pieces?"

"His limbs and head have been…I guess…severed in some way."

"In some way?" said Morgan.

"It doesn't look like they were cleanly cut. It's more like they were ripped off. There are all kinds of muscles and I don't know, bones or tissue sticking out from the limbs. The medical examiner is already there. He's waiting for us."

"Could it be an animal? A bear attack?"

"I don't know, sir."

"What about the parents?"

"They're at the hospital."

"The hospital?" puffed Morgan.

"The first thing the kids did was call the police. But then one of them recognized the…ya know…the head. They realized it was Brian Delmore. After calling us they called the family. The parents got here just a little bit after we did. The mother went totally apeshit: absolutely out of her mind hysterical. The first ambulance strapped her down, shot her with tranquilizers and brought her to the hospital. The husband went with them."

The trio finally reached the crime scene. The medical examiner, Dr. Wyatt, was standing there. His face was pale with shock. He looked like he was in a daze, his mouth hanging open. Morgan immediately went to the body. It was unlike anything he had ever seen in all his years of police work. As the patrolman described, it appeared as if the limbs and head were literally ripped away from the body. Blood was everywhere. The torso had a deep gash down the center.

Morgan twisted around sharply, grabbed the doctor by his shirt and barked, "What did this?"

"I…I…um…"

"Answer me dammit! Was this an animal?"

Wyatt finally composed himself enough to speak. "I don't think so. Despite the savagery there are no claw or teeth marks. I don't see any animal fur or tracks. There also doesn't appear to be any cuts, like from a knife, or a blade of some kind. I'll know for sure when we bring the remains in, but right now, I have no idea what did this."

Morgan shot off orders to the two patrolmen. Wyatt took a deep breath and interrupted him. "There's more."

"What? What else?" asked Morgan.

"The heart and genitals are missing."

"WHAT?"

"The heart and genitals are missing. Just like the limbs, they look as if they were torn from the body. I know this doesn't make sense, but it looks like someone just grabbed them and ripped them out of the body. I don't know what else to say; I'll know more when I examine the remains in the lab."

Morgan called in every officer who was off duty. He enlisted the help of officers from neighboring towns. He even contacted the State Police. Morgan didn't have an ego when it came to something this crucial. He didn't care whose case it was, whose turf it was, who got the credit, or any nonsense like that. He wanted every man on the job he could get.

Over twenty officers, four of them with dogs, spent two days combing the woods. It was the largest search party Crestwood Lake had ever seen. They found nothing. Not one shred of evidence that could explain what happened to Brian Delmore. They encountered no bears or significant animal tracks in the area. They interrogated every one of the kids who discovered the body. In fact, they questioned every kid in the high school. They didn't turn up a single motive, suspect, or explanation. Even more frustrating, the medical examiner couldn't offer anything more than the impressions he had at the crime scene: no sign of an animal or any kind of a weapon, and no bruises on the body consonant with being grabbed, strangled, bitten, or bound. Morgan was overwrought, the parents were disconsolate, and the mayor was demanding answers.

• • •

Morgan sat at one of the tables at Toby's drinking his usual bourbon. He'd been working on the Delmore case practically nonstop for days, and needed a break to keep his own sanity. Morgan ordinarily sat at the bar, preferring to be at the center of things and of course, closer to Vicki. But tonight he was waiting for Gil to meet him and wanted some privacy.

Vicki brought him another drink. She could sense his burden, seeing it in his eyes. Vicki put her arm around him, placed her head next to his and pulled him inward. Although always warm to Morgan, she was being more comforting than usual. She withdrew her head, left her hand on his shoulder and said, "I'm sorry, Butch. I know you're going through hell. You wanna come by my place at some point and talk?"

Morgan looked at her and answered, "Yeah, I would. Can't say when, but I would."

She patted his back and offered, "Anytime, hon, you let me know if you need anything else, OK?"

Morgan gazed into her eyes. The look on her face was even more soothing than her embrace. At that moment he realized that he really did love her. "Thanks, Vick."

A few sips later and Gil sauntered in. He sat down, took off his hound's-tooth flat cap, looked at Morgan and said, "You look like hell, man."

"I feel like hell," replied Morgan.

They continued to exchange pleasantries and platitudes. Morgan waited for Gil to get his drink so they could really start talking. He didn't have to wait long. Vicki promptly appeared with Gil's favorite rye.

"Hey, sugar," said Gil with a smile and a twinkle in his eye.

"Hiya, Gil. Take care of my friend here. He needs more than just bourbon tonight."

Gil thought about what she could give Morgan that he couldn't. But he kept his thoughts to himself and offered, "Don't worry. He's in good hands."

Gil had bright blue eyes and a full head of white hair. It had a few pale gold twinges, vestiges of the blond locks he used to sport. He looked good for his age: lean, but not gaunt, having been active throughout his life. With the help of some good genes he was quite spry for a seventy-two-year-old.

Gil was extremely intelligent and an avid reader. He had two master's degrees, one in English and one in history. Throughout his life he taught high school, wrote books, and tutored. He had also been an administrator at the county library for a number of years. He was most fascinated with early American history.

But for all his brains it was generally another part of his anatomy that did most of his thinking. Gil was an inveterate hound dog. It cost him three marriages. He got caught with a hooker once by an under-cover cop. Morgan got him out of that one. He also got blackmailed by a councilman's wife he was fooling around with. Morgan came in handy there too.

Gil was no stranger to fermented beverages either. He wasn't quite what most people would call an alcoholic, but he definitely was a regular. If anyone did confront him about the addictive dangers of alcohol he would quickly parry with: "I've been drinking for over fifty years and I've never found it to be habit forming." That was Gil: if he wasn't writing a treatise on the American colonial period, or between the sheets with the slut du jour, he was enjoying his rye whiskey.

"Gil," Morgan began, "something dire is going on in this town and I know you know something."

"Now wait a minute, Butch—"

"Shut up," Morgan growled. "You listen to me. There are all the frigging people who died in that house of yours."

"I wish you'd stop saying that house of *mine*."

Morgan bristled. "Will you just fucking listen to me?"

Gil relented.

"In addition to all the people who croaked in that house that *used* to be yours, there's been a lot of other weird shit going on. Too many deaths—bizarre deaths—like Ron Millhouse. A perfectly normal guy suddenly goes bonkers and throws himself in front of a train. Or the nun—a nun no less—slashes her wrists and jumps in the lake last year. Then that doctor and his wife stab each other to death. Now Brian Delmore is in pieces in the morgue. I don't know what to tell his poor parents. The father wants me to get the axe and sue the town. Then there's all these…just plain crazy things happening. Like that schizo who was hiding in that house terrorizing that woman. I forgot her name…" Morgan shook his hand in front of his head and squinted…

"Patricia Dukowski," Gil said.

"Yeah. She ended up shooting the whack job. Then, have you noticed there seems to be a lot more road kills and dead animals lying around?"

"Well, now that you mention it…"

"There are," asserted Morgan. "What's up with that? And then we've been getting lots of peculiar reports from the townspeople: screams coming from the graveyard, gunshots, two unexplained fires, and definitely an increase in psychiatric related calls. I even got a report of a large, hairy, two-legged beast in the woods. Now we have a goddamned Bigfoot. What the hell is going on here?"

Gil leaned over and said, "Why are you asking me?"

Vicki stopped by with two additional drinks. She placed them on the table as she surveyed their faces. Morgan gritted his teeth behind his pursed lips, bobbed his head and stared at Gil. Vicki immediately picked up on the tension.

"Be nice now, ya hear?" she said, and walked away.

As soon as she was out of earshot Morgan unleashed: "Ok Gil, we're gonna play this fucking game a little more? Fine. I'll tell ya why I'm asking you. I'm asking you because between you and your parents, your family goes back one hundred years in this town. You're a damn historian for God sakes. No one knows as much about this town or its history than you. I know you studied the occult and other off-the-wall shit. You published a frigging book on the Salem Witch Trials. And—just to refresh your memory—you're the one who told me that the house you sold Burke is haunted. So can we please dispense with the bull?"

Morgan's voice had steadily risen during his little tirade. More than one person at the bar, including Vicki, was staring at him. Gil had the sense not to push the issue any further. He gulped down his first drink, moved the glass to the end of the table and slid over his second. Gil spoke softly, hoping Morgan would do likewise.

"Look…I don't know exactly what's going on; all I have is suspicions, theories."

"Go on," demanded Morgan.

"I don't know for an absolute fact that the house I sold Burke was haunted, but it sure seemed that way to me. My father used to tell me stories about creepy stuff and ghostly apparitions that appeared in the house. Then there's all the people who died in it, who all sensed their deaths in one form or another. I don't know about you, but I believe in the paranormal."

"What about everything else that's been going on?"

"How much do you know about Crestwood Lake's early history?"

"Not much," said Morgan.

"Well, I'm not the one who knows more about it than anyone else, as you say, but we'll get to that in a minute. Let me tell you what I do know."

"Go ahead."

"Crestwood Lake was originally established by a group of Puritans who broke off from the infamous Puritans of Salem. They were even more fervent about their faith than the Salem Witch Trial zealots. They left the Massachusetts colony sometime after the witch trials to start their own colony. They ended up in Crestwood Lake, only it was called Scalford back then. The Scalford Puritans were reclusive, and not much is known about what took place in their enclave."

"Something happened to them, right?" said Morgan.

"Yeah. In 1713 there was a fire. Supposedly, every building in the village was burned to the ground. But here's the real bizarre part: not a single body was ever found, not even charred remains. Nor were any of those people ever seen again. They just vanished, like the colony in Roanoke in 1587."

Morgan sipped his bourbon and said, "Yeah, so what."

"Well...what caused an entire settlement, every single building, to burn down, and how do you explain the complete disappearance of all those people? It generated all sorts of scary rumors. Neighboring peoples avoided the area because of the folklore. Time and nature gradually obscured the settlement, and it reverted back to the state."

"What were the rumors?"

"That Scalford was bewitched just as Salem was. They think the Scalford Puritans even had their own series of witch trials and burned people at the stake."

"So what are you saying, that Crestwood Lake is haunted by the ghosts of those people?"

"I'm saying more than that, Butch."

"So what the hell are you saying?"

"This is where you'll think I'm nuts, which is why I'm hesitant to share these things—"

"Cut the crap and go on."

"Well, the suspicion is, that there are people in Crestwood Lake today who are actual witches."

"What…like those, what do you call them…Wiccan I think. Some kind of pagan religion. Those kind of witches?"

"No, not Wiccans, Butch—*Real* witches—people colluding with the Devil."

"What? Are you for real?"

"Yes, I am. That's the current hearsay. Listen, I'll tell you what. There's someone I've been planning to meet. I started looking into these things more deeply not too long ago. At first I thought I'd write a new book, but now it seems there are more vital issues at stake. I've been in contact—email and phone calls—with Professor Doug Aaronson. He's a parapsychologist and a historian. He teaches at Boston University. Real smart guy, lots of experience, has done a ton of research, primarily into the lost colony of Scalford. He knows even more about these matters than I do. You and I should go see him. What do you say?"

Morgan thought for a minute. Anything having to do with mysticism definitely went against his grain. But after recent events, most notably Brian Delmore's death, and the lack of leads, he concluded there was nothing to lose. Morgan believed that real-life people were doing these horrendous things. But perhaps they belonged to some kind of kooky cult, and maybe Aaronson's insights could help him find them.

"OK," said Morgan, "I'll go along. Set it up, but do it soon. I have to get to the bottom of this shit as fast as possible. And now, if you don't mind, I need a serious break from all this crap. I'm gonna go sit at the bar and talk to Vicki."

Gil got a look on his face like a teenage boy unfolding a Playboy centerfold. "Sure man, I completely understand that. You gonna get something working there or what?"

Morgan glowered at Gil and said, "Take the dick out of your brain. She's a decent woman and I'm not looking to just mark some territory like you do."

"OK, OK. Don't get your balls in a knot."

Morgan stood up, put his index finger on the table and said, "Just get a hold of that witch doctor and let me know when we can go see him."

Gil nodded, finished his rye and walked toward the door. He waved at some woman sitting in the corner of the room. Morgan took a seat at the bar.

• • •

Sharon O'Connell was in the middle of her daily five-mile run. Only this time, instead of running around town, she was in the woods on the eastern side of the lake. She had, of course, heard about the killing and dismembering of a local boy. But Sharon had enough naiveté to believe that nothing like that could happen to her. She was also cocky enough to believe that nobody could catch her anyway. She was twenty-eight years old, and had innumerable racing triumphs under her belt, including many triathlons. She was 102 pounds of lean muscle with a resting heart rate of forty-nine. Nobody was going to catch her.

Sharon resided in a small cottage a few blocks from the lake's east shore. She lived a rather isolated existence: no husband, boyfriend, kids, or pets. Her father was deceased and her mother lived in another state. She was a freelance writer, editor and copywriter, and did virtually all of her work from home. Writing and running were her passions. She enthusiastically merged them by writing a book about cardiovascular exercises.

One of the reasons she liked running in the woods was because of the frequent inclines along the trail. These provided a more strenuous workout. Lay people, or "non-runners" as Sharon referred to them, would argue that the uphill effort was offset by the declines. But as Sharon contradictively pointed out, going downhill stressed certain muscles to prevent oneself from falling forward; muscles that would not be fully challenged on a flat medium. She devoted a whole chapter to the concept in her book.

Sharon was jogging her way up the steepest hill when she felt an uncustomary degree of fatigue, as if there was a five-pound weight on her chest.

Her calves began to ache as well, much to her confusion. She was only two miles into her routine, a scintilla of her capacity. The land plateaued at the top of the slope, and in extremely uncharacteristic fashion, she decided to rest for a few minutes. Her breathing was abnormally labored.

Trying to regain her breath, Sharon stopped, bent over, and massaged her calves. She stood up and took in the scenery. It was just past the height of autumn. The forest was beautiful, even though the leaves were beginning to fall. A disturbing sensation crossed the back of her neck, like a passing hand. She grabbed her neck, but nothing was there. Sharon looked backward and for a split second, thought she glimpsed something moving through the trees. She did a double take but saw nothing. Her calves continued to ache. She looked all around, but saw only trees—no animals, not even a bird or a squirrel. That sure seemed odd. The pressure on her chest continued.

Sharon took her pulse. It seemed a little fast, even after a two-mile run. She thought about walking the rest of the way, but then rebuffed the idea. She could not accept that her body wasn't performing as well as it should. She would give herself a few more moments and run as usual.

The sensation on the back of her neck returned. She smacked her neck, as if swatting a mosquito, spun around, and saw her. Sharon instinctively clasped her chest and gasped. She was horrifying! This absolutely monstrous looking woman! A fiendish gorgon! Pale, sallow skin, with gray teeth, semi-clenched. She had red eyes with pronounced blood vessels radiating outward from her pupils. She looked enraged. Paradoxically, her hair was lush and feminine. Long and dark gray, it flowed over her body, enveloping her shoulders. Sharon noticed it had streaks of other colors running through it.

She wore a wrinkly, dark purple and black dress that hung loosely over her entire body. Around her waist was a belt made of hemp. A dead bird, with a little noose around its neck, dangled from the belt. The woman started to hiss: "sssssssssssssss."

Sharon just stood there in fear. The woman's eyes bored into hers. Sharon wanted to run but couldn't; her muscles wouldn't move. She felt mesmerized, as if an electric current was running through her body, terrorizing and paralyzing her simultaneously.

"Who…who…are you?" Sharon murmured.

The woman said nothing. She raised her wrinkled hand. Her fingers terminated in long, black talons. She hissed even louder.

She lunged forward, thrusting her thumb into Sharon's mouth and her two middle fingers into Sharon's eyes—all the way to her brain. Sharon reflexively gagged, and then uncontrollably convulsed. Blood poured out of her mouth like a spigot. The woman took her free hand and slashed Sharon open from her throat to her crotch. Then she withdrew the hand from Sharon's head, allowing her lifeless body to slump to the ground. The demon licked the blood off her claws. Then she claimed her trophies from Sharon's body.

• • •

Morgan walked out of the local variety store. He had been interviewing the owner about Brian Delmore's death. The owner's son was in Brian's class. Desperate for leads, Morgan was questioning everyone with any tie to Brian. As he walked toward his truck he noticed Grand Vin half a block away. Now was as good a time as any to check out the newcomer. Maybe he'd get lucky and the owner would know something about Brian, or the people who mutilated him.

The brick building that housed Grand Vin stood alone. The rear and right side of the structure were bordered by a tree-lined brook. The left side harbored a few parking spaces that gave way to a small vacant lot. The front of the building abutted the street.

Morgan approached the store slowly, attempting to get a good look at it. He was inspecting it for any legal improprieties, zoning violations, building code anomalies, etc. Morgan never hassled law abiding people over petty infractions, but he didn't forget them either. He was shrewd. You never knew when you might need something important from somebody and it was always advantageous to have leverage.

As he entered he saw Van Haden quietly conversing with Cassandra Voorhees. Cassandra was definitely an oddball. Vicki, who rarely spoke ill of people, called her the "deranged hippie." No one knows if she was once an actual hippie. She was the right age, being in her sixties. She certainly dressed like one, always wearing psychedelic, flowing dresses, with all sorts of accessories: gaudy beads, necklaces, bracelets, and sometimes a headband. She had long gray hair, sometimes with strips of colored fabric woven into it, down to the small of her back. Sometimes she dyed streaks into her mane creating a striated, kaleidoscopic montage. She was retired, but had a variety of sidelines such as pet sitting, providing astrology and psychic readings, and selling weird shit on eBay. She lived in a small, dilapidated, lake-front house and was frequently seen walking around town. She was harmless, but everyone thought she was a kook.

As soon as Van Haden saw Morgan he said, "Good afternoon, Captain, I'll be right with you. Please have a look around."

That's exactly what Morgan did. Morgan's initial impression of Grand Vin was contempt for what he perceived to be ostentation and pretentiousness. *The nerve of this asshole,* Morgan thought. It was bad enough a decent man like Ron Millhouse had to die so terribly. But to see his traditional sports-oriented liquor store, with all its beers and whiskeys, turned into a stuck-up, pompous wine shop really pissed Morgan off. And if that wasn't bad enough, now he had to drive to the next town to buy his bourbon. That was it. Van Haden was a total jerk-off in Morgan's book, virtually an irredeemable designation. Van Haden and Voorhees had a few more whispered exchanges and then she hastily left the store.

"Captain, how good it is to finally meet you. I am Luther Van Haden, the proprietor of Grand Vin. How may I serve you?" Van Haden extended his hand.

Proprietor? Morgan thought, *what a douchebag. Why can't he just say owner?* Even though Morgan had the brains, he hated it when people used highfalutin words. He wasn't impressed by Van Haden's dressy image either. He thought his pocket square was for sissies. He disliked the man immediately.

"How do you know who I am?" said Morgan.

"Well, my good man, it's simple deduction. First, I read about you in the local paper. Dreadful thing what happened to that boy. Earlier, I observed you getting out of your pickup truck, as opposed to a standard police cruiser. That reveals that you are more than a simple patrolman. The badge on your shirt is gold. The regular policemen wear silver badges. Your age also suggests the requisite years of service to be in a position of command. And while it's just my subjective impression, your overall demeanor, your swagger, your commanding presence, all evince a man of status and authority." Van Haden re-extended his hand.

"I'm not your *good man*," said Morgan in a confrontational tone. "I am Captain Morgan and I would appreciate it if you would address me as such."

Morgan's testosterone was in full force, much as the alpha male in a herd letting all the other challenging males know who's boss. With Van Haden, it wasn't so much that he felt intimidated—it was more disdain.

Van Haden bristled in return. At this point Morgan had taken his hand. Van Haden squeezed and stared him directly in the eyes, as if X-raying Morgan's skull. Morgan squeezed back even harder and met his gaze without wavering. They were the same height, eye-to-eye, hand-to-hand: two goliaths squaring off. Only Morgan, mortal as he was, wouldn't back down to anything in this universe. Nothing could break him. You'd have to kill him first.

Van Haden eased his grip, withdrew his hand and smiled. "Captain, my apologies for being too colloquial. I assure you that I meant no disrespect. I am very glad to meet you. I want to cultivate positive relationships with everyone in Crestwood Lake. Can I interest you in a bottle of wine?"

"I don't drink wine," said Morgan, dialing down his tone a notch. "I don't suppose you sell any bourbon in this joint?"

"I'm sorry, Captain, I am exclusively a wine vendor."

That's because you're so full yourself, thought Morgan. Then out loud: "Mr. Van Haden, look, I stopped by today because I make it a point to know everyone in town. This is a small community and it's important for me to *cultivate* good relationships with everyone as well."

"Why of course, Captain. I'm delighted that you're here. Let's talk, but give me just a minute. I need to go in the back for a moment. I have something that I'm sure will pique your interest."

"Go ahead," said Morgan.

Van Haden slipped through the narrow doorway behind his counter. Morgan checked his cell phone to see if anyone had called or left a message. It was a superfluous action. It would have rung if anyone called, or dinged if anyone left a message. Certainly the station would have contacted him immediately if anything significant arose. Morgan was a little on edge. He felt tremendous pressure to find Brian Delmore's killer. He strolled around the aisles looking at the bottles and the prices. "Hmmmph," he kept muttering to himself.

Van Haden emerged from his back room with a bottle and two snifters in his hands. He placed them on the counter. "Captain, please join me."

Morgan sauntered over.

"Captain, please have a drink with me. I don't sell anything but wine, but I do reserve a few special bottles of assorted spirits for occasions such as this. You mentioned you like bourbon; this one here is exquisite. It has a deep flavor and is sublimely smooth. You must try it. Please, be my guest."

You would think Morgan would be a stickler about something such as drinking on the job. But Van Haden had lowered his guard first, and in Morgan's mind, the gentlemanly thing to do was to accept his offer of a drink. Besides, Morgan didn't perceive having a belt or two to be an infraction anyway. A real man can hold his liquor.

Van Haden filled the two glasses halfway, handed one to Morgan and said, "To your health, Captain."

"And yours," Morgan said. He drank his glass with one swig. He cocked his head and raised his eyebrows. "That's damn good bourbon." Morgan grabbed the bottle and inspected the label.

"Jim Beam Devil's Cut," proclaimed Van Haden. "It's my personal favorite."

"Not bad," said Morgan glancing to his right. On the wall next to the counter he noticed a small curio made of dark, sumptuous wood; American black walnut, Morgan concluded. It had a single glass door. The wood was highly polished and the glass was crystal clear and unadorned. It housed an unusually large bottle of wine. "This some kind of special bottle?" asked Morgan pointing his thumb at the cabinet and shaking his hand back and forth.

"Indeed it is," Van Haden proudly exclaimed. "That's a double magnum of the 1961 Chateau Latour."

"You want to translate all that into English?"

"Very well, Captain. I'll commence with the bottle itself. It's a double magnum. The term *magnum* means something quite different in the wine world as compared to your realm, Captain. A wine bottle that is twice the size of a standard one is called a magnum. Hence, a double magnum, as you see before you, is the equivalent of four regular bottles of wine.

"This here is Chateau Latour, considered by many oenophiles to be the most preeminent Bordeaux in all of France. The 1961 vintage was arguably the best of the twentieth century, although some would say 1945. In any event, Captain, you are beholding a quadruple-sized bottle of one of the best wines in the world today."

"Oh yeah?" said Morgan, unimpressed. "What's this go for?"

"Oh it's not for sale. It's a personal keepsake. But I imagine it could easily fetch thirty thousand at auction, probably more."

"Hmmmph," huffed Morgan. "So where you from Van Haden?"

"I've been abroad for many years, mostly Europe. But now I've come back to the states."

"What brings you to Crestwood Lake?"

"I know a good opportunity when I see one, Captain. It's an idyllic community and so rich in history. It's an enchanting place, wouldn't you agree?" Van Haden refilled Morgan's glass.

"Hmmmmm," said Morgan. Van Haden's enigmatic answer didn't escape his detection, but he had more important things to interrogate him about. And he didn't want to put Van Haden on the defensive by pressing him about extraneous details. But he did need to poke him just a little bit further.

"So explain something to me, Mr. Van Haden."

"I am at your disposal, Captain. Ask anything you like."

"How do you expect to make any money selling nothing but hoity-toity wines in this small town? These are simple folk: beer drinkers, cheap wine, regular liquor. Most of the people here aren't rich. They don't have money to piss away on fancy, overpriced wine."

"My good man—I'm sorry—I mean, Captain. My establishment is more of a passion than an entrepreneurship. I am a man of diverse means. My circumstances do not necessitate that my endeavors here prosper financially. It flourishes in other ways."

"Well while you're 'flourishing' [Morgan made air quotes], I have to drive to Concord to buy my bourbon."

"Captain, it is not my intention to inconvenience anyone. Come by any time you need a bottle of bourbon. I always have this one on hand in the back. I would be more than happy to supply you with some if you're ever in a pinch."

"Did you know Ron Millhouse?" asked Morgan, ignoring Van Haden's pleasantries and enticements.

"Not directly no. Terrible tragedy."

"What do you mean not directly?"

"I never met him in person. I knew of him through some mutual acquaintances, but that's all. I met his widow when she put the store on the market. I gave her a very generous price; more than what the premises were worth. I felt it was the least I could do."

"How gallant of you, Mr. Van Haden," Morgan said with a tincture of sarcasm. "What's upstairs?"

"Those are my quarters, Captain. I prefer the convenience of being in close proximity to my wares."

"Did you know Brian Delmore or any of the members of his family?" inquired Morgan, mixing up the questions in an effort to catch Van Haden off guard.

"No I did not, Captain. Remember, I'm fairly new to Crestwood Lake."

"Yes I'm well aware of that. But I know many of the locals have already visited your store. Maybe you overheard something that might be useful to me?"

"I'm sorry to say that I did not."

"You seem to know Cassandra Voorhees well. She doesn't strike me as a wine snob. What did she want?"

"You're quite direct, aren't you, Captain? But I guess you have to be in your business."

"You didn't answer my question."

"Cassandra was confiding in me about a personal matter. I am not at liberty to discuss it, but I can assure you it has nothing to do with the crimes you are investigating."

"I didn't know you were friends with Cassandra."

"As I professed, I wish to foster positive relationships with the townspeople."

"Like the Jorgensens?" said Morgan

Van Haden shook his head and looked down. "Another terrible tragedy."

"I understand they bought wine from you."

"How did you know?" asked Van Haden.

"From one of their guests who was at their house the night they killed each other. Dr. Jorgensen told one of his colleagues about your store and the wines he bought from you. Did Jorgensen share anything with you that would explain that night?"

"No, Captain. All we talked about was wine."

"What about the wife. Was she ever in your store?"

"Why yes. She came by once to purchase another bottle of the wine that I originally sold to her husband. She loved it. And no"—said Van Haden with increasing irritation—"she also did not reveal anything that would hint toward the horrendous violence she was capable of. I am afraid that I can't help you with these matters, Captain."

Morgan could see his conversation with Van Haden was going nowhere so he went for broke: "Well excuse me for pointing this out, but it just seems a little funny to me. The guy who owned this store before you throws himself at an oncoming train, and two of your customers stab each other to death, on the same day that one of them was in your store."

Van Haden leaned forward, frowned, looked Morgan dead in his eyes, and spoke firmly, "Captain, I think I have been more than gracious. I see no reason to impugn me by implying that I had some form of affiliation with these unfortunate coincidences. I am a simple wine merchant. Moreover, I am new to this town and have minimal connections to its citizenry. I never met Millhouse, and the Jorgensens were nothing more than customers."

"I have to do my job, Van Haden. Don't forget that," said Morgan.

"Your *job*?" repeated Van Haden. "Don't you mean your ego?"

"What?" snapped Morgan.

Van Haden's eyes suddenly seemed larger. He glared at Morgan. "You approach my store looking for some picayune violation, you proffer an aggressive hand shake and attempt to stare me down, and you display palpable contempt for my merchandise, my dress, and my choice of words. Yet despite my acquiescence to your authority and my courtesies, you tacitly inculpate me in crimes against people with whom I had only a fleeting or indirect relationship. Captain, I had hoped to ingratiate myself with you. But I can't help wondering if I've unwittingly provoked some of your personal sensitivities and not merely your professional ones?"

Morgan was thrown off guard. He wasn't accustomed to people confronting him in return, especially with some of his innermost thoughts or motives. How the hell could Van Haden know he was scoping out the outside of his store for any violations? Or know what he felt about his dress?

Morgan's intuition sensed that something was wrong—very wrong—about Van Haden. He had assailed him with extremely flimsy coincidences, mostly to see how he'd react. Now he knew. If he had anything more substantial on Van Haden he would have really let him have it. Yeah, Morgan had an ego. And Van Haden had tunneled right into it. But Morgan also had a good head on his shoulders. He didn't want to alienate Van Haden any further. Without anything tangible, any additional confrontations on Morgan's part would indeed appear more personal than professional and play right into Van Haden's hand. He rarely did it, and he hated it, but he wisely chose to retreat and finish the engagement on a diplomatic note. Not a weak diplomatic note—but a Morganized one.

"Relax Van Haden. I check out every new business owner or public figure in the town. I'm the head of the police and it's my job to know the people I serve. You know there's been a series of horrible deaths here. The mayor and the townsfolk are crawling up my ass and down my throat to come up with answers. The man you bought this store from inexplicably kills himself in a gory fashion. Then two of your customers stab each other to death. Now tell me the truth…what kind of cop would I be if I didn't ask you about it?"

"Why yes, Captain—"

"And yeah, maybe I do have a little bit of a bug up my ass. I liked Ron Millhouse—everybody did—and everyone liked his store. It was the only liquor store in town and it was down to earth. Now you come in here with these expensive wines. And it's not like you kept the beer and liquor and just added some fancy shit—oh no—you had to get rid of the ordinary stuff. It's off-putting to the community, sir. Now the whole damn town has to drive to the next damn town, just to buy a bottle of booze. It's like you're saying 'fuck you' to Crestwood Lake. Do you get where I'm coming from Mr. Van Haden?"

"You're right, Captain." Van Haden placed his hand on Morgan's upper arm. Morgan looked at his hand and then glared at Van Haden, who promptly withdrew it. "I understand, Captain. You have to do your job. Perhaps my ego got in the way a little too. And I'll tell you what—I'm going to give some thought to adding some beer and liquor to the store. It is absolutely not my wish to offend Crestwood Lake. It's just that…I've always been a wine lover. I've always had a dream of owning my own wine store. And now that I'm getting up in years, I just wanted to spend whatever time I had left fulfilling that dream. But I don't suppose a shelf or two of bourbon and vodka and maybe some beer would prevent that."

Morgan gulped down his drink and said, "Nice meeting you, Mr. Van Haden. Thank you for the bourbon. Here's my card, call me if you do come across anything that you think might help me."

"You have my word. It would be my pleasure to assist you, Captain." Morgan started walking out. When he was halfway out the door Van Haden said, "Be sure to say hi to Vicki for me."

Morgan reflexively said, "OK," as he let the door close. Now on the street his thoughts swirled: *How the hell does he know Vicki? How does he know her well enough to call her by her first name? And how does he know that Vicki and I have any kind of relationship?* He didn't feel like storming back in and starting it all over again with Van Haden. He knew that wasn't the last time he'd see him.

Inside Grand Vin, Van Haden gritted his teeth, squeezed his snifter and stared at Morgan until he was out of sight. The glass shattered into hundreds of shards.

"He can't be turned," echoed a woman's voice from the back room.

"No he can't," replied Van Haden. "But we can break him with who he loves."

THE PERFIDY

Being an airline pilot sucks. Especially before you achieve any appreciable seniority. Rookies like me get the shittiest routes and the worst hours: four, sometimes five, days in a row on duty. To make matters worse, you could live on one coast, but your route could terminate on the other coast. Now to get home, you're just like any poor schmuck forced to fly: subject to delays and flight cancellations. Whatever number of days your current schedule was, you always had to add a day, sometimes two, before you were physically walking through your front door. The up side was you then had a stretch of days, five if you're lucky, all to yourself. The routine was grueling and not worth the pay.

I remember as a little boy, thinking that being a pilot was the coolest thing in the world (next to being an astronaut). I went to college, joined the air force, and spent eight years flying transport aircraft like the C-5 Galaxy. Not hot-shot fighter jets, but big, lumbering, boring, cargo planes. I guess my transition to commercial airliners was a natural progression. I felt like a bus driver, only with my life and many others at stake. There's nothing cool about sitting in a cramped cockpit for fourteen hours flying to the other side of the world. There's nothing glamorous about eating insipid airline food, constantly being jet-lagged, and dealing with insufferable corporate bullshit. I got to bang a stewardess here and there, but it still wasn't worth it.

Anyway, I never owned a permanent home; I always rented. What was the point? I was in the air half the time. I wasn't intending to be a commercial pilot for the rest of my life. I planned on eventually getting a normal job, most likely in the aerospace industry. Then I'd buy a home and settle down.

My current route ended at Newark Airport in New Jersey. Thanks to the geniuses who do the scheduling, there was a three-day layover before I had to be back at the same airport. Three days. I lived in Bangor, Maine, and would have to waste a good portion of the first and third days just to go home and back. It wasn't worth the hassle. But then, what the hell do you do in a state like New Jersey for three days? Sell drugs? File a cockamamie disability claim? Maybe participate in a drive-by shooting? At least I had enough time to get loaded and sleep it off before the next route.

One of my colleagues recommended this upscale restaurant that had a large barroom, well known for catering to single professionals. So I decided to check it out. Sitting at the bar, I spied this hot blonde. Her girlfriend became absorbed in a conversation with some other guy at the bar, and now the blonde was flying solo. I didn't waste any time, offering to buy her a drink, to which she agreed. Her name was Karen Gardner. We talked for hours, had dinner, and then screwed our brains out for the next two days. Karen grew up in Jersey and was in town visiting old friends and relatives. She owned a florist shop in some small town in Vermont called Crestwood Lake.

Our relationship intermittently evolved. My schedule wreaked havoc on it. And it was such an ordeal getting to her town: a four-hour drive from my apartment to her. Even with five or six days off, it was still a long haul. We always met at her place, since I had extended periods of free time, and she had a business to run six days a week. But I really liked her, and was starting to fall in love. Eventually, as we got closer, I wouldn't even go home. I would just fly to the Burlington, Vermont airport, drive the two hours to Karen's, and stay with her.

But staying at Karen's had its problems too. Karen and her roommate Liz rented their house. It was obvious that Liz wasn't thrilled about me being there for days at a time. Karen offered her extra rent, but Liz still dropped subtle hints about us getting our own place. Karen couldn't afford her own home. Nobody makes a fortune selling flowers, especially in a small town.

Then one day, Liz, not so subtly, left the newspaper on Karen's desk, open to the real estate section. She had circled an ad for a neighborhood house that was available for sale or rent. Karen and I discussed it and decided to rent it and move in together. Renting was fine with me. I didn't want to purchase anything yet, being uncertain of my occupational future. Karen was also amenable to renting, but probably for different reasons. I never asked her directly, but I suspected she wasn't quite as committed to the relationship as me. My feelings were a little further along than hers. Extracting yourself from a lease is easier than a mortgage, and I sensed that Karen still wanted to be able to reach the rip cord. So we went forward with the rental despite my twinge of uneasiness.

The house was a midsize colonial on Crestwood Lake Road, which encircled the lake. It was on the street side, not the lake side. Being right on the water would have been preferable, but it was only a rental. Some old spinster, a Mrs. Cleary, lived there her entire life. Her daughter (our new landlord), found her dead one day. She had apparently overdosed on her numerous medications. They couldn't tell if it was intentional or not. Her daughter insisted that her mother wasn't senile, but she was just as opposed to the prospect of suicide. She professed that her mother always seemed content with her life, and sometimes beamed like a woman in love. Assuming the daughter's reports were accurate, it sure was one hell of a mystery. I was a little creeped out about moving into a home where someone died, but Karen seemed oddly indifferent.

I took two weeks' vacation to complete several chores on the house. From the moment we moved in, weird things began to happen. On the first day I found a freshly killed squirrel in the basement. It appeared to have been partially eaten. It looked as if someone or something held it like a piece of fried chicken and started munching. There was no blood, just the carcass. How was that possible? If the squirrel had been eviscerated outside, it clearly wouldn't have been able to crawl inside. If it was attacked and partially consumed in the basement, where was the blood?

And more disturbingly: what the hell was in my house that could tear bite-sized chunks out of a squirrel? I told Karen about the gruesome discovery, but she was more concerned that I disposed of it, than the disconcerting implications.

Two days later I woke up early and spent five hours painting two rooms. Karen was at her florist shop. Feeling tired, I made some lunch and took a nap on the living room couch, only to be awoken by this loud, resounding growl. It sounded like a monstrous, rabid dog was in the next room, seconds from lunging. I sprang off the couch like my ass was on fire. The growling immediately ceased. I bolted into the next room but nothing was there. I stood there, looking around, stupefied. I grabbed our biggest kitchen knife and went through the house room by room. I found nothing, not even the sanity I thought I was losing. Assuming it had been a bad dream, I chugged a beer and got lost in putting up shelves in Karen's new walk-in closet. I didn't tell Karen about it; she'd think I had a screw loose.

Karen had one part time employee, a woman named Sherri. On the days Sherri worked, Karen would leave early to assist with the house. Otherwise, she needed to be at the shop until early evening. The after-work window was naturally a prime sales time and she couldn't afford to lose any business. The local supermarket sold flowers cheaper, and she couldn't give potential customers any more reasons to bypass her shop.

Whenever she did get home, she certainly pitched in. It was mostly cleaning, painting, and minor repairs. Old Mrs. Cleary hadn't exactly kept up with the place in her elder years, and her daughter didn't want to be bothered, so she gave us a break on the rent to fix the place ourselves. Karen did her share, but seemed to be irritable a lot. I wasn't sure what to make of it. I asked her about her testiness, but she attributed it to having to work all day at her store, and then all night on the house.

My sleep was erratic. Obviously, as a pilot, your schedule prevents you from ever establishing a regular sleep regimen. I usually woke up very early. My morning routine was to plop on the couch with my coffee and watch the news, easing into the day. But now I had a bevy of household tasks.

One morning I got up at four thirty. Karen was dead asleep and didn't have to get up until seven thirty. I groggily staggered down the stairs toward the kitchen to turn on the coffee pot. The house was dark except for the meager amount of light that distant street lights and the moon provided. It was sufficient to see a rough outline of the rooms and larger pieces of furniture. I weaved through the living room and then abruptly stopped. On the other side of the room stood a dark figure. Even with the limited light, I could ascertain a rough human form. I froze in fear, not knowing what to do. Maybe it was just something in the room that resembled a person in the dark. But what if it was a person? I ran to the light switch and flicked it—nothing was there: nothing in or near that spot that could account for it. Maybe it was some kind of optical illusion. So I turned the light back off, but it was still gone. That was even more vexing. So I blamed it on the hour and my pre-coffee bleariness, but that still didn't take away my willies.

I headed straight for the kitchen, turned on the lights and discovered a dead mouse on the floor. Or should I say…half a dead mouse. Imagine if you would, clutching a mouse by its haunches, inserting its head into your mouth, viciously bisecting it with your teeth, and disposing the posterior on the floor. Sorry for the graphic detail, but now you have a perfect image of what confronted me in the kitchen.

I called an exterminator that day. In the absence of a cat or a dog, he couldn't provide an explanation for the partially devoured mouse or squirrel. He nevertheless set all kinds of traps and baits in the cellar, attic, and outside. I told Karen about the mouse but not the dark figure. She didn't seem too fazed. How could she be so indifferent to finding half-eaten rodents in our dwelling?

There was an array of other oddities, some of them so minor that they could be easily explained away. What couldn't be explained away was the number of them, and the fact that they didn't happen to Karen. I would come up from the basement after turning off all the lights, become occupied elsewhere in the house, return to the basement later, and find a light on. Obviously it slipped my mind—or I'm going psychotic—or I'm transposing between parallel universes—or there's a little goblin in the house eating rodents and messing with my head. See the dilemma? The brain's forced to accept the "forgot the light" excuse even though it simultaneously knows it didn't.

I would place an object in one room and a day later it would appear in another. Karen swore she didn't touch it. Did she forget? Did I forget? Did neither of us forget and the goblin borrowed it? One day I heard the distinct sound of footsteps in the attic. Like an overweight man stomping his way across the beams. I flew up there with a flashlight and a kitchen knife, searched the entire attic, and found nothing but another dead mouse. This one was missing all four legs. I was about to go mad. In what universe does this make sense?

As a pilot, we study science, mathematics, and aeronautics. Our brains are reality-based. We deal with irrefutable facts and the laws of nature. How the hell does a mouse end up in your attic with no legs? It certainly didn't walk there. And what pulled, chewed or otherwise wrested the legs from the hapless creature? And if it was eating it, why just the legs? The questions were roiling over and over in my brain.

The next day I found a string of dead wasps on the dining room table—arranged in the shape of an upside down pentagram! It was so eerie... so discomposing. I left them there to show Karen. As soon as she walked through the door that night I escorted her to the table.

"Ewwwwww," she whined. "Why didn't you get rid of them?"

Why was she not getting how bizarre this was? "I will," I replied, cocking my head and looking at her as if *she* was brain-damaged. "Don't you think this is strange? It's not just one dead wasp on the floor. How could a whole bunch of them die on the table, and arrange themselves in the shape of an upside down pentagram?"

"A pentagram?"

"Yes. A fucking pentagram! An upside down pentagram. Do you know what a pentagram is? It's a five-pointed star. It's used as a symbol in religion and spirituality. But it's also a symbol in devil worship, particularly when the star is upside down, as it is here."

Karen looked at me as if *I* was the one who was fruit loops. "What are you talking about?" she asked.

"Look here. If you draw a line between the wasps you get a perfect five-pointed star, only upside down. The center point of the star, which is usually on top, is on the bottom, and the two bottom points are on the top. That's a symbol of Satanism. I know this because we had this Haitian whacko in the service. He believed in voodoo, the Devil, and other demented shit. He had a T-shirt with an upside down pentagram on it. He eventually ended up in a psych unit and got discharged. Anyway, forget the pentagram. Don't you think it's strange that a bunch of wasps would all die in this neat little arrangement on our dining room table?"

"I don't...know," muttered Karen. "Yeah I guess it's a little peculiar, but I think you're acting a little kooky about it too."

"That's because this isn't the only weird thing that's happened around here. I haven't said anything because I didn't want you to think that I was nuts."

"What else has happened?"

"Well, one day I was sleeping, and distinctly heard a large dog growling in the house. Another morning I saw a dark figure in the house, but when I turned the lights on, it was gone. Then there are all the different objects that magically relocate to other rooms. I also heard footsteps up the attic, and when I investigated, I found another dead mouse, only this one had no legs. Now why would a mouse, even a dead one, be missing its legs and nothing else?"

Karen took a piece of paper, scooped up the wasps and threw them in the garbage. Then she took my hand and sat me down at the dining room table. She looked at me and said, "Honey, listen to me. Now please don't think I'm pooh-poohing your concerns. Yeah it's a few unusual coincidences, but all explicable. If you were sleeping when you heard this dog, you could have been dreaming, or maybe heard some noise outside that in your sleepy state sounded like it was in the room. As for the figure in the dark...baby, it's easy to mistake things or see shadows in the dark. And the objects showing up in other rooms? With all the work you've been doing in the house, inevitably you're going to misplace some items, or forget where you put them. The footsteps on the roof? Who knows? An animal? Local kids throwing a rock or a baseball that hit the roof and bounced? I'll give you that the mouse with no legs and the wasps are kinda freaky. But not freaky enough to start talking about voodoo and devil worship."

Now I really felt like a mental case. Maybe I *was* a little stressed. Maybe it was my underlying anxiety that Karen was not as invested in our relationship as me. Maybe I was pissed about doing most of the work on the house. I didn't know what to say. I just looked at her sheepishly.

"C'mon baby," she said. "We need a break. No work tonight, no cleaning. Let's grab a bottle of wine and go to the local pizzeria. Whadda ya say? Pizza and wine."

"Sure, that sounds wonderful."

"I have this wine I want to try." She walked into the kitchen, slipped a bottle out of the rack, returned to the dining room and handed it to me. "I went to that new wine shop in town. The owner recommended this bottle of Barolo."

"Barolo?" I said, examining the label.

"It's a fine wine from the Piedmont region in Northern Italy. The owner claims it's hailed as the King of Italian wines. You've flown to Turin right?"

"Yeah, a few times. In fact, I'm going there on the route after the next one."

"It's from that area," said Karen. "Turin's the capital of Piedmont. The Italians call it Torino."

"Sounds expensive."

"It can be pricey. This was his last bottle of this particular one, and he gave it to me cheap. Let's go eat."

So we went to the pizzeria in town. The wine was exceptionally good. So was the pizza. So was getting out of the house of horrors and relaxing for a little while. A five-day schedule awaited me in two days. I dreaded it and looked forward to it at the same time.

The next day I took it easy, doing only a few miscellaneous things on the house. I had to be up early the next morning and get to the airport. That evening I spent time packing and getting ready for my five days of bouncing all over the world. I tried to get amorous with Karen, but she said she had her period. I told her it was fine with me, "that we have to earn our wings every day," but she ignored my crack and said that was gross. She didn't seem inclined to please me in any other manner either. In fact, ever since we got the house, she seemed much less physical than usual. More things for me to worry about at thirty thousand feet.

That night I had trouble sleeping. What a surprise. Finally I drifted off but had a terrible dream: my plane was going down. People were screaming, the instruments were going berserk, and the plane was in an uncontrollable dive. Suddenly I awoke, covered in sweat with my heart racing. What a ghastly dream! Every pilot's worse fear. Don't ever believe or trust any pilot who tells you he doesn't think about it.

I turned on the light, located my tranquilizers (unofficially obtained), and took one. I checked the alarm to make sure it was set properly, turned off the light and lay there. Waiting for the pill to kick in, I decided to go to the bathroom. I didn't really have to go, but figured it was better than being woken again with a full bladder. I didn't turn the light back on, not wanting to wake Karen, even though she always slept like a corpse. Didn't this woman have any anxieties?

I made my way to the bathroom, creeping down the hallway, running my hand along the wall to guide me. I peered down the corridor and saw it again! The same dark figure from the living room the other morning. My heart started to race again. I frantically scoured the wall with my hand, searching for the light switch. A gentle breeze of warm air slid across my face, as if someone was breathing on me. I heard the growl again, and then heard—in an angry whisper—"*Get out!*"

I freaked! I ran back to the bedroom, turned on the night table light, and then ran back to the hallway. It was now bright enough for me to see the light switch. I turned it on and saw nothing. Nothing! Absolutely nothing. Feeling unhinged, I went back to the bedroom to check on Karen, who was fast asleep. I left the bedroom and proceeded to check every other room in the house, finding yet another dead mouse. Only this time the eyes were missing! I didn't know what to do or think. What was happening to me? How to make sense out of it? I *had* to make sense out of it.

I saw three possibilities. One, I was going crazy. Two, I wasn't going *crazy* per se, but had some kind of medical condition that was affecting my brain. Or three, the house was truly haunted. I ruled out number one immediately. Number two wasn't a hot choice either. I had no physical symptoms of disease. Pilots undergo regular medical testing to ensure we are fit to fly. All my results came back normal, as they always did. That left three, but three was outright insane, especially in my $E=MC^2$ world. That returned me to number one.

But then I thought of my previous rationale: it was stress, just stress. But I didn't completely buy it. I've certainly had more trying times than patching up an old house and doubting my relationship, and didn't lose it then. And stress didn't place mutilated rodents and symbolically arranged bugs in the house. Nevertheless, I continued to try and convince myself that most of it was due to stress. Then I thought that maybe it was good I'd be gone for a while. Get my mind off the house and Karen and see where things stood upon my return. I threw the mouse into the side yard and went back to bed.

The next morning, I woke up feeling like I had a hangover. I showered, got dressed, fetched my bags, and went down to the kitchen. Karen was making breakfast.

"Hey, baby," she said in a cheerful voice—unusually cheery.

What was she so goddamned happy about?

"Want some eggs?" she asked.

"No. I'm not hungry. I didn't sleep well, and just want to get to the airport before the traffic starts."

"Oh, I'm sorry." She gave me a big hug and a kiss, and rattled off various important items to make sure I didn't forget anything. "Don't worry about the house. I'll take care of everything while you're gone. You just come home safe and don't forget to call me."

We said our final goodbyes and I left.

It was an exhausting stretch: numerous flights around the east coast ending in Florida, then to the Caribbean, Texas, and finally Memphis. However, the Memphis flight got cancelled. Thank God. This would mean I'd get home a day early. I decided not to tell Karen in order to surprise her. To be frank, I also liked the idea of showing up early and unannounced to see what she was up to.

I got into the Burlington airport Sunday at noon. This was perfect: Karen would be home on Sunday, or at least she should be. I got to my car as fast as possible and sped home.

The road next to our house was on a sharp incline, peaking near our bedroom window. Heading over the top of the hill, one could gaze into the bedroom if the shades were up. Karen usually kept the one window uncovered. The moon normally rose on that side of the house and she liked to lie in bed and look at it.

Sure enough, cresting the hill, I peered through that window. My stomach sank. Although it was only two, maybe three seconds, I saw Karen, lying on the bed naked with the dark figure on top of her between her legs! I zoomed into the driveway, jumped out of the car, unlocked the door, and dashed upstairs to the bedroom. Karen was alone! She was on the bed startled, sweating, naked, looking surprised. Her vibrator was on the nightstand.

"Honey!" she exclaimed, wheezing and out of breath. "Why didn't you tell me you were coming home?"

"What's going on here?"

"Nothing," she panted. "I was…I was…I was just…"

I quickly darted into the closet, then into every upstairs room. Nobody was there. I returned to the bedroom. Karen was putting on her pink, silk robe.

"What are you doing?" she asked. "What's wrong?"

"What were *you* doing?"

She started to catch her breath. "I…I…I was just"—she turned her head toward the vibrator—"you know…"

I wasn't sure how to act or what to say. Nobody could have left the house, or even reached the downstairs in the time between when I first saw them and when I entered. Clearly nobody else was upstairs. What the hell? I just get home and I'm imagining phantasms already? I just stood there like an addled idiot.

Karen strolled over, put her arms around me, gave me a kiss and said, "Honey, what's wrong? Are you mad at me for pleasuring myself?" Then she started acting and talking like a submissive little coquette. "Maybe you could take over now," she said in a little girl voice, running her finger down the side of my cheek to my chest. She undid her robe and practically threw it off her body. God she looked beautiful, standing there with her thick blonde hair mussed up so sexily. And she was obviously still aroused. No man in his right mind could refuse that. My demons would have to wait.

It was good to be home…or so I thought. But my arrival was so discombobulating. I could have sworn I saw the dark figure with Karen. Then it vanished leaving me to wonder again about my perceptions, my sanity, or something else. Then the sex with Karen was rapturously intense. She was so lustful and enticingly servile. I was dumbstruck, not knowing what to think. I had been shocked to the extreme, then seduced and ravished, all within minutes.

I spent the rest of the day trying to get my bearings and relax. Karen slowly transitioned from sensuous, to aloof and slightly irascible. It confused me, but I didn't say a word; better to give her some space and avoid any confrontations. I only had until Thursday before my next schedule began. As I told Karen, I was flying into Turin, Italy, then on to various European destinations. The next couple of days had to be peaceful.

The next day, I tinkered on a variety of minor projects. All the major work on the house was completed. I was in the basement organizing my tools and came across yet another dead mouse. Its tail and ears were missing. Here we go again. The whirlwind in my mind commenced. What creature could have done this? And why would that creature only remove its tail and ears? Why didn't it just eat the whole damn mouse? And why weren't all the traps and baits the exterminator deployed working? I focused on the latter question only because it seemed to be more tangible than the others. I called the exterminator, who stated the baits don't work immediately…the poison works days after it's consumed…the dead mice probably had already been poisoned…and so forth. That still didn't explain the condition I was finding them in. In any event, the exterminator was booked that week, but offered to send someone out next week. I would be halfway around the world by then, but told them OK. Let Karen worry about it.

The next day, Tuesday, was extremely unnerving: plagued with one quirky event after another. I could have sworn I left my coffee cup in the living room, but found it in the bathroom. Once again, I left the basement certain the lights were all off, only to find some on later in the day. Two dead wasps appeared in the sugar bowl. I heard water running through the pipes even though nothing was on that used water. One window in the dining room kept fogging over while all the rest were crystal clear. Throughout the day, a number of my items were missing, the most important being my airline ID badge. I searched everywhere, but couldn't find it. Immensely frustrated, I gave up and had a glass of wine to calm my nerves. Upon finishing the last sip I explosively vomited all over the kitchen counter. I cleaned the mess and just curled up in the recliner with a blanket, afraid to do anything. I tried to take a nap, but couldn't unwind. I was genuinely regretting moving in with Karen, or at least into this house.

Finally I got up, went into the kitchen, and started making dinner; it would give me something to occupy my mind. The main kitchen window overlooked the deck. In the middle of the deck we had a small table and two outdoor chairs. Looking out the window my gaze was met by a large gray cat with piercing green eyes, perched upon the table. It stared straight at me, not moving a muscle. An unnatural stare—an evil stare—as if every brain cell in its head was fixated on my being. I felt like it wanted to kill me—to destroy me. I stared back, not out of anger or even defiance, but more out of dismay. The cat didn't flinch; it just continued to stare me down. I stood there, transfixed.

Suddenly, something sharp stung my neck. I smacked it, but got another sharp jolt in my palm. Opening my hand, a wasp, still buzzing, fell to the floor. "God damn you!" I yelled, stomping it, and grinding it with the ball of my foot. I looked up and saw the cat, hissing viciously at me, so loudly it could be heard through the closed window. Its head was bent forward and every hair along its arched back was on end. Its mouth was wide open, teeth fully bared, nostrils flaring, demonic green eyes penetrating my soul. I ran to the bathroom, washed the stings, put some ice on them, and looked out the kitchen window. The cat was gone.

I called Karen and told her what happened. She was dismissive, instead focusing on the Chinese takeout she wanted for dinner. By the time she got home my stings were easing. As we ate I told her about the cat. Karen denied ever seeing it before. She asked me a number of detailed questions about my next route: when I was packing, the precise time I was leaving the house, etc. It seemed like Karen was looking forward to my departure.

Wednesday morning Karen told me she had to stay at the store late that night to catch up on some tasks. It irked me, but I didn't say anything. I was only home until Thursday evening—couldn't she put her work off until then? And other than the ravenous escapade the previous Sunday, she hadn't been in the mood for sex. Something was brewing, something was wrong between us. There was no point in bringing it to a head with less than two days to go. It wouldn't be wise to begin an extended journey, with numerous flights, on the heels of an eruption in our relationship. After this next schedule I would be home for nearly a week and could address it then.

The remainder of the day was strangely calm. No dead vermin, no missing articles, no lights left on, no psycho-cats from hell giving me the evil eye. I did some preliminary packing and took care of a few loose ends. I thought about calling Karen and offer to pick up some dinner and bring it to her shop. It would be nice if we could at least have supper together, but then I changed my mind. She obviously didn't care about working late the day before I was supposed to leave. She might be in a mood. Or maybe whatever was fermenting in the bowels of our relationship would regurgitate itself all over our dinner. It had been an uneventful day and I decided to leave it that way.

Karen got home about eight o'clock. She scrounged up some leftovers and made a makeshift meal. Her mood was better than expected, but she made it very clear that she was tired. I didn't need a cryptographer to break that code. A wet dream was the only potential action in my immediate future. Nevertheless, we chatted while she ate. I threw out some suggestions of things we could do together when I returned. She reacted positively on the surface, but I surmised she was just humoring me.

We went to bed early. Karen was fatigued, and I definitely needed a good night's sleep. I was leaving at 5:00 p.m. the next day, driving three and a half hours to Boston's Logan Airport, and flying the red-eye to Turin. Karen zonked out immediately. I however, lay there for hours, my mind a tempest of ruminations. I thought about our relationship and if we had a future, but mostly I obsessed on all of the bizarre incidents in the house. All of the plausible explanations in the world could not satisfy the maelstrom in my mind.

I was developing a headache. My aspirin was in the kitchen. I went downstairs, entered the kitchen, but before turning on a light, heard: "*Get out*," only this time it was hoarser and louder. It came from outside the kitchen—from the deck. I scrambled to the wall and flicked on the deck lights. There, to my horror, was the gray cat, glaring at me with those hellish green eyes! I wanted to wring its neck. I unlatched the sliding door and practically threw it off its track. The cat sprang away far quicker than I could react. I was terrified and furious at the same time. I swear to God, if I had gotten a hold of it, I would have killed it with my bare hands.

I turned around, about to storm out of the kitchen when I almost stepped on a dead squirrel! Half a dead squirrel! The front legs and head were gone, the back legs, hindquarters and tail lay on my kitchen floor. Assorted entrails oozed their way out of what was left of the torso. I hollered so loud that Karen came running down the stairs into the kitchen.

"Look! Look at this shit! I'm sick of this fucking shit!"

"Calm down, calm down," she kept saying, but it was too late.

I was screaming: "I will not fucking calm down! I'm sick of finding dead animals and mutilated animals, and dead bugs, and getting stung by bugs, and that frigging cat was just here. I heard something yell 'Get out' on the deck, so I turned on the light and the gray cat was there staring at me." My voice got louder and louder. "I turn lights off, and then they're on. I put things in one room, and they appear in another. I'm hearing dogs growling, water running, footsteps in the attic, and I know I saw some kind of creature between your legs when I got home Sunday!"

Karen nervously put her arms around me and said, "Honey, please calm down, please, I love you. Take it easy. Come here, get out of the kitchen." She led me to the dining room. "Please, sit down a minute."

As I sat, she stroked the back of my head and kissed me on the cheek. "I'll take care of the squirrel, baby, please just sit and take a breath for a moment. You have to get some sleep tonight. You have to fly tomorrow. Let me get you a drink." She went to the kitchen, opened up a cabinet and poured something into a glass. She came back and said, "Here, take this. It's whiskey."

I did start to calm down. It was soothing just to have Karen be so nice to me. She even said she loved me. I wasn't completely sold on that, but it felt good nonetheless. Sipping the whiskey, I heard the sliding door open, and Karen walking out onto the deck. Karen walked back in, closed the door, and returned to the dining room.

"I got rid of it, baby."

I finished the rest of the whiskey and collected my thoughts. "I'm not staying in this house anymore, Karen. Whether we stay together or not, I'm not living here anymore. Something is going on in this house, and I don't give a shit if it's something explainable or not. I've had it. I hate this house."

"OK, OK, baby," Karen said, obviously trying to placate me. "We'll work it out when you get back. Please, let's go to bed. You have to get some rest."

I took a sleeping pill. Pilots aren't supposed to take medications like that, but I didn't care. I had to sleep. The next day I'd be flying all night. It would be more dangerous for me to be up all night. Besides, the sleeping pill would wear off well before I was in the cockpit.

With Karen's solace, the belt of whiskey, and the pill, I finally dozed off, sleeping straight through to the morning. I awoke and heard Karen in the kitchen. I sat up in bed and thought about the night before…then went downstairs.

Karen greeted me with a jaunty good morning and said, "Here's your coffee, baby. I have to finish getting ready for work." Then she went into the bathroom.

I finished my cup by the time Karen came back into the kitchen.

"Karen, listen to me. I'm going to say goodbye to you now. I can't sit in this house until five o'clock tonight. I'll go crazy. I'm going to pack and leave early. The pilots have their own lounge at the airport. I can rest, watch TV, get something to eat, whatever."

"No problem, honey."

She gave me a big hug and a kiss and wished me well. I told her again that I wasn't staying in this house anymore. She said she understood and that we'd discuss the details when I got back. She gave me another hug and reminded me to call her.

Karen left for her store. I had some breakfast and started getting ready. I packed everything I owned that was important, or highly valuable, even if I didn't need it: jewelry, my checkbook, my birth certificate, social security card, etc. I just felt safer having my most vital possessions with me.

I had a carry-on bag. I emptied it out completely and then repacked it. I put all my assorted work-related paperwork in it, then my documents, valuables and toiletries. Also some medications, permissible stuff like aspirin and my heartburn pills. I still couldn't find my ID badge, but had all day to get a new one at the airport.

I was almost ready to leave, but had to use the bathroom. I certainly didn't want to stop somewhere on my way to the airport. Sitting on the toilet I noticed the roll of paper was empty. Dammit! Is it so hard to replace the roll when you're done? I reached around the back of the toilet where Karen usually kept an extra roll. Groping aimlessly I heard a high-pitched shriek and then felt a sudden, sharp pain. The cat had sunk its fangs into my wrist! I yanked my arm back as the cat darted out of the bathroom. Two unusually strong streams of blood squirted out of the punctures and sprayed the wall. "You motherfucker!" I yelled. I grabbed a nearby bath towel, clamped it on my wrist, and applied pressure. Removing it to inspect my wounds, I saw two distinct perforations. Then I looked where the blood had sprayed. With my mouth agape, utterly aghast, I stared at the wall. The blood had formed itself into the words: *get out!*

I've never been so close to a complete nervous breakdown. I hurriedly pulled my pants up. I punched the mirror on the medicine cabinet door, smashing it into pieces. I charged through the house, grabbing my stuff, knocking over anything in my way. I was crazed. It took all my psychological strength to remember everything, because there was no way on this earth I was ever setting foot in this house again. And at that moment, I didn't care if I ever saw Karen again either. I tore out of the house, not even bothering to turn off lights or close the door. I sprinted to my car, threw my stuff into the back seat and screeched out of the driveway like a madman.

I raced to the airport, hazardously weaving in and out of traffic. I needed to feel safe. The airport and my job were separate from the house. They were the secure part of my life. I didn't start calming down until parking my car and entering the terminal. It was eleven hours until the flight, but I didn't care. I went to the lounge and just rested all day. I watched TV, read magazines, took a walk around the airport, bullshitted with other pilots, and got something to eat. The wound on my wrist was sore, but wasn't bleeding and didn't look infected.

A couple of hours before the flight I called Karen, only because I had promised her. I actually didn't feel like talking to her. Anything having to do with that house was making me feel dangerously unbalanced. Not wanting to relive it, I didn't tell her what happened in the bathroom. We had a short conversation. I used the excuse that I had to get ready for the flight. I told her that I loved her, but actually wasn't sure. I just wanted to end the conversation on a positive note. She said, "I love you too," and hung up.

We took off on time, and without any issues. The weather was clear and our destination wasn't reporting any delays or problems. My mind however, bubbled with thoughts and fears. For the first time in my life I was actually considering the possibility of the supernatural. There was no rational explanation for what my blood did that morning. What disturbed me the most was, a preternatural force had permeated my body—my essence. I felt violated from the inside out—like I was possessed. And was this the end of it? Or would it follow me throughout life? Was it just the house? Did it have something to do with Karen? It was driving me nuts. I had no way of knowing. The ambiguity and uncertainty of it all was painfully perplexing. My preoccupation must have been observable, as my copilot asked me a few times during the flight if I was all right.

If I broke up with Karen how would I get my things? Conversely, if I didn't break up with Karen how would I get them? I wasn't going back in that house. Could I tell her about what happened this morning? If I told her what happened she'd think I was crazy, but if I refused to go home without an explanation, she'd think the same. Maybe I should just end it with her and move on. Or, stay at a hotel when I got back, lay everything on the line to her, and see what happened. Or maybe we—

"Captain, we're about ready to start making our descent," said my copilot interrupting my tortured train of thought. "Mind if I hit the latrine first?"

"Sure go ahead, I'll wait for you."

While he went to the can I seized my carry-on bag to look for my aspirin. I had a whopper of a headache, and didn't want my copilot to know about it. When you're in charge of an aircraft, you can't afford to look the slightest bit off your game. And he already knew that I was stewing over something.

I swished my right hand around the bottom of the bag, feeling for the aspirin bottle, when I touched something furry and gooey. I clenched the object and pulled out my hand. It was the first half of the squirrel! I was holding it by the shoulders, front paws and entrails dangling onto my palm. Suddenly it came to life! It cocked its head, as the eyes lit up into two fiery red orbs! It stared directly at me! And in the same voice as the cat last night, it looked me square in the eyes and growled: *"You're dead!"*

And that is when I lost my mind.

• • •

Karen lay on the bed in her pink, silk robe, head propped against a pillow. She reached over to the nightstand and turned on the radio, just in time to catch the top of the hour news:

"There has been a plane crash in Europe this morning. New England Airlines flight 420, a Boeing 737, left Logan Airport last night, and went down in the French Alps, just south of Lake Geneva, en route to Turin, Italy. Witnesses say the plane nosedived into the mountains and exploded in a tremendous fireball. All 174 passengers and crew are presumed dead. The cause of the crash is yet unknown, but authorities report there is no suspicion of terrorism at this time. Rescuers on the scene report that it was a powerful impact as evidenced by the small pieces of wreckage in the debris field. The plane had apparently just begun its descent—"

Karen turned off the radio and smirked. She scratched the gray cat's head with her long nails. It purred wildly. Then she threw something on the floor and said, "Go play." The cat leapt off the bed and clenched the ID badge in its teeth.

Karen undid her robe and pulled it open, exposing her naked body. She spread her legs and began touching her breasts. A claw-like hand placed a string of dead wasps on the dining room table in the shape of an upside down pentagram. A large, dark, figure materialized on top of Karen, inserting itself between her legs. She wrapped her arms and legs around it and said, "Now we can be together forever, baby."

THE LAKE

Morgan was cruising along Interstate 91 in his pickup on his way back to Crestwood Lake. It was half past three in the afternoon. He had spent the day traveling to a number of nearby towns. He was still investigating possible leads, and interviewing people with even remote connections to Brian Delmore. The mayor was exerting unrelenting pressure and Morgan was exploring every possibility. Unfortunately, not a shred of evidence had surfaced as to whom or what had butchered the poor teen.

He had heard about the plane crash two days before on the news. The next day he received a call from a federal air marshal. The marshal informed him that the pilot was from Crestwood Lake. It didn't take the Feds long to ascertain he was living with Karen Gardner, whom they had already contacted. They planned to interview Karen and examine the residence to determine if anything in his personal life might shed light on the crash. The marshal acknowledged that the pilot had officially resided in Crestwood Lake only about a month, but nonetheless asked if Morgan knew anything about him or Karen. Morgan had no knowledge about the pilot. He did know Karen (as he did every business owner in town), but not well. He explained that she had never been on his radar for any reason. The marshal didn't require Morgan's presence or assistance with interviewing Karen. The only reason he deigned to contact Morgan was in case he might be useful to his own investigation.

Had nothing else transpired in Crestwood Lake recently, Morgan probably wouldn't have given the plane crash much thought. But this was yet another perturbing coincidence involving his town. Karen Gardner wasn't an immediate priority, but she was now on the agenda in Morgan's head.

Suddenly, a black Dodge Charger with tinted windows zoomed by at nearly one hundred miles per hour.

"Jesus Christ!" hollered Morgan. He slammed the accelerator and placed his flashing light on his dashboard, but the Charger was unimpressed. As Morgan started to gain on it, he radioed the state police for backup.

The Charger wove back and forth across the two-lane highway struggling to lose the pickup, but Morgan was unshakable. As the car swung to the right, Morgan floored it and shot up along its driver side. The Charger's driver-side window opened, followed by a gunshot. The bullet pierced Morgan's passenger-side window, just missing his face. Morgan hit the brakes and careened around the back of the car to its right flank. He closed back in, opened his driver-side window, grabbed his Ruger .357 magnum with his left hand, and fired all six shots at the Charger's right rear wheel. The tire exploded. The Charger fishtailed to the right, flipped, slid on its side, and then spun sideways. It twirled countless times, then upended, finally resting on its passenger side.

Morgan pulled over, grabbed his double-barreled shotgun, pointed it at the car and started walking. Nothing could have survived that tumble, but he was ready to shoot. That was Morgan—never taking chances. He was about twelve feet from the vehicle when the driver suddenly stood up through the driver side window! He was scrawny, with pale-white skin, wild, shoulder-length black hair, and dark, sunken eyes. Blood was streaming down his face. He raised his hand and pointed his pistol. Morgan blasted him, blowing away half his head.

"Eat that shit!" exclaimed Morgan.

Morgan heard the sirens of approaching police cars. Two state troopers appeared on the horizon. They pulled up and ran out of their vehicles, guns drawn.

"Sorry, boys, but the party's over," said Morgan smugly. Morgan knew the older one. The young one was a rookie, brand new to the force. When the rookie got a look of what was left of the culprit he started to heave. As he was doubled over, retching and spitting, Morgan patted his back proclaiming, "Looks like I busted your cherry, boy."

After the rookie collected himself Morgan began relaying the sequence of events. Just then his lieutenant, Jack Dougherty, called him on his cell phone.

"Butch, it's Jack. A couple joggers found another body in the woods. One of them knew her. Her name is Sharon O'Connell, a local resident. Do you know her?"

"No I don't."

"It's the same thing as the Delmore boy. I mean, she's not dismembered but she's mutilated—slashed completely open. Medical examiner's on the way. I'm sure he'll want to remove the body before it gets dark. Can you get here before then?"

"No I can't. I'm on 91 with the state police. I just shot some punk who tried to kill me."

"Jesus, Butch, how the hell did—"

"Shut up. Listen, I want you to go over that crime scene with a fine tooth comb. Do as much of it as you can before it gets dark. Let Wyatt take the body when you're done. Meanwhile, we have to get another search party organized. Get on it right now. I'll call ya as soon as I'm done here."

"OK, Butch."

Hours later Morgan was on the phone with Dr. Wyatt. The doctor described his findings: "She had multiple wounds to her head and abdomen. They were all fatal so any one could have been the cause of death. They appear to have been inflicted at the same time so I can't pinpoint which one killed her."

"Go on," said Morgan.

"Well, some kind of object, with multiple, long, pointy projections penetrated both eyes and the mouth, all the way through to the brain. Then she was slashed from her throat to her vagina. I don't know by what. It wasn't a knife. Now listen, I didn't find any traces of an animal on or near the body. But the gash down her torso looks as if it was done by a claw."

"A claw?"

"Yeah, it looks like the same kind of gash that you see when a bear slashes a body. But it's not a bear."

"How can you be so sure?"

"Aside from the fact that we didn't find any animal hair or tracks, there are two reasons. First, a bear tends to slash more wildly. It certainly doesn't insert its claw into your face, and make a methodical, straight line all the way down to the pubic region. The victim has a controlled gash. Moreover, a bear would use its teeth as well, but the body didn't have any teeth marks on it."

"And the second reason?"

Wyatt paused and finally said, "Her heart and uterus are missing."

Morgan's stomach instantly sank, as if he had just drunk a glass of wet cement.

"Captain, no animal is going to remove specific organs. Like the Delmore boy, they were ripped from the body, but they were ripped out intact. An animal couldn't be that focused or discriminative. Now we have *two* bodies from which the reproductive organs and hearts were extracted. This is some kind of ritualistic killing. It has to be some kind of psycho."

"So how could a person do this? They'd need some kind of weapon. You said it wasn't a knife. What was it then?"

"Well...uh...uh..."

"Oh for Christ sake, Wyatt, can you please just tell me what you think?"

"Look, I don't know for sure, OK? There's not enough evidence. All I can do is speculate and I know you, Captain, anything from left field and you start getting pissed off."

In a gentle, but firm voice, Morgan said, "All right, Doc, I promise not to be a jerk. I need your help. I have two appalling murders and nothing to go on. I know we're dealing with something crazy. Please, I'll take your speculation."

Wyatt took a deep breath and let out a long, audible sigh. "It looks like some kind of claw, but not an animal claw. It's as if someone has a long hand, with long, pointy, sharp fingers. As I said, the holes in the eyes and mouth are the diameter of a finger. Only the one in the mouth is just a little bit wider. Underneath and to the side of each eye is another hole, as wide as a finger but not as deep. So it looks as if someone or something, inserted its middle two fingers in her eyes, and its thumb in her mouth simultaneously. The pinky and forefinger partially penetrated below the eyes. Then it took the other claw and ripped her open and took the organs. That's what it looks like even though I don't know what on this earth would have a hand like that."

Morgan kept his word, thanked the doctor, and enjoined him to contact him immediately with any new developments. As he got off the phone Officer Edwards knocked on his door.

"What is it?" asked Morgan.

"Uh, sir, I have the information about that guy you tangled with on 91."

"Go on."

"Well it looks like you did society a favor, sir; he was a drifter from Colorado."

"Colorado? What the hell was he doing out here?"

"Don't know, sir, but he's got quite an arrest record: drugs, shoplifting, assaults, drunk and disorderly, tons of traffic infractions, an animal cruelty charge he did a year for, one weapons charge he did three years for, and get this: he was arrested and tried for the murder of two teenage girls. Two jurors died under suspicious circumstances during the trial. He got a mistrial, but the prosecutor never re-filed the charges because in the interim, evidence that was in custody mysteriously disappeared. Oh, and the Charger he was driving was stolen."

"Hmmmph," snorted Morgan, "just when I thought I couldn't feel even better about blowing him away. Thanks, Edwards."

Later that night the police inspected Sharon's home, but discovered nothing that could demystify her murder. The next day, Morgan and other officers visited or called people who knew Sharon to interview them. They questioned every possible person with any link to Sharon. And once again, police canvassed the woods with numerous personnel and dogs. But just as in the Brian Delmore case, the paucity of clues was startling. Morgan was exasperated beyond words.

The following day Morgan received another call from Dr. Wyatt. "Captain, you instructed me to call right away with anything unusual. I just got done doing the autopsy on the guy you shot."

"Yeah?" said Morgan.

"He was somewhat malnourished and anemic. Clearly his diet had more drugs and alcohol than nutrients. Must have been in a lot of fights. I found quite a few old bruises and previously broken bones. But what's even more intriguing is the tattoo he had on his back. I mean, he had tattoos all over, and a few piercings, but spanning the entire width of his back, from shoulder to shoulder, was a large circle. Inside the circle was an upside down pentagram, and superimposed on the center of the pentagram was a sinister looking ram's head."

"So what does that mean?"

"Well I saw this before when I used to work in Manhattan. It's a symbol of the Devil or devil worship. This guy was some kind of mental case and into some very weird stuff. Lord knows why he was here from Colorado, but I'm sure it wasn't to go antiquing in quaint New England villages."

Morgan thanked the doctor, put his feet up on his desk, and rubbed his forehead. His satisfaction over eliminating a dangerous criminal was now turning into a festering consternation. Too many creepy elements had come into play. Morgan didn't like creepy. Not because he was afraid of it, but because he didn't believe in it, or at the very least, didn't understand it. It was too much of an unknown; a capricious variable that could unpredictably derail his logical and diligent methodology.

● ● ●

Debbie Kurzmann was a divorced, forty-year-old freelance photographer, bird watcher, hiker, and nature lover. She lived in upstate New York.

Reliable and skilled, her work was always in demand by magazines, books, and other forms of media. The diversity of her clients' needs afforded her the opportunity to venture throughout the country to myriad scenic areas. She felt that she had the best job in the world.

Debbie was married for seven years to a corporate executive. His job necessitated frequent travel as well, often to overseas destinations. In the beginning of their marriage they had hoped they could coordinate their itinerancies to ease the separations. Unfortunately, that proved to be infeasible. Their son also suffered, often spending more time with the live-in nanny than his parents. Eventually the marriage collapsed. They shared custody of the boy, but when he reached his teen years, he demanded to stay with his father. Debbie's ex had moved to Los Angeles and naturally, their son found L.A. more exciting than the sticks of upstate New York. This arrangement afforded her more time for her career and other passions. But she chronically missed her boy, and now had nagging doubts about whether she should have abandoned her occupation.

Her current assignment was for a publisher producing a book entitled *Colors of New England*. It was a pictorial guide to the natural beauty of New England during the four seasons. Debbie was crisscrossing her way through Vermont and New Hampshire on her way to Maine. Her publisher had given her precise locations to photograph, but also encouraged her to explore, and choose some of her own. Crestwood Lake was one of her personal selections. Debbie had visited it before during one of her previous New England jaunts. She still had months to complete her assignment. Nobody was expecting her any time soon, or knew exactly where she was.

The fall foliage had peaked, which was exactly what she needed. Debbie already had plenty of photos bursting with bright autumn hues. Now she wanted some shots of the transition to winter. Specifically, she desired a picture of Crestwood Lake with the sun setting between the thinning trees.

Debbie scoped out various spots and selected one on the northeast side of the lake. It was one of the more isolated and quieter sections of the shoreline, sprinkled with only a few homes. Debbie was trying to avoid any people who could distract her, or worse yet, enter her field of vision as she took pictures.

The sun had just reached the perfect angle. She crouched at the water's edge, the toe of one boot just touching the water, and began to shoot: click...click...click...click...click. She moved her body slightly, click...click...click. She rotated just a few degrees, click...click. She leaned forward just a little more, click...click...click...SPLASH! The water erupted violently. A large black creature lunged out of the lake and landed its hook-like claws into each of Debbie's thighs! She was so shocked she couldn't even scream, sucking in breath so hard she choked herself. Blood squirted from her femoral arteries, but Debbie was too terrified to even process the pain. The monster growled and dragged her back toward the water. Now she screamed with all her might, but it was too late. Debbie tried to dig her hands into the ground, but she was no match for the demon. He yanked her below as a swirl of blood and water formed a macabre eddy; an ephemeral, yet morbid residue signifying the last moment of Debbie Kurzmann's life in this realm.

• • •

The townsfolk were alarmed and on the edge of panic. Prior to the deaths of Brian Delmore and Sharon O'Connell, they were merely on edge. They knew that strange occurrences were increasing in their town, but their apprehension was still limited. The suicides of Ron Millhouse and the nun were grim, but not as frightening as murders. The people weren't overly concerned about Burke (who they assumed died of natural causes), Angus Miller (written off as a lone whack job), or the Jorgensens (rich, philandering snobs, who thought they were better than everybody, and probably deserved their fate). And virtually no one knew that the pilot of the recent plane crash was from Crestwood Lake. But now, after the horrid murders in the woods, the citizenry were justifiably affrighted, and demanding to know what was being done.

Clyde Burrows was the thirty-eight-year-old mayor of Crestwood Lake. His office was flooded with phone calls and unannounced visitors insisting on information. And as expected, the rebel rousers within the population were accusing the police and Burrows of incompetency, if not worse. Burrows feared that the fomenting unrest would undermine his next election. As with all politicians, votes meant more than anything else. So he announced that there would be a town meeting at the municipal building, headed by none other than Captain Morgan. He declared that Morgan would provide the town with an update on the investigation and answer all of their questions.

Morgan was livid that the mayor was putting him in this position. The investigations of both murders hadn't turned up anything. They had no promising leads and definitely no suspects. What was he supposed to tell the restive community?

Well here's the deal folks: we got some kind of psycho, or maybe a bunch of witches from the seventeenth century—not quite sure yet—on the loose out there. Either way, someone or something is running amok slaughtering innocent people and ripping out their gonads. Oh and by the way, we don't have any frigging clues. So we have no idea if it's going to happen again, or how to stop it. Thank you all for coming though. Have a good night.

Morgan put up an ardent protest, but Burrows was inexorable. Escalating to a shouting match, it reached a brink that if Morgan had said one more word his job would have been in jeopardy. He came very close to telling Burrows where he could go—and what he could do to himself once he got there. But Morgan, as much as he hated doing it, knew when to pull back. He was not going to be denied the chance to find the killer by losing his job.

Actually, based on the bylaws of the Crestwood Lake Town Charter, the mayor couldn't fire Morgan unilaterally. He needed a majority approval of the town council to terminate the chief of police. But if Morgan became outright insubordinate, it could sway enough members of the council, especially under the current circumstances. Bottom line: Morgan had to acquiesce to the mayor's demands.

The meeting room was packed with agitated residents. Morgan had to be on his best behavior with the townspeople. If he lost his cool with them he was done. The attendees weren't exactly unruly, but they were angry, unrelenting with their questions, and somewhat implacable. Morgan reached deep down inside himself. He thought about the men under his command and his responsibility to them. If he became defensive, loud, or confrontational in return, it would reflect poorly on all of them. He thought about Vicki—and telling her that he loved her. And most of all, he thought about heading to Gil's after the meeting and benumbing himself with some bourbon. Having relief in sight facilitated his equanimity.

And so he did his best. He let people vent without interrupting. He answered their questions as best as he could, calmly, and with civil language. He packaged the lack of leads in statements like "the investigation is still ongoing," and the "entire force would not rest until the killer was found." He stressed the overtime the police were working, the extra patrols, and their collaboration with the state police.

By the end of the meeting he had an oppressive headache, and a sweat-drenched shirt. On his way out he noticed Luther Van Haden, sitting silently in the back of the room, staring at him. He had been seated there the whole time, quietly listening to the meeting. It unnerved Morgan.

Gil was waiting for Morgan; he had their usual rye and bourbon ready. Morgan arrived, collapsed onto Gil's couch, and let out a long, depleted sigh. He was completely effete. Gil poured their drinks and took his usual spot on the loveseat. Betsy jumped up and plopped next to his lap. Stroking Betsy's neck, in a hesitating voice, Gil said, "Should I ask how it went?"

"It went exactly how I expected it would. They were on the verge of torches and pitchforks." And then with gritted teeth: "And Burrows, that cocksucker! I'd like to smash his skull into a bloody pulp. All he cares about is reelection. He forces me to take the heat to make him look good. Oh, and another thing. That fancy-pants, stuck-up douchebag who owns the new wine store was there. Luther Van Haden's his name. Have you met him?"

"No I haven't. What's his deal?"

"He just sat there in the back the whole time. Didn't say one word. I stopped in his shop the other day to check him out. You should see his store."

"I heard about it. No more beer or booze."

"It's even worse than that." Morgan took a sip of his bourbon. "Nothing but pretentious, expensive wines. He's got one huge bottle in a special cabinet worth thirty grand. I mean who the fuck does he think he is? And he's hiding something. I could tell that he knows more than what he's admitting to. Oh and get this, as I'm walking out of his store he tells me to say hi to Vicki…ya know, in a provocative kind of way. Now how the hell does he know Vicki, or that I have a connection with her? I don't like him, Gil. I don't like him one single bit. I get a very bad vibe from him. There's something about him (Morgan made a fist and shook it), I don't know what, but something."

"So what are you going to do next?" asked Gil. "I mean about the murders."

"I don't know." Morgan let out another long sigh. "I honestly don't know. We've pretty much exhausted every possible lead. We've talked with practically everybody in the victims' lives. There was nothing helpful at either crime scene. We searched their houses, their computers, their phones, their cars, the woods, all of it. Nothing."

"So what does that tell you?"

In a real snotty voice Morgan whined, "I don't know, Gil, what does that tell me?"

"Let me ask you an honest question. You've been a cop a long time. Does it make any sense to you, that two horrible murders like this could be perpetrated without any clues. I mean, absolutely nothing to go on as you've described?"

"No it doesn't. There would have to be something. Maybe not enough to find the killer, but at least something to go on, like tracks around the body or evidence of the kind of weapon he used, or suspicious people in the victim's life, but yeah, something."

"Then you need to start considering the alternatives. You need to at least consider what we talked about."

"I told you I'd go with you to see the witch doctor."

"He's not a witch doctor. He's a respected historian and parapsychologist."

"What exactly is a parapsychologist?" said Morgan with a derisive tone and a sneer.

"It's a branch of psychology that deals with psychic abilities. But many of them also extend their research into the occult and supernatural phenomena."

"So when are we going?"

"He can see us on Sunday. He lives in Cambridge. A little over three hours' drive."

"Yes, I know how far the Boston area is from here," said Morgan, once again sarcastically.

Gil just looked at him.

"I'm sorry. I'm really stressed out. I had a terrible night. I don't mean to be a prick. What's this guy's name again?"

"Doug Aaronson. He's quite accomplished. Two PhDs: one in psychology and one in history. He teaches both subjects at Boston University. He's written a number of books on the psychology of various eras in American history. His psychology specialty is parapsychology and his history specialty is the American colonial period. But he has a fervent interest in the occult, devil worship, witchcraft, and so on."

"So what's he gonna tell us, how to scare a ghost?"

"Forget the ghosts and witches for now. Even if it's just regular people into some kind of black magic, he could certainly provide information about their behaviors, rituals, motivations, etc. Undoubtedly that could help you with your investigation. You know, the investigation where you don't have *any* clues?"

"We have one clue," said Morgan.

"Oh really?"

Morgan hadn't planned on sharing with Gil what Wyatt divulged about the long, five-fingered claw that ravaged Sharon O'Connell's body. He didn't want to give Gil the satisfaction. But the bourbon was loosening him up, so he told Gil everything about O'Connell's autopsy.

"Bet you didn't share that at the town meeting, huh?" said Gil with a smile.

"Are you outta your mind? And there's something else."

"What?" asked Gil.

"Don't say I told you so. Don't even fucking *look* like you're thinking I told you so."

"OK, What?"

"Ya know that dirtbag I blew away the other day on 91? The medical examiner reported he had a huge tattoo across his back. A sign of devil worship: a ram's head in an upside down pentagram. You ever hear of anything like that?"

"Sure, that's a classic symbol in Satanism. You think he's connected with any of the events in Crestwood Lake?"

"I don't know. I just don't know. There are just too many bizarre things piling up. It's making me more and more nervous. Let's have another drink and talk about something else."

"OK," replied Gil, "Have you seen that new little brunette at the customer service counter in the supermarket? Oh my God what an ass!"

Morgan let out a brief snort. Reaching for the bottle of bourbon he said, "Ya know Gil, if they ever cracked open that head of yours they'd find three things: a giant pussy, a dictionary, and a bottle of rye."

"Are you saying I'm a dipsomaniacal Lothario?"

Morgan shook his head and poured another drink.

● ● ●

The next day Morgan was in his truck, driving to *Roses Are Red*, the florist shop owned by Karen Gardner. He turned down a side street from the police station which led to one of the town's two main thoroughfares. He saw Cassandra Voorhees walking out of St. Matthew's Catholic Church, holding some kind of container. He thought that was odd. He never knew Cassandra to be a church goer. In fact, he never saw her anywhere near St. Matthews, or any other church for that matter. But there she was, in her flowing, mottled clothing, with strings of beads and multicolored hair. Even her walk was queer: it had a quirky little bounce, as if she stepped on a stone every other stride.

Morgan planned to call on Cassandra as well. He still wanted to know what she was talking about with Van Haden. He decided to see her after Karen Gardner. His first impulse was to pull over and ask Cassandra if she was headed home, and if he could swing by. Then he quickly changed his mind. Better to catch her off guard. He'd just stop at her house unannounced after Karen. If she wasn't home he'd try another day.

Morgan strode into *Roses are Red* setting off one of those little tinkling bells above the door. Immediately he was inundated by "that smell." To him florist shops always smelled like funeral parlors. For Morgan, flowers were almost as stupid as fancy wine: fleeting and overpriced. The shop appeared to be empty. "Hello," he called out.

"Be right there," Karen's voice echoed from the back room.

Morgan continued to look around with his scanners on full. He didn't notice anything unusual, with the exception of a three-foot-wide pot, bursting with a plant he'd never seen before. It had silvery-green stems and greenish-gray leaves. The leaves looked as if they had little hairs or spikes coming out of them. The flowers were yellow, tiny, and formed into tight, round clusters. He heard Karen's footsteps approaching.

"Hello, how can I help…oh, hi, um…you're, Captain…"

"Captain Morgan, ma'am, chief of police. We've met before but it's been a while."

"Well it's nice to see you, Captain. Is this official business or can I assist you with some flowers?"

"Flowers aren't my thing, ma'am. I think you know why I'm here," said Morgan testing her.

"Uhhhhhhh, oh, I assume you're referring to the plane crash and my boyfriend, the pilot." Karen shifted from her chipper intro to noticeable solemnity, almost as if she knew she was supposed to look doleful and was forcing it. "The federal authorities already came to see me. Like I told them, I have no idea what might have caused him to crash. Everything was fine at home: He wasn't acting peculiar, he didn't use drugs, and we were getting along great. That's why we moved in together. This has been exceedingly hard on me." Karen's eyes became a little teary.

Morgan smelled dissimulation. "I'm sorry for your loss, ma'am. Look, I'm not the FAA. It's not so much the crash per se that I'm interested in. It's just—I'm sure you know—there's been a lot of troubling events around here lately and this is one more eerie coincidence. The pilot of a major plane crash just happened to live in Crestwood Lake. Now what are the odds of that?"

"I understand. It's uncanny."

"How long did you know him?"

"About six months."

"Did he have any connection to this town other than you?"

"Not that I'm aware of."

"How long have you been in Crestwood Lake?"

"Oh, about seven years."

"And what brought you here? I mean, this is a small town, basically in the middle of nowhere. You're originally from Jersey if I'm not mistaken. Why would you come here?"

Karen wanted to ask how he knew where she was from, but she assumed the Feds had looked into her background. Still, she didn't like it. With a slight tone in her voice she said, "Captain, it sounds as if you're investigating me. Have I done something wrong, other than lose the man I loved in a catastrophic way?"

"You didn't answer my question, Ms. Gardner. What brought you to Crestwood Lake?"

Karen rolled her eyes.

Morgan noticed how quickly her grief had ebbed.

"I didn't plan on coming to Crestwood Lake specifically. I'd been to Vermont a few times as a girl and loved its peace and quiet. Jersey's over-populated: nothing but traffic, strip malls, crime, and outrageous taxes. So I was looking for a place in this area to settle down. This shop became available and the rent was reasonable, so I decided to move here, Ok?"

Morgan wasn't sure what else to ask her. He had already elicited what he was curious about: she was a phony, had an attitude, and he didn't trust her. And, as Morgan thought to himself: *If Gil's Twilight Zone crap was true, this bitch could be part of the freak show.*

"I'm not trying to give you a hard time, ma'am. Like I said, there have been a lot of inexplicable things happening around here lately. The people want to feel safe. I have to keep my eyes and ears open. And as you can imagine, there's been a lot of pressure on me lately." Morgan appeared to soften to play on her sympathies. It was just a ploy to acquire information and judge her character further.

"I understand, Captain," and with a slight, but still detectable tone she asked, "Anything else?"

That told Morgan something. Even when he dropped his guard, she maintained hers. Little did she know that her behavior just elevated her from a blip on Morgan's radar to a beacon.

"No, ma'am, that's all…Oh by the way, have you been to the new wine store in town? Grand Vin I think it's called. I heard it's quite interesting."

"You don't strike me as a wine connoisseur, Captain."

"Occasionally I indulge…so have you been there? Because I thought I saw you coming out of there the other day."

Morgan was bluffing of course, but Karen didn't know that. And if Morgan had seen her, she certainly didn't want him catching her in a lie. She took the bait. "Why yes, Captain, I got a bottle of wine there. It was the last one my boyfriend and I shared before the tragedy."

Bingo! thought Morgan. He also noticed her attempt to turn the tables and play the sympathy card again.

"So you met the owner?" said Morgan. "What's his name again?"

"Luther," replied Karen

Oh, so now we're on a first name basis with the asshole, thought Morgan. Then out loud: "So what'd ya think?"

"It's a delightful little shop."

"Really? And the owner?"

"He's a charming man. Very distinguished. *He* has good manners, Captain."

"Well excuse me, Ms. Gardner, but social graces don't mean shit. What matters is what's in a person's heart and mind. Someone can be polished and charming, yet still be harboring treachery."

"Maybe you're threatened by him, Captain. No offense, but he's an educated, sophisticated gentleman who owns a reputable, upscale business. Maybe that's off-putting to someone of your background."

Karen had no idea who she was dealing with.

Morgan took a step closer to Karen and leaned his head forward, drilling her eyes with his. "I don't give a damn about his background, his manners, his fancy clothes, or his pretentious wines. That crap doesn't make anyone a better person. That snobby persona that you applaud could be nothing more than a pretense. Someone who seems refined can simply be a wolf in sheep's clothing."

"Captain, I was just—"

"Take you for instance. You *seem* like a nice lady with an outwardly harmless business. But who knows what's really in *your* soul? Given your insinuations that I am ill-mannered and low class, all these pretty adornments you sell, could merely be the facade of something darker in your heart." Morgan maintained his stare.

Karen was flustered and intimidated. She leaned back and said, "Captain, I wasn't trying to be offensive, I was just—"

"Thank you for your time today, Ms. Gardner." Morgan headed toward the door, stopped, turned around and pleasantly asked, as if the previous exchange never occurred, "Excuse me one second, but what plant is this?" Morgan pointed toward the yellow flowers that had caught his eye before.

"That's wormwood."

"Wormwood?" said Morgan. "I never heard of it."

"It goes back many centuries in Europe. It's supposed to have all sorts of medicinal qualities. They use it to make the liquor absinthe. Have you ever heard of absinthe?"

"Yeah, it tastes like licorice. It used to be illegal. They thought it caused madness or hallucinations."

"Wormwood has many properties. Some mythical, some not," said Karen.

Morgan thanked her again and left. Karen watched him walk away. The gray cat strolled out from behind the counter, hissed in Morgan's direction and then rubbed its face on Karen's leg and purred. Karen looked down at the cat and whispered, "All in good time Lilith. All in good time."

• • •

Morgan still intended to go to Cassandra's house, but he wanted to ensure enough time had elapsed for her to get home since seeing her earlier. She might have had errands, or other kooky tasks to complete. So he got gas, went to the ATM, got a sandwich, and parked a few doors down from Grand Vin, but on the same side of the street. Last time Van Haden had spied his truck across the street. Morgan couldn't see directly into the store, but then nobody could see him. He just wanted to observe who might come or go. So he sat there, ate his lunch and watched.

Nobody entered or exited the premises. Morgan wasn't surprised. How many idiots could there be dumping that kind of money on wine? Which of course made him wonder all the more why Cassandra Voorhees was in the store the other day. And just the way that she was talking with Van Haden seemed suspicious—THUMP! "Shit!" yelled Morgan. A large, dead, pitch-black crow landed right on the hood of his pickup. The body came to rest so that its eyes met Morgan's in a cold, lifeless stare. Morgan stuffed the rest of his roast beef sandwich into his mouth, took the paper wrapping, exited his truck, grabbed the bird with the paper, and chucked it toward the curb. "Sonnavabitch," he mumbled through his meat-filled maw.

Morgan got back in his truck, took a long swig of his Pepsi, and composed himself. He picked his nose, cracked his neck and farted. He continued to watch Grand Vin for a while. Nobody went in or out of the store. Finally, he decided it was time for his surprise visit.

Cassandra's shack was on the southwest corner of the lake. Her property was quite enviable: a small peninsula jutting out into one of the smaller coves. It afforded privacy, splendid scenery, and a degree of individuality. It was one more disparate fabric woven into her unconventional tapestry.

Her house was equally atypical, but unlike her property, for unfavorable reasons. The exterior of the building was decrepit. Clearly it hadn't been painted in many years. The once white surface was now a dingy, light gray. One awning hung diagonally across its window, two boards were missing from one side, the foundation sported numerous cracks, and the roof lacked a number of shingles. Another window was broken and had cardboard taped over it. The lawn was utterly overgrown with weeds, vines, and brush. It looked like a stereotypically haunted house. Her spooky domicile, combined with her own bizarre appearance, earned Cassandra the sobriquet *Wicked Witch of the West* from the local children.

The driveway was a rocky, rectangular patch, dappled with weeds. It extended only a third of the way into her property, necessitating a short walk to the house. As Morgan pulled up he saw her old Volkswagen Beetle. The hood and trunk were pink while the sides and top were an offbeat shade of light green. All sorts of whacky stickers decorated the rear of the vehicle. Every Goosey Night the local kids would soap its windows.

Morgan parked on the street, strolled down her driveway, spit, and approached the house. The doorbell didn't work so he knocked. Failing to glean a response he knocked a second time. Finally he called out, "Hello. Ms. Voorhees, it's Captain Morgan of the Crestwood Lake Police." Still no answer. He knocked a third time, harder than the last two.

Morgan walked around the house trying to get a peek inside. Various items were strewn about the property: a rusty watering can, flower pots, a pile of bricks, a statue of a frog, an old children's wagon with assorted rocks in it, etc. Then there were the garden gnomes. Morgan counted seven of them. They popped out of the underbrush in a seemingly random pattern. The trees nearest the house had wind chimes and assorted ribbons in them.

Morgan climbed the back stairs to a screen door, which led into an enclosed porch. He peered through the grimy wire mesh. Morgan thought it looked like a haphazard flea market. The walls were covered with all sorts of pictures, designs, and weird gewgaws. The shelves and table were littered with bric-a-brac. Numerous boxes and containers were scattered about the floor. Various star and planet-like objects hung from the ceiling. The porch also had this unusual odor, as if some kind of incense had just been burning. Morgan called out and knocked on the back door, but again, without response. Finally he gave up.

On his way back to his truck he saw a dead black cat in the tall grass next to the house. Its mouth and eyes were wide open, as if the last thing it saw was the Devil. Morgan cringed, inspected the immediate vicinity for any other surprises, and then returned to his truck. *Fucking freak*, he thought to himself. Morgan got back in his pickup and left.

The whole time Cassandra Voorhees watched him from a small window in the attic.

● ● ●

The next morning, Morgan was sitting in *The Bagel Hole*, savoring his salted bagel with cream cheese and large black coffee when his cell phone rang. "Goddamnit!" he snarled. He hated being interrupted when he ate. He looked at the caller ID. Of course, it was the station.

"Captain, it's officer Wesley. I'm working dispatch. We just got a call. They found a floater in the lake."

"Where?"

"Arthur Teasdale called. He found it under his dock. His address is—"

"I know where Teasdale lives," said Morgan. "Get on the horn and get things rolling. You know what to do."

"Yes, sir," replied Wesley.

Morgan decided to finish his bagel.

Arthur Teasdale lived on the northwest corner of the lake, the last house before a patch of woodland broke up the begirding of lakefront homes. Due to the topography and local climate, the wind nearly always blew toward the northwest. Naturally, it drove a gentle current across the water in the same direction.

Teasdale was a fifty-nine-year-old jack-of-all-trades, who eked out a living doing odd jobs. His wife June worked as a cashier in the local supermarket. Their children were grown and married. They were a simple and congenial couple and led a quiet life.

Teasdale had two huge Irish wolfhounds. On their hind legs they stood taller than a man, but anyone who got within striking distance only got licked to death. As long as the weather permitted, they were kept outside in a fenced-in area of his yard. They barked relentlessly if anyone walked by, more for attention than anything else. As Morgan pulled up, they began their canine chorus.

Morgan didn't bother ringing the bell. He simply just walked around the house (on the other side from the dogs), and headed down to the water. Police, EMT's and Teasdale were all standing around the dock. They had pulled the body out from under the dock and eased it to the water's edge.

"What's the deal, Arthur?" said Morgan.

"Hey, Butch. I was just telling your men. I came out here this morning to do some work on the dock. When I looked underneath to check the pilings I saw this body. Gave me the scare of my life. I've never seen anything like it. I ran up to the house and called you guys. Who is it?"

"How the fuck do I know? I just got here."

Addressing Teasdale, one of the officers stated, "It's obviously a young female. She probably drowned further down the lake and sank. As a body decomposes gases in the body cavity are created, causing buoyancy. When she became a floater, the wind and current drifted her up this way."

Teasdale looked like he wanted to puke.

Morgan took a few steps toward the body and gave it a cursory look. It was disgusting. Tough ol' Butch Morgan was actually a little squeamish when it came to stuff like this. He figured it was the medical examiner's job. Let him do the dirty work. He'd get the report later.

"Arthur," said Morgan, "has anything—and I mean anything—unusual been going on around here lately? No matter how trivial, anything out of the ordinary?"

"Well…no…not really," said Teasdale looking around his property. "Well, actually, the dogs have been barking more, especially after sunset."

"Your dogs always bark."

"Yeah, but not too much when it's dark. It's usually during the day if people or cars go by."

"You leave them out all night?"

"Not when it gets to this time of year. We bring'em in after supper. But they spend a couple hours outside after the sun goes down, and recently they just seem, I don't know, more twitchy than usual. Once or twice I came out with a flashlight and looked around, but didn't see anything. Oh, wait a minute, there was one time when I came out and found half a raccoon."

"Half a raccoon?" said Morgan.

"Yeah, it was the damnedest thing. Looked like something ripped it right in half. The bottom half was missing. It was outside the fence so I know my dogs didn't do it. It wasn't in the road or flattened so it wasn't a car. I don't know what did it—really strange."

"You ever been to that new wine shop in town?" asked Morgan.

The sudden segue caught Teasdale off guard. He looked baffled, thought for a moment and said, "You mean Ron Millhouse's old store? That new uppity place?"

"Yeah."

"Nah I don't drink. But I heard all he sells is wine. So everybody who wants anything else has to drag their ass over to Concord."

"All right, Arthur, the medical examiner will be here, then they'll fish her body out. My men here will get some info from you for the report. If anything else happens you think I should know, call me, ya here?"

"Sure thing, Butch."

Morgan rattled off a bunch of orders to the patrolmen including to search the area. Normally he'd have put the immediate vicinity under much greater scrutiny. But he knew the girl had been dead for weeks and died elsewhere on the lake. He also knew Teasdale had nothing to do with it. His property was just where she came to rest, not where her demise occurred. What he truly needed to know was who she was, and how her body ended up in the lake. He'd have to wait for that answer.

• • •

Father Mark Santoro was an Italian-Irish priest from Boston and the recently appointed pastor of St. Matthew's Church. He did not appear or act very "priestly." He had a strong personality, sort of a lighter version of Morgan. However, he was never scurrilous and had more diplomacy and tolerance. But he definitely wasn't meek either. His inside joke to his friends was that he was *not* one of the scions of the earth.

He was a young-looking forty and handsome, with wavy black hair and brown eyes. The women loved him. He was charming and always kissed each one on the cheek after mass. Many rumors circulated about his dalliances and they didn't involve altar boys. One purported that he had a fling with the nun who drowned herself.

Father Mark rode a Harley, which only contributed to his bad boy image. The elder members of the community thought it distinctly unholy and indecorous. The kids thought it was cool, and the young women thought it was hot.

The archbishop was conflicted about Father Mark. He deplored his wild side. But Father Mark performed his duties well, did what he was told, and virtually everyone not on social security liked him. So when Father

Mark became eligible, the bishop compromised within himself and gave him his own parish, but in the remote precincts of Crestwood Lake. Father Mark wasn't exactly thrilled. He was born and raised in Boston and had always hoped his ministry would remain there. But Boston was only three and a half hours away and he visited as often as possible.

St. Matthews was a small and rudimentary church. The diocese of Burlington barely had enough money to build it, let alone embellish it. St. Matthew's primary garnitures were a few stained glass windows and a statue of Mary. Even the large crucifix on the wall behind the altar was devoid of a sculpture of Jesus. On the left side of the altar was an impressive series of multi-tiered racks of red votive candles. Parishioners made small donations in the accompanying metal box and lit a candle in support of their cause. The candles provided one of the few splashes of color in the sterile surroundings—not to mention some revenue—hence their multitude.

On the right side of the altar was a reproduction of Guido Reni's *Michael*. The classic painting depicts the archangel Michael wielding a sword, and stomping on Satan's head as he casts the fallen angel out of heaven. Father Mark had purchased it in Rome when he was in the seminary. It was a cheap replica and the colors had faded markedly over the years. Nevertheless, it resonated with Father Mark's basic—some would argue simplistic—view of the world: there was good and there was evil, and he was a champion of good.

When Father Mark arrived at St. Matthews he purchased eight jugs of inexpensive wine (for his personal use and the church ceremonies), at Crestwood Wines & Liquors. Because it was for the church, Ron Millhouse charged him only slightly above cost. Father Mark hadn't kept track of his supply and now suddenly realized there wasn't enough wine for that week's services. He had heard that the new shop focused only on collectibles and not inexpensive wines. He didn't feel like driving to Concord so he decided to give Grand Vin a shot. Maybe they'd have something serviceable and save him a trip.

Father Mark walked the half mile from St. Matthews to Grand Vin. He liked walking around the town center. He thought it was beneficial for people to see him in public, and relished opportunities to connect with them. But he still harbored some insecurity about being a Bostonian, recently transplanted to this small, Vermont town. He was afraid people might view him as a city slicker or an outsider—maybe even distrust him. He knew the Harley didn't help.

As he approached Grand Vin Father Mark inexplicably started to feel nervous. He wasn't prone to anxiety. He pressed the four fingers on his right hand to his heart and took a deep breath. As he was about to enter the store a middle-aged, stern-faced man marched out, almost knocking him over.

"Oh I'm sorry," Father Mark immediately offered.

The man stopped, looked the priest up and down, sneered, and walked away without a word.

Perplexed, Father Mark meandered into the store, still looking back in the man's direction, wondering what had elicited his cold reaction.

"Did you turn the other cheek, Father?" a resonant voice bellowed.

Father Mark whipped around, completely off guard. With his mouth half open he stared at Van Haden with a degree of awe. There he stood, towering above the clergyman, in his black three-piece suit, with a fiery red tie and pocket square. In his right hand was a large, smoldering, cigar. Van Haden took a puff and blew out the smoke in a cloud that billowed over the priest's head.

"What?" said Father Mark, still off balance.

"I said," responded Van Haden, "did you turn the other cheek? That gentleman almost ran into you and then returned your unwarranted apology with antipathy."

"Oh…uh…that's OK…uh…hello." He extended his hand. "I'm Father Mark. I'm the pastor of St. Matthew's Church."

"And I am Luther Van Haden, the proprietor of Grand Vin." Van Haden shook his hand firmly. "Need some wine for your Sunday celebration I imagine?"

"Well…uh…yes. How did you know?"

"You're a Catholic priest, yes?"

"Yes."

"This is a wine store. You require wine for the transubstantiation that you allege occurs during your ceremony. So unless you're planning on easing your conscience with alcohol, I assume you need wine for your mass."

Father Mark was stupefied. His thoughts raced: *How did he know the term transubstantiation? What did he mean by "allege?" And why does he think I need to ease my conscience?*

"Are you Catholic?" explored Father Mark.

"Oh no," chuckled Van Haden with an amused smile.

"Then how do you know—"

"Transubstantiation—whereby bread and wine are supposedly transformed into the body and blood of your Messiah."

"Yes."

"Father, I am a lettered man. I have studied many things in my time. Religion in particular fascinates me."

Father Mark felt his heart skip a beat. He ignored it and focused his thoughts. Van Haden's subtle challenges about his "alleged" and "supposed" beliefs engendered just enough irritation to facilitate the vanquishing of his dismay.

"Do you adhere to any established faith?" queried Father Mark.

"I have faith in myself, Father, and in the shortcomings of man—but not in the putative infallibility of his Gods."

"So are you an atheist or an agnostic?"

"What's the difference?" said Van Haden with a smirk and a dismissive wave of his hand.

"Well, an atheist doesn't believe in God while an agnostic is merely skeptical."

"Well, my dear Father, based on your own antinomian beliefs, faith is indispensable for salvation. The atheist is certainly condemned. But even the skeptic does not possess enough faith to ensure his eternal redemption."

"Well it's not just about faith."

"Oh really?" retorted Van Haden. "Matthew 21:21: 'Jesus replied, I tell you the truth, if you have *faith* and do not doubt, not only can you do what was done to the fig tree, but also you can say to this mountain, Go, throw yourself into the sea, and it will be done.' 1 Peter 1:5–9: 'for you are receiving the goal of your *faith*, the salvation of your souls.' Ephesians 2:8: 'For it is by grace you have been saved, through *faith*, and this not from yourselves, it is the gift of God,' ...should I continue, Father?"

"No," said Father Mark with a grave countenance and voice. "I've heard enough. Are you familiar with Shakespeare, Mr. Van Haden?"

"Why of course, Father."

"*The Merchant of Venice*, scene III: 'The Devil can cite Scripture for his purpose. An evil soul producing holy witness is like a villain with a smiling cheek.'"

"Are you calling me the Devil, Father?"

"If the cloven hoof fits..."

"Very droll, Father, very droll. But what I find even more amusing is your hypocrisy. You think you can dispense reclamation with your stale bread and cheap wine. You think some insignificant prophet who died two thousand years ago is going to be reborn and bestow salvation on the desperately immoral species known as mankind. You wear that white collar and preach your delusions like a paragon of virtue. Yet you can't even get your own soul in order. Were *you* producing *holy witness* when you *borrowed* that five hundred dollars out of the Sunday collection last year to get your motorcycle repaired? No, you justified it by telling yourself you needed it to travel to conduct your ministrations."

"You evil scum," growled Father Mark.

"Oh I'm scum?" said Van Haden raising his eyebrows. "And that Hustler magazine you keep hidden in your drop ceiling, that you jerk off to now and then, what does that make you? A choirboy? Or what about that little blonde you defiled the week before your ordination. Since you weren't an official 'priest' yet [Van Haden momentarily popped his cigar in his mouth and made air quotes], you could rationalize that one away, eh?" He removed the cigar, leaned his head forward, and beamed with a cocky grin.

Father Mark composed himself, even though he was fuming inside. It was just enough fury to suppress the sheer terror he also felt at coming face to face with pure evil. An evil he'd only read about in books and scripture...until now.

"You know what Mr. *Van Haden*," Father Mark articulated the last name slowly and mordantly. Suddenly his thought processes ground to a halt. "v-a-n h-a-d-e-n," he repeated slowly out loud. Then he scoffed. "I should have seen this a mile away. Take away the 'n' and substitute an 's' and you get Van Hades...*from hell!*"

Van Haden raised his eyebrows and smiled close-lipped, as if he was saying, *no shit, stupid.* "Took you a while huh? Is that collar cutting off the blood supply to your brain?"

"You know what you just did, you vile heathen? You helped spell your own doom."

"And how did I do that?" mocked Van Haden puckering his lips.

Father Mark stiffened and said, "Proverbs 16:18: 'Pride goeth before destruction, and a haughty spirit before a fall.' You let your contempt and your narcissism get the best of you. You should have ingratiated yourself and deceived me, cloaking your true identity. Then you could have operated from the stronger position of anonymity. But you couldn't contain yourself. The instant you saw who I was you became confrontational. You used your omniscience to vindictively counter me. But as you radiated in prideful *vengeance*, you simultaneously exposed your hand.

"You just quoted various scriptures affirming how faith is paramount for salvation. But by revealing yourself to me, you just increased my faith tenfold. Because now I know with certainty that if an evil like *you* can exist, the opposite *has* to exist. It's the ultimate irony. Your evil has given me the faith to withstand your evil. I will see you again, Van Haden!"

Father Mark spat on Van Haden's shiny oxfords and stormed out. Van Haden gritted his teeth and clenched his fists, crushing the lit cigar into his palm. "You haven't *seen* vengeance yet, Father," he muttered.

• • •

Dr. Wyatt phoned Morgan at his office in the station. Morgan was eager for his call. The police had found nothing on the dead girl in the lake that could identify her. He was hoping Wyatt had matched the dental records.

"Hello, Doc. Whadda ya got?"

"You're lucky. She's a missing person and her dental records were just put in the system. She's been missing thirty days, which is completely consistent with the state of decay, given the water temperature."

"Who is she?"

"Her name is Jill Morton. She's a twenty-two-year-old from Bristol. She recently graduated from the University of New Hampshire, degree in psychology. No criminal record, living with her parents, working in a local department store."

"How did she die?"

"I don't know."

"What do you mean you don't know?" said Morgan.

"I didn't find any marks on the body—a body that's been decomposing in water for thirty days, mind you—that would suggest an external cause of death. As best as I can tell there was no gross pathology internally either."

"Did she just simply drown?"

"Can't say for sure. There was water in her lungs, but even if she didn't drown there'd be water in her lungs after thirty days in the lake."

"So basically you're calling me to tell me you can't tell me anything."

"I'm sorry, Captain."

Morgan hung up and assigned one of his men to follow up with the Bristol Police to check for any leads. And then, in quite uncharacteristic fashion, he left work early. He was meeting Vicki at her place for dinner. It was Friday night and she had traded with another bartender to get the night off. Morgan decided to avail himself of her offer to come by and talk. But it wasn't just his romantic feelings that were motivating him. Right now, he was genuinely in need of a friend he could trust.

Vicki lived in a small, but utterly charming cottage a few blocks from the lake. She assiduously maintained her home and property. Gardening was her primary hobby, as evidenced by her verdant lawn and artful landscaping. She had a small recirculating pond that emptied into a babbling, narrow waterway that meandered its way back to the pond. It was surrounded by tastefully designed flower beds and manicured shrubbery. There were no tacky statues, ceramic animals, or wind spinners. A luxurious stone walkway wended its way from the driveway to the front door.

Her house had a carapace of white vinyl siding, highlighted by dark green shutters, shingles and trim. She had it power-washed twice a year. Her backyard contained a variety of fruit and flowering trees, a well-organized shed, and a small, brick patio.

The inside of her home was just as fastidious. She kept it clean, neat and tactful. The décor was conservative but elegant. A beautiful grandfather clock marked the spot where her drunken ex had literally shoved her through the wall. A paradoxical loveseat rested above the spot where she bled on the floor when he broke her nose. Various pictures obscured the sites of the times he perforated the sheetrock with his fist. Vicki had repaired the damage and repainted everything years ago. The portraits and paint helped her gloss over the painful memories, and provided a veneer of rebirth.

Vicki fixed Morgan one of his favorite meals: a hearty meatloaf, mashed potatoes with gravy, and creamed corn. During dinner they talked about everything except recent events. Morgan didn't like discussing critical matters when eating. In depth conversation distracted him from his meal. Nor did he want food, or other activities encroaching on his concentration once he became embroiled in something serious. Tobacco and alcohol were the only acceptable accessories to sobering discourse.

After the meal they retired to the living room. Vicki had a bottle of Four Roses that she kept just for Morgan. She poured him some of the bourbon and a white wine for herself. Morgan sat on her soft, cream-colored couch, legs spread, one hand holding his drink, the other arm sprawled across the top of the couch. Vicki was next to him, in her teal blue sweats, sitting on her calves, holding her wine with both hands. Her lush, red mane was down and softly flowed over her shoulders.

"What should we talk about?" said Vicki whimsically.

Morgan scoffed. "Vicki, I've never seen shit like what's going on in this town in all my life. I don't know what to make of it—well maybe I do—but that's neither here nor there. The town is freaking out about Brian Delmore and Sharon O'Connell. Now a missing girl turns up dead in our lake. And that's on top of all the other weird deaths and coincidences that have been going on."

"I know, I hear it every day at Toby's. Did you know all of Ben Willoughby's chickens were slaughtered?"

"No. What?"

"Yeah, something killed them all. Butchered them—ripped them into pieces."

"An animal?" asked Morgan.

"They don't think so. None of them were missing or eaten. All of their carcasses, although in pieces, were still there. Any animal that would have killed them would have done so for food. Animals don't kill just for the sake of it."

"Ya see, that's what I'm talking about. In some ways, that's even crazier than the murders. What the hell is going on? And then there's that jerk-off who owns the new wine store." Then, in an acerbic tone Morgan enunciated, "*Grand Vin*. What the hell does that even mean?"

"Great wine, in French," replied Vicki.

"Whatever," said Morgan. "Have you been there yet?"

"No."

"Yet somehow he knows you, and also knows that you and I are friends."

"What do you mean?" asked Vicki with a look of concern on her face.

"The day I went to see him at his store, as I walked out he told me to say hi to you. Now how does he know you, and that you know me?"

"That's weird. But then again, people talk. A lot of folks in town have gone there to check the new place out. It's not inconceivable that someone might have mentioned me or our friendship."

Morgan let out a low growl. "That still doesn't add up for me. The way he said to say hi to you, I don't know, it was like some kind of parting shot. There's something about that guy...I just don't know."

"What? Put it into words."

"I don't know," repeated Morgan, only louder. "The best way I can describe it is…he seems…ya know how they portray a mafia boss in the movies? The Godfather's a guy who's a pure psychopath. He'd kill his own brother if it meant protecting his interests. Yet he dresses like a Wall Street banker, hobnobs with the affluent, eats at fancy restaurants, and acts like he's Mr. fucking charming. He's a smooth talker with a gentle exterior, yet underneath lays a monster. That's what Van Haden reminds me of."

"Did you run him through your computer, or database, or whatever you call it?"

"Of course. Nothing came up." Morgan took a long sip of his bourbon.

"Why don't you have him tailed?"

"I can't take away resources from murder and missing persons investigations for a hunch. You hear anything about him at Toby's?"

"Yeah, but it's all the same: guys complaining that they have to drive to another town just to get booze, cracks about his snooty business, a couple guys think he's gay, ya know, stuff like that. But you mentioned something before when discussing all the events in general…that you don't know what to make of it, but maybe you do. You sounded like you had a suspicion."

"Look, Vicki…" He looked right into her eyes. Vicki tilted her head and ran her hand through her hair. *Damn she's a lovely woman*, thought Morgan. And she looked at him so softly. He didn't want that tender gaze in her eyes to change into staring at him like he was nuts.

"What, Butch? Talk to me."

Morgan knew he could never say no to this woman. He would do anything for her. He wanted to kiss her so bad. Vicki put her right hand on his shoulder and rubbed his upper arm.

"You know about the history of Crestwood Lake?" asked Morgan.

"Only what I read in Gil's book."

"Sunday Gil and I are driving to Cambridge to see this professor. Some kind of shrink who specializes in witchcraft and history, and all that crap.

Gil thinks there's something to it, and that it might be behind the bizarre stuff happening here."

"He thinks there are witches in Crestwood Lake?" Vicki raised her eyebrows in disbelief.

"Yeah. He thinks there are people who are witches and conspiring with the Devil."

"Well, ya know," said Vicki, "I don't know if there's some guy with a pointy tail and women riding brooms, but there could certainly be some kind of kooky cult. It might explain the mutilations, the murders, the chickens, etc. It wouldn't be the first time that reputed Satan worshipers were terrorizing a community and committing vicious crimes. I think you should go hear what this guy has to say. He might know things that could help you flush out the whackos committing all this stuff."

"Yeah. That's what Gil thinks." Morgan looked at her intently and said, "How've you been, Vicki?"

Vicki bobbed her head and half-smiled, almost as if Morgan had brought up something silly. "I'm fine. Really, I'm OK."

"How long has it been since I dragged his ass out of here? Nine years?"

"Yeah, almost ten."

"And what about you?" said Vicki quickly changing the subject. "Connie died only a year and a half ago."

"I keep myself busy with work, especially lately. But being alone is starting to get to me." Morgan was testing the waters. He was hoping Vicki would respond likewise.

Instead, Vicki rubbed his arm again and said, "Being alone's not so bad." Then she pulled back. "Of course my situation was different. I didn't have a loving partner who died." Vicki finished her wine in one gulp. "I had a drunken degenerate who beat the piss out of me."

Talk about a mood killer. So much for Morgan's fantasy of Vicki kissing him followed by *Butch, you don't have to be alone anymore.* Maybe he needed to be more direct with Vicki. Or maybe his feelings were unrequited. Morgan wasn't quite ready to be more proactive. He allowed the moment to fade and the evening to come to a close. On his way out he gave Vicki a big hug, a kiss on the cheek, and a heartfelt thank-you for her cooking and her support.

As he stepped out onto her porch she said, "Be careful, Butch. I don't want anything to happen to you. I might get tired of being alone some-day too."

Now Morgan was really befuddled. He started his truck and pulled away, all the while trying to decipher whether Vicki was giving him a green light or not.

• • •

Neil Pasternak was an avid fisherman. He didn't care what time of year it was. Even in the winter, as long as the temperatures remained above zero, he'd be on the lake ice fishing. He was forty-three and had worked in the Crestwood Lake Post Office for most of his adult life. He lived on the south shore of the lake with his wife and teenaged daughter. They, however, were at his sister-in-law's in Rhode Island for the weekend, attending a cousin's bridal shower. Neil was delighted. He had the whole weekend to fish.

Neil had a simple rowboat with a battery powered motor. He loved puttering around the lake stalking his favorite quarry: smallmouth bass. It was the last Saturday in October and the sun had shined all day. Dusk was approaching and Neil was near the center of the lake, where naturally the water was deeper. He knew that as the season unfolded and the water got colder, the bass retreated from the shallows. He had a new chartreuse jig, and had already caught four fish with it that afternoon. He wanted to get in a few more casts before heading home.

Neil was probing the depths when his jig got snagged on something. He yanked and tugged, but it wouldn't come lose. He was afraid of pulling too hard and snapping the line. "Dammit!" he yelled. He had just pur-chased that jig—eight bucks for a single lure. Thus far it was earning its keep. Nevertheless, he hated losing lures, particularly pricey ones. Neil moved the boat toward the lure in order to get right on top of the snag, hoping that would help dislodge it. He alternated between engaging the motor and reeling in the line. Finally the boat was poised directly above the stuck lure. He pulled the pole straight up and side to side, but still couldn't set it free.

Neil laid the pole down, grabbed the line with his hand and stuck his head over the side of the boat. A ghoulish face confronted him from the water! Long white hair on top of a skull-like head, with large, black eyes. Its mouth was wide open, baring its jagged and pointed teeth. Neil gasped and instinctively withdrew, but it reached out with its long arms and claws and grabbed him by the head, digging its talons into the back of his scalp. The creature's head then emerged from the water. Two red pupils fluoresced as it emitted a low-pitched hiss. Neil grabbed its arms and pulled frantically, but it was futile. The monster now squeezed Neil's head from the sides. He felt like his skull was in a vice. The pressure became unbearable as the bones just under his ear started to crack. Neil screamed with all his might. Neil's right eye popped out of its socket and dangled from a bloody nerve. The demon thrust itself up and engulfed the eyeball with its mouth, severed the nerve with its teeth and swallowed it whole! It then twisted Neil's head 180 degrees…*slowly*. Neil felt each and every vertebrae snap. The last thing he saw was the lake directly behind him. The demon then pulled his body into the water and disappeared.

At that precise moment, four other events were taking place. Father Mark was struck on his motorcycle by a car barreling through a stop sign. Karen Gardner was drinking a strange concoction made from her wormwood flowers. Cassandra Voorhees scraped the dead cat from her yard and brought it to her attic. And Van Haden sat in his parlor above Grand Vin sipping a wine from Provence: Chateau Malherbe, Pointe du Diable, French for *The Devil's Point*. He sat there with his eyes closed, snickering sinisterly, almost orgasmically, as a slideshow of all of the dreadful happenings in Crestwood Lake flashed through his twisted mind.

THE PROFESSOR

It was Sunday and Morgan was planning on driving to Cambridge with Gil to see Professor Aaronson. But as he always did on Sunday mornings, he went to the station for a few hours first. As he walked in he saw Lieutenant Jack Dougherty buried in something at his desk.

"What's going on, Jack?"

"Oh, Butch. I was gonna call ya, but I figured you'd be in at some point this morning. We've got another problem."

"Now what?" moaned Morgan.

"Well, after we found that girl floating under Teasdale's dock, we proceeded to visit every lakefront house to determine if anybody saw anything. A couple residents on the north side pointed out this van with New York plates that's been parked in the same spot for almost a week. We ran the plates. It belongs to a Debbie Kurzmann from Waverly, New York."

"Where's Waverly?"

"Not far from Canada. It's within Adirondack State Park. It's a small town, only about a thousand people. I just got off the phone with the local police. One of their officers knows her. She's a nature photographer. They said she travels a lot, often in New England, taking pictures for magazines and stuff. She lives alone, hasn't been reported missing, and isn't in any kind of trouble as far as they knew. However, no one's heard from her in a while either."

"So what's the problem?" asked Morgan.

"Something might have happened to her. I had two of our guys comb the area where her van is parked. They found this expensive camera by the water's edge. We went through the pictures: all shots of the lake, the trees, and the scenery in general. Then we came to the last picture. I just printed it out." Dougherty handed the photo to Morgan.

"What the hell is that?" asked Morgan. In the photo was this large, black, monstrous-looking creature exploding from the water. It was fairly blurry, but appeared to be pouncing on whoever was pointing the camera at it.

"I don't know. I have no idea what that is. It doesn't look like it was staged. You can tell by the other photos and time stamps that she was rattling off a succession of shots when all of a sudden this *thing* appears. And it's the last picture. But how can this thing be real?"

"Who the hell knows," responded Morgan. "Get a hold of the state boys. We need a diver to look in the lake. Make copies of all the photos on the camera. Impound and search the van. We're officially treating this like a missing person. And we need some kind of expert to look at the camera and these shots, especially the last one to determine if they're authentic or not. I'm sure the state police have someone like that. Check the local hotels. See if she was staying in any of them."

"I'll get right on it."

"Listen up, Jack. I'm going to Cambridge today with Gil Pearson. It has to do with the two murders. We're interviewing this professor who might have information about them. If something really important comes up you can call, but otherwise I'll be gone all day. So hold down the fort."

"You got it. I'll take care of everything."

Morgan had known Jack Dougherty a long time and trusted him. But he wasn't going to reveal the details of why they were seeing Professor Aaronson. The last thing he needed was for his right-hand man to think he was on a witch hunt.

Dougherty was the same age as Morgan and had been on the force almost as long. He became a Crestwood Lake police officer the year after Morgan did. They rose through the ranks together until they were both lieutenants. Then their captain retired, and the mayor at that time gave the job to Morgan, who had one year more seniority. Lieutenant Dougherty was a fine officer with a meticulous record, but the mayor felt that Morgan had more of what it took to be captain. Of course, the only reason told to Dougherty was the seniority issue. Dougherty accepted it and maintained his devotion to duty, serving Morgan faithfully as his second in command. But Morgan was still reticent about sharing any of his unearthly suspicions with him. He didn't want to take any chance of appearing irrational.

● ● ●

"So how do you know this guy, Gil?" asked Morgan as they drove south along Interstate 93 in Gil's Ford Focus.

"Well, I first came across his work when I was writing my book on the Salem Witch Trials. I read two of his books and many of his articles. I attended one of his lectures, but didn't meet him in person. I was still compiling my book when I first contacted him directly. We spoke on the phone a couple of times back then. Then we e-mailed back and forth over the years; always talked about getting together but never did.

"Then, out of the blue, he calls me about a month ago. We were already e-mailing about Crestwood Lake, about all the weird happenstances here. But now he calls me asking if the strange events were escalating. I was astonished. I asked him how he knew. He said he had reasons to suspect an increase in supernatural activity and thought we should meet in person. I told him about you and he strongly urged me to bring you along."

Morgan then told Gil about Debbie Kurzmann and showed him the photo.

"What the hell?" exclaimed Gil, momentarily swerving into the next lane.

"Watch the road!"

Gil took the photo from Morgan's hand and held it over the steering wheel. "This was the last photo on the camera?"

"That's right. It was taken a split second after the ones just before it."

"So whatever this thing is, we're presuming it killed her? Dragged her into the lake?"

"I guess," said Morgan.

"You *guess?*"

"Look, Gil, I don't know what to say or think. If this was a picture of a real person then I'd say yes, this is the killer, or at least the person who abducted her. But no, it's a picture of some kind of monster. I don't believe in shit like this. So to say yeah, this *thing*, is what killed her means I have to accept a whole new way of looking at the world."

"That's what Aaronson and I are counting on," replied Gil.

Morgan just looked at him.

• • •

Professor Douglas Aaronson was a forty-eight-year-old bachelor. He lived in a stately Victorian house in West Cambridge. He came from a wealthy Boston family that owned a large textile firm with sundry manufacturing plants. Much to his father's chagrin, he preferred academia to the family business. Upon his parents' deaths the bulk of their holdings went to his two older brothers, who managed the family empire. Nonetheless, Aaronson was still bequeathed a sizeable inheritance. It allowed him to pay off his student loans and pursue his intellectual goals without having to worry about financial stability. Not that he needed much of a buffer. He was a tenured professor at Boston University, wrote a number of successful books, and was frequently called upon to lecture, for which he was handsomely compensated.

Rumors were always circulating about his sexual orientation. He didn't appear or act feminine, but when you're pushing fifty, have never been married, and don't seem to have any lady friends, people inevitably talk. Truth is he was more asexual than homosexual.

He was moderately handsome, with long brown hair that fell below his ears, and a well-trimmed beard. His brown-rimmed glasses almost matched his eyes. His countenance, his status, and his affluence, could easily have fetched him more female attention. But Aaronson was in love with his scholarship. If he wasn't teaching, writing, or reading, then he was sleeping. Even meals were an encumbrance to his studies.

In addition to psychology and history, his primary disciplines, he was absolutely intrigued by the macabre, and by man's fascination with it. As a child he loved scary movies and had all kinds of horror related collectables. As he got older his focus shifted to books, both classic and modern works. He read everything Edgar Allan Poe ever wrote.

Despite his engrossment with the supernatural, Aaronson was nevertheless, a rational man. He was well-grounded in science and reality. He conducted psychological experiments, crunched numbers, read exhaustively, and constantly searched for facts—his opinions always discursively derived. Thus, as beguiling as the supernatural was, Aaronson never actually believed in it, until lately—or more specifically—until the recent occurrences in Crestwood Lake crystallized everything he had studied about American Colonial witchcraft.

Gil and Morgan pulled into Aaronson's cobblestone driveway. As they got out of the car, Morgan scanned the house up and down and then stared at Gil, who ignored him. Morgan pressed the doorbell. A series of reverberating chimes echoed from within. Morgan rolled his eyes. An elderly woman in a maid's black uniform with a white apron opened the door.

"Hello, I'm Gil Pearson and this is Captain Morgan. We're here to see Professor Aaronson."

"Why yes," the woman replied in a British accent. "He's expecting you. Do come in please. It's very nice to meet you gentlemen. I'm Mrs. Clarkson, the housekeeper." As they stepped through the vestibule she said, "Please follow me. You can wait for the professor in his study."

She ushered them into a large room encompassed by book shelves. A large fire roared in a capacious stone fireplace. At one end of the room a massive oak desk was littered with books and papers. Upon it sat a traditional banker's lamp with a green shade. The far corner of the room was dominated by an antique escritoire, equally brimful with papers, stationery, and the like. In the middle of the room were two brown leather couches, matching chairs, and a rectangular coffee table. A few standing lamps placed strategically around the room contributed an ambient light.

"Please have a seat," said Mrs. Clarkson. "Is there anything you require, gentlemen? May I offer you a beverage?"

Gil opened his mouth, but Morgan quickly said, "No thank you, ma'am, we're fine."

"The professor will be with you shortly." Mrs. Clarkson bowed her head and left the room.

Morgan looked at Gil and said, "Are you fucking kidding me?"

"What?" said Gil with feigned innocence. He knew exactly what was irking Morgan.

"Look at this place. He's even got a limey housekeeper answering the door for him." Morgan started bobbing his head from side to side. "And we're waiting for him in the *study*," he said with an affected whine.

"You know, Butch, you got a real problem."

"*I've* got a problem?" said Morgan raising his eyebrows and touching his chest with his fingers.

"Yeah, you do. The man's a professional—a professor. And yes, he's got some money. So he has a nice house. So he has a housekeeper. So what? You haven't even met the man yet and already you're bristling. You got a real hang-up about any kind of prosperity or sophistication. Would it provoke your ego less if he lived in a tenement, answered the screen door in his underwear, holding a can of beer, and farted?"

Morgan pointed at Gil and growled, "Now that's not what I fucking—"

"Gentlemen," exclaimed the professor suddenly appearing in the doorway. "I've been eagerly looking forward to meeting you. I'm Professor Aaronson, but you can call me Doug," he said looking directly at Morgan. Aaronson was clad in a camel hair blazer with brown trousers and penny loafers. The light stripes on his brown, open-collared shirt matched the color of his blazer.

"Hi, I'm Gil," he said, exuberantly springing from the couch and extending his hand. "It's so good to finally meet you."

"Likewise," replied Aaronson. "And you must be, Captain Morgan."

"Yes," said Morgan shaking his hand.

"I've heard a lot about you, Captain."

"Yes, I'm sure you have," said Morgan, glancing at Gil.

"Gentlemen," said Aaronson, "please let me get you a drink. Some Scotch or maybe some cognac? I just acquired some lovely Bordeaux."

"Oh no, you too?" said Morgan.

Aaronson looked confused. Gil quickly spoke up: "There's a new wine shop in town. I think I told you about it. The previous owner killed himself. Now some new guy, this snobbish character—"

"A total asshole," interjected Morgan.

Gil continued: "He took over the place, got rid of the beer and liquor, and now sells nothing but expensive wines. As I'm sure you've deduced, Butch doesn't like him. He suspects there's something suspicious about him. That's what he responded to, not your Bordeaux."

"Understood," said Aaronson. "Now how about that drink?"

"I wouldn't refuse a glass of bourbon," said Morgan.

"My pleasure," said Aaronson. "And you Gil?"

"I'll try some of that Scotch you mentioned."

"Very good." Aaronson walked to the far wall where a large armoire stood. He opened the doors to reveal an ample liquor cabinet. A light automatically came on as the doors opened. He turned and said, "Ice?"

Gil and Morgan nodded.

The professor filled three glasses with ice cubes and placed them on a tray. In his other hand he grabbed two bottles and proceeded to the table. He poured Gil and himself some Scotch and Morgan some bourbon. Aaronson raised his glass and said, "To things that go bump in the night."

They clinked their glasses and sipped.

"So, Captain," Aaronson began, "tell me about this highbrow scoundrel who commandeered your local liquor store."

"Well, he's only one part of it. There's a whole bunch of things. First of all, Gil told me that he's brought you up to speed on all the bizarre crap and murders that have happened, right?"

"Yes, Gil told me everything," replied Aaronson.

"OK, so you know the backdrop, which is why we're all here in the first place. One of the previous incidents was the apparent suicide of Ron Millhouse, the guy who used to own the liquor store. A completely normal guy with a wife and family and no significant problems."

"Threw himself across an oncoming train," said Aaronson.

"Yeah. So then douchebag shows up. You should see this guy. I went to his store and had a drink with him. Looks like some kind of fancy aristocrat. Wears a black three-piece suit with a red tie and one of those stupid red handkerchiefs in his pocket...whatever you call them."

"A pocket square," said Aaronson.

"Whatever. Anyway, he sells nothing but expensive wine in a small, lower income town like Crestwood Lake—says it's his hobby and he doesn't need the money. He's kind of elusive about his background. Comes across as suave and polished, but I can't help feeling like I'm talking to a smarmy con man. Anyway, two of our residents buy wine from him and end up stabbing each other to death."

"Dr. Jorgensen and his wife, correct?" said Aaronson.

"Yeah. Now maybe that's just a coincidence, but I still don't like it. And another thing, he seems to be, I don't want to say psychic, but knowledgeable about things. Like he knew who I was before I even introduced myself. Yes, you can explain it in various ways, but it still seemed funny. Oh, and he knew I was inspecting his store for violations. Yeah it might have been obvious that I was checking the place out, but he didn't know why. And he knows Vicki even though she's never met him. She's the barmaid in town and a good friend of mine; told me to say hi to her as I left the store."

"Butch has the hots for her," said Gil with an impish smile.

"Shut up," barked Morgan.

"You said you had a drink with him?" inquired Aaronson.

"Yeah he had a bottle of this bourbon, pretty good stuff: Jim Beam's Devil's Cut—ever hear of it?"

"That's a little on the nose," remarked Aaronson. "What's this gentleman's name?"

"Luther Van Haden," said Morgan with a ridiculing tone.

Aaronson scoffed. "And you had a drink with him?"

"Yeah, why?"

Aaronson leaned over and said:

"'Tis Satan drinks with thee tonight,
    Take heed brother! Sister beware!
    Your whiskey and gin, they are poisoned with sin,
    If you drink with the Devil tonight."

Morgan looked at him as if he was speaking a foreign language.

Aaronson explicated: "It's an old stanza from an 1895 issue of *The Churchman*, an evangelical journal. I stumbled upon it during my studies."

"So what are you saying?" asked Morgan. "That this guy is the Devil?"

Aaronson looked at Gil and slowly enunciated, "v-a-n h-a-d-e-n."

"Oh my God," said Gil. "Why didn't I see it?"

"Will one of you two please tell me what the hell you're talking about?" demanded Morgan.

Gil spoke up: "Van is 'from' in Dutch. Take the word Haden, replace the 'n' with an 's' and you get 'from Hades.' In Greek mythology Hades was the underworld and eventually became synonymous with hell. Van Haden is a barely encrypted alias for *from hell*."

"Are you guys for real?" asked Morgan.

"We have much to discuss, Captain," said Aaronson. "Let me freshen all of our drinks."

Aaronson stood up and refilled their glasses. He then called for Mrs. Clarkson. As he waited for her he turned and asked, "Gentleman, do either of you require anything? A snack, some water, anything at all? The lavatory is just down the hall."

"I'm good," said Morgan.

"Me too," said Gil.

Mrs. Clarkson approached.

"Mildred, we won't need anything for a while. Please see that we aren't disturbed."

"As you wish, sir."

Aaronson closed the doors to the study. He then added a few logs to the fire. He retook his seat, sipped his Scotch, leaned over, looked directly at Morgan and said, "Your town is haunted, Captain."

"Haunted?"

"Deeply haunted," said Aaronson. "Ghosts, witches, demons, and of course…the Prince of Darkness himself."

Morgan grimaced. "C'mon, Professor, give me a break. You're saying that *all* those creatures exist, and *all* of them are in Crestwood Lake? And what the hell is the difference between them all anyway?"

Gil interrupted: "Butch, please…just listen for now. We came all this way to hear what the Professor has to say. Hear him out. You need to at least consider the possibilities."

"All right, all right," said Morgan, raising his hands as if surrendering. "Go ahead, Professor, I'm all ears."

"Allow me to outline Crestwood Lake's history, then we can proceed to the cast of characters. Is that acceptable gentlemen?"

Morgan nodded.

"Gil said, "Yes, I think that would be helpful for Butch."

Morgan gave Gil a dirty look.

Aaronson began: "Much of what I'm about to relate can't be proven, as it is largely based on folklore and second hand accounts. There are documents testifying to some of it, but that still doesn't prove it irrefutably. A few assorted details are known facts, but the kernels of reality are enshrouded in the mythos transferred over the generations."

Aaronson looked at Morgan. "However, Captain, I've done extensive research into this area. I'm not trying to vaunt, but no one has studied the Scalford lore more than me. I've sifted through countless files, personal communiques, rare books, theological texts, old legal documents, you name it. Between that and my general studies of the supernatural, I believe I have amassed the most plausible synthesis of Scalford's bewitched history.

"Let's commence with what is undisputed. We do know that a sub-group of Puritans splintered off from the Salem colony, shortly after

Massachusetts governor Sir William Phips abolished the witch trials in 1692. Apparently, this trenchantly zealous faction of Puritans was outraged. They fervently believed that witches remained in Salem, and protested that the evil had yet to be completely purged. So approximately 90 of the roughly 550 original Puritans abandoned Salem and ventured into the wilderness. They settled in Crestwood Lake, which they denominated Scalford after their leader's birthplace in England. All of that is documented from numerous sources throughout history. Now things start to get a little nebulous.

"A variety of verbal accounts and a few documents—mostly personal letters—attest that the Scalford Puritans gradually came to believe, that even members of their ultra-devoted sect, had become witches."

"But I thought they were so religious," said Morgan.

"Villainy wears many masks, none so dangerous as the mask of virtue," responded Aaronson. "Just as you distrust the intentions of your debonair wine merchant."

Morgan slowly nodded.

Aaronson continued: "So the Scalfords set out to eliminate the witches amongst them. Unfortunately, they mistakenly believed they had valid tests for identifying witches, such as throwing the suspect into water. Water was considered pure, and supposedly rejected evil. Thus, if the person floated, he or she was inculpated as a witch, and often forcibly drowned forthwith. Without a doubt they utilized Crestwood Lake. As expected, innocent people who couldn't swim drowned, but their deaths were glorified as divine proof of their sanctity. Conversely, some guilty parties who could swim, and weren't immediately drowned, lived to ravage another day. They may have been tried and acquitted, or escaped prosecution through some villainous means. Others were charged with witchcraft based on spectral evidence, as in Salem."

"Spectral evidence?" said Morgan.

"A person's dreams," said Gil.

"Yes," said Aaronson. "If one individual avowed that another had haunted them in their dreams, this was sufficient justification to charge the haunter with witchcraft. Some people, as in Salem, were accused because of miniscule doubts about their religious devotion. Anyone who was the slightest bit odd, heterodoxic, emotionally unstable, or perceived as the slightest threat to the natural order, was incriminated as a witch.

"This ultimately led to anarchy and the eventual breakdown of Scalford. People were impugning and recriminating one another. Executions abounded. They resorted to fire and water, the time-honored means of killing witches. As I stated, some were drowned, their bodies left to decompose in the lake. Others were burned at the stake, just as in medieval Europe. Purportedly, their ashes were scattered in the woods surrounding Crestwood Lake. Again, as with the drownings, innocent people died. Some guilty ones were killed, and some survived.

"Legend has it that the real witches who had escaped imputation began killing the non-witches. The witches finally corralled all the non-witches and gave them a choice: join us or die. Either way, every virtuous Puritan met his end. Supposedly, the refusers were killed, eviscerated and burned, inevitably during the coven's ceremonies."

"Eviscerated?" exclaimed Morgan, nearly jumping out of his seat. "Gil must have told you that the two bodies found in the woods were missing their hearts and sexual organs."

"Indeed," said Aaronson. "Witches and demons use bodily organs in their rites—hearts and sexual organs in particular—but other body parts as well. Typically, a coven will meet around a large bonfire. The members will toss the body parts into the fire as they chant their incantations. And that's not to mention their necrophagous behaviors."

"Necrophagous?" repeated Morgan

"Feeding on the organs, or other dead body parts," explained Aaronson.

Gil took a deep breath and a long sip of his drink. Morgan refilled his bourbon and mumbled a series of profanities.

Aaronson returned to his disquisition: "These events took place over two decades and culminated in the devastating fire in 1713 that annihilated the entire settlement. It's assumed that the surviving witches who had murdered the last Puritans incinerated the village. The witches then spread out across New England, assimilating into various communities. When outsiders eventually visited the area, all the buildings had been blazed, no human remains were found, the witches were long gone, and the mystery of the lost colony of Scalford was begotten.

"Interestingly, there's a recorded increase in suicides in the area, in the years following the 1713 fire. Witches have been known to drive people to suicide. It's one of their exceptionally twisted ways of tormenting mortals. But, we know that some of the Puritans who had converted to witchcraft to escape death could not live with themselves, and needed no help from the witches in their self-castigation. There's an extant letter from 1715, a suicide note actually, kept in the archives of the Massachusetts Historical Society, from a William Phelps to his daughter. He describes insurmountable guilt for 'turning to the Devil,' and states that his only recourse is to terminate his life and accept the fires of perdition."

Morgan looked at Gil with a half-smile and said, "Do you think if I became a witch I could get the mayor to kill himself?"

Gil remarked, "No need for that…just be yourself."

Morgan leered.

"The *mayor*?" queried Aaronson.

"Just another jerk-off in the mix," said Morgan. "Professor, you said Crestwood Lake is haunted by ghosts, witches *and* demons. You wanna give me a rundown on all these freaks, like what exactly are they? Gil says these are people in cahoots with the Devil?"

"My pleasure," said Aaronson, "but first we must understand the concepts of body, spirit, and soul."

"Isn't someone's spirit their soul?" asked Morgan.

"No, not technically. Lay people, and even some clergy, equate the terms spirit and soul. However, they are truly separate entities, most notably when the soul is disengaged from the spirit through the handiwork of maleficence. First there's the body, the definition of which is self-evident. Next is the spirit, our incorporeal life force. Finally there's the soul, also incorporeal, and indubitably a force, but more importantly, a spiritual energy bestowed upon us by God. The soul is immortal, eternal, and transcendent of every other human facet. The idea of the spirit and the soul being separate has its roots in the Old Testament, Hebrews 4:12 for example.

"According to theological postulates, if you have lived morally, and die peaceably, your spirit and soul enter the hereafter harmoniously entwined. If, however, you are morally conflicted, sinful, or beset by crippling psychic anguish, guilt, hatred, etc., then your spirit and soul are left in limbo. Some theologians refer to this state as purgatory. Researchers such as me would argue this is how ghosts are born. A ghost's soul is traumatized, either by malevolence executed upon them, or by iniquities they have wreaked upon others. A ghost is trapped between the realms, struggling to find peace, reconcilement, or redemption. They can languish indefinitely, haunting the places where they lived on earth.

"For example, there are the Scalford Puritans who shunned evil, but were brutally murdered. These are troubled spirits, viciously thrust between the realms. They could be well-meaning: endeavoring to thwart the malefactors and protect humanity. Then there are tortured spirits such as William Phelps, condemned to writhe in limbic agony, penitential for his sins, but devoid of recourse since the Devil owns his soul. The motivations of these wraiths are unknown. Their remorse would imply benevolence for the sake of redemption. But, with their souls under the auspices of hell, it's anyone's guess how their behavior will be dictated.

"Next in the pecking order, unequivocally wicked, are the aforementioned witches. A witch is a male or female, although some call male witches warlocks, who has bartered his or her soul to the Devil in exchange for supernatural powers. The most common necromancy is the infliction of harm on non-witches, casting 'spells' to use the colloquial vernacular, 'runes' in technical parlance. Lucifer particularly enjoys instilling them with that capability. But they may possess other faculties as well, such as telepathy, telekinesis, immunity from disease, the ability to transform into animals or disappear, the list is practically endless.

"Inevitably there are current citizens of Crestwood Lake who are witches. Some may be descended from the witches of Salem and Scalford. You gentlemen probably know many of them, having had countless interactions with them, without ever knowing their true identity."

"Can they be killed?" asked Morgan.

"Yes and no. Their bodies can be extinguished, but their spirit lives on, and their soul as well, only in the possession of the Devil. When you kill a witch, an even greater terror awaits, for now you have unleashed a soulless spirit, an *evil* spirit, onto the world. Fueled by sinister rage, they seek the destruction of those who have not relinquished their souls, namely, mortals. These vengeful revenants are now known as demons. They are diabolically vindictive, especially if they were executed witches. They appear as gruesome monsters and have ghastly powers. They inflict unspeakable pain and suffering and frequently work in concert with living witches. Serial killers, infanticide, genocide, war atrocities, disfiguring diseases, horrendous accidents, many of these horrors are the work of demonic influence in our world. Captain, I believe that the two poor people who were mutilated in your woods encountered a demon."

Morgan and Gil just sat there, speechless. Even Morgan was taken back.

"Another drink gentleman?" asked Aaronson.

They both nodded no. Gil shifted in his seat.

Morgan said, "The medical examiner couldn't figure out what killed them. There were absolutely no clues: no signs of a weapon or an animal, no footprints, fibers, DNA, teeth marks—I mean nothing. It's like an unseen entity just materialized, shredded them, took the body parts, and vanished."

"That's precisely what happened," said Aaronson.

Morgan looked at Aaronson, swallowing hard as the sinking feeling in his stomach returned.

"Ascending our hierarchy of infamy," said Aaronson, "we now arrive at the pinnacle of evil, the being pulling all the strings: Lucifer himself—the keeper of all of the souls."

"Are you sure it's Van Haden?" asked Morgan.

"Well, Captain, based on your descriptions of him, his uncanny insight, the ominous play on words of his name, the tragedies associated with his store, I'd say he's the prime suspect."

"But why now?" questioned Gil. "There must be covens of witches all over the world. Why would he come to Crestwood Lake at this time? And why are these malicious activities accelerating now? You specifically asked me if more strange phenomena were taking place in Crestwood Lake. What made you suspect that?"

"It's been three hundred years since the climactic fire of 1713. It's the tricentennial," answered Aaronson.

"Of course," said Gil.

"Wanna clue me in?" said Morgan looking back and forth between Gil and Aaronson.

"It's been three hundred years," said Gil. "The number three is significant in religions all over the world, the quintessential example being the sign of the Trinity in Christianity. But the number three is also important in witchcraft and the black arts. Some view it as the Devil's countercharge to the Trinity."

"Exactly," said Aaronson.

"Now it all makes sense," said Gil. "The Devil, the demons, the witches, the whole lot of them, are becoming more active now to celebrate. It's the three hundredth anniversary of the obliteration of Scalford. They're rejoicing for God sakes—reveling in their wickedness."

"Precisely," said Aaronson. "And possibly even more. They're probably seeking to revitalize the coven, and maybe even destroy Crestwood Lake, just like Scalford."

"So how—I mean why—Jesus the questions are endless," said Morgan. "So if there's a devil, then there must be a God, right?"

"That's what dualist theologians and Manichaeists would say," responded Aaronson.

"You wanna put that in English, Professor?" said Morgan.

"Dualism and Manichaeism are philosophies that go back two thousand years. Their underpinnings can be traced to Egyptian cosmology.

Dualistic theories posit that both good and evil exist, and there's an eternal struggle between them: a timeless clash that's infinite, and brings order and stability to the world. Others, such as the Christians, believe that God and the legions of good will eventually vanquish evil. The short answer to your question is yes, many theologians and philosophers contend that the presence of one, particularly the presence of evil, implies the existence of the other."

"Did he say that slow enough?" asked Gil looking at Morgan.

Morgan gave Gil the finger.

"Personally," said Aaronson, "I agree with the dualist point of view, for a very simple reason: if only evil existed, it would have triumphed millennia ago, wiping out humanity in its infancy. Thus, the dark side does not possess unlimited power, but I'm not convinced, like the Christians, that good will eventually trump evil. If that's the case, what is good waiting for?"

"So if there's a God," said Morgan, "why does he allow evil to exist?"

"That's the inescapable question," said Aaronson. "When you ask clergymen that question you inevitably receive evasive responses such as 'God works in mysterious ways' or 'It's part of God's plan,' etc. They don't know the answer. It's a very rational question, and it challenges their faith. If God is omnipotent why not just exterminate evil? Why even allow it to come into existence in the first place? If God *loves* us, why cause man to suffer? These questions defy logic, which is why clerics proffer 'God works in mysterious ways' types of answers."

Gil said, "According to Martin Luther, 'Reason is that greatest enemy that faith has.'"

"Quite true," said Aaronson. "Clearly we are dealing with forces and motivations beyond our comprehension. And despite being a man of science and reason, I have become convinced that evil exists, as well as its counterpart. But neither side can dominate, or one would have conquered the other by now. It truly is an eternal battle with incessant, alternating victories."

"So," said Morgan, "even if there's no winning the war, we can still win individual battles—keep the bad guys in check."

"Yes, I would agree with that," replied Aaronson.

"So how do we save Crestwood Lake?" asked Gil.

"You have to free the souls that the Devil has expropriated," answered Aaronson.

"Come again," said Morgan.

"Every witch and demon has surrendered his or her soul to the Devil. If you reclaim the souls from his possession, they can be restored, but *only* if the individual is truly repentant. If so, the evil dissipates, the soul and the spirit are rejoined, and they are emancipated from the shackles of hell. The souls of the demons—who are dead witches—are free to enter the life hereafter, while the souls of the living witches are returned to their bodies. The witches become whole again: body, spirit and soul. The *unrepentant*, however—witches or demons—are doomed to hell.

"I must emphasize this point: being contrite is insufficient, if the Devil still owns your soul. You *must* wrest the souls from Satan's clutches first. Then each being's conscience will determine his or her fate from there."

"And just how do we get the souls back from the Devil?" asked Morgan. "Ask him to close his eyes and count to a hundred?"

Aaronson smirked and then offered, "We're getting a little ahead of ourselves. First, we should probably discuss who is vulnerable to evil and who is not."

"I think that's a fascinating topic," said Gil. "May I offer my apotropaic insights?"

"Please," said Aaronson, "it would afford me time to attend to my Scotch that I've been neglecting."

"Apo-what?" said Morgan to Gil.

"Apotropaic. It means having the capacity to ward off evil," responded Gil.

"Why didn't you just say that?" snapped Morgan.

Gil ignored him. "When I was working on my book about the Salem Witch Trials I became engrossed in how one opposes evil. I researched it for months, reviewing numerous religious texts. I interviewed priests and theologians, including two who had performed exorcisms. I arrived at the following conclusions:

"First, many clerics contend that faith shields you from the Devil's influence. It seems to make sense. Obviously the Devil can't just swoop in, take your soul, and make you start hurting people. Nor can he just slaughter humans at will, or as you pointed out, Doug, the battle would have been over eons ago. And your faith needn't be in one particular God. If that were true, then all the other souls, from all the other religions, would already belong to Satan, and that's plainly ludicrous. So it's not faith in a specific god, but faith in a higher power and virtuousness: a resolution that good exists, and a determination to embrace that holiness and reject iniquity.

"In addition to faith, a man's overall rectitude is vital. People who are morally principled are more recalcitrant toward evil than those of dubious character. Individuals who are selfish, jealous, unscrupulous, or vindictive, are at risk. So are people who are emotionally unstable or have a feeble constitution. These psychological shortcomings are chinks in one's armor, little portals by which evil can worm its way in.

"It also helps to be outright antagonistic toward evil. Butch will love this one, but to employ a crude paradigm, having the mettle to tell the *Devil* to go to hell."

"No fucking problem," said Morgan.

Gil snickered, shook his thumb at Morgan, and said to Aaronson: "My coarse friend here, while definitely not a social ambassador, may actually possess a real strength, one that can repel evil. To quote Martin Luther again: 'The best way to drive out the Devil, if he will not yield to texts of Scripture, is to jeer and flout him, for he cannot bear scorn.'

"And one last thing: love. Pure love can deter evil, because love is the ultimate goodness. Nothing agonizes the Devil more than people loving each other. It causes him pain to the core of his being."

"Superb," proclaimed Aaronson. "I completely concur. I have encountered every one of those ideas in my examinations as well. They are part of the orthodoxy for combatting all things ungodly."

Morgan spoke up: "Look guys, that's all very nice, but something tells me we need a lot more than a conscience and warm fuzzies. Not that I'd mind telling Van Haden to kiss my ass, but I think we have to take action.

Professor, you said we have to steal the souls of the coven back from the Devil. Can we move on to how we're supposed to do that?"

"Of course, Captain, by all means. Let me start by making one quick point which I think will assist you in that endeavor."

"What's that?" asked Gil.

"The Devil may be pansophic, but he's not truly omniscient and he's certainly not prescient."

"English, Professor, English," said Morgan.

Gil leaned over toward Morgan and softly said, "That is English. Eight hundred thousand years from now when your species begins walking upright, you'll be able to understand it."

Morgan leaned even closer to Gil and said, "Eight seconds from now when I'm through with you...*you* won't."

"You two are quite amusing," remarked Aaronson. Then he looked at Morgan and said, "*Pansophic* means universal knowledge or wisdom. The Devil knows a great deal about earthly subjects, and even more about the spiritual realm. He is cognizant of many things that have transpired on earth and in peoples' lives, especially their sins. But he doesn't know *everything*. Thus, he is not *omniscient*. He doesn't know what you're thinking, even though he is extremely intuitive. He can't read your mind. And probably most importantly, he can't foretell the future. Thus, he is not *prescient*: he doesn't know what you will do, or what will happen."

"How do you know?" asked Morgan.

"Very simple; same logic as before. If he knew everything that was going to happen he would have already overcome the earth. If he was prescient he could obviate every move against him and spell humanity's doom. But aside from my ratiocination, it has been noted by several writers and theologians, some who claim to have confronted Satan, that he never knew what would happen. This is a vital piece of information."

"Indeed," said Gil.

"You see gentlemen," said Aaronson, "if we assume Christianity is correct, the Devil is merely an angel—not a god—and therefore not omnipotent. He was one of the original angels in heaven. He and his followers turned against God and were routed by the archangel Michael, who expelled them from Paradise."

"The legend of St. Michael and Lucifer," said Gil, "suggests that the forces of good can overcome evil, even if not permanently."

"Quite right," said Aaronson. "Now on to the business of reclaiming souls. Years ago, while conducting research in Jerusalem, I met a priest and a rabbi, who were both exorcists. We discussed witchcraft and the selling of souls to the Devil. Satan preserves all the souls of each individual coven in a separate and special container. To be clear, each receptacle represents one coven, the number of souls within which may vary."

Gil said, "Many people think that a coven is always twelve witches, plus the Devil to equal thirteen, but that's apocryphal."

"That's correct. The actual number of witches in any one particular coven can vary greatly."

"So what's the criteria for a coven?" asked Morgan.

"There could be a number of different parameters," answered Aaronson. "It's often a geographic location, but it could be a temporal differentiator. Sometimes the specifications are elusive. I'm pretty sure though, that every witch and demon from Crestwood Lake, past and present, would represent one coven. Covens meet regularly and perform various rituals. It's a foregone conclusion that the Crestwood Lake coven assembles deep in the woods surrounding the lake.

"The souls of the Crestwood Lake coven will be stored in some kind of vessel, surely in close proximity to wherever the Devil is operating from. The container must be confiscated—and here's the tricky part—transferred to hallowed ground, opened, or better yet smashed, thus allowing the souls to escape within holy surroundings."

"Such as a church," said Gil.

"That's pretty much the only option in Crestwood Lake. If you were in Jerusalem or Rome there'd be other alternatives, but for our purposes, yes, a church."

"St. Matthews," said Gil to Morgan.

Morgan looked at Aaronson. "We talked about all the personal strengths necessary to resist evil, and how to clean up the whole damn mess. But you haven't said anything about how to deal with a specific creature. In other words, if I come face to face with any of these assholes we've been discussing, how do I kill them?"

Gil chimed in with a smile, "Butch is a practical and somewhat concrete man. He wants to know if he should put silver bullets in his .357."

"Damn straight," said Morgan. "I need a backup in case I can't bore them to death with your theories."

Aaronson smiled briefly, but then said, "Well, actually, the Captain does bring up an important issue. First of all, Captain, a witch is still a live human being, and therefore, can be killed like any other human. The archaic assumption that they can *only* be destroyed by burning or drowning is just a myth. However, as I said before, they possess any number of powers, which renders them more formidable. They might have abnormal strength, or the ability to teleport, but suffice it to say, they'll be no need to exchange the ammunition in your firearm."

"And what about the demons?" asked Morgan.

"Much more dangerous. A demon is already dead, and invested with even greater supernatural power. According to individuals who have confronted demons, the fire and water myth now holds veracity: these are the only two methods that can destroy them. However, no demon is going to stand there passively as you endeavor to set it on fire. So unless you have a blowtorch, or a means of trapping the demon in a conflagration, fire is not very practical. And as for water, it is not normal water that is counteractive, but *holy* water. It must have been blessed by a priest, or some other church official, who has been consecrated by ecclesiastical authorities. The clerics I met in Jerusalem claimed that they had literally dissolved demons by splashing them with holy water.

"Holy water can also be used against witches. You can certainly drown a witch in regular water, *but*, destroying a witch with *holy water* is the only way to prevent it from becoming a demon after death. They needn't be submerged in it, only touched by it, like the demons. So it would behoove you to visit this church you mentioned, meet with its priest, and arm yourself with some holy water."

"Doug," said Gil, "earlier you said the Puritans had no reliable means of determining who was a witch. Why didn't they just splash suspects with holy water?"

"Because, as is so often the case with humans, their myths and preconceived notions obscured the truth. They believed that water in general was noisome to witches, which is why they used it as a test for witchcraft, and for executions. They didn't know that holy water was the key. In all fairness, having your community infested by witches is not an everyday occurrence. The Puritans, just like most modern humans, were not familiar with these phenomena. Naturally their ideas about evil were based on fables and misconceptions."

"And what about dealing with Lucifer?" asked Morgan.

"Well, Captain, as for combating the Devil himself, obviously he cannot be destroyed. He is an eternal being and nearly as invincible as his heavenly counterpart. He cannot be killed, only repelled. And that can only be done if you possess the various strengths that Gil previously reviewed. But I wouldn't focus on the Devil per se; I would focus on finding his receptacle, releasing the souls on hallowed ground, and terminating the entire coven. That will keep the Devil at bay."

Morgan was deep in thought. Gil and Aaronson sat there waiting for him to say something.

"Butch?" said Gil.

Morgan snapped his fingers. "I think I know where the Devil keeps the souls!"

"Indeed, Captain," stated Aaronson. "Do tell."

"Well, if Van Haden is Lucifer, it's in his store. He's got this giant bottle of some special wine in its own cabinet next to his counter. He said it's not for sale, but bragged that it's easily worth thirty thousand or more. I take it you know about fine wine, Professor?"

"Yes I do."

"The bottle's called a double magnum; I remember that because of my gun. Do you know what that is, Professor?"

"Yes, a double magnum contains four standard bottles of wine. It equals three liters."

"Right," said Morgan. "It's from 1961. I remember that because it was my birth year. The name was…chateau some-shit. It had a castle with a lion on it."

"Oh my!" exclaimed Aaronson. "You mean Chateau Latour!"

"Yeah. That's it."

"What a complete and utter defilement!" proclaimed Aaronson. "You've just described one of the greatest wines in the world, in a quadruple-sized bottle no less, from one of the best vintages of the twentieth century…abominably befouled by the vile souls of witches and demons."

"Yeah *that's* the problem," said Morgan. "A fancy bottle of wine got ruined."

"Forgive me, Captain. Of course there's much more at stake here. The epicure in me reacted viscerally."

"Yeah, whatever," said Morgan. "So how do I steal it?"

"Good question," said Gil. "We'd have to know a time when we could be positive that Van Haden was away, but how could we?"

"You wait until Thursday night," replied Aaronson.

Gil and Morgan both looked at Aaronson with astonishment.

"Thursday is Halloween—at sundown, the New Year on the Druid calendar begins. Supposedly, the barrier between the earth and the underworld is thinnest at this time. You can be certain that your coven will be having a special ceremony, deep in the woods on that night. If Lucifer is in Crestwood Lake, he will definitely be leading it."

"That's it, Butch," said Gil. "We'll break into Grand Vin that night, bring the bottle to St. Matthews and smash it on the altar."

"We're gonna have to meet with Father Mark to arrange this," said Morgan. "We have to make sure nothing else is going on in the church that night. And I don't feel comfortable breaking into a church. We need him to be on board."

"What if he thinks we're crazy?" asked Gil.

"I got an even better question," said Morgan. "What if we're wrong about all of this shit and the chief of police is found guilty of breaking and entering, stealing thirty grand worth of private property, and vandalizing a church? I won't just lose my career and look like a nut-job, I'll go to jail."

Gil leaned over and said to Morgan, "I'm going to do this. If you want to join me that's fine. If we fail, and someone catches you with me, you can always say you were apprehending me. I'll swear to it."

Morgan nodded, but still looked conflicted.

"Butch, what does your gut tell you?"

"I guess something tells me that this is the right thing to do. Why did that son of a bitch tell me to say hi to Vicki? She's never met him. I got a bad feeling, Gil. I'm afraid he's going to hurt her—I don't have any evidence or proof—just a feeling in my bones. And I will NOT let that happen. I love her, Gil. That's it. Let's do this."

"Allow me to warn you gentlemen," said Aaronson. "The Devil is not stupid. He has the entire coven at his disposal. Even if he is far from his wine shop, even if a major ceremony is taking place, there are likely to be witches, maybe even demons, in the vicinity guarding the receptacle. You should expect to encounter resistance."

"We understand," said Gil.

"Oh, I almost forgot," added Morgan reaching into his shirt pocket. He handed the photo from Debbie Kurzmann's camera to Aaronson and said, "What do you make of this?"

"What in God's name is that?"

"We have a missing woman, a photographer who was at Crestwood Lake taking photos. We found her camera at the water's edge. That was the last picture taken on it."

"Then I'm afraid, Captain, this is the demon that killed her. As a matter of fact, this is starting to make more sense."

"What do you mean?"

Aaronson expounded: "The Scalford witches who were executed were either drowned in Crestwood Lake or burned at the stake, their ashes scattered in the woods. Those witches became demons, who now inhabit the lake or the woods. It explains the grisly nature of the murders in the woods, and this photograph."

"Are the demons confined to the lake or the woods?" asked Gil.

"That I don't know," said Aaronson. "But I wouldn't take any chances. I would assume they can manifest themselves anywhere and I would be prepared. You need to see this Father Mark as soon as possible. You must present all this to him, secure the use of his church for Halloween night, and acquire some holy water. He might also be able to provide some additional spiritual protection."

"Professor, can I ask you to clarify some points because I need to make sure I'm clear on all this," said Morgan.

"Of course, Captain."

"So…all the weird stuff that's been happening in the town is related to this coven?"

"I can't say with assurance that every single peculiarity is the work of the coven. Remember, there are numerous ghosts rampant in your town as well. They may not be baleful, but they're not going to be having tea and cookies with you. Their mere existence, in addition to the motivations that drive them, will result in unusual events, such as Gil's old house, whose occupants sensed their own death. Clearly it's haunted. Is it due to these ghosts or some other pernicious spirits, or both? It's hard to say. There's much about the spiritual world we don't know."

"And there's been a lot of animals showing up dead or mutilated," said Morgan.

"In addition to human organs, witches use animal innards and parts in their ceremonies as well."

"How about the suicides, like Ron Millhouse and the nun who slashed her wrists and jumped in the lake?"

"I don't think there's any guesswork here, Captain. They came to be possessed or tormented by the Devil or his agents. They had something about them, some chink in their armor as Gil explained earlier, that allowed evil to permeate them. Much like the Jorgensens. You mentioned they bought wine from Van Haden. He probably poisoned it with a potion of some kind, a common tactic in witchcraft. However, I wouldn't be surprised if there was already bad blood festering between them."

"A potion? Maybe like from wormwood?"

"Wormwood?" said Aaronson. "Why yes, that's been reputed to be used in various witches' brews for centuries. Why do you mention it?"

"Remember that recent plane crash, the flight from Boston to Italy?" Aaronson nodded.

"The pilot lived with this woman in Crestwood Lake. I got a bad vibe about her too. She owns a florist shop in town and speaks highly of Van Haden. She has these strange yellow flowers in her store, and when I asked her what they were, she said wormwood."

"Good Lord, Captain. Your town is completely infiltrated by evil."

"We better start getting back," said Gil. "We don't have that much time before Thursday."

"Indeed," said Aaronson. "If you need me, call me, no matter what time it is."

"One last thing," said Morgan. "So if we're able to free the souls, that means all the dead witches, namely the demons, will go to heaven, and the live ones will revert back to their normal human self?"

"Yes, but only if they are truly repentant," responded Aaronson. "A cornerstone of Christianity is forgiveness of one's sins. If their contrition is sincere, the deceased souls are reclaimed by heaven. The live witches will resume their normal humanity that existed prior to their fall from grace. Their body, spirit and soul will be reunited. But if they are *not* penitent—demon or witch—they will be banished to the bowels of hell for all eternity, and will no longer haunt the earth. In essence they will be eradicated."

"Got it," said Morgan.

"I would also expect the chaos to increase this week," said Aaronson.

"Can you be more specific?"

"As Halloween approaches the demons and witches will become increasingly active. They will be engaged in activities instrumental to their ceremony, or simply amplifying their heinous acts for pure exhilaration. You should anticipate assorted mayhem, probably more deaths or missing people. They'll be harvesting organs and eliminating anyone they think is a threat."

Morgan and Gil expressed their gratitude and the three men bade each other farewell. Morgan and Gil got back on the road. For the first fifteen minutes they barely talked, each one trying to assimilate all that had been discussed. Finally, with the sun setting on the horizon, they began to work on their plans.

● ● ●

Near the north-central part of Crestwood Lake was a small island. It was largely marshland with some solid earth. Crouching over Neil Pasternak's body were two faceless creatures, clad in white shrouds, clawing him open from his scalp to his ankles. They removed various bodily organs. A few they consumed, others they placed in a large urn. One demon grabbed the urn, the other picked up what was left of Pasternak's body. Then they both vanished.

THE MEMOIR

I hate humans. Or should I say mortals? Same thing really. Useless creatures. Fatuous, benighted, and irrational—oh, so irrational. And so incorrigibly arrogant. Every one of them thinks he or she is so enlightened and everybody else is mistaken. Every one of them attempts to convert or control others. Every one of them has this obsessive need to foist their beliefs and misguided religion onto the rest of their sorry lot. They fight each other over their delusions, massacring each other in the name of their gods. Each one assumes his or her cause is just and anyone who thinks differently is a heretic. Humans are evil—that's right—mankind is inherently evil.

Abducting a mortal being and setting his or her body on fire is evil. And when it's performed under a banner of divine righteousness, it's an even more loathsome atrocity. How dare they profess their virtuousness while murdering me? Setting me ablaze to writhe in unendurable agony, as if *I'm* the pestilence in this venal realm called Earth.

Do you know what it's like to burn to death? The English language doesn't possess words adequate for describing the pain. The torture is unbearable: hot, searing, seething pain. You can smell your own flesh scorching. You thrash and scream and beg for death. But you don't die with alacrity. The heat needs time to penetrate your charring skin and eventually stop your heart, more from the agony and shock than the actual physical damage. And all the while those goddamned sadistic fiends are crowing over your suffering. The last thing I remember is the look of satisfaction on their faces. And they consider *me* unholy?

Hypocrites! Their so-called Bible asserts that they are forbidden to seek vengeance, that it belongs to their God. And yet they dispense their vengeance with impunity. And now I dispense mine! I will never cease repaying the debt of revenge that they bestowed upon me.

My name is Thomas Ramsey. I was born in London in 1678, the eldest of four children. My youngest sibling and my mother died during childbirth when I was eight. My father worked as a blacksmith and occasional tanner and struggled to provide for us. He was a miserable bastard, frequently intoxicated, and regularly beat my mother and the children. Being the oldest, I got the worst of it. Any infraction (and the drunker he was, the slighter it could be), was met with a beating. He relished forcing us to disrobe, holding our heads down to the floor, and flogging us with a specially fabricated strap until he drew blood. Maniacally religious, he routinely professed how the "Devil needed to be beaten out of us." One day when I was five years old, I stole a piece of fruit from a neighborhood vendor. When the merchant informed my father, he took my hand and pushed my index finger back until it snapped. "Your hands will no longer be instruments of the Devil," he angrily proclaimed.

After my mother died, his drinking worsened, but strangely, not the whippings. He would drink himself into such a stupor that he was incapable of assaulting us. Only an unmitigated hypocrite could conflate Puritanism and alcoholism.

Between his two crafts my father earned a moderate income, but we lived as if we were destitute. We never had enough to eat, but he always had enough to drink. Our clothes had to be reduced to rags before he purchased new garments, and they were often used. Little did we know my father was stashing away money to finance our emigration to the colonies. My father had friends and a brother who had already left England and settled in the colonies for religious reasons.

In 1689 we abandoned London for good. We settled in Salem, the capital of the Massachusetts Bay Colony, which, after merging with the Plymouth Colony in 1691, simply became known as the Massachusetts Colony. Life was hard; we had few of the conveniences that living in

London had to offer. We had fewer varieties of foods, greater fears of starvation, and much more physical labor.

But the worst part was the fanatically religious and overbearing culture. In yet another monumental example of human hypocrisy, the Puritans escape England to eschew persecution, and then proceed to persecute their own. The moral climate minimized our comforts, even more than the barren nature of our circumstances. Anything that fostered relaxation or merrymaking was prohibited, since idleness was viewed as a route to the Devil. Everyone knew everyone's business; each citizen was under constant scrutiny. The only benefit to this merciless milieu was that it forced my father to be temperate.

Children and women were subject to the harshest standards because they were assumed to be more susceptible to the forces of evil. Unlike London, where I occasionally had brief periods to gallivant with my peers, in Salem, every child's whereabouts was always known and supervised. Children were never allowed to play.

Samuel Parris was the newly appointed minister for Salem and a contemptible scoundrel. He was the most arrant embodiment of hypocrisy and self-righteous indignation that ever walked the earth. After church on Sunday he would line up all the children and order them to hold out their hands. Brandishing a switch he would go down the line catechizing each child about the Bible. Every incorrect answer was rewarded with a painful lash across the palm.

I was not well versed in their Biblical fiction. Oh I was exposed to their dogma and sententious pontificating on a regular basis, but I refused to waste my energies studying their doctrine beyond the times it was thrust upon me. Subsequently, I often failed to answer Parris's questions and was a frequent recipient of his discipline. I would have my revenge in 1720.

Once more I must highlight their hypocrisy, for it is such a stark, pervasive, and ubiquitous feature of the Puritans. In all honesty I have rarely encountered a deist who wasn't also a hypocrite. Sanctimony and religious devotion are indissoluble, but reach their apex in Puritanism. One further example of the Puritans' hypocrisy was their abject lack of compassion and empathy. Those who prospered, or simply had better luck, were enviously perceived as unworthy, or the beneficiary of some tryst with the Devil. Conversely, those beset with inordinate misfortune were judged as deserving of their anguish. Clearly they must have offended God and incited his wrath. So much for the Christian concept of goodwill toward man and lending a hand to those less fortunate than you.

In sum, whether you succeeded or failed you were reprobated. Everybody despised, condemned, distrusted, or begrudged someone else. You can only imagine the enmity that was fostered. I thought it was a laughing stock—Christianity in all its glory. Naturally this pernicious acrimony set the stage for the inquisition to come.

From the moment we arrived in Salem there were stirrings about witchcraft. Gradually, more and more colonists began accusing each other of being witches. As mentioned, successful individuals were always suspect, but multitudinous other criteria were also deemed incriminating. Miniscule deviations from the Draconian order, or the slightest lapse in one's religious fervor and you were considered an apostate. Anyone who seemed odd, unduly emotional, impulsive, or driven by anything other than "Godly" forces was questionable. One day, one of the single men gazed a little too long at one of the married women. He was summarily escorted to Parris's office for a stern lecture about the sin of desire, as well as a browbeating about any associations to Satan.

And God forbid if you *did* commit an actual offense of some kind. Punishment was swift and meted out with severity. I'll never forget the poor woman who spent a full day in a stock for missing church on Sunday. The entire community gawked and laughed at her. More than a few assailed her with rotting food or fecal matter. Afterward a group of the elders subjected her to a grueling interrogation about her possible affiliation with witchcraft.

The accusations and recriminations continued to spiral out of control. Then in January 1692, Parris's daughter and niece began having these fits. My Master has since explained to me that they were merely ill and experiencing seizures. They were smitten with ergotism. Ergot is a fungus that had infected the rye crop in Salem. Ergotism produces an array of symptoms including seizures, hallucinations and even psychosis. Not surprisingly, the ignorant mortals interpreted these reactions as proof that witchcraft had indeed infiltrated their community. They were right of course, but for the wrong reasons, which again proves what imbeciles they were.

Things really started getting out of hand at that point. I was fourteen at the time, but remember it well. To this day we still rejoice in the fact that it was the imputation of Parris's own family members as witches that triggered the ensuing pandemonium. The vilifications were flying. Countless people were inculpated and dragged into the church for questioning. If Parris and his coreligionists still had the slightest doubt, the individual was formally indicted. Ultimately, twenty-four people died. Nineteen were hanged, four died in prison, and one hapless eighty-year-old was crushed to death by stones for not entering a plea. Half of those terminated really were witches. But even more fascinating were the dozens of witches amongst them who were never even suspected. Again, imbeciles.

In October of that year, Governor Phips intervened and ended the witch trials. Interestingly, the governor's wife had also been implicated in witchcraft. I'm not sure why they blamed her, but they were right that time.

But the cessation of the trials certainly didn't halt the suspicions, the indicting, and the infighting. Friends and relatives of the executed were outraged. A number of physical assaults and two unsolved murders took place in the wake of the trials.

Meanwhile, a growing subgroup was absolutely convinced that witchcraft was still in our midst. They wanted to defy the governor and restart the trials, despite his interdiction. A few even argued that he and his wife should stand trial. But most of the elders did not want to incite a rebellion and stood their ground against the seditionists.

The deadlock broke in the spring of 1693. The ultra-zealous contingent, led by Minister Alexander Pitt, decided to leave Salem and create their own colony. My father was one of them. Since I was only fifteen, my sister thirteen, and my brother eleven, we had no choice but to accompany him.

What a horrendous journey. Ninety-one of us, with animals, wagons and supplies, trekked nearly two hundred miles into the vast and forbidding wilderness. We couldn't bathe, slept in makeshift tents, and ate whatever wild game the men could shoot. Two of the older members died along the way. The nights were terrifying. There were all sorts of eerie sounds, unearthly screeches and sickening wails. Pitt claimed they were the cries of witches and demons, but assured us of our safety if we remained steadfast in our faith.

Finally we came to the crest of a mountain that majestically overlooked a beautiful lake. Heady with its splendor, Pitt announced that he was overcome with divine inspiration. He proclaimed that providence had guided us to this divine location and this lake would be the heart of our new colony. He named our virgin settlement Scalford, in honor of his birthplace in England.

That season was the hardest of my life. Every soul who was able worked day and night: chopping down trees, producing lumber, cutting firewood, building houses, finding food, planting crops, and many other chores. It took a couple of years to fully establish the colony: years of interminable labor, disease, hunger, and occasional skirmishes with the lingering Abenaki Indians.

And of course, the same insufferable religiosity that had strangulated Salem pervaded our community as well. Pitt was even more hidebound and evangelical than Parris, as impossible as that may seem. Amazingly, despite the ascetic and theocratic culture, only occasional references to, or suspicions of, witchcraft arose during the first decade of our colony. I suppose that was because everyone in our faction viewed themselves as free of demonic influence when they deserted Salem. But it was just a matter of time before the paranoia permeated Scalford as well. Just as in Salem, trivial offenses, jealousies, intolerance of others who were different, or emotionally troubled, spectral evidence—all could lead to charges of witchcraft.

It began with the winter of 1703–1704, ushered in by an unusually early frost that decimated our crops. Food was scarce and seventeen members of our settlement, mostly elderly, but all malnourished, perished from influenza or other infections. Pitt and his retinue of ignoramuses attributed it to the work of the Devil and asserted that witchcraft had finally come to Scalford. From that point on the hysteria steadily grew. Over the next decade there were numerous accusations and executions. Pitt felt that we had to return to the classical methods for exterminating witches, namely fire and water. Hanging was insufficient as he felt that it extinguished the body but not the evil. Thus, if the church elders were convinced of someone's guilt, they burned the poor soul at the stake and spread the ashes in the woods. If any doubt existed, the accused was brought to the center of the lake in a small boat and thrown into the water. If they drowned they were beatified, as it proved their soul was pure. If they floated (or in reality swam), it was considered proof of their wickedness and they were often forcibly drowned.

In 1712, the colony's population was dwindling from a combination of natural causes and official executions; not to mention the individuals who my Master's acolytes eliminated. That's when the plague hit. To this day I don't know if it was the exact same illness as the Black Death in medieval Europe, but that is inconsequential. The symptoms and course were similar. People would develop fever, followed by vomiting or coughing up blood. Then—buboes—the iconic symptom of the plague: swollen, infected lymph glands most commonly in the armpits and groin. A small percentage of the afflicted, as in Europe, was able to recover for unknown reasons.

The plague killed my father, my wife, and was now ravaging my poor six-year-old daughter. I loved that little girl more than anyone or anything in my entire life. I stayed at her bedside day and night, knowing I would become infected. I didn't care, as long as I got to see her live. She shook in agony, febrile, hacking up blood. I prayed to God incessantly, pleading with him to take my life, if only he would spare hers. But heaven had no mercy for my innocent child. She continued to deteriorate and finally succumbed. I was inconsolable, wailing in unimaginable grief. That's when Minister Pitt and two other church officials called on me. Pitt stood over her bed, looked at her emaciated body with contempt, turned to me and disdainfully professed:

"Your father, your wife, and now your child. Clearly your clan has betrayed the Lord. Only witchcraft could justify such punishment on one family."

I was enraged! Incensed beyond madness! "You bastard!" I screamed, throwing myself at Pitt, and knocking him to the ground with so much force his bones cracked. I clenched my hands around his throat choking him with all my might, with all my grief, until his face turned blue and his neck snapped. By that moment one of his cohorts had grabbed a fireplace poker and swung it into the back of my head.

I awoke in shackles, naked, anchored to a wall, in one of the dark, dank, excrement-laden cells of our stockade. I had a tremendous headache, and could feel dried blood on the back of my neck. I called out repeatedly, but no one answered, no one attended me—no one brought me food or water for two full days.

On the third day, one of the church officials came to my cell. He declared that I had been unanimously found guilty of cold-blooded murder and witchcraft, and would be burned at the stake the next morning. I protested, but he turned around without uttering another word and left. He ignored my pleas for sustenance.

Oh did I seethe. I've never had so many agonizing and twisting emotions simultaneously in my wretched life. I felt unbearable grief over my family. I couldn't stop picturing my little girl dying. Weeping uncontrollably, I felt completely forsaken. How could a supposedly loving God allow such egregious distress and injustice to befall an innocent man? And then I felt rage. Homicidal rage! What I did to Pitt was nothing. I wanted to kill every denizen of Scalford. As loud as possible, I screamed:

"You hypocrites! You worthless blackguards! I will make each and every one of you pay. You think my burden is because of the Devil? I *wish* the Devil were involved because even our God couldn't save you from my revenge!"

I yanked at my shackles with all my strength, but succeeded only in breaking my wrist. Fatigued from my fury and the deprivation of food and water, I passed out. I awoke in the middle of the night. Except for the scurrying of an occasional rat, it was ominously silent.

Suddenly a candle effloresced in my cell. It was Mary Pickford, one of the women from our colony. She was crouched down, sitting on her ankles, holding the candlestick in one hand and a mug of water in the other.

"Mary, how did you get in here?"

"There, there," she whispered in a soothing voice. She placed the candlestick on the ground. She raised the mug to my lips. I gulped it down furiously.

"How do you get in here?"

"That's not important, Tom. I don't have much time. I'm here to help you."

"Help me…I'm so weak…can you get me out of here?"

"No, I cannot. But I can see to it that after the torment that awaits you, you will live again. Live again to exact your vengeance on these horrid beings."

"What do you mean?"

"My Master can grant you eternal life. He can grant you awesome powers. After tomorrow, you'll never have to suffer again. Instead, you can righteously partake in the retaliation against your crucifiers."

"What do you mean by Master? Do you mean…"

"Yes, Tom…Lucifer. He will not ignore your pleas like their inclement God. He will not forsake you; he sympathizes with your pain, your family's pain—your *daughter's* pain. You cannot let her death, and most of all, their callous disregard for her death, go unavenged."

At that moment my rage returned. I felt a fire burning inside. She was right. How dare they show such gross insensitivity to my family's crucibles? And to insinuate that my pure and sinless little girl deserved her fate. I would fulfill my vow and make them pay!

"Mary, they're going to burn me at the stake. Can you save me?"

"No I can't. But it's actually better that you endure this ordeal."

"Why?"

"Because, if you join us in life, your powers will be greater than any mortal's, but still limited; you will still be at their mercy. But if you surrender your soul now to my Master, and *then* die, you will be given the fiercest capabilities. You will be practically indestructible. And, Tom—this is very important—by accepting your fate, by relinquishing your body to the fire and your soul to him, you will prove your fealty. And unlike their so-called God, your new Master will reward that loyalty."

"Done," I proclaimed. "Tell me what to do."

Mary reached into her dress pocket and produced a small knife. She cut herself on her arm and allowed a few drops of her blood to drip into the mug. She returned the knife to her pocket and then withdrew a small vial. It contained a yellow liquid which she mixed with the blood.

"What is that?"

"Wormwood," she answered. "Now drink this."

She put the mug to my lips and tilted it. I sipped down the bitter concoction. A strange sensation swept through my entire body, as if something left, but was replaced at the same time.

Mary put her hand on my chest and stated, "Your soul now belongs to him."

"Now what?"

"There is nothing more to be done at this time. I must bid you farewell. Tomorrow will be terrible, but it will be your last ordeal, and it will be your rebirth. When it is over, you will be with us."

She leaned over and kissed me on my forehead. Then she stood up and vanished, candle and all. At that moment, I didn't fear my fate anymore.

Sunrise arrived. Three guards entered my cell. They bound my ankles together. Then they unshackled me and tied my wrists behind my back. I didn't say a word. Neither did they. They dragged me out of my cell, up the stairs, and out of the stockade. They did not do so with care. In the courtyard outside the prison, virtually every adult citizen of Scalford had gathered. In the center of the courtyard was a large stake. At its base was a pyre of firewood, topped with hay and straw. On the ground were also several piles of firewood and kindling. Standing next to the stake was the magistrate and the church elders, including the newly appointed minister. Another guard held a lit torch.

The crowd began jeering and cursing me, shouting all kinds of invectives. Some yelled that they couldn't wait to see me burn. Others hollered that I was worthless and deserved to go to hell. A few threw stones at me. These were the people who were my friends less than a week ago. How quickly their allegiance had evaporated. I think I would have died from despair were it not for Mary Pickford. I saw her in the crowd, sympathy in her eyes. She gently nodded, giving me the strength to face my doom.

The guards tied me to the stake. They then wrapped a series of chains around my body, binding me to the stake from my ankles to my chest. They placed iron shackles on my wrists, since ropes would burn and allow a possible escape. The magistrate made a formal declaration of the charges and the sentence to be carried out. The minister went into a nauseating diatribe about the dangers of sin, and the penalties that awaited heretics and transgressors, especially those who turned to the Devil. He then directed his rant at me, loudly and angrily deriding me and my entire family for our despicable abandonment of God. He gave me one last chance to admit my alliance with the Devil and beg for God's forgiveness. I spat in his face. The crowd went wild. The minister hollered, "Proceed with the execution."

The guard with the torch set the hay and straw ablaze, while the other guards added kindling. The conflagration began. The crowd was frenzied. My rage and hatred reached new heights. I was so infuriated. Liars! Pharisees! Every one of them. These are your people, Lord: they preach your forgiveness and good will with their lips, but shun such virtues with their hearts. They perversely revel in the torture of their fellow humans. I didn't regret the deal I had made for one second. I swore to my new Master that I would do everything within my new powers to destroy these hypocrites. I would transform their sadistic satisfaction into indescribable anguish.

The flames reached my feet. The burning was so intense. I screamed and flailed, but the chains allowed no leeway. They continued throwing wood on the fire. The flames grew and engulfed me to my waist. My feet were sizzling, the skin blistering like meat on a spit. I squirmed and screamed. There are no words for the pain. They tossed more wood on the fire. The flames enveloped my entire body. My body hair crackled. My groin caught fire. It was excruciating! I could smell my skin burning. The hair on my head caught fire. My heart pounded. I thought it would burst from my chest. I screamed and screamed. They cheered and cheered. I screamed! They cheered! I screamed! They cheered! I screamed…

I awoke on a stone slab in what appeared to be an underground chamber. A number of torches projected from the walls. I was surrounded by people clad in hooded brown robes. They looked like monks. Frightened, I tried to sit up. One of them placed a hand on my shoulder and removed her hood. It was Mary Pickford.

"It's all right, dear," she said. "You're safe. It's over. Just lie there for now."

"Where am I? What happened?"

"Hush now," said Mary. "Everything is all right."

I looked down. I was still naked. Only my flesh wasn't burnt. I felt no pain, no heat, no cold… physically, I felt nothing.

"Am I alive?"

"Not in the mortal sense. You exist now in the netherworld, but you will soon be able to transpose between the realms at will." She peered behind her toward a dark passageway with a slightly surprised look on her face. Then she turned back to me and whispered, "Our Master approaches. Be quiet."

Mary replaced her hood on her head. The witches surrounding me promptly broke in two, forming a line on each side of the slab. I heard footsteps. A tall dark figure effused from the darkness. He wore a black cape and had brilliantly white hair, piercing brown eyes, and a ruddy complexion. When he reached my slab the witches all kneeled.

"Stand," he commanded in a deep and domineering voice.

The witches immediately complied.

He looked at me. He looked *through* me. "Sit up," he ordered.

I shifted down to the end of the slab and took a seated position. He moved to within arm's reach and met my eyes with his. He appeared as if he was barely restraining his ferocity.

"Do you know who I am?"

Afraid, I murmured, "Yes…I think so. You're…you're…Lucifer?"

"From now on I am your master! You will address me as such. Do you understand?"

"Yes, sir, I mean, Master."

"I have given you eternal life. And I can take it away at any moment. Do not forget that."

Still timorous, I nodded.

"Shortly I will be giving you an arsenal of other gifts. Powers you can't imagine. Do you see these witches before you?"

Again I nodded.

"They are still mortal. They have yet to earn the rewards you will receive. Rewards you earned by surrendering your soul and then dying. Especially dying so horrendously at the hands of those treacherous Puritans. You do remember your tormentors, do you not?"

My fear dissipated as my anger returned. "Yes. I do remember them, Master. God damn them!"

"Oh it won't be God who will be damning them, I assure you. It will be you! You and all of the other members of our coven."

"I look forward to that opportunity, Master."

He reached out his hand, its long black fingernails extending to a fine point. "Kiss my hand," he ordered.

I did so without hesitation.

He grabbed my throat and squeezed. His pupils turned red as he spoke: "For the rest of eternity your soul belongs to me. You will do my bidding, or I will abrogate that eternity and you will burn again, only this time in the infinite fires of hell. From this moment on you are greater than just a witch. You are deceased from the mortal world. You are now a demon!"

Maintaining his grip on my throat, an overwhelming wave of energy coursed through my body. I began to metamorphosize! My bones and muscles enlarged. My skin became gray and leathery. My vision became keen, my hearing acute. My eyes turned red as my teeth extended into an array of fangs. My fingertips sprouted talons. I felt fierce! I felt murderous! I felt a massive surge of rage! I growled. The witches all stepped back.

My Master's mind and my own became one. I instantaneously understood all that I was, and all that was required of me—and the penalties for failure. Nothing more needed to be said. He released his grip and vanished. The witches withdrew. I was reborn.

Soon thereafter, I joined my demonic brethren and the witches of our coven in our two principal objectives: convert as many of the Scalford Puritans as we could, and second, make life miserable for the remainder. I particularly relished the latter half of our agenda which was in complete concordance with my new being. You see, the duty of converting mortals largely falls to the witches. They were still "human," at least in appearance, and thus better equipped to cajole vulnerable subjects. The demons—hideous but powerful—were charged with the malevolent functions, although the witches certainly assisted us with those as well.

We had countless mechanisms at our disposal. Of course, the demons would savage hapless mortals at times, usually when we needed organs for our rituals. But it was the innumerable minor torments which were so much more gratifying. Instead of eradicating them outright, we could luxuriate in their suffering. We caused disease, gave them nightmares, destroyed crops, stole their possessions, killed their pets, and placed rats in their dwellings and beds. The witches slipped potions into their food and drink. One potion caused a man to defecate in public. He was whipped for it the next day. Another prompted a woman to betray her husband. She eventually committed suicide. A child was bewitched into urinating all over her parents' clothes. Another woman was compelled to strip naked and prance into church. You should have seen the thrashing she received.

And of course, we created an invidious and internecine environment so that the townsfolk would point fingers at one another. The witches spread gossip, rumors, and false accusations. Meanwhile, we committed various infractions and petty crimes, and then placed evidence on people's property so they could be inculpated. Sometimes the victims were blamed for the tribulations that we caused them. As in Salem, anyone stricken with undue adversity was construed to have offended God, who was now taking his penance. Nothing gave my Master more pleasure than subjecting some innocent Puritan to hardship, only to have his fellow pilgrims blame him for his plight.

We weren't always inciting depravities. At times we were dormant, awaiting the Master's orders. We also had recurring ceremonies to attend—and no one dared to miss any of our Master's rituals. We held our services deep in the woods in the middle of the night. Our rites were diverse and included sacrificing animals, burning human or animal organs, and chanting endless incantations. Every now and then we would have a wild orgy. Sometimes my Master would transform himself into a wolf and fornicate with the female witches. Other times he would preach and educate us about cosmology and religion—*his* religion—not the biased, expurgated version the Christians had been brainwashing us with since birth. Sometimes we drank each other's blood, or the blood of animals or humans. Occasionally, we would take the body of one of our victims and consume it entirely: flesh, bones and organs. We routinely discussed whatever sinister activities were ongoing or upcoming. And in every ritual, in one form or another, we always paid homage to our Master.

As my Master's congregation (and our treachery), increased, so did Scalford's persecutions for witchcraft. By the following year, 1713, deaths by natural causes, our doing, and executions, had reduced the population to twenty-eight individuals (and nine of those were witches). The citizens feared that their numbers were too low to sustain themselves, and they planned to return to Salem, or join some other colony. We could not let that happen. We had gone too far in our pestiferous deeds, many of which had been witnessed by the remaining Puritans. Occasional malfeasance could be attributed to a variety of factors, but at this point, we left no doubt that the Scalfords were haunted by a coven. If they went to a populated area and told their story, we could have faced a large scale backlash.

So one Sunday, when every member of the remaining community was in church, we set fire to the building. The witches amongst them revealed themselves. I and the other demons stormed the building. We offered them all one last chance to join us or die. Some surrendered to our side. A few, however, somehow managed to escape. There always seemed to be a minority of humans who were immune to our powers. Those who refused us, but didn't escape, were burned to death. We collected all of their ashes and spread them around our ceremonial sites in the forest. Then we burned the entire town to the ground. It was the final act of retribution that I watched with the utmost contentment.

The escapees ultimately made their way to other colonies and revealed the events that had taken place. By the time outsiders had decided to investigate and entered Scalford, everything was gone. Our witches had traveled far to avoid running into any of the escapees. They blended into larger cities such as Boston and New York. The news about Scalford spread throughout the colonies and the entire area was avoided for many generations.

In 1720 my Master granted me permission to travel to Sudbury, Massachusetts. I still had a debt to repay, namely Samuel Parris, the original minister from Salem. Parris was on his deathbed, but that made no difference to me. My aim was to ensure he was terrorized before he breathed his last, much as he had terrorized Salem.

First I haunted his dreams, giving him terrible nightmares of bloodshed and his own death. My favorite was to cause him vivid images of his wife committing unspeakably lewd sexual acts with other men and animals. Then I aggravated his physical maladies. I weakened his rectal muscles so he would regularly soil himself. I beleaguered him with nausea, vomiting, and spasms of pain. One day I ripped his dog into two pieces and left the carcass on his bed.

Finally I couldn't wait any longer. One afternoon while his wife was in town and he lay debilitated in bed, I appeared before him. He gasped at the gruesome sight of me. He knew immediately what I was, but not who I was. Clasping his neck I compressed his throat just short of strangulation, but enough to prevent him from speaking. I moved my ghastly face to within a foot of his, and in my demonic voice growled: "I am Thomas Ramsey."

His eyes lit up; clearly he remembered me.

"*You* are the monster," I said, "because it was your sadism, your hypocrisy, and your sanctimony, that contributed to my bitterness of the world, and my disgust with human beings. You helped make me what I am. And now I will exult, knowing that you will take that knowledge to your pathetic grave!"

I then slowly squeezed my hand and listened to his throat crumble as I choked out the last vestiges of his life. I felt fulfilled to the core of my being.

After dealing with Parris, our coven was relatively dormant for more than two centuries. The witches, as stated, had left for the large cities, but the demons remained. Those who had been drowned in the lake when they were witches resided there. Those like me, who were burned, and whose ashes were scattered in the woods, made the forest their home. We still had ongoing ceremonies, and regularly slaughtered animals and stray travelers for our rituals. Occasionally we were called upon by our Master to perform deeds in neighboring communities. But with Scalford and the immediate vicinity remaining largely uninhabited, few individuals were available to bring into the coven.

In the twentieth century, as the new town of Crestwood Lake emerged, so did our revival, but it's more difficult for us to operate in the modern world. We can't get away with the malefactions we could in a more backward and ignorant society. Our activities bring more attention from the authorities and the police. It is burdensome, as evil always operates best covertly.

Nevertheless, in the years leading up to our tricentennial, our undertakings have increased. The induction of new witches has reinvigorated our coven. Some of them were culled locally, and some are descendants of the Scalford witches who were living elsewhere. The latter were ordered back to Crestwood Lake with the express purpose of resurrecting the coven.

I have returned to what I do best: inflicting suffering on human beings. I wander deep in our woods ambushing unsuspecting hikers and campers. I love the terror on their faces as I materialize in front of them. Now with the town renewed, instead of taking forest animals, I can butcher individuals' pets. I acquire blood and organs and the added bonus of people's misery. How wonderfully evil!

I am proud to boast that I have instigated three suicides, several divorces, two epidemics, a number of fires, countless traffic fatalities and a plane crash in Italy. I am particularly thrilled about a priest, whose abdication of his faith I engineered, and a nun whose suicide in our lake I incited. Hypocrites! The nun was a drug addict and the priest was a pederast. I was more than happy to steer some victims his way before his fall.

And now in our tricentennial year, I have been summoned for an important mission. We are holding a major ceremony on Halloween night, our most sacred holiday. The boundaries between the underworld and the realm of the living temporarily disperse. Heavenly restrictions on our capabilities are weakened, and all sorts of demons can be unleashed on the earth.

For a celebration of this magnitude, the normal sacrifices will not suffice. Oh, we will still employ animal and human organs, but on Halloween night, in commemoration of our three hundred years, my Master insists that we burn the bodies of three human infants. I have been commanded to acquire the newborns. I am absolutely delighted that he has chosen me and not any of the other demons for this task. I will avenge my daughter for the Puritans' gross heartlessness toward her death.

My Master alerted me to a house on the southwest corner of the lake. The wife gave birth two weeks ago to triplets. I am to enter the dwelling at night, slay the babies, and hide the bodies in our woods for Halloween night.

It is now predawn on the Sunday before Halloween. I derive extra gratification by committing such heinous acts on the Christians' Sabbath. I arise from my woodland sanctuary at three in the morning. I'm invigorated by my rage and vindictiveness, and titillated by the carnage I am about to inflict. Drifting through the woods, invisible, but mightier than any perceptible force, I come across a raccoon. I snatch the beast, rip off its head with my talons, and squeeze the blood from its still convulsing body into my mouth. I am so excited, I am celebrating even before the deed is done.

I reach the end of the woods at the north end of the lake. The moon is in its last quarter, yet bright enough to cast a sheen on the slightly rippled water. I can see through the lake and spy my demonic colleagues in their aquatic lair. I wonder if they are envious of me. What demon wouldn't salivate at the chance to assassinate newborn children, especially for a cause as momentous as ours? They see me but make no motion. We do not acknowledge one another as humans do. We do not engage in silly, superficial customs. We know each other and our intentions. That is sufficient.

I close in on the southern end of the lake and turn westward. I know exactly where I'm going, having already visited the house on two occasions. When my Master first informed me of the plan I set out to behold my quarry. I was tempted to dispatch them then, but it would have been premature. The second time, I ventured around the outside of the home, basking in the thoughts of what was yet to come.

At last I come to the house and land on the roof. From my previous reconnaissance I know the exact spot that lies over their bedroom. I descend through the structure and materialize inside the room. Three individual cribs are lined up against the wall. The babies are sleeping, completely oblivious to their fate. I snicker uncontrollably. This will be one of the most glorious moments since my rebirth. I open both hands and extend my talons to the fullest. I step toward them, hesitating only to decide which one to strike first. I raise my hands and hiss—a sudden splash! I'm burning! It's holy water! NO! I writhe in excruciating agony. It's more painful than when I was burned at the stake! My body is dissolving, steam and smoke erupting as I disintegrate. Oh the pain! THE PAIN! I'm screaming in pain! Where is my Master? Even he forsakes me. Who did this to me? The pain…

The demon diffused into a smoldering, bubbling mass on the floor, discharging multiple bands of smoke. A foul stench emanated from the vile ooze.

The parents, awakened by the demon's cries, bolted into the room and flipped on the light switch. They were immediately accosted by the odor. They saw the puddle of smoking muck in the middle of the floor. Cassandra Voorhees stood above it with an empty, dripping container in her hands. They ran over to the cribs. The babies were still sound asleep.

The parents then turned to Cassandra, aghast, yet relieved. The mother burst into tears. The father started to speak, "Was it…a…a…"

"Yes," responded Cassandra. "It was the demon whose forthcoming I warned you about during your reading. You should be safe now. But we can do another reading later to be sure."

The mother was still crying.

"I don't know how to thank you," said the father. "I'll get you the other half of your money tomorrow."

"You can keep it," said Cassandra. "Thank you for trusting me."

He nodded and held his wife. He started weeping as well.

Cassandra crouched down and removed a lingering talon from the edge of the slime and placed it in her container. "This will come in quite handy," she remarked.

THE CABALS

"Do you know why I summoned the two of you?" asked Van Haden.

"To Crestwood Lake?" said the woman meekly.

"No," said Van Haden making a fist, "to my quarters."

The three of them sat in Van Haden's small, austere parlor above Grand Vin, lit only by candlelight.

"No, my Master," replied the man. "We were only told of the anniversary celebration and the larger plans to reclaim this domain."

"I have a problem," said Van Haden, "and the two of you are going to solve it for me."

"Yes, my Master," they said in unison.

"Shut up and listen. You two are going to kill the captain of the local police. He's a menace who could complicate our plans."

"Why us, Master?" the man asked.

Van Haden leaned forward with an angry look on his face, palpably annoyed at being questioned. "Because…I cannot rely on the coven members who live here. If they were to fail, he would know who they are and possibly connect them with me." Then he stuck his index finger in the man's face and said, "And YOU have yet to prove your worthiness."

"We will not fail, Master," asserted the woman.

Van Haden rose, approached the woman, and leaned down, practically putting his face in hers. In a frighteningly soft and dour voice, without blinking an eye he stated, "No…you won't, because if you do, your body parts will be amongst the ones we burn or consume Halloween night."

The woman didn't move a muscle. She just looked at him terrified. Van Haden turned toward the man, clutched his shirt just beneath the neck and yanked him forward. "Do you understand as well?"

"Yes, my Master," said the man, nervously nodding his head.

Van Haden released his grip and suddenly transitioned to the genteel demeanor he normally reserved for the general public. It actually made the two of them even more afraid.

"One more thing," added Van Haden in a nonchalant, almost light-hearted manner, "if the captain kills either of you, I will leave your bodies to rot as your souls go straight to hell." And then with a quirky smile he asked, "Now, do we all understand each other?"

They both nodded like bobble-head toys.

"I don't think we do yet," said Van Haden in an unnervingly somber tone. He walked across the room and grabbed a square metal box about the width of his chest. The top was ornately designed with silver filigree. He placed it on the floor between them. He opened the top, plunged in his hand, and pulled out a head by the hair. The neck was jagged, as if it had been ripped off the body. Veins and mangled strips of tissue dangled from it. The blood was partially clotted. He thrust the head into the man's face and barked, "Do you know this man?"

"No, Master." He started to tremble.

"Do you know why I'm holding his head?" asked Van Haden raising his voice, looking back and forth between them.

"No, Master," they both said.

"Because he failed to kill the priest!" said Van Haden. "His head will now be an offering at our Halloween ritual. NOW do we understand each other?"

They simultaneously repeated "Yes, Master," and then babbled anxiously about how they wouldn't fail.

"Enough!" Van Haden stared at them, and then reverted once more to his polished deportment. "Relax. I'm sure you will both serve me well." Van Haden returned the head to the box and retook his seat. Then he turned toward a doorway at the end of the parlor and hollered, "Goog."

A ghastly, decrepit old man slunk into the room. He looked nearly skeletal: his thin, sallow skin barely encasing the protuberances of his bones. His eyes were black and deeply recessed. The skin on his face was completely wrinkled: an unbroken expanse of fine creases. His ears were pointed. He was bald on top, with a semicircle of thin, straggly, long, white hair projecting out of the sides and back of his skull. He wore a black suit with an eighteenth century, white ruffled shirt. He stood a mere five feet.

In his bony hands was a bottle of wine and two folders. He refilled the glass resting on the small table next to Van Haden's seat and placed the bottle on a nearby shelf. He then approached the couple and handed them each a folder. He never spoke.

"Goog has just handed each of you a dossier on Captain Morgan. It contains his photos, address, information about his home and work, and other pertinent data. Leave me now. Study the material and make your plans. Make sure it is done before Thursday. Bring his heart and genitals to the Halloween ceremony. Now go."

The two subjects promptly left. Goog retreated whence he came. Van Haden sipped his wine, closed his eyes and snickered wickedly.

• • •

Upon returning from Cambridge, Morgan went straight to the police station. He was anxious to know about any developments in any of their multiple investigations. He didn't call from the car. He was too engrossed with absorbing the professor's words and discussing plans with Gil. Lieutenant Dougherty was still on duty when Morgan hurried in.

"What's happening, Jack?"

"Not too much. We have ascertained that Debbie Kurzmann was staying at a local motel. She was on assignment, taking pictures for a book about New England, but we have nothing else to go on. We have no idea what happened to her, other than that bizarre photo. Once again, we're canvassing the area and knocking on doors to see if anybody saw anything."

Morgan picked up on Dougherty's tone. "Once again?" he said.

"Naturally we have to investigate. We have to ask everyone who lives in the area if they saw anything. But people are really getting freaked out. We've questioned the townsfolk about Ron Millhouse, the Jorgensens, Brian Delmore, Sharon O'Connell, Jill Morton and now Debbie Kurzmann, not to mention countless other minor incidents. People are scared. There are too many deaths and murders piling up. The anger and outrage is fomenting again. We need some answers—hell—we need arrests, and soon. Because it's going to take more than a town meeting to pacify the citizenry this time."

"I know, I know."

Dougherty continued: "I contacted the State Police. A diver's coming tomorrow to check out the section of the lake where the pictures are from. They also have an expert who can look at the camera and the photos, especially the last one, and determine if they're authentic. But he has to examine the location where the photos were shot and he's in Burlington on another assignment—so that could take some time."

"I'm not too worried about that," said Morgan. "The photo's real."

"How do you know?"

"I just do. Anything new on Jill Morton—why she was here or how she ended up in the lake?"

"No. We talked to the Bristol police and her family, and I know this is an old story, but there are no leads. She was last seen leaving her job at a department store in Middlebury over a month ago. The family said she has no connections to our town: never been here before, as far as they know. No known drug use, no criminal record, no psycho ex-boyfriends, no nothing. I don't know what to tell you, Butch."

Normally Morgan would have been more demanding of his second-in-command to dig deeper and uncover something. But now he knew what his men were up against. He knew they weren't going to turn up leads as they would in a normal murder, or missing person case.

"Anything else going on?" Morgan asked.

"No. It's been pretty quiet. Oh there was a hit-and-run Saturday night. Someone rammed Father Mark, the priest from St. Matthews, while he rode home on his motorcycle."

"What?"

"He's OK. He was very lucky. Some car sped through the stop sign at the intersection of Auburn and Second Ave. The car hit his back tire, but still knocked him for a loop. He's got all kinds of contusions and a broken finger. He spent Saturday night in the hospital. Went home today."

"And the driver of the car?"

"Don't know. They took off. There were no witnesses and it was somewhat dark, right around sunset. Father Mark only got a glimpse of the car. A dark sedan is the best he could come up with."

Morgan just stood there, slowly shaking his head, looking at the wall, his mind racing. He assumed the hit-and-run was intentional. He'd go home, call Gil, and tell him what happened. Then they would go see Father Mark tomorrow.

"You OK, Butch? You don't seem like yourself."

"Got a lot on my plate. It's been a long day. I'm going home. See you tomorrow."

• • •

Morgan lived in a modest waterfront home on the east side of the lake. He and his wife bought it just after getting married. He paid off the mortgage with her life insurance money. His plan was to eventually sell it, but for the moment he was conflicted. On one hand, the house was a constant reminder of his loss. But on the other, selling it would mean having to sift through all their belongings…all *her* belongings, igniting a surge of grief. And Morgan just wasn't ready to face that yet. So in yet another irony of the human mind, the feelings that made him want to leave were the same feelings that made him want to stay.

In the interim, Morgan tried not to think about her death. She had developed an aggressive form of uterine cancer. By the time it was diagnosed it was too late. He watched her wither away in agony until the very end. The last few weeks she was practically oblivious from the morphine. On her last day on earth he stayed up all night holding her hand. He felt it would ease her transition. He wanted her to know that he would be there until the end; that she would not die alone. She was only forty-nine years old.

Maybe his grief was why Morgan hadn't told Vicki he loved her, as opposed to fearing his feelings wouldn't be reciprocated. At times he wondered whether his love for Vicki was merely loneliness in disguise. But when they were together, his heart said otherwise. What made him realize his feelings were genuine was that he truly cared about Vicki. He didn't just think about the void she would fill in his world, he thought about how he could make *her* happy. Morgan wanted Vicki to be happy. That was the linchpin in deciphering the conundrum in his heart and mind. Ultimately he came to the epiphany that he could have love for someone, and feel grief for someone else at the same time.

As Morgan walked through his door and flicked on the light he decided to call Vicki. He wanted to talk to her, but at the same time was leery of delving into the details of his conversation with Aaronson. Maybe instead of explaining—Morgan stopped in the middle of his living room. A chill went through him. He immediately drew his weapon. He had the distinct feeling that someone had been, or was in, his house. It seemed as if things had been moved slightly from where he had left them.

Morgan cocked his .357 and began to search his house. He slowly, very slowly, and stealthily moved from room to room, his magnum held at arm's length. The most risky moments were inspecting rooms or closets with closed doors. Someone could easily be inside waiting to strike. He came to the closed bathroom door. Instead of standing in front of it, he leaned against the wall next to it. He crouched down, snatched the doorknob and flung the door open. Nobody was there. He repeated the process with the closets. He surveyed the basement and found nothing.

He then headed to the second floor. He skulked from room to room, but they were all empty. Lastly, he approached his bedroom. He could see his bureau from the hallway. Articles of clothing he had left on it had been moved. He reached the bedroom doorway. He cautiously leaned in to view the entire room. Nobody was there. But he had one more place to check: the bedroom closet. At this point Morgan was fed up. He summarily walked over to the closet, flung the door open incautiously and pointed his .357 at—nothing. Retreating from the closet Morgan abruptly stopped. On his bed were numerous dead wasps arranged in the shape of an upside down pentagram.

Morgan didn't know what to make of it, other than it was more evidence someone had been in his house. He was tired, hungry, and now apprehensive. Instead of calling Vicki, he phoned the station, and ordered they make additional patrols past his house. Then he heated up some leftovers. Afterward, he checked every door and window and went to bed, as always, with his trusty magnum by his side.

His sleep was mercilessly restless. He awoke multiple times with the jitters. He didn't want to have a drink or take a pill. He was actually afraid of falling too deeply asleep. During one of his awakenings he searched the house again, gun in hand.

Morning finally arrived. He had so much on his mind he didn't know what to do first. He called the station to see if anything was going on. Officer Wesley answered. He said there had been a few minor incidents overnight, but nothing serious.

"What do you mean by minor?" inquired Morgan.

"Well, some homeless guy, a mental case, caused a disturbance. He was in the center of town half naked screaming about God and the Devil. We brought him to the psych ward at the hospital. There were also two break-ins. One man reported that someone broke his window and threw a dead cat into the kitchen. Another couple came home and found someone had thrown animal feces around their living room. Nothing was stolen. Sounds like kids playing pranks for Halloween.

"Anything else?" asked Morgan.

"Oh, and crazy old Edith Banks called. She claimed there were strange lights coming from the lake. We told her it was probably nothing. She called back later and said there was a fire in the center of the lake and some weird chanting and screeching. We dispatched a car, but the officer didn't see anything. That's about it."

Aaronson was right, Morgan thought. Things were starting to escalate. While conferring with the station he spied the blinking light on his phone. He hadn't noticed it last night when he got home. After talking to Wesley, Morgan pressed the message button:

Hey, Butch, it's Vicki. I guess you're not back from Cambridge yet. Just wanted to hear what that professor had to say, and let you know that I was thinking of you. Call me. Oh, Tuesday night I'm off if you wanna get together for a drink or something. Bye.

Morgan sat there with a warm feeling inside and a gentle smile on his face. He was definitely going to take her up on Tuesday. He'd call her later. It was early in the morning and she probably worked late the night before.

His first order of business, however, was getting ahold of Gil. They had to go meet Father Mark. He called Gil. After several rings he drowsily answered, obviously just awoken.

"Hello?"

"Get up, sweetheart, we have to go see the priest."

"Jesus, Butch, what time is it?"

"It's time to get our shit together. We've got three days till Halloween and there's going to be a lot of other things going on, pulling me in various directions."

"Fine," said Gil, looking at his alarm clock; it was seven thirty. "How about I meet you at the church at nine?"

"OK."

"Are you going to call him first?"

"No," responded Morgan. "You know I don't like giving people a heads up. It's better to catch them off guard."

"Of course, why did I ask?"

"Someone tried to run Father Mark over."

"Huh?" said Gil.

"Saturday night someone went through a stop sign and clipped him on his motorcycle. No serious injuries. They took off. I'm sure it was purposeful. And that's not all. Someone was in my house yesterday."

"What?"

"When I got home I had a distinct feeling that someone had been here. Some of my stuff was moved. Then I found a bunch of dead wasps on my bed, arranged in the shape of an upside down pentagram." Morgan heard nothing but silence on the other end of the phone. "Gil, you still there?"

"Yeah I'm here. You're right; we gotta get going on this. They know about you."

"No shit! I already had a drink with the frigging Devil."

Gil rolled his eyes. Never too early for profanity he thought. "All right, all right. I'll see you at nine."

Morgan showered, dressed, and then went to the local diner to get some breakfast. He couldn't function without food. He ordered a Taylor ham and cheese sandwich, home fries, and a coffee. He got it to go. He didn't want to be accosted by any townsfolk questioning him about recent events or ongoing investigations while he ate. He'd eat in his truck where he could have at least a few moments of peace, or so he thought. Half way through his sandwich his cell phone rang.

"Butch, it's Jack. Just letting you know the diver's here to check out the lake. You coming by?"

"No. I have to go see Father Mark."

"The *priest*?" said Dougherty.

Morgan wished he had thought, before blurting out his plans. Not that he needed to explain himself to a subordinate, but why would he be looking into a non-fatal hit-and-run when a possible murder investigation was looming? He certainly wasn't going to tell Dougherty the real reason he was going to visit Father Mark. So he offered, "Yeah, it's not every day that someone tries to run over a priest in our town. I'm gonna check it out. Call me as soon as you know anything from the diver."

"No problem. There's one other thing. You know Neil Pasternak?"

"Yeah I know him."

"His wife just reported him missing."

"Now what?" moaned Morgan.

"His wife and daughter came home yesterday. They were away for the weekend in Rhode Island. When they got back he wasn't there. Didn't come home all night. His wife said he never acts like that. They weren't fighting, he didn't call or leave any messages—nothing. They've been repeatedly calling his cell phone, but there's no answer. Last time they talked to him was Saturday morning. He was going fishing. I've got a man in a boat combing the lake."

Morgan took a deep breath and punched the dashboard. "All right, I'll see you as soon as I can. Call me with any updates in the meantime."

"You got it."

Morgan wolfed down the remainder of his breakfast and headed for St. Matthews. He decided to drive by Grand Vin on his way, just to check it out. He was beginning to feel a little unglued. He thought about every death, missing person, and freaky incident that had taken place. He pondered everything Aaronson said. And he thought about the demonic symbols being left in his own home. The last shred of doubt he had about the involvement of the supernatural was now evaporating.

As Morgan approached Grand Vin he slowed down. He didn't know what he was looking for, he was just looking. As he passed it, he spied Luther Van Haden standing motionless in the front window, staring directly at him with a scowl on his face. Van Haden followed Morgan with his eyes as he drove by. Morgan gritted his teeth and mumbled "motherfucker." He almost stopped. Morgan felt like storming over and confronting Van Haden right then and there, but he controlled himself. Losing his cool would only tip his hand. He couldn't provoke Van Haden before Thursday. It would only make Van Haden more cautious, and possibly thwart his plan to steal the bottle of souls.

• • •

Andy Dalton sauntered through the woods with his 12-gauge shotgun. He wasn't a serious hunter, he just liked stalking around with a gun. It made him feel cool and powerful. Occasionally Andy would shoot a turkey or a pheasant, but he never kept it for himself. He would give it to other hunters who ate what they killed. He thought cleaning the carcass was gross.

Andy was twenty-seven and still lived with his mother. His parents divorced when he was four. Over the course of his childhood he had sporadic contact with his dad, who now lived in another state and hadn't seen him in five years.

Andy worked full time in the local auto parts store. He had aspirations of attending a technical school and becoming an auto mechanic, but never genuinely pursued them. He always had an excuse. He usually blamed it on money, but the real reasons were his immaturity, indolence, and excessive partying. He'd had a few girlfriends, including two who he dated for almost a year. But the relationships never evolved into a solid, long-term union. His lack of direction certainly didn't help.

Andy worked Saturdays and had Mondays off. Monday was his day to smoke pot, watch TV, or like today, traipse through the woods with his big bad gun. He had hiked about a mile from the lake when he stopped to rest. He took out his phone, checked his messages and began texting a friend:

C if U can get some stuff 4 Fri night. I'm out. Is that chick Chrissy & her friend comin?

As Andy hit the "send" button he heard a deep growl. He turned around and was face to face with a large black bear. Only this was unlike any black bear he had ever seen. It had fiery red eyes that glistened, almost as if they were emitting tiny red laser beams. And it had fangs, like a saber-toothed cat. It was hunched over, mouth slightly open, ears pointed up, and growling.

For a moment Andy was paralyzed in shock. What the hell kind of bear was this? And how did it get so close without him seeing or hearing it? Andy dropped his phone, grabbed the shotgun with both hands and quickly raised it, aiming directly at the bear. But he was still inhibited, more from his dismay than anything else. Should he just shoot it? Should he see if it walked away? Should he back off?

Then the bear came closer. Andy fired directly into its face. The shotgun blast threw Andy back two steps. The bear was unscathed! It stopped, but didn't have a single mark on him. Andy was horrified and stupefied at the same time. *How? How?* He kept saying in his mind. Andy threw the gun at it and ran. The bear was on him in an instant. It lunged onto his back slamming him into the ground with so much force his breastbone snapped. Andy screamed in pain! The bear clamped its jaws on his right shoulder and ripped away his arm. Blood gushed out of the stump as the bear greedily lapped it up. Andy screamed like a wild man! The bear opened its mouth wide and sank its fangs into Andy's head, puncturing his skull and brain. Then the screaming stopped…and the feeding began.

● ● ●

Morgan pulled up to St. Matthews at five minutes to nine; he was always early. He despised people who were chronically late. Six minutes later Gil was late. Morgan's annoyance was building. Five minutes later Morgan called Dougherty for an update.

"Hey, Butch, the diver's in the water as we speak. Meanwhile, our guys found Pasternak's boat. It drifted to shore with all his gear on board, but there was no sign of him."

"When the diver's done looking for Kurzmann, have him search the section of the lake where you found Pasternak's boat," ordered Morgan.

"Yessssss, Butch. I kind of thought of that on my own."

"Call me when you know anything."

Nine fifteen rolled around and no Gil. Morgan called him.

"Hello," said Gil in his usual carefree tone.

"Where the fuck are you?"

"Right behind you."

Morgan looked in his rear view mirror and saw Gil pulling up. He scowled and got out of his truck. Before he could berate Gil for being late, Gil said:

"You talk to Vicki?"

"No. Why?"

"She just wanted to know how you were doing and how things went yesterday."

Morgan cocked his head and said, "You talked to her?"

"Yeah, last night. She left me a message. I called her when we got back from Cambridge."

Morgan squinted and peered right at Gil's face. "What'd you tell her?"

"Not much. I said we had an interesting discussion with the professor, and that you went to the police station as soon as we got back, and that you'd probably call her today."

"Did you tell her what we plan to do?"

"No, I didn't," said Gil.

"Well *don't*. I don't know what she'll think about it. Might think I'm off my rocker. Plus the less people who know the better." Then Morgan said, "Why did she leave *you* a message?"

"I guess because she couldn't reach you so she thought she'd try me. Will you relax; I'm not horning in on your girlfriend."

"OK, first of all, she's not my girlfriend. And second, you never know with you, Gil. You couldn't keep it in your pants at the zoo."

"How do you think you got spawned?"

Morgan just sneered.

The rectory of St. Matthews was attached to the back of the church. Morgan rang the bell; a nun answered the door. She was dressed in a traditional nun's habit, with a coif that covered her head and the perimeter of her face. She also wore dark glasses.

"Morning, ma'am. I'm Captain Morgan, chief of police. This is my associate Gil Pearson. We're here to see Father Mark."

"Oh I'm sorry, he was hurt in an accident and he's resting. I'm taking care of him and the place for a while. I don't think he's in any condition to see anyone."

"I'm sorry too, ma'am, but this is police business and it's urgent," said Morgan stepping into the doorway. The nun could tell he was determined.

A voice called out from another room: "Who's there, Cecilia?"

"It's the police," responded the nun.

"Send them in."

The nun stepped back and stretched out her arm. "He's in the parlor."

"Thank you, ma'am," said Morgan.

Morgan and Gil walked into the room. Father Mark was in a brown, upholstered recliner. He had two large bruises on his face. His pinky was in a splint. A number of plain, wooden chairs had been arranged around a small table. The room was humbly decorated. Various religious pictures and crucifixes adorned the walls. A small TV stood silent in the corner. Next to Father Mark's recliner was a folding tray table with an assortment of bandages, Advil, and other medications.

Morgan and Father Mark knew each other, but not very well. They had crossed paths at a few town functions, but never in St. Matthews. Morgan wasn't a church goer. Until yesterday, he barely believed in anything spiritual.

"Father," Morgan began, "thank you for seeing us. You know Gil Pearson, right?"

"Yes, we met once before," said Father Mark shaking Gil's hand with his uninjured one.

"How you doing, Father?" asked Gil. "What happened?"

"I was at Copley Hospital Saturday afternoon visiting patients. It was starting to get dark as I headed back to the church. I took my bike. It wasn't that cold Saturday; I bundle up, and it saves gas. I was going through an intersection when a car went straight through the stop sign without slowing down, almost as if he wanted to hit me. I had a split second to react. I gunned it, and luckily he only rammed the rear of my bike. I still went flying. I had a slight concussion. If it wasn't for my helmet it would have been much worse. I broke my finger, and you should see the rest of my body: I'm black, blue and purple all over.

"You're lucky you didn't break anything else," said Morgan.

"Sure feels like I did. My whole body hurts. Please, sit down. Can I have Cecilia bring you two a drink?"

"I'm good, thank you," said Gil.

"Me too," said Morgan.

"What can I do for you gentlemen?"

"Father," Morgan began, "I don't know how to say this, and I'm usually not one for beating around the bush, so I'm just gonna come out and say it."

"Please do."

"Our town is haunted by a coven of witches that goes back to colonial times. And we're pretty sure that the guy who owns that new wine store in town, Luther Van Haden, is the Devil."

"I know," said Father Mark with composure.

Morgan and Gil looked surprised.

"You know?" said Gil.

"Yes, I know who he is."

Morgan and Gil just looked at each other.

"All right," said Morgan, "let's start comparing notes."

Morgan and Gil proceeded to enlighten Father Mark about all the events that had transpired recently in Crestwood Lake. Most of them he was aware of, but didn't know the particulars. Then they recounted their meeting with Aaronson, sharing everything the professor had outlined. Father Mark concurred with everything Aaronson espoused. Father Mark told them that he had consulted an exorcist he knew in Montreal. The Canadian priest had similar insights about witches, demons, and the Devil, and how to combat them.

Morgan then told Father Mark about their plan to steal the bottle of souls Halloween night and destroy it on St. Matthews's altar. Father Mark was in complete agreement. Father Mark then elucidated how he came to meet Van Haden and the interchange he had with him.

"Father," said Morgan, "during the course of these events, various people have come to my attention. Like Karen Gardner, the girlfriend of the pilot who crashed. She owns the florist shop in town. She's all warm and gooey about Van Haden. She also keeps wormwood in her store. I never heard of it until I paid her shop a visit the other day. Aaronson said wormwood is a classic ingredient in witches' brews."

"She is undoubtedly a witch," said Father Mark. "No regular florist would have wormwood in their inventory."

"Hmmmm," said Morgan. "There's someone else I need to ask you about too."

"Go ahead."

"Do you know Cassandra Voorhees?"

"Yes I do. Why do you ask?"

"Well, a couple of reasons. First of all, there's something weird about her. The way she behaves, her hair, her clothes—she looks like a freak. I don't know if you ever saw her house, but it's off the wall. The day I met Van Haden she was in his store having a hushed conversation with him. Then I saw her coming out of your church carrying some sort of canister. Why was she in your church? Can you tell me anything about her?"

"She's a witch," said Father Mark.

"AHA! I knew it!" proclaimed Morgan.

"No, you don't."

"What do you mean?"

"She's not the kind of witch you're thinking of Captain. She's a *white* witch."

"What the hell is a white witch?" asked Morgan.

"It's a witch who uses supernatural powers for the betterment of mankind," said the nun standing in the doorway. The three men just looked at her.

The nun removed her glasses and coif. Long multicolored hair flowed everywhere.

Morgan and Gil were speechless. It was Cassandra Voorhees.

Morgan looked at Father Mark and said, "What the hell's going on here?"

"Cassandra, come over here and sit down," said Father Mark.

Cassandra took the chair next to Morgan. Morgan looked at her as if she was from another planet.

Father Mark turned to Gil and Morgan and said, "Gentlemen, I'm sorry for the deception. Cassandra and I have to be extra careful. For starters, there are witches—evil witches—amongst us. Anyone in this town could be a witch. We had to make sure that you two were safe. Moreover, the dark forces are cognizant that we, the forces of good, are also here in Crestwood Lake and opposing them. My accident was no accident. They were trying to kill me."

"They're also trying to kill you, Captain," said Cassandra. "Give me your hand."

Morgan looked at Gil, somewhat uncertain, then reached out his hand to Cassandra.

She clasped it firmly and closed her eyes for about ten seconds. Then she analyzed his palm. "You're in grave and imminent danger, Captain."

Morgan withdrew his hand and said, "Last night when I came home, I had the distinct feeling that someone had been in my house. It seemed like things had been moved from where I left them. On my bed I found a bunch of dead wasps arranged in the shape of an upside down pentagram."

"You've been marked for death," said Cassandra.

"Cassandra," said Gil. "You're a white witch?"

"Yes."

Gil could see Morgan was still reeling from Cassandra's prophecy, and was also confused as to what exactly she was. He looked at Morgan and said: "White witches are beings who have supernatural abilities, like divination, healing, communication with other realms, and spells to ward off evil. As Cassandra pointed out, they are benevolent and seek to safeguard mankind. The early European church, however, in their ignorance and fanaticism to eradicate malevolent witchcraft, subsumed all supernatural forces and practitioners under one rubric. Despite their goodwill, white witches were condemned and their practices banished. Many white witches were unjustly put to death. It was a terrible tragedy which only served to strengthen the forces of evil."

"Our numbers decreased over the Middle Ages and the Renaissance," added Cassandra. "Those of us who remained hid in the shadows. It wasn't until the modern era that we began to flourish again. The irony is staggering. Modern man's disbelief in witchcraft is precisely what allowed us to reestablish ourselves."

Morgan looked directly at Cassandra, pointed at her, and with a skeptical tone said, "Why were you in Van Haden's store that day?"

"My intuition told me that Lucifer had returned to Crestwood Lake. I needed to know for sure. We immediately recognized each other. He tried to entice me, to convert me. Over the ages a few white witches have been led astray. Converting a white witch to Satanism is a significant triumph for the dark side. When you walked in, Captain, he was in the middle of cajoling me, offering me all sorts of rewards for joining his coven. Although being in his presence is extremely painful, I acted as if I was considering his offer. I was merely buying time. The longer I linger in his company, in his domain, the more I can ascertain of his intentions."

"What do you mean you recognized each other?" queried Morgan.

"We have met before."

"Where?"

"In Europe."

"When?" pressed Morgan.

"During the Black Death in Italy."

"What?" exclaimed Gil. "*The* Black Death? The infamous bubonic plague of the fourteenth century?"

"Yes," said Cassandra. "In 1348 in Venice."

"You're full of shit," snapped Morgan.

"I assure you she's not," said Father Mark, reaching for the Advil.

"When were you born?" asked Gil.

"1214 in Rouen, France," replied Cassandra.

"You're immortal?"

"Not exactly. I will never die of disease, but I can be killed. However, that would be an arduous task. I've acquired significant powers in my years."

"How is that possible?" asked Morgan.

"I am a descendant of an angel. I don't have the full capabilities or the immortality of one, but I am far more than a regular human being. I would be quite a prize for Satan. Unfortunately for him, I will die before turning my back on my heritage."

Morgan and Gil just looked at each other with their mouths open. They looked at Father Mark. He raised his eyebrows knowingly, and then washed down his pills with some water.

"So you can tell the future and know what everybody's thinking?" challenged Morgan.

"No," said Cassandra. "Nobody has that power, not even Lucifer himself. Only God is completely omniscient. But I can perceive things beyond normal human limits, and get a sense of things to come. For example, I know they're trying to kill you, Captain, but I can't tell you exactly where, when, or how. I can also impart all three of you with some degree of protection. I can't make you invulnerable, but I can make it more difficult for the witches and demons to harm you."

"I was at your house last week," said Morgan.

"I know," said Cassandra.

"Why didn't you answer the door?"

"I wasn't certain yet whose side you were on."

"*Me?*" blurted Morgan as he pointed to himself and opened his eyes wide.

"Please don't take offense, Captain. After all, you thought I was an evil witch. I believe you also said I was weird, and a freak."

"So what were you doing coming out of the church that same day with some kind of container?" questioned Morgan.

"That was holy water," said Father Mark. "I gave it to her."

"I used it to dissolve a demon," said Cassandra.

Gil sat up in his chair. "I assume you overheard our conversation before. Professor Aaronson told us that holy water can kill a witch or a demon."

"Indeed," said Cassandra. "Fire or holy water can slay a demon. As for witches, your professor was also correct: anything that can kill a human can kill a witch. However, holy water, obviously benign to humans, can also destroy a witch, but because it is blessed, it will prevent a witch from becoming a demon after death."

"You dissolved a demon?" asked Gil.

"Do you know the Kendalls? They live a few houses over from me. The wife recently had triplets."

"Yeah I know them."

"Lucifer dispatched one of his demons, an old one from Scalford, to slaughter their babies, probably for their ceremony this coming Halloween. I was waiting in their bedroom with the holy water."

"How did you know?" asked Morgan.

"I had conducted a psychic reading for them and sensed the impending danger."

"So you met Lucifer in Venice in 1348?" asked Gil.

"Yes."

"Humor me for a moment, Cassandra," said Gil. "It's not every day we're asked to believe that someone is eight hundred years old. I'm a historian. Who was the Doge of Venice in 1348?"

"Andrea Dandolo," she replied.

"And what event in Venice that year was imputed to be the cause of the Black Death there?"

"The earthquake of January 25."

"During Dandolo's reign Venice was at war with Romania. What other power allied with them against Venice?"

"Venice was at war with the Hungarians, not the Romanians, and it was Genoa who was one of their allies."

"You said you were born in Rouen in 1214. What happened in Rouen in 1204?"

"Rouen was part of Normandy. In 1204 Phillip II annexed Normandy to the French Kingdom."

Gil looked at Morgan and said, "She's right."

"When did you two," said Gil pointing back and forth between Father Mark and Cassandra, "discover you were on the same team?"

Father Mark spoke up: "As you know, I was only assigned to St. Matthews six months ago. I met Cassandra at our church, but I didn't know who she was."

Cassandra interrupted, "I have to be extremely careful as to whom I reveal myself. Although I can get a sense about people, I can't read minds, and anybody can be aligned with the Devil. Since Van Haden knows me, my identity is known to the entire coven. He is awaiting my response to his temptation. Once he is certain I will not accept I will be in immediate peril, much like you, Captain." Turning to Father Mark, she said, "I'm sorry, Father, please go on."

Father Mark resumed: "Last Thursday I observed Cassandra filling a container with holy water from the receptacle in church. I asked her what it was for. She stated she didn't have time to explain, but needed to see me soon to address some urgent matters. The next day is when I went to Grand Vin and met Van Haden. Early yesterday morning Cassandra unexpectedly came to the rectory. She explained to me who she was and everything that was happening in Crestwood Lake."

"Cassandra," said Morgan, "please forgive me, but you have to understand that in less than twenty-four hours I've gone from the reality I knew for fifty-two years to a horror movie. Just since yesterday I've been asked to believe that there's a God, a devil, angels, witches, demons, and now you. You're telling us you're this eight-hundred-year-old 'good witch' [Morgan made air quotes]. So excuse me for asking, but how am I supposed to believe this? How do I know you didn't just study your history like Gil has? How do I know what you are, and whose side you're on, even if all this crap is true?"

Gil leaned over and said to Cassandra, "You'll have to excuse Butch. Jesus Christ himself could come down off the cross and he'd still want to see some ID."

"I understand," said Casandra. "What normal person could accept all this at face value? I can't prove to you what's in my heart, Captain. The unfolding of the events to come will demonstrate that. But I can prove to you what I am."

"Now *that*, I'd like to see," said Morgan.

With that Cassandra disappeared.

Morgan gripped the arms of his chair with both hands and gasped. It was the first time in his entire life he had been so alarmed. He turned toward Gil, who looked as if he had literally just seen a ghost. He just sat there, wide-eyed, with his mouth agape. Morgan looked at Father Mark.

Without batting an eye Father Mark said, "I saw the holy water splash her when she filled her canister. I know she's not an evil witch."

Cassandra reappeared.

"Are you satisfied, Captain?" she asked.

"Cassandra," said Gil, "there's so much I want to ask you. My God… what you must have witnessed in all your years! There are innumerable historical myths or uncertainties that you could disentangle."

"There are more pressing issues at hand," said Father Mark.

"I know you were a history teacher, Gil," said Cassandra. "Let's focus on what we need to do. The entire town is at stake. In fact, even more than that. Every foothold that evil acquires increases their strength, and their chances of eventually dominating the earth. If we survive past Thursday, then maybe you and I can have a little chat."

"What do you mean *if we survive*?" asked Morgan.

"Captain, we are up against Lucifer himself and an entire coven of witches and demons. Lord knows how many of the townsfolk have already been inducted. It's only the four of us—and no offense—but the three of you are mere mortals. They've tried to kill Father Mark once. They will try again. And, Captain, you are surely in their sights."

"Let's work on our plans," said Father Mark. "There's nothing going on in the church Thursday night. I will lock all the doors by sundown. Cassandra and I should stay here to guard the church and ward off any unplanned visitors or mischief-makers. I'll turn off all the lights in the church and especially the rectory to discourage any trick-or-treaters.

"You and Gil can go to Grand Vin. Wait until it's completely dark to ensure Van Haden and the bulk of the coven will be in the woods. But as your professor friend admonished, inevitably there will be coven members there protecting the bottle."

"We will give each of you vials of holy water," said Casandra. "While you can use them on a witch, try to save them in case you encounter a demon, since witches can be killed by traditional means."

"According to the professor the witches look normal but the demons don't," said Morgan.

"That's quite right," said Cassandra. "Demons are hideous monsters. They cannot transform into normal looking human beings. Waste no time dispatching them. They can kill you swiftly, even without touching you. But even the witches can be dangerous. As you have been informed, they do possess powers that normal humans do not. How will you get into Grand Vin, Captain?"

"Gil and I will figure that out."

"I strongly recommend that you approach with stealth and employ the element of surprise," said Cassandra. "Treat it as if you were storming a building harboring armed criminals waiting to ambush you."

"I can bring extra men from my force," said Morgan.

"NO!" cried Father Mark and Cassandra together.

"You cannot tell another soul about this," said Father Mark.

"My men are not witches, Father."

"Captain, there's no way you can know that with absolute certainty, and even if you're right, it doesn't matter. You can't guarantee that one of them won't say something to someone else. You also can't prevent them from acting in some way that draws suspicion from one of our enemies. We can't take any chances."

"What am I going to tell Vicki?" said Morgan looking at Gil.

"Who's Vicki?" asked Father Mark.

"She works at Toby's. We've been friends for many years. She knew Gil and I were going to see the professor and basically what for. She's waiting for me to call her, to hear what's going on. I know I can't tell her all this. I'm just not sure what I can tell her."

"You can't tell her anything," cautioned Cassandra. "You'll not only risk our safety, you can endanger her life."

Morgan nodded but was visibly perplexed.

Cassandra reached over and touched his shoulder for a few seconds and then withdrew her hand. "You love her," she said.

Morgan looked at her, surprised, but then lowered his eyebrows and humbly said, "Yes."

"Then she is already in jeopardy," said Cassandra.

Morgan's eyes widened again. He said, "The day I met Van Haden, as I left his store, he told me to say hi to Vicki, even though they had never met. It unnerved me."

Cassandra scoffed. "If I can apprehend that you love her so can he. The Devil absolutely loathes love. If you want to protect her you must not tell her anything, and focus on the mission at hand. If Lucifer discovers that you love her, or that she knows anything about us or our plans, she will definitely be targeted."

Morgan rubbed his forehead for a moment and said, "So all we need to do is smash that bottle within the church and that will put a stop to all of this?"

"Quite dramatically," said Cassandra.

"How do you know?"

"I've seen it happen before."

Gil perked up. "You've seen it before?"

"Yes," Cassandra replied, "How do you think the Black Death ended?"

Gil didn't know what to say.

"Are we sure this bottle is the vessel holding the souls?" asked Father Mark.

"I can't be totally sure," said Morgan. "It seems like the most logical choice. Actually, it's the only choice we have. Is there any way of knowing for sure?"

"No there is not," said Cassandra. "But I think you're right, Captain. I know the bottle you are speaking of. I stood right next to it and sensed something...something indescribable...yet still forbidding."

"You mentioned you could give us some protection against evil," said Gil.

"Here," said Father Mark. He removed a small wooden box from a shelf on the wall. He opened it and removed two sets of rosary beads. He handed a set to Gil and one to Morgan. "These have been blessed. Put them on and don't take them off."

Gil and Morgan each slipped them over their head and under their shirts.

"I have also cast a spell of protection, gentlemen," said Cassandra.

"We shouldn't speak or see each other again until Thursday," said Father Mark. "Again, it's too easy for one of Satan's disciples to see us together."

"Cassandra," said Morgan, "one last thing. You stated I was in imminent danger. Can you be any more specific?"

"No, but considering what we do know, combined with some logical reasoning, I'd say this: I would definitely expect them to make an attempt before their Halloween ritual. I would also expect them, like any other murderer, to find a time and a place with no witnesses. If I were them, I would ambush you at night in your domicile."

Father Mark gave Morgan and Gil several vials of holy water and wished them well. Morgan stood up and thanked Father Mark, as did Gil. Then Morgan extended his hand to Cassandra. As she shook it he said, "I'm sorry for thinking you were a witch...you know...a bad witch...or calling you weird. I didn't know."

"It's fine, Captain. I've been around long enough to not get offended by such things. You just watch yourself; be very careful."

Gil walked over and shook Cassandra's hand. "I *will* take you up on that post-Halloween chat. I want to hear all about the Borgias."

"Oh good Lord!" said Cassandra. "What a bunch of depraved heathens. There was more than one witch in that family as well."

"Really?" said Gil as his eyes lit up.

"C'mon, Gil," said Morgan grabbing his arm. "You guys can play Trivial Pursuit on Friday."

"What about the lost colony of Roanoke?"

"Witches," said Cassandra.

"Enough," said Morgan, now tugging at his arm. "I have to get going."

As they were walking to their vehicles Gil asked, "How are we going to break into Grand Vin?"

"I have a couple of ideas. But I need some time to collect my thoughts. I also have to go to the station. We've got multiple investigations going on and I have to at least act like I normally would under such circumstances. We'll discuss it later. I got to get ahold of Vicki too."

"Butch, you can't say anything to her."

"I know, I know. But I already told her before Sunday about your ideas regarding witches and why we were seeing Aaronson. I need to know what you said to her about the professor yesterday so we can get our stories straight."

Gil replied, "I played it cool on the phone with her last night. I knew we couldn't disclose the specifics of what we conferred with Aaronson about. So I nonchalantly commented that he had some interesting thoughts on witchcraft, and Crestwood Lake's history, but I doubted he could shed much light on current happenings. So if I were you, given your personality, I'd act as if you thought it was crap, and a waste of your time. Sprinkle your comments with your typical vulgarity and your customary sneer. That should sell it."

Morgan shot Gil a derisive look.

"Just like that," said Gil.

• • •

Morgan went to the police station to oversee the various activities. The Brian Delmore and Sharon O'Connell cases were basically at a standstill, as all their leads had been exhausted. Nor could the Bristol, or Crestwood Lake police, uncover how or why Jill Morton ended up dead in the lake. Morgan also wasn't surprised that the diver found no traces of Debbie Kurzmann or Neil Pasternak in the lake, and his men found no clues in Kurzmann's van or Pasternak's boat. The New York police were assisting with Kurzmann's investigation on their end. Morgan knew they wouldn't find anything either. Meanwhile, Morgan had officers interviewing Neil Pasternak's family, friends and associates. If Aaronson was right, Pasternak was already carved up somewhere by Van Haden's henchmen. Nevertheless, he had to go through the motions as if he knew nothing. If he didn't investigate Pasternak's disappearance, how could he explain his inaction to the family, the mayor, or the rest of the force?

At lunchtime Morgan called Vicki, apologizing for not getting back to her sooner, and blaming it on work. She completely understood. He basically parroted what Gil had said about Aaronson. They made a date for Tuesday night. Then he called Gil and suggested they meet at Gil's house later in the afternoon to discuss their Grand Vin plans. Finally he called his neighbor Dennis. He would need his help with outwitting his assassins.

That afternoon a suspicious fire broke out in an old barn, on a small farm on the fringe of Crestwood Lake. The barn was destroyed, but the firemen were able to prevent the blaze from spreading. While the firemen were fighting the fire, the police received a frantic call from residents on the west side of the lake. Twenty-nine-year-old kindergarten teacher Paula Swindlehurst had hanged herself from a tree in her backyard. In her hand they found wormwood flowers.

• • •

Morgan arrived at Gil's late in the afternoon. They took their usual seats in Gil's living room. Gil could see the effect of the accumulating strain on Morgan's face.

"You OK, Butch?"

"What do you think?" said Morgan. "Did you know a teacher named Paula Swindlehurst?"

"No."

"I didn't think so. She was young. Started teaching after you retired. She hung herself in her backyard today. She had wormwood flowers in her hand. I was the only one who knew what they were. Naturally I didn't say anything."

"It's starting to unravel. I'm worried about you. They're out to get you and will make their attempt before Thursday. Why don't you stay at my place until then?"

"No," said Morgan shaking his head.

"Then how about you at least let me stay with you."

"I don't need a damn babysitter."

"They're trying to kill you."

"I've already got it covered. It's gonna be dark soon. I have to get back to my place before night falls. I can handle them coming after me. Let's discuss Thursday night OK?"

Gil nervously relented. "Wanna drink?"

"No," said Morgan. "I need to be completely sharp."

That's when Gil felt assured that Morgan was taking the threat seriously. Clearly Morgan was scheming a countermove. Gil poured himself a drink. Then the two of them devised their attack on Grand Vin.

● ● ●

Morgan drove home and parked his truck in his driveway. He fetched a small duffel bag from his closet, turned on the floodlights in the back of his house, and headed to his neighbor Dennis's house. He had explained to Dennis that he had received death threats and wanted to stakeout his home from Dennis's window. The two had known each other for many years and Dennis was happy to assist.

Morgan's home was "lakefront," but it was the back of his dwelling that faced the lake. The front of Morgan's house was on Crestwood Lake Road. The expanse of land in Morgan's vicinage was on a steep slope stretching down to the water. Dennis's house was across the street from Morgan's, perched about sixty feet above and two hundred feet beyond his. From Dennis's living room window, which faced Morgan's house, Morgan could see the front and sides of his house, but not the lake side.

Morgan placed a chair in front of the window and partially closed the curtains, leaving a foot or so of space. Out of his bag he took a folding tripod, and a pair of military-issued, night-vision goggles. Morgan had a friend who was a lieutenant colonel in the army and provided him with special equipment. Morgan attached the goggles to the tripod and began his surveillance. He assumed his assailants, be they witches or not, would not approach the house from the back, given that it was well lit, and bordered by the water. If this supposition was correct, then they couldn't converge on his abode without his notice. He also hoped that whoever was coming would arrive on foot, and not by materializing inside his house. After what he saw Cassandra do, anything was possible, but he couldn't control every single contingency. He also had no idea if they would arrive tonight: they could come Tuesday or Wednesday. Nevertheless he was prepared to stake out his home all three evenings. He didn't know what he was going to do for sleep for three days. For the moment he was taking it one night at a time.

Dennis assisted Morgan with his mission. He periodically kept watch to allow Morgan time to eat, relieve himself and recharge. About midnight, however, Dennis went to bed. Morgan sat there, watching his property assiduously. All kinds of thoughts were racing through his mind. He thought about the plans he made with Gil. What would happen if they failed? And for that matter, what would happen if they succeeded? He expected some degree of messiness to the aftermath. How would he explain his actions to those who were clueless about the truth of Crestwood Lake? And how could he prevent it all from happening again?

And of course, he thought about Vicki. He suddenly recalled that he was meeting her tomorrow night. How could he watch his house if the murderers didn't show up tonight? He'd have to cancel with Vicki, but then what would he tell her? He already had to lie to her about his meeting with Aaronson, now he'd have to concoct an excuse for tomorrow night. Maybe he could—something moved along the right side of his house. Morgan blinked a few times to clear his eyes and looked again. He didn't see anything. Then he saw the brush move on the right side. He zeroed in on the oscillating branches. Out popped a deer. Then a second one. Morgan exhaled sharply, placed his hand over his heart and took a deep breath. But he still kept watching closely. It was possible that someone was there and had frightened the deer. Fifteen minutes went by—no more movement.

His mind drifted back to Vicki. What could he tell her to get out of tomorrow night? He thought of various work-related excuses. "Dammit," he murmured to himself. He actually wished the killers would show up tonight. At this point he wanted them more than they wanted him. It was bad enough they intended to kill him. Now they were screwing up his plans with Vicki and that really pissed him off.

He thought about telling Vicki the truth, but then abruptly suppressed the idea. He kept thinking about Cassandra's warning. The mere fact that he had feelings for Vicki could place her in danger. And if he told Vicki what he knew, and the dark powers found out, he could imperil her even more. And besides, would Vicki even believe him anyway? What if she thought he was losing it? He could never prove it to her. What would he say, even if he could tell her?

Hi Vicki it's Butch, I can't see you tonight. I have to stake out my house. I'm expecting a couple of witches, maybe even a demon or two, to sneak up in the middle of the night and kill me. Oh, have you heard? The whole damn town is haunted by a coven of witches and demons going back to the seventeenth century. And that prick Van Haden is the Devil. Oh, and by the way, Cassandra is not a "deranged hippie" after all. She's a good witch. I saw her disappear yesterday. Thursday Gil and I are going to steal this big bottle of wine from Grand Vin. Ya see, the souls of all the witches and demons are in the bottle. So we're gonna take it and smash it in St. Matthews church. It has to be on hallowed ground. This will release all the souls and send the demons to the afterlife. The witches will go to hell or return to normal—all depends on if they're repentant or not. So I hope you understand, I'm kind of busy this week saving the world from the powers of evil. Maybe we could hook up on the weekend?

Yeah, right. Morgan scoffed. He could never tell Vicki what was going on, even if he and Gil were successful. In yet another ironic twist, one of the reasons he couldn't tell Vicki was one of the same reasons he loved her. Vicki was intelligent and rational. She didn't believe in any nonsense: no astrology, no psychic hokum, no herbal remedies, no aromatherapy, no reincarnation...none of it. She had a good head on her shoulders and was firmly grounded in reality. She would never believe the truth about Crestwood Lake.

Morgan reflected on the other things he loved about her. She was a kind soul. She was far more apt to try to understand people than criticize them. She was also more tolerant of people who were different. Morgan knew he needed more of that in his personality. He thought Vicki was good for him in that regard. He thought she could make him a better man.

But he also wanted to be good for her. He knew he could love her like she had never been loved before. He knew he could make her happy. Morgan was fiercely loyal, a true one-woman man. He knew he could show Vicki what a marriage was supposed to be like.

It tore Morgan up inside, watching Vicki go through the misery that her ex-husband put her through. He would see fresh bruises on her at Toby's. Each time Morgan was ready to lock him up, but Vicki would stop him. She hoped to work it out, that he would change. Morgan could never understand how someone as rational as her could put up with that kind of abuse. Maybe that was the down side of being too nice: it could cloud your judgment. Morgan needed a little bit of Vicki in him, but Vicki needed a little bit of Morgan.

Ultimately the abuse escalated and climaxed. One night in a drunken rage he was beating Vicki worse than ever. He broke one of her ribs and knocked out a tooth and still wouldn't stop. She thought he was going to kill her. She managed to grab a long-handled flashlight and swung it right into his head, cracking his skull and knocking him out cold. She called Morgan. Her ex spent two months in a hospital and a rehab recovering. Then he went to prison for five years on a pleaded-down sentence. Just before he was released Morgan went to see him. Morgan told him straight out that if he ever set foot in Crestwood Lake again he would shoot him dead and claim self-defense. He knew Morgan would do it, and more importantly, he knew Morgan could get away with it. That was the last they ever saw of him.

Vicki never got involved with another man. She focused on healing herself, refurbishing her house, and in general, restoring her life. And while she had done much to accomplish those goals, the scars undeniably remained. She still had bad dreams, flinched at sudden noises, and endured painful memories whenever something reminded her of him.

It was during those years after her marriage ended that her friendship with Morgan grew deeper. Now with his wife gone, Morgan's feelings for Vicki blossomed into love. He wished there was a way of determining whether she felt the same without exposing himself. And then Morgan came to a conclusion. As he stared into his goggles, waiting for psychos to come and kill him, he decided that when all this was over, he was going to tell Vicki he loved her.

Morgan's entire universe had changed overnight. Everything he knew, or thought he knew, about the world was turned upside down. He was still trying to assimilate everything. If any good was to come out of the incomprehensibleness of it all, it was that life is short and often beset by tragedy and pain. If one is lucky enough to even have a chance for love or happiness, it must be taken. Morgan then realized the ultimate irony: that an evil like Van Haden, the eternal nemesis of love, had actually influenced him to pursue his love for Vicki. Maybe that's why evil was allowed to exist: to paradoxically promote love and goodness. Maybe that's why in all this craziness—*something moved.* Morgan did a double take. This time it definitely wasn't a deer. Two people, one carrying what looked like a crossbow, and the other a sawed-off shotgun approached Morgan's house from the left side, which was adjacent to a strip of woodland. They did indeed avoid the lighted rear side of the dwelling. Morgan watched as they effortlessly entered through a ground floor window without breaking it. He was flummoxed. He had locked every door and window in the house.

Morgan waited until they were both inside and then hustled over to his house. He had his .357 in his right hand. But he also had a Smith & Wesson M&P 9mm with a seventeen-round clip in his belt. He loved his magnum, but it was limited to six rounds. In his pocket, were two vials of holy water. He crept over to the same window the intruders had entered. It was wide open. He was still confused as to how they opened it so easily.

Morgan slowly stepped through the window, gingerly planting his foot on the floor. Then he pulled his other leg through. Right next to the staircase, he heard the floors creaking above him. His plan was to be still and waylay them on their way back down. That's when he felt a sharp point against the back of his head. It was the arrow cocked in the crossbow.

"Good evening, Captain," a velvety female voice cooed. "Why don't you drop your pistol so I don't have to unload this arrow into the back of your neck." Then she shouted, "Rolf, get down here. I got'em." Then, she calmly repeated, "Drop the pistol, Captain."

Morgan released his grip on the gun's handle and dangled it by the trigger guard from his thumb and forefinger. But instead of dropping it, he tossed it directly behind him. She flinched. He felt the arrow withdraw from his head. Morgan whipped around as fast as he could, hitting the crossbow with his right forearm. She fired. The arrow grazed Morgan's right temple, slicing the skin and impaling the wall. Morgan gave her a left hook to the jaw, knocking her back. Then he pulled the 9mm from his belt and put two slugs in her face. She was done.

He whipped back around with both hands on the 9mm aiming at the staircase, standing silently. Not a sound emanated from the upstairs. Morgan crouched down and picked up his magnum. He returned the 9mm to his belt and put both hands on the magnum…waiting. Nothing. Then he called out, "Listen up, boy, I'm about to call in the cavalry. You can't escape. So either throw down your gun, and walk down these stairs alive, or I promise you, I will shoot you dead just like your partner. Now what's it gonna be, boy?" Blood was seeping out of the right side of Morgan's head.

A shotgun blast went off, peppering the base of the stairway. Morgan wasn't stupid enough to stand within firing range of the upstairs landing. "I'm still here, asshole," Morgan hollered. "Drop your gun or die."

Morgan heard footsteps running across the upper floor and then a rear window shatter. The attacker was obviously escaping through the back of the house. But which direction would he head? Morgan surmised that he wouldn't run straight back for the same reason as before: the lights and the lake. Nor would he run to the left side of the house where he entered, as Morgan was still by the window on that side. So Morgan gambled and darted out the front door and toward the right side of the house. Along his property line on the right side was a thick hedgerow with ample sticker bushes. It blocked passage to the adjacent property. The intruder would have to come between the house and the hedgerow to get to the road.

Morgan reached the right front corner of his house. He crouched against the foundation and waited. The rear floodlights emitted a residual light into the side yard. Morgan, however, was in complete darkness… listening. Sure enough, someone was running full speed around the right side, toward the front of the house. As he reached the right front corner Morgan fired. The man screamed and collapsed. Morgan sprang to his feet and ran over to him. He was on his back, blood pouring from his right hip. The man reached for his shotgun, but Morgan kicked it away.

He stuck his magnum in the man's face and barked, "Who sent you?"

The man groaned in pain, but didn't say a word.

Morgan stepped on his wound and yelled, "Who sent you?"

The man screamed. "I can't. He'll kill me."

Morgan shoved the barrel of the gun into the man's crotch, leaned over and softly said, "You either tell me who sent you or I'm gonna kill you right now. First I'll blow your cock off. I'll stand here and watch you suffer for a while. Then I'll put one in your face. But if you tell me who sent you—I'll put you under arrest—but I'll also give you protection. Now for the last time, who sent you?"

"It was Van Haden," whined the man.

"Luther Van Haden, the jerk-off who owns the wine store?"

"Yeah," said the man.

"I hear he's Lucifer," said Morgan

"Yeah, man, he's the one."

"Are you a witch?"

"No, not yet. I had to kill you to prove my worthiness."

"Interesting. And your female friend in there?" inquired Morgan.

"Yeah, she's a witch."

"Where does Van Haden keep the souls of all the witches?"

"Look, man, if he finds out…"

Morgan stepped on his wound, only harder. The man screamed in pain.

"Where does he keep the witches' souls?" demanded Morgan.

"He's got a big bottle of wine in his store in a special cabinet."

"How do you know?"

"My partner, she told me."

"I understand there's a big ceremony Halloween night," said Morgan.

"Yeah, that's when I was supposed to become a witch."

"Where is it?"

"Somewhere in the woods—I don't know where—I haven't been to one yet."

"Who else were you supposed to kill beside me?"

"No one. Just you."

"How about a woman named Vicki Larson?"

"I don't know any Vicki, man."

Morgan pushed the gun harder into the man's crotch. "What else can you tell me about Van Haden's plans? I'm not letting you live until I'm satisfied you've told me everything."

"He wants to retake Crestwood Lake or destroy it if all else fails."

"Destroy it how?"

"I don't know. He doesn't share things like that with me."

"Anything else?"

"That's all I know, man, I swear. He hasn't told me anything else."

Morgan withdrew his gun from his crotch. The man grabbed his hip and moaned. Morgan put his free hand in his pocket to retrieve his cell phone. Suddenly, the man reached into his pocket and withdrew a snub-nosed revolver! He raised his arm to fire…

Morgan shot him right between the eyes.

"Asshole!" decried Morgan.

THE ANAGNORISIS

Morgan got no sleep whatsoever Monday night. First, he had to go to the ER and have his scalp stitched. Meanwhile, by the time his men and other personnel had arrived, inspected the crime scene and removed the bodies, it was almost sunrise. He tried to sleep after they left, but he couldn't stop thinking about seeing Vicki that evening. He lay in bed staring at the ceiling, thoughts whirling through his mind. What in the world was he going to tell her? He already knew her questions: Why were these people after him? How did he know they were after him? What did the professor have to say? And probably many others. He couldn't tell her the truth—at least not yet. He lay there contriving the best plausible answers conceivable. Finally, he abandoned any hope of sleeping and went forth with his day.

Morgan had already answered some of those nagging questions to his fellow officers when they arrived on the scene. He denied any knowledge about why the perpetrators wanted to kill him. He chalked it up to revenge from any of the countless criminals he had arrested over the years. Morgan considered not revealing that he was staking out his house, since that would invite queries about how he knew. He could have simply offered that he heard them break in and got the jump on them. But Morgan didn't want to get caught in a lie. Sure, he could have asked Dennis not to say anything, but nobody can be entirely trusted, at least not in Morgan's book. And what if someone saw him going to or from Dennis's house? No, Morgan was not going to take any chances. So he told the truth: Sunday night he came home and discovered that someone had been in his house and thus decided to start surveilling his property from afar.

It was a grueling day. Morgan was inundated with paperwork and the same questions from additional people, including Mayor Burrows. Initially, Burrows acted concerned about the attempt on Morgan's life, but his tone quickly changed as his focus shifted to the continuing mayhem in Crestwood Lake. Morgan dodged him for the moment, claiming he was too busy, but promised to see him later in the day. Then he blew him off. He was in no mood for any of the mayor's asininity.

The police had yet to uncover anything about Morgan's failed assassins. Their fingerprints were not on file; nor were they carrying any identification, or anything else that could trace them. The serial numbers on their firearms were filed off. Their photos were being sent to state and federal authorities to see if anything turned up. Morgan didn't honestly care who they were. He knew who sent them and what he still had to do. Of course he had to act as if this was a "normal" attempt on his life. He continually reminded himself to act as if they were average hoodlums, and not disciples of Satan. The psychic energy it took to maintain that facade, on top of all the other stress, was exhausting.

Morgan called Gil and informed him about what had happened. Gil insisted that Morgan stay at his place until Thursday. Gil was shocked when Morgan agreed. Morgan knew he couldn't remain awake around the clock for two more nights watching his house. Besides, he had to deal with Van Haden, not waste time on his minions.

The end of the day came, and it was time to go to Vicki's. Morgan had mixed emotions. As he drove to her house he rehearsed his statements one last time. The mere fact that he had to do that was perturbing, and out of character for him. Morgan was as straightforward as they came. He told you the truth whether you liked it or not. And if he had a reason to withhold it, he wouldn't lie about it. He'd simply inform you that he wasn't telling you. But he didn't want to lie or hold back the truth from Vicki. He wanted Vicki to be that one person in the world whom he could talk to about anything. He was so frustrated. He clenched his fists and pictured ripping Van Haden's head off.

Morgan pulled into Vicki's driveway. She was already standing in the doorway, clad in jeans and a pink sweatshirt, arms wrapped around herself from the cold. Her long red hair was down and free. *Even shivering she looks like a doll*, thought Morgan.

"Whaddaya doing outside?" asked Morgan as he exited his truck.

"I couldn't wait to see you. I heard about what happened last night." She threw her cold arms around him and gave him a big, unusually long hug. Then she saw the side of his head and gasped. "Butch, your head!"

"I know, I know. I'm OK. Let's go inside." Morgan noticed her eyes. She looked as if she'd been crying.

Vicki promptly ushered him in. Morgan collapsed on the couch.

"Can I get you a drink?" she asked.

"No."

Vicki looked at him as if he was from Mars.

"You can get me three or four," said Morgan.

Vicki smiled knowingly and fetched a bottle of bourbon. She poured them each a glass. Soft, classical music flowed from her stereo. A purple candle burned soothing, lavender aroma into the air.

"Not having your white wine?" asked Morgan.

"No, I need something stronger today." She sat down next to Morgan on the couch and gave him another hug. "What happened?"

"We don't know yet exactly. Sunday night when I got back from Cambridge I discovered that someone had been in my house. I assumed they'd be back, so I kept an eye on the place from my neighbor Dennis's house last night. I saw them enter my place: some punk with a shotgun and a woman with a crossbow. So I turned the tables on them. The woman took a shot at me. Her arrow grazed my scalp—my bullets grazed the center of her brain," said Morgan with a cocky smirk.

Vicki sat there with her mouth open. Then she finally asked, "Who were they?"

"We don't know. Prints aren't in the system. They had no ID. We're working on it. They're probably related to, or hired by, someone I put away sometime."

"What happened with that professor in Cambridge? Gil didn't say much."

Morgan groaned and waved his hand dismissively. As Gil had advocated, he had to sell it. So then he sneered and said, "It was just what I expected: lots of this hocus-pocus horseshit. He talked about all these weird supernatural theories and witchcraft. Bottom line, it was just a bunch of bookworm hogwash that has nothing to do with what's going on here."

"Did he think what was happening in Crestwood Lake was the work of some kind of cult?"

"He said it could be, but there's no way of knowing for sure. All in all, it was a waste of my frigging time."

Vicki looked like she was sold.

Morgan and Vicki began discussing other recent occurrences. She had heard about Father Mark's motorcycle accident and the disappearances of Neil Pasternak and Debbie Kurzmann. Morgan only shared the official version and was cautious not to reveal what he actually knew. In fact, he even curtailed some of the official information, such as the creature's photo in the Kurzmann case. He had to get past Thursday first. Then he and Vicki were going to discuss *a lot* of things. After a few more bourbons the conversation moved away from Crestwood Lake. Morgan threw out some preliminary ideas as a prelude to telling Vicki that he loved her.

"I think I'm ready to sell my house," said Morgan.

"Really?"

"Yeah, ya know, at first I couldn't because of the memories of Connie. And I just didn't feel like being bothered with it. It's such a hassle to sell a house, pack up all your stuff, move, and set up a new place. But I feel like I've reached a turning point, like I'm ready to start over somewhere. Even though it's going to provoke all sorts of memories, going through everything in the house, I've decided I need a fresh start."

"Where would you go?"

"I guess I'd stay here, although I have had thoughts about retiring somewhere warmer."

"Retiring?" exclaimed Vicki. "You wanna quit your job too?" Vicki took a long sip of her bourbon.

"I got twenty-nine years in. I don't know, I mean, I'm happy with my job, but part of me would like to retire and maybe see the world a bit, while I'm still young enough to enjoy it. Maybe with the right person. I've always wanted to see more of the West. I've never been to the Grand Canyon or Yellowstone Park. I want to see the Rockies."

"I want to go to Paris," said Vicki. "I've wanted to go there since I was a little girl. I want to stroll down the Champs-Élysées, go to the Louvre, take a boat ride on the Seine…oh, and the Eiffel Tower. I've always wanted to go to the top of the Eiffel Tower. I want to go to Paris so bad."

"I'll take you to Paris," blurted out Morgan. "We can do all those things. I mean, the French are nothing but a bunch of snobs, but I'll take ya."

Vicki looked at him quizzically and said, "*You'll* take me?"

"Yeah I'd…" Morgan realized the implications of what he just admitted. He thought of trying to backpedal, but he'd had enough dissembling for one night. So he looked her straight in the eyes and said, "Yes Vicki, I would take you to Paris. I would take you anywhere."

Vicki's eyes became teary. Then she turned away.

Morgan became perplexed. Were they good tears or bad tears? Was she not ready to hear that he had feelings for her? Had her ex traumatized her beyond repair? Should he pursue the issue or back off? Women and emotions! It was the only thing that Morgan was diffident about. So he just simply asked, "Vicki what's wrong?"

Vicki finished the bourbon in her glass, stood up, and wrapped her arms around herself. Only this time she wasn't cold. She struggled to contain the tears.

"Vicki, I'm sorry. Did I say something wrong?"

"No, No, No," she said, "It's not you, Butch. You don't know what I've been through. I can't make any big changes in my life right now. I'm not ready. And I…" Vicki stepped back, closed her eyes tightly, clenched her fists, and pressed her arms to her body.

"And you what?" probed Morgan.

"I…I…Butch…I'm just not handling what happened to me well. It's too late for me. Too much damage has been done…You don't know what I've been through! I can't just start over as if nothing ever happened. I still suffer with the choices I made in life. I still see his face in my head. I still hear him coming up the stairs at night. I still wake up sweating and screaming. I hate what he did to me! I hate what I became because of him! Oh if I could only go back in time. What I would give to be young again…to do it all over again."

Morgan didn't know what to do. He felt like holding her but was afraid of making it worse. So he just gently said, "I'm sorry if I upset you, Vicki."

Vicki approached Morgan, stroked her hand across his cheek, and said, "No, no, it's not your fault, Butch. I just have so much pain, and so much regret. I wish I could do it all over again. Maybe then I'd let you take me to Paris."

Morgan's mind was going in so many directions. The conversation with Vicki had clearly gotten out of control. He shouldn't have broached the issues he did, especially after how many drinks they had. Morgan didn't realize how tormented she was. He was two days away from a showdown with the Devil, and this was no time to open Vicki's wounds, or divulge his love for her. He had to get through the next couple of days without any emotional burdens, and a clear head. He had to put Vicki back together again and put this discussion on hold.

"Vicki, please…sit down. Let me talk to you."

Vicki retook her seat, and then reached for the bottle of bourbon, but Morgan stopped her.

"Hold off on the bourbon for now. Just listen to me for one minute."

Vicki looked at him wistfully through her weepy eyes.

"Vicki, I'm sorry if I stirred up any of your pain. You're the last person on this earth I want to hurt. Listen…there's something really big going down this week. It involves all the things that have been happening here in Crestwood Lake. I'm not at liberty right now to tell you what it is, but trust me, it's huge.

"I've got a lot to deal with right now, even though I would like to talk to you more about how you're doing. But I have to get through the next couple of days. So I was wondering…maybe this weekend, we could get together again and talk? I'll have a lot more to tell you then, and *I'm* definitely gonna need someone to talk to."

"Sure, no problem. Are you OK?" she asked.

"For the moment."

"Jesus, Butch, now I feel like a real shit. People tried to murder you just yesterday and I'm here bawling about crap that happened years ago. I'm so sorry."

"You have nothing to be sorry about. Just give me till the weekend. But I *do* need to talk to you some more, OK?"

"Of course, Butch."

They went on to chat about trivial things. Finally Morgan got ready to leave. Vicki walked him to the door and gave him a long embrace. Then she looked at him earnestly and said, "I wish I could go back in time."

Morgan replied, "Regrets are not for promoting grief. They're for learning about the changes we need to make in our lives, so our futures will be without regret."

Vicki twitched her head, opened her eyes wide and said, "That's pretty profound, Butch."

"I'll see you in the future—and I'm sure we won't regret it."

● ● ●

Morgan went home, checked on his house and packed a small suitcase. He grabbed his duffel bag of weapons and equipment, and then went to Gil's.

Gil answered the door smiling like a frat boy, greeting his roommate the morning after.

"So how was the big date?" Gil was practically drooling on himself.

"Don't be a douchebag," said Morgan as he walked through the doorway.

"C'mon, man, gimmie the dirt. What happened?"

Morgan sighed, rolled his eyes and sat down.

Gil pranced over and sat next to him, still smiling.

"What do you think I'm gonna say, Gil? That I went over Vicki's, she answered the door in a negligée fondling herself, and we boffed our brains out all evening?"

"Oh God!" exclaimed Gil. "*Please* tell me that's what happened!"

"You're worse than a dog in heat. Wipe the smile off your face because it was *not* that kind of evening."

"Sorry, man. What *did* happen?"

Morgan proceeded to tell Gil about how he indirectly told Vicki he loved her and she had a meltdown. He explained her trauma from her ex-husband was still painfully fresh. He described how he calmed her down and managed to postpone their conversation.

"You did the right thing, Butch. We don't even know if we're going to be alive in two days. First things first, then worry about Vicki."

"Do you think we'll be alive in two days?"

Gil took a long, deep breath and said, "I'm not sure."

Morgan felt a twinge of consternation. "You say that more like you think we won't than we will."

"Look, many individuals over the course of history have challenged the forces of evil. Some of them make it and some of them don't. Despite Aaronson's insights and Cassandra's spells, we have no guarantees. Priests have died performing exorcisms. White witches have been burned at the stake. People holier than us have been murdered by evildoers."

Morgan bristled and said, "I aint going down without a fight."

"I understand, but that may not be enough."

"Meaning what?"

"If we've learned anything in the last couple of days it's this: there are good and bad powers beyond our comprehension that ultimately control all of this. Just as Aaronson said, there's a balance of those powers, an enduring seesawing of victors. All of our plans and safeguards are merely weapons in a battle. They help, but they don't assure us of triumph. And even if we win, how do we know that sacrificing our lives isn't part of what's necessary to win?"

"So you think we're going to die?"

"I don't like our odds. For starters, Satan can't be defeated, only held at bay. And as for the coven, it's been in existence for three hundred years. What makes us think that the likes of you and me, a police officer and an old fart, can destroy them? We're not gods. We're not some spiritual being like a white witch. We're not even men of the cloth. Shit…my behavior alone would get me a front-row seat in hell. So do I think that two insignificant mortals such as you and me can kick Lucifer's ass and come out smelling like a French whorehouse? No, Butch, I don't."

Morgan stared at Gil for a moment and said, "I liked you better when you were in heat."

• • •

Morgan entered the police station Wednesday morning and was immediately accosted by Lieutenant Dougherty. "The mayor's here and he wants to see you immediately. He's really pissed that you dodged him yesterday."

"Good morning to you too, Jack."

"I'm just trying to give you a heads up."

"Where is he?"

"He's in your office."

"MY office?" exclaimed Morgan. "That son of a bitch. What else is going on?"

"You know Elmore Stinson, owns that small farm on the edge of town?"

"Yeah."

"Well someone went psycho on his property. Half of his animals were slaughtered and the other half are missing. Chickens, couple of goats, some pigs, a horse, even his goddamned dog."

Morgan opened his mouth to ask a question, but Dougherty quickly interrupted: "We don't know who. We don't have any leads yet; it was just called in a couple hours ago. It looks like someone, probably a few people, sneaked on to his farm in the middle of the night and killed the animals with large knives. Meanwhile, he and his entire family, wife and kids, are all sick. They were all vomiting this morning. The whole family went to the ER to be checked out. Things are getting weirder and weirder."

"Does the mayor know about this latest incident too?"

"Of course."

And then, just for appearances, Morgan said, "And I don't suppose there's anything new on the scumbags who tried to kill me?"

"Not at this time."

"All right. Let me get this bullshit with the mayor over with."

Morgan approached his office. There was Burrows, leaning his butt against Morgan's desk, legs stretched out straight and his arms folded across his chest. He looked ready for a fight.

"Would you mind getting your *ass* off my desk?" growled Morgan.

Burrows stood up, walked past Morgan, slammed his office door shut, spun around and growled back, "Would you mind telling me what the hell is going on in this town, and why you and your men can't seem to solve any of it? We've got an unprecedented string of murders, disappearances, fires…even animals being slaughtered, and you can't close one stinking case. What the hell are you doing?"

"What the hell am *I* doing?" Morgan said pointing at himself. "What the hell do you think I'm doing? I'm not the one sitting in his office all day, playing with himself, crawling out occasionally to kiss the citizens' asses, and bullshit them into voting for me again."

"I'm warning you, Butch—"

"I've got every man on the force working on these crimes. We've even got the state boys assisting us and nobody's turned up anything. We have scoured this town, questioned everyone, analyzed every crime scene, cross-referenced the state and federal databases, conducted stakeouts and increased patrols. I myself have been on duty virtually nonstop."

"Well clearly that isn't enough to—"

"And just to refresh your memory, Clyde…*I'm* one of the people they tried to kill. I don't see anyone creeping in your house at night trying to murder *you*. And you know why not? Because I have extra patrols, specifically canvassing your residence every day and night protecting your unappreciative ass. I'm also the one who had to manage a hostile town meeting because you don't have any fucking balls."

Burrows bristled and pointed at Morgan. "I am the *mayor*, and I have every right to know what's being done, and why there's no results. I have to answer to the people and you have to answer to ME, and YOU will show me some respect."

"Respect's a two-way street. How *dare* you come in here and ask me for a status report the way you have, as if we're not doing our jobs. You don't know the first thing about police work. You weren't even a bottom-feeding lawyer before you took office. All you did was own an auto dealership, throw some money around at fundraisers, and kiss enough ass to get elected. I've been doing this job for twenty-nine years."

Burrows snorted and said, "That's because you haven't had anything to do for twenty-nine years. Now that we have some real crimes, we get to see just how incompetent you are."

Morgan slowly approached Burrows until he was right in his face. You could see a glint of fear in Burrows's eyes.

"Now you listen to me, slime ball," said Morgan in a chillingly quiet voice. "This is my town and my police force. I was on the job when you were still wetting your bed. I don't give a *fuck* what office you bought your way into. You have no standing to question how I do my job the way you have. And I'm not going to take that crap from some spineless, swindling car hawker."

"I'll have your job!"

"Oh yeah?" trilled Morgan whimsically as he raised his eyebrows. "You think you can get enough council members to agree with that?"

"I'll do whatever it takes. You're finished. And you can kiss your pension goodbye too."

Morgan stared at Burrows with sheer contempt. Then he walked over to his filing cabinet, unlocked it, and retrieved a large brown envelope with a clasp. He opened the envelope and spilled the contents onto his desk: a dozen pictures of Burrows with a blonde, stockings-and-heels-clad prostitute.

Burrows's jaw dropped.

Morgan picked out one shot of the prostitute performing fellatio on Burrows. "This one's my favorite. I wonder if your wife would agree?"

"You bastard!"

Morgan got in his face again. "Oh I can be much more than that, Clyde. I can be your worst fucking nightmare. Because if you mess with my job, or my pension, it won't just be your wife receiving a copy of your little photo album. I'll make sure every citizen in Crestwood Lake sees it. And then after you're divorced, forced out of office, and totally disgraced…then I'll break every fucking bone in your body."

Burrows stared at the pictures again.

Morgan scooped up the photos and handed them to Burrows. "You can have these as a token of my affection. I've got multiple copies stored in more than one location with people I trust. Anything happens to me, they still go public."

Burrows was speechless.

"Now," said Morgan, extending his right hand toward the door, "you go back to playing with yourself, and I'll go back to doing my job and investigating the crime spree in this town."

Burrows gritted his teeth and headed straight out of Morgan's office.

● ● ●

That afternoon Morgan's neighbor Dennis heard his doorbell ring. He opened the door and was greeted by Karen Gardner holding a large vase of flowers.

"Hi! You're Dennis Norwood right?"

"Uh, yes, that's me."

"I'm Karen Gardner. I own the florist shop in town. I think we met once before. You were in my store last year sometime."

"Yeah, I think so."

"I have a delivery for you," said Karen with a big smile.

At first Dennis thought that maybe Morgan had sent them as a thank you, but then quickly realized that sending flowers, especially to a man, would not be Morgan's style. "From who?" he asked.

"I'm not sure. My assistant took the call. There's a card with the flowers. May I come in and set them down?"

"Sure." He ushered Karen in, eager to find out who his benefactor was.

Karen stepped into the foyer.

"You can put them right there on the coffee table in the living room," said Dennis.

Karen placed them on the table. Dennis walked over, grabbed the card taped to the side of the vase and opened it. It simply said:

WATCH YOUR BACK…

Dennis spun around, just in time to see Karen shove a long bladed knife into his lower abdomen. He let out a harsh shriek. Karen withdrew the knife. He clutched his body and fell back on the floor, blood flowing from his wound.

Karen kneeled over him, holding the bloody knife in her right hand. She had a maniacal look on her face and raging yellow eyes.

Dennis's heart raced, his breathing was labored. In-between breaths he wheezed and choked, grasping his wound with both hands.

Karen reached into her left pocket and removed a sprig of wormwood. She placed it on Dennis's chest and said, "We know you helped Captain Morgan murder two of our coven members. I'm here to avenge their deaths."

"What?" gasped Dennis, doing his best to feign ignorance.

"I think I'll eat your liver at our ceremony tomorrow," said Karen.

Dennis alternated between panting and groaning, his teeth clenched. He was beset by waves of pain. "What are you?" he moaned, looking into Karen's bright yellow eyes.

"I'm your redeemer," proclaimed Karen. "I am here to cleanse you of the sin you committed against my Master. The offering of your body parts to our ritual will be your restitution."

"What?" Karen plunged the knife into Dennis's heart. His body sharply contorted as blood spurted from his mouth. He quivered with his mouth agape, as if trying to scream, but all he could do was grunt: "ack…ack…ack…ack."

Karen's smile grew wider and her eyes shone brighter. The draining of Dennis's life seemed to energize hers.

She waited for his body to stop twitching…then she started extracting his organs.

• • •

That evening Morgan went to Gil's house to spend what would be, one way or another, his last night there. They had porterhouse steaks and salad for dinner. Morgan called Vicki to confirm their date for the weekend. They had a brief conversation. Vicki seemed oddly aloof.

They retired to Gil's living room where they reviewed their plans one last time. Morgan opened his duffel bag containing his arsenal. He removed his Smith and Wesson 9mm and the cleaning supplies. He withdrew his Ruger .357 from his holster and unloaded the ammo. He then proceeded to clean the two handguns. As he did so he told Gil about his interchange with the mayor. Gil was one of the people who had a copy of the photos.

With a twinkle is his eye Gil said, "I would have loved to see the look on Burrows's face when you spread those pictures over your desk."

"It was priceless," responded Morgan.

"How did you get them again? You know the madam at the cathouse, right?"

"Yeah. When you've been on the force as long as I have, you make a lot of connections. It's always wise to make the local house of ill repute your ally. I made sure the law never bothered them, and they provided me with incriminating evidence on all kinds of people. I save the photos just in case I ever need leverage with somebody."

"You're sure Burrows won't retaliate in some way?"

"No way. First of all, he has way too much to lose: his marriage, his job, his reputation. And second, that scummy little twerp doesn't have the balls to do anything. It's good that he knows what I got on him. I'll need him on my side after the stunt we're gonna pull tomorrow."

Morgan finished cleaning the guns and then reloaded them. He held up the 9mm and said to Gil, "This is going to be your toy for tomorrow's festivities. I'll have my shotgun and my magnum." Morgan pulled a few more objects out of his bag. He held up a beige colored rectangular block and said, "This is the plastic explosive, otherwise known as C-4. And these little babies are the stun grenades."

"Tell me about them again."

"They're not like a normal grenade, which is designed to project shrapnel. Stun grenades simply produce an incredibly loud boom and a blinding flash of light. Anyone in the immediate area will be disoriented, deaf, and blinded for a few seconds. We can't use a traditional grenade. If the shrapnel were to break the bottle of souls, spilling its contents on non-hallow ground, the jig would be up. Once we have the bottle in our possession, then we're gonna raise hell."

"What do you mean?"

"You'll see tomorrow," said Morgan with a devilish look.

Just then the phone rang. Gil looked at the caller ID. "It's Professor Aaronson." He picked up the phone. "Hello."

"Gil, it's Doug Aaronson."

"Hey it's good to hear from you. I'm here with Butch. We're going over our strategy for tomorrow."

"That's why I called. I wanted to see if the plan is still on, and if so, to wish you well.

"It is, and thank you. Boy, do I have stuff to tell you. We met an eight-hundred-year-old white witch: this woman who lives in town who Butch thought might be an evil witch. She was with the priest we talked about. The four of us are working together."

"How do you know she's a white witch?" asked Aaronson.

"We saw her disappear and reappear right before our eyes."

After a long pause Aaronson finally said, "But how do you know she's a white witch and not one of Satan's cohorts?"

"She took holy water from the church and claims to have dissolved a demon with it. Father Mark saw some of the water splash her with no ill effects." There was another long pause. "You there, Doug?"

"Yes. Is there anybody else with you beside the Captain?"

"No."

"Put me on speaker so the Captain can hear me too."

Gil turned to Morgan and said, "I'm putting him on speaker. He wants to talk to us both."

Morgan nodded.

"Hello, Captain."

"Hi, Professor. What's up?"

"Listen, about this woman who is supposedly a white witch. Just because holy water didn't affect her doesn't mean she's on your side."

"What are you talking about? I thought you said that holy water can kill a bad witch."

"Yes it can. But the problem is this: not everyone allied with Lucifer is a witch. A witch, meaning an evil witch, is someone who has bartered their soul to the Devil. But one can certainly conspire with the Devil without having traded their soul. He may have offered them something for their services, but that doesn't mean he made a contractual agreement with them involving the relinquishment of their soul. Even if this woman is a white witch, even if she has powers as Gil described, that doesn't mean she is not a secretive servant of Satan. She could be one of his agents without becoming an evil witch."

"Jesus Christ!" yelled Morgan. "If that's the case we're walking right into a trap!"

Aaronson continued: "I would proceed with extreme caution. I would proceed as if she, and even Father Mark for that matter, can't be fully trusted."

"They tried to Kill Father Mark by hitting him with a car while he was on his motorcycle," said Gil.

"Anything can be a ruse," replied Aaronson. "Look, all I'm saying is, you never know. Be careful, take every precaution, and assume anyone can be your enemy. Call me tomorrow night when this is over."

"Will do, Doug," said Gil. "Good night."

"Good night, gentlemen, and Godspeed."

"Now what the hell do we do?" barked Morgan.

"I'm not sure."

"What if," said Morgan, "we break into Grand Vin tonight? We steal the bottle and take it to some other church instead of St. Matthews?"

"It's too risky. Van Haden will probably be there and we can't over-power him. We'll never get the bottle."

"And what if Cassandra is working for him? She'll have told him about our plans. They'll be waiting to ambush us tomorrow."

"We have to stick with the plan," said Gil.

"Why?"

"Look at it this way: if Cassandra is a traitor, we're dead either way. Because that means that Van Haden and his entire coven know about us and our plans. They'll all be out to kill us. Without the bottle there's no way we can fight off an entire coven of witches and demons. If Cassandra is on our side, however, then our plan is still viable."

Morgan thought for a minute and reluctantly said, "I guess you're right, but I still don't like it. Based on your logic, Cassandra is the deciding factor in our destiny. I prefer to have my fate in my own hands."

"But it is. You could choose to withdraw…to not fight."

"That ain't happening," asserted Morgan. "I'm taking these pricks down if it's the last thing I ever do."

"Then your fate is in your own hands."

• • •

Halloween arrived. As a cop Morgan dreaded Halloween. Even in a small town the police were inundated with additional duties, such as extra patrols to monitor the trick-or-treaters. But that was only the beginning. They had to contend with assorted pranks, vandalism, drunk drivers, raucous parties, and the inevitable crackpots that Halloween always seemed to arouse. However, given recent events, fewer children would be trick-or-treating and more parents would be convoying the ones that were. This would ease the police's burden, but nevertheless, Morgan had the entire force on duty. He suspended all work on the ongoing investigations Halloween night. Lieutenant Dougherty and one other officer would man the station. Every other officer was going to be in the community, on foot or in a vehicle. Morgan told Dougherty that even he would be patrolling the town. This would provide a plausible excuse for his absence from the station.

Morgan again had to be careful as to how he conducted himself. After the phone call with Aaronson he was doubly paranoid. He kept hearing the professor's warning in his head: *assume anyone can be your enemy.* He thought before he did anything at the station, ensuring he acted as natural as possible.

Neil Pasternak's wife called, demanding to speak to Morgan. Obviously still distraught, she pressed Morgan for any information about her husband's disappearance. Morgan did his best to assure her of their efforts to find him. He felt guilty and painfully conflicted since he knew they never would. But she needed hope to deal with her pain.

One person Morgan didn't see all day was the mayor. Apparently he was keeping his distance. It was one less hassle to worry about on what was probably going to be the most monumental day of Morgan's life.

The day unfolded quieter than a normal Halloween. A few calls for vandalism and other juvenile related activity came in, but nothing more harrowing. Morgan expected chaos, but there were no deaths or suicides, no fires or explosions, and no serious accidents of any kind. *The calm before the storm*, Morgan thought to himself. He was itching to drive past Grand Vin, but didn't want to take any unnecessary chances. Maybe he'd ride by after nightfall.

Around six thirty Morgan ordered some takeout for himself, Lieutenant Dougherty and Edwards, the other officer assigned to the station that night. Feeling tense, Morgan ate by himself in his office. He hated the waiting. Whatever was going to happen—good or bad—he just wanted to get it over with.

The switchboard was unusually quiet. More than one patrolman had radioed in to say that almost no trick-or-treaters were left. Virtually all the parents who did allow their children to partake in the ritual limited them to the daylight hours.

Sometime after eight o'clock Morgan informed Dougherty that he was leaving to join the patrols for a few hours and then go home. Morgan got in his truck and took a brief cruise around the center of town, just to make a general reconnaissance. He decided to drive past Grand Vin. It was utterly dark: not a single light on in the store, or in the rooms above where Van Haden lurked. Then he drove past St. Matthews. As Father Mark promised, all the lights in the church were out. He could see a faint light inside the rectory. He assumed Father Mark and Cassandra were waiting there. He thought about driving past Vicki's, but was fearful of endangering her if anyone was following him. He might have run into the three witches who were currently descending on her house.

Morgan dialed Gil's cell phone, blocking his number from the caller ID. When Gil answered he hung up. That was the signal. Morgan drove to a secluded area on the opposite side of the brook that ran along the back of Grand Vin. It was about a hundred yards downstream from the store. At that spot the brook was only about ten feet across and shallow. It also contained a number of large rocks which allowed one to cross without getting wet. Trees lined each side of the stream.

Morgan parked his truck. He turned off the interior light so it would not illuminate when he opened the door to exit. His duffel bag was on the passenger seat, alongside his shotgun. He held his magnum in his right hand. The 9mm was in his belt. He waited, constantly looking around him with his night-vision goggles. No lights were on in the immediate vicinity, but distant streetlights imparted a faint luminescence. He turned off his cell phone and police walkie-talkie and left them on the seat.

Morgan heard sirens in the distance. As part of their plan, Morgan had given Gil a throw-away cell phone confiscated from a drug dealer. After getting Morgan's signal, Gil called 911 to report a fire on the opposite end of town. Headquarters would dispatch most of the patrol cars to it. It was a risky maneuver, but it nearly ensured that there would be no police in the immediate area of Grand Vin. The last thing Morgan needed was police interference with what he was about to do.

Morgan looked at his watch. Finally he saw Gil, a few minutes late of course, dressed in black, walking briskly toward his truck. Morgan holstered his magnum, tossed his goggles in the duffel bag, snatched the bag and shotgun, and got out of his truck. Gil approached.

"I'm thinking of having a sex change operation," said Morgan.

"What?" said Gil.

"Because maybe then you'd be on fucking time!"

Gil just rolled his eyes.

Morgan handed him the 9mm and said, "That's ready to shoot." He reached into the duffel bag and gave Gil a flashlight. Morgan slung the duffel bag over his shoulder and placed both hands on the shotgun. "Follow me quietly," he said.

Morgan wended his way down to the brook. He could just make out the outline of the rocks. As gracefully as his 270 pound frame would allow, he stepped from rock to rock, traversing the stream without incident. Gil followed easily. They walked up the embankment and stopped. Morgan scoped out their heading with the night vision goggles, but saw nothing. They proceeded upstream, using the trees for cover. They encountered no one.

They reached the back door of Grand Vin. The building remained dark. Morgan leaned his shotgun against the brick wall. He laid down his duffel bag, returned the goggles to it and withdrew sundry other items. He handed Gil a small penlight and instructed him to shine it between the deadbolt and the doorknob. Morgan then pressed the C-4 into the edge of the door. He inserted a blasting cap with a long fuse.

"Put away the penlight," said Morgan. "Have the regular flashlight and your pistol ready." Morgan slung the duffel bag back over his shoulder, grabbed his shotgun, and took a lighter out of his pocket. He lit the fuse and said, "Go!"

They ran around the side of the building. Morgan pulled a stun grenade out of his jacket pocket. The C-4 exploded. It was more powerful than Morgan expected. It blew the door right off its hinges. Morgan ran to the door as fast as he could and threw in the stun grenade. He and Gil stood on the side of the doorway outside the building holding their ears. The detonation was absolutely deafening, louder than the C-4, accompanied by an intense flash of light.

"Flashlight," said Morgan.

Gil ran in and scanned the room with his light. Morgan was next to him, ready with the shotgun. They were in the storeroom behind the sales floor. Morgan had another stun grenade ready. Gil found a light switch and flipped it on. Morgan spied the doorway leading to the counter on the sales floor. He couldn't see it from his angle, but next to the counter was the curio with the double magnum of Chateau Latour. Morgan hustled over to the doorway and threw another stun grenade out into the middle of the sales floor. It landed between the freestanding racks of wine. Gil and Morgan withdrew from the doorway, closed their eyes and held their ears. Another devastating explosion and blinding flash of light ensued. Most of the bottles in the racks adjacent to the stun grenade shattered from the shock wave. Wine and pieces of glass were all over the floor.

Morgan ran back to the doorway and behind the counter. He turned toward the curio. It was empty! "The bottle's not here!" he yelled to Gil.

"What?"

"It's not here," cried Morgan. "The cabinet's empty!"

Gil screamed! A searing pain sliced through his brain. Something grabbed him by the sides of his head and jolted him up into the air toward the ceiling. Gil dropped the 9mm and his flashlight.

It was Karen Gardner! She was behind Gil, holding him up in midair, compressing his skull with her hands. Her brilliant yellow eyes were fuming with rage as her long blonde hair flowed wildly about. She hissed and gritted her teeth.

"Butch, help! The pain!"

Morgan dropped the shotgun. It was impossible to shoot her with it, without also hitting Gil. He drew his magnum instead. But he couldn't get a clear shot. Karen used Gil as a shield, effortlessly darting and twisting him in any direction as they both levitated.

"Let him go or I swear I'll blow you away bitch!" shouted Morgan.

"I don't think so," said Karen.

"Look out!" hollered Gil.

Morgan felt a tremendous blow across his back, as if someone clobbered him with a refrigerator. He hit the floor so hard he was stunned for a few seconds—then he turned over.

Looming over him was a grotesque demon! His skin was gray and leathery. His long legs ended in hooves. His outstretched arms terminated in rows of long, black talons. His bald scalp was covered with disfiguring markings, some oozing blood. He had bright red eyes, and fangs. Morgan, still holding his magnum, fired twice into the demon's face. Nothing happened.

In an extremely deep voice the demon blared, "Your earthly firearms won't help you this time, Captain. Do you remember our first encounter?"

Morgan didn't respond. He was trying to think. With his magnum in his right hand he started crawling back across the floor on his elbows. The demon followed. Karen, still holding Gil by the head, cackled.

"I'm actually in your debt, Captain," said the demon. "When you killed me on the highway you allowed me to transform from a witch, into what I am now."

"You're the piece of shit I shot on 91?" asked Morgan, still elbowing away from the slowly approaching demon. Karen and Gil were now directly above him.

The demon furled his brow and bellowed, "And now I wish to express my gratitude."

"Mortimer," cried Karen to the demon, "castrate him first. I want to see the look on his face."

The demon raised his arm to strike, but let out a terrible howl! His trunk collapsed on his thighs as smoke and steam surged from his body. A putrid stench consumed the air. He dissolved right before Morgan's eyes.

Morgan looked up. Gil was holding an empty vial of holy water.

"NO!" screamed Karen.

Morgan instantly twisted around and shot Karen in one of her legs that was dangling between Gil's. As Karen and Gil plummeted to the ground, Morgan scrambled to his feet. The demon gasped his last. Gil rolled away from Karen—Morgan shot her in the stomach. Karen wailed! Blood streamed from her abdomen.

"Where's the bottle of souls?" demanded Morgan.

"Fuck you!" snarled Karen.

Morgan shot her in the other leg. She screamed, removing one hand from her stomach to hold her fresh wound.

Morgan looked at Gil. He was on his knees holding his head with a dazed look.

"Are you OK?"

Gil grunted, "I'll live."

Morgan turned his attention back to Karen.

"Let me explain to you how this works, bitch. Every time you don't answer my question I put another bullet in you. I've been told if you repent, you can still save yourself. So you either cooperate, or become my new ammo container."

Karen's eyes became an even brighter yellow, as blood vessels throbbed throughout her face. She cocked her head up and growled, "Go ahead and slay me, Captain. I will become a demon, and the first thing I'll do for my Master is torture you to death!"

"Is that so?" said Morgan in a nonchalant tone, raising his eyebrows.

Morgan reached into his pocket and removed a vial of holy water. He bit off the cork and spit it out. He held the bottle over Karen. A petrified look came over her face.

"One last chance. Where's the bottle?"

"You go to hell!"

"You first," retorted Morgan, as he splashed the water on her body.

Karen let out an inhuman squeal. She writhed and screamed, smoke emanating from all over her body. Her skin evaporated and her bones and organs liquefied. She didn't expel the same stench as the demon, but she was annihilated just the same. In less than a minute she was reduced to a smoldering pile of ooze.

Gil said, "We have to get to the church."

"Yeah. We have to alert Father Mark and Cassandra. Maybe she can use her powers to tell us where the bottle is."

"If she isn't one of them," replied Gil.

They were collecting their weapons and equipment when Gil commented, "If the bottle's not here, what were the witch and demon doing here?"

"I don't know. Van Haden lives upstairs. Maybe he always has some of his thugs guarding the place."

"Or maybe they knew we were coming."

"Either way, we have to get to the church," said Morgan. "If Father Mark and Cassandra are on our side they could be in danger. Let's get out of here before the police arrive. Someone had to hear the explosions."

On their way out the door Morgan stopped and said, "One more thing." He reached in his bag and pulled out two sticks of dynamite. They were taped together and had a conjoined fuse.

"Are you nuts?" asked Gil. "You're going to blow up the whole building?"

"Damn straight I am."

Gil started to warn Morgan about the possible collateral damage, but it was too late. Morgan lit the fuse and threw the dynamite through the doorway into the sales area.

"Run!" he shouted.

Morgan and Gil bolted along the stream. The blast was enormous. All the windows in the building blew out, debris was ejected in all directions, and a fireball erupted. Car alarms from vehicles peppered with projectiles started going off.

They were negotiating the rocks in the brook when Gil slipped and fell on his side in the foot-deep water. "Shit!" said Gil.

Morgan grabbed Gil's shirt by the armpit, "I gotcha," and pulled him up with one hand. "You OK?"

"Yeah," said Gil. "Let's go."

They continued across the rocks, ran to Morgan's truck, and got in. Huffing and puffing, they slowly regained their breath. Morgan started his pickup and sped away as fast as he could. Morgan noticed Gil staring at him with a shocked look on his face.

"What?" asked Morgan.

"You need some serious psycho-mental help, you know that?"

"Me?"

"Yeah you, ya frigging lunatic. What if an innocent passerby got hit with shrapnel? What if the fire gets out of control?"

"I had to take that chance. We might not be able to stop Van Haden. I had to at least destroy his base of operations. Plus, blowing up all the fancy wine is a bonus."

Gil just shook his head with his mouth open.

Morgan turned down a secluded side street.

"Where you going?" asked Gil

"I have to stay off the main roads. All the police and firemen know my truck."

After snaking his way through various side streets, Morgan turned toward St. Matthews. He killed his lights, shut off the engine and allowed the truck to silently roll to a stop along the curb. Morgan reloaded his magnum. Gil had the 9mm ready. Morgan retrieved a flashlight from his bag. He left the shotgun in the truck.

They approached the door of the rectory. The small light he had seen before was still on.

"Don't knock or ring the bell," said Morgan reaching for the doorknob. It was unlocked. He slowly opened the door. Morgan and Gil stepped inside. It appeared to be empty. They heard nothing. Morgan shined his flashlight in a few of the rooms, but no one was there.

"Maybe they're in the church," whispered Gil.

Morgan nodded. They went down a hallway and found a door that faced the church. Morgan opened it. They stepped into the left end of the sacristy. The sacristy was long and narrow, curving behind the altar, and spanning the entire width of the church. They couldn't see the far side. Near each end of the sacristy was an entrance to the altar.

"I don't think anyone's here," said Gil.

Morgan shined his flashlight on the wall. He found a panel with what appeared to be the main light switches for the church.

"Turn the lights on," said Gil. "We can't scour the entire church in the dark with flashlights. It's too risky. Someone could be waiting for us. Turn the lights on and flush'em out."

Morgan flipped all the switches, producing a series of loud clicks. The church lit up. Morgan and Gil charged into the left side of the altar, pistols brandished, and stopped dead in their tracks.

"Good evening, gentlemen," bellowed Van Haden. "We've been expecting you."

A roar erupted from the congregation. The pews were filled with witches and demons! At the far left corner of the altar was Van Haden standing in the pulpit. Clad in a black cape, he gleamed with a wicked smile. To his immediate left was Daniel Nye, the owner of the local hardware store, holding Father Mark, who had been severely beaten. He held the priest's arms behind his back. Next to them was the female demon who slaughtered Brian Delmore and Sharon O'Connell. It was Mary Pickford, the witch from Scalford, now a monstrous gorgon. In her right hand was the bottle of souls. In her left hand was Cassandra's head, hanging from its hair, leaking blood. Behind her were the racks of burning, red votive candles.

Morgan and Gil were aghast. They looked at the crowd. Half of them were witches. They still looked normal except for their yellow eyes. Many of them were wielding weapons: knives, swords, crossbows, and maces. Morgan knew most of them. They were people from Crestwood Lake. People he had known for many years: schoolteachers, merchants, nurses, tradesmen, a council member, and more than a few fellow policemen. They all glared at him as if *he* was the Devil incarnate.

The other half of the attendees were grotesque demons. No two looked alike, except for their fiery red eyes. They were different sizes and colors, each evincing revolting deformities: fangs, pointed ears, claws, tails, horns, etc. One had four arms. One had the head of a snake, another a bloody ram's head. One had insects crawling in and out of its orifices. One stood silently, enwrapped in a white shroud, with a black void for a face. Even the demon who slew Debbie Kurzmann was in attendance. He was wet and bedecked with algae. It was a cornucopia of the macabre. And they all glared at Morgan, most of them hissing, growling, biting, or waving their claws.

Morgan looked back at Father Mark. He was barely standing. His left eye was gone. Most of his teeth were shattered. Blood streamed from his broken nose and both of his ears. His broken finger was now missing.

"Was this what you were seeking, my dear Captain?" said Van Haden gesturing to the bottle in Mary Pickford's hand. She stared at Morgan, gritted her teeth and hissed.

"They ambushed us, Captain," muttered Father Mark. "They were already here when Cassandra and I entered the church. We didn't stand a chance. They took our holy water."

Van Haden snickered. "You idiot," he said to Morgan. "Did you really think we were that stupid? Did you really think I had no idea what you were up to? Do you think you're the first mortal in history to defy me? Do you have any idea what I'm going to do to you? DO YOU, CAPTAIN?"

Morgan just glared at him.

"I'm going to eat your testicles during our ceremony...while you're still alive!" said Van Haden, followed by a hearty laugh.

"They're holding their Halloween ceremony here in the church," whimpered Father Mark, "not in the woods."

"How dare you desecrate a church, you worthless fucking asshole," snarled Morgan.

Van Haden guffawed maniacally. "I know, it's wonderful! It's such a delightful twist! And it gets even better, Captain. Instead of you spilling the souls on hallowed ground, I'm going to drink the entire bottle on this hallowed ground! Tell him what that means Father."

Father Mark looked at Morgan with his remaining eye and said, "If he consumes the contents of the bottle, the souls within it can never be set free. They will be his for all eternity. Even the ones who wish to repent."

"I've never been so proud of myself!" proclaimed Van Haden with a crazed grin.

Father Mark looked at Van Haden and said, "Remember Lucifer, pride goeth before destruction, and a haughty spirit before a fall."

"You're so right," said Van Haden. "It is time for the fall." Van Haden turned toward the witch holding Father Mark and said, "Daniel, would you be kind enough to remove the priest's head?"

Daniel released Father Mark's right arm and drew a machete from his sheath. Father Mark suddenly elbowed him in the ribs. Daniel gasped and bent over. Mustering all the strength he had left, Father Mark threw himself at Mary Pickford, knocking the bottle and Cassandra's head out of her hands, and Mary into the racks of candles. Using his body weight to hold her against the flames, her raggedy, purple and black dress ignited like newspaper. In seconds she was enveloped in flames, shrieking in agonizing pain. The bottle rolled on the ground toward Morgan. Daniel swung his machete and decapitated Father Mark. Morgan leaped forward and grabbed the neck of the bottle with his left hand while still holding his magnum in his right. Smoked surged from Mary's body as the flames consumed her, reducing her to a heap of ashes. Someone in the congregation fired their crossbow at Morgan, but hit Gil in the left shoulder. Gil jerk-ed and grunted. Daniel started toward Morgan. Morgan pointed his gun at the bottle. Van Haden hollered "Stop!" holding his hands out to keep Daniel and the coven at bay. Then he yelled, "Lieutenant!"

Morgan was about to shoot the bottle, but then Vicki's voice shouted, "Butch, help me!" Lieutenant Dougherty emerged from the right side of the sacristy. He had Vicki by the hair, with his revolver jammed against her head. She was crying and flailing her arms. Dougherty walked her over until they were about eight feet from Morgan.

"Jack! You too?"

"That's right, *Cap-tain*," enunciated Dougherty scornfully. "Drop the bottle or I'll spray her fucking brains all over this church." Vicki whined and grimaced.

Van Haden started snickering again.

"You son of a bitch," snarled Morgan to Van Haden.

"You stupid fool!" retorted Van Haden. "You think we didn't know about your feelings for her either? Where do you keep your brains, Captain? In that fat ass of yours? Or maybe you don't have time to think, since you're so busy beating your chest and throwing your weight around." Van Haden beamed in complete satisfaction.

Morgan looked at Dougherty and said, "How could you Jack? I've known you almost thirty years. I trusted you."

"Yeah and for almost thirty years I had to play second fiddle to your bullshit. I deserved to be Captain more than you. But nooooo, they gave it to the almighty Morgan. Well I got news for you, *Cap-tain*: being pig-headed, overbearing, and contentious is no substitute for competency. So now you can kiss my ass, *Cap-tain*." Dougherty tightened his grip on Vicki's hair, causing her to yelp.

Morgan flinched.

"Go ahead, superman," said Dougherty, "see if I don't blow her brains out on your sanctimonious uniform. Now put the bottle down or she dies."

Van Haden's snicker intensified to a steady chuckle. "I love jealousy!" he proclaimed as he opened his arms to his followers and exulted.

Cries of approval swept over the crowd.

Morgan looked at Gil. He had dropped his gun and was now holding his bleeding shoulder with his right hand, the arrow sticking out from between his fingers. Gil had a panicked look on his face. "Don't do it, Butch," he said.

Morgan looked back at Dougherty. "OK," said Morgan, "OK...just don't hurt her." Morgan extended the bottle forward and then slowly downward toward the floor. He watched Dougherty's eyes. For a moment Dougherty followed the bottle and not Morgan...

Morgan fired...hitting Dougherty right in the mouth. The back half of his head exploded. He collapsed...dead before he hit the ground.

Morgan placed the bottle on the floor and went to reach for Vicki, but she grabbed the bottle and pulled back! Her eyes turned bright yellow as her hair became drier and wilder. She clutched the bottle's neck with one hand and wrapped her other arm around the base of the bottle, pressing it against her chest.

"NO!" yelled Morgan. "NO!"

Van Haden roared with laughter. The congregation cheered!

"Once again, you stupid fool!" said Van Haden.

"Vicki!" said Morgan, "Why? Why?"

"I told you before," cried Vicki. "You don't know what I've been through. You weren't the one who was brutalized every day of your life. You don't know my pain!"

"Pain is such a wonderful motivator," said Van Haden. "Wouldn't you agree, Captain? I never know which I love better: pain or jealousy!"

Gil looked at the congregation; they were getting restive. A few had moved closer.

"How long, Vicki?" asked Morgan.

"Not long after you took him away. Nine years ago. I swore I would never be a victim again." Twitching her jaw toward Van Haden she said, "He guaranteed me that no human being would ever harm me again. He gave me peace of mind."

"More than you ever gave her, Captain," said Van Haden with a cocky smile.

"Did he, Vicki?" said Morgan. "Because you didn't seem to have peace of mind the other night. You seemed to me to be full of regret: wishing you could be younger, wishing you could do it all over again, tortured by the fact that you can still hear him coming up the stairs. You still wake up sweating and screaming. Is *that* the peace of mind you're referring to?"

Vicki's eyes filled with tears.

"Don't listen to him Vicki," commanded Van Haden. "He doesn't know your pain."

"He's right," said Morgan. "I don't know your pain. But I do know that you're still *in pain*. He can't take away your pain," said Morgan pointing to the pulpit. "All you got for your soul was an illusion of security. You still suffer from the abuse. And now you have to live with the added regret of the deal you made—the blood by association that's now on your hands. And I *know* you feel that remorse."

Vicki completely burst into tears. "It's too late for me. I'm so sorry. I never meant to hurt you."

"I love you, Vicki."

"I love you too, Butch."

"You're making me sick!" said Van Haden. "I've had enough of this nauseating human weakness. Seize them!" he shouted to the coven.

The witches and the demons surged toward the altar.

"Vicki!" cried Morgan.

"Butch!" cried Gil watching the crowd descend on them.

"It's too late," said Vicki. "I'm so sorry."

Morgan pointed at Van Haden and screamed: "YOU GO TO HELL!"

Then he turned toward Vicki and fired.

His bullet pierced the bottle and then Vicki's heart. Vicki fell back. The bottle shattered, spilling its contents all over her body and then onto the church floor.

"NOOOOOO!" wailed Van Haden, gnashing his teeth and shaking his fists in fury. Flames erupted from his skull.

A barrage of white, wispy filaments burst from the wine, billowing and expanding in all directions. The soul of every witch and demon in the coven was released. A few ascended skyward and disappeared through the church's ceiling, and a few blazed toward the pews. But most fluttered momentarily before plunging straight down, in a chorus of shrill and painful cries.

One filament hovered above Vicki and then sank into her chest. Her torso lurched. She suddenly gasped—her eyes and mouth wide open. Morgan and Gil watched in amazement. The sickening yellow hue drained from her eyes. Their emerald radiance returned, only now more dazzling than before. The wound on her chest sealed over. Her hair turned lush and rich. Her wrinkles receded. Her skin became clearer and tighter. Her body, soul, and spirit, regenerated, returning to their former state, nine years ago.

Morgan and Gil quickly looked in every direction. Van Haden was gone, as was Father Mark's body, Cassandra's head, Dougherty's body, and the vile remains of Mary Pickford. The entire coven had vanished, except for a few bewildered and obviously penitential individuals. They ran to the painting of St. Michael, dropped to their knees and started praying.

Gil looked up at the painting. Its colors were now so vibrant it almost seemed alive. For a second he thought he saw St. Michael's left leg push the Devil's head into the ground. Above St. Michael's likeness appeared Father Mark and Cassandra from the waist up. They were smiling.

Gil franticly tapped Morgan on the shoulder, pointed his finger and said, "Look!"

Morgan gazed at the painting. Cassandra raised her hand, as if extending a blessing. Father Mark made the sign of the cross. Then their images faded. That's when Gil realized that the arrow in his shoulder had disappeared.

Vicki was still on her back and somewhat in shock. Morgan kneeled down and embraced her.

"I love you," he said.

"I love you too."

"Are you OK?" he asked.

"I…think…so."

"Now can I take you to Paris?" said Morgan with a radiant smile.

"Yes," said Vicki. "You can take me anywhere."

THE EPILOGUE

Morgan, Vicki and Gil sat in a corner table at Toby's, drinking and celebrating. Morgan had his arm around Vicki. It warmed his heart to be able to freely show his affection for her.

Gil was completely shit-faced.

"He had the hots for you for a long time," said Gil, leaning on his elbows, pointing at Vicki, and of course, referring to Morgan.

Vicki blushed. Morgan rolled his eyes and shook his head with a smile. Normally, this would have been the point in the conversation where he would have told Gil to stop being a douchebag. But he was in such a good mood that Gil could get away with anything. Well, almost anything.

"I kinda knew," said Vicki averting her gaze, and then furtively grinning at Morgan. Morgan smiled even wider and pulled her in closer.

Gil took a long sip of his rye and asked, "So did you guys do it yet?"

Now Vicki really blushed.

"All right, all right that's enough," said Morgan raising his hands.

"What?" said Gil innocently with a dumb look on his face.

"Why don't you go to the bathroom and get a *grip* on yourself," quipped Morgan.

"Good idea," responded Gil. "Maybe I'll use both hands and go on a double date!"

Vicki and Morgan burst into laughter.

"Gil, you're a piece of work," said Morgan

"That's what my third wife used to say. Or was it the second? Yeah, the second. Used to nag me about my drinking all the time too. She'd say, 'I thought you were cutting down on the booze?' I'd say, I am…there's ice in the glass!'"

"Awwww, she was probably concerned for your health," said Vicki. "And the money. Do you know how much money I've seen people blow at the bar over the years? Not that I should talk. Lord knows I'm not completely innocent."

"Let me tell you something," said Gil. "Over the course of my life I probably spent eighty-five percent of my money on booze, women, a little pot, and general carousing."

"And the rest?" asked Vicki.

"The other fifteen percent I pissed away!"

Vicki chuckled. Morgan shook his head again.

"Oh," said Gil, "I spoke to Aaronson again the other day. He's still ecstatic. He keeps saying he wants us to go see him again—practically begged me. I already told him all the details, but he wants to chat in person—wants information for his studies. We should all plan a date to go visit him."

"Of course," replied Morgan. "We will."

"Not to change the subject," said Vicki looking at Morgan, "but on a more serious note…how are you doing with all the questions being raised about the disappearance of so many townsfolk?"

"I just act as bewildered as everyone else. Once again I have to go through the motions like I'm clueless. Investigations are ongoing, numerous authorities are conducting inquiries. I just go with the flow. The one good thing is, now that all the pandemonium has stopped, there's somewhat less pressure on me. In fact, a lot of individuals are attributing all the recent chaos to the people who have vanished. Little do they know that they're mostly right."

Morgan took a sip of his drink. "I made Edwards my new lieutenant. At least I know he's clean. The diocese sent some new priest to take over St. Matthews. The town removed the remaining debris from Grand Vin. Don't know what they'll do with the property. I'm assuming Van Haden won't be showing his face. I guess the town will ultimately appropriate it. Oh, and speaking of not showing his face, the mayor is still keeping his distance from me, which suits me just fine. I just can't wait for everything else to settle down."

"It will," said Gil. "And I'll tell you why. Because people.will eventually forget about it. It'll be this *big mystery* [Gil widened his eyes and waved his hands], but it will ultimately settle down and people will go on with their lives. Especially if there are no more murders, or animals being slaughtered or any other crazy shit."

"I suppose you're right," said Morgan. "But what if it starts up again?"

"What do you mean?" said Vicki.

"Well, the Scalford Puritans thought they cleaned house—started a brand new community. But eventually evil returned. What makes us think it couldn't happen here again?"

"Because we kicked their ass!" said Gil like a wild-eyed cheerleader, followed by another swig.

"Did we?" questioned Morgan. "Or was Van Haden responsible for his own undoing? Ya know, Father Mark was right: pride goes before the fall. The only reason we defeated Van Haden was because of his pride. He didn't just want to win—he wanted to rub everybody's face in it: mine, the church's, the town's, maybe even God's. He knew what we were up to. He could have taken his coven and the bottle into the woods and drank it there—game over, we're dead. But no—he had to have his ritual in the church just for spite. And therein lies his weakness. His pride allowed him to be vulnerable by bringing the bottle onto hallowed ground. That gave us a chance. Even an evil as powerful as he, still has its fatal flaws."

"OK, that's enough of that shit," slurred Gil. "This is supposed to be a celebration."

"I agree," said Vicki firmly, raising her glass.

"You're right, I'm sorry," said Morgan.

"You need to drink more," said Gil as he pointed a slightly trembling finger at Morgan. "Unless you guys are gonna do it tonight, then you better not." Gil smiled like he was getting a lap dance.

Morgan looked at Vicki and said, "Do you have any girlfriends you could fix him up with? I'm afraid he's gonna start humping people's legs."

Vicki cocked her head, looked at Gil and said, "I know I'm going to be sorry that I asked this...but what's your type?"

"Anything with a skirt and a pulse," said Morgan.

"What can I say," remarked Gil, "I'm a true philogynist."

"Philogynist?" said Vicki.

"A lover of women," answered Gil.

"Sure you don't mean philanderer?" said Morgan

The three of them laughed.

Gil raised his glass and proclaimed, "I want to propose a toast."

Morgan and Vicki raised their glasses.

"To my two best friends and their love. May you have many years to cherish each other."

"Hear, hear," said Vicki.

"Thank you, Gil," said Morgan.

They all clinked their glasses and sipped.

Gil placed his glass on the table, pointed at Vicki and said:

"Now about those girlfriends of yours..."

• • •

In a cold, dank, candlelit, subterranean chamber, far below the bottom of Crestwood Lake, Goog poured two glasses of wine.

"This is Musigny," Van Haden said. "It's one of the top Grands Crus of Burgundy. This is the 1713, one of my favorite years."

"1713?" said his guest. "And it's still good?"

"Oh yes. I assure you, wines from my collection do not age beyond their peak."

"How did you come by a bottle of the 1713?"

"The family who owned the vineyard at the time, the Bouhiers... were...shall we say, associates of mine."

They sipped the wine. Van Haden briefly closed his eyes and hummed in satisfaction.

"Very good," said the man.

They sat in two of three French bergère chairs, ornately upholstered in blue and gold, with a round, walnut, single-pedestal table between them. On the center of the table was a flambeau with a large, blood-red candle. It cast an unearthly light upon the room.

"So," began Van Haden, "I assume it is now clear to you why I insisted you maintain possession of your soul until now."

"Yes."

Van Haden leaned forward. "Or else it would have perished with all the others! This is why I am discriminating about who can become a witch, and when. You can't just casually barter with me at will. And if it wasn't for my discernment, your soul would be rotting in the bowels of hell as we speak."

"I understand, sir."

"Master!" roared Van Haden, springing forward and seizing his throat. The man felt a powerful jolt and lurched. A surge went through the center of his body as Van Haden extricated his soul. Still clutching the man's throat he said, "From this moment on I am your master and you will address me as such. Do you understand?"

"Yes, Master," he said, choking out the words.

"You owe me your life!"

"Yes, Master."

Van Haden released his grip and sat back in his chair. "Drink the wine," he commanded. His newly christened proselyte nervously took a sip.

"Our contract is now initiated." Van Haden stared at him for a moment. "Did you notice the slab in the other room?"

Still a little unsettled, the man hesitated.

"The room with the torches on the walls," said Van Haden raising his voice.

"Yes, my Master. I saw it when we arrived."

"If you obey, if you do not fail, if you do NOT incur my wrath, I will allow you to evolve into a demon someday. On that slab you will make your final transition. Do you understand?"

"Yes...yes...my Master," said the new warlock, vibrating his head up and down.

"If, however, you disappoint me, your suffering will know no bounds. Are we crystal clear on this point?"

"Yes, Master," he repeated, continuing to nervously nod his head.

Van Haden looked at Goog and said, "Bring him in."

Goog turned and withdrew into a black passage.

Turning his attention back to his new convert Van Haden said, "I want this town back. We have much work to do. We are going to rebuild the coven."

"Of course, Master. I will do whatever is necessary. But, Master, please tell me I will get to kill Butch Morgan."

Van Haden smiled. "He will die a gut-wrenching, terrible death. But first he must suffer. We MUST make him pay—him and Vicki Larson."

The warlock snickered in agreement.

Footsteps approached. Goog returned with another man. He was tall, sported a salt-and-pepper crew cut, and looked like he was in his late forties. The warlock vaguely recognized him. Goog topped off Van Haden's wine, poured another glass for the new attendee, and then retreated. The man sat in the third chair and took a sip of his wine.

Van Haden looked at the first warlock and said, "I am pairing you with another new member to our coven. This is Derrick Larson. He already knows who you are."

The first warlock shook his hand and said, "Derrick Larson? Weren't you married to Vicki?"

"I was...until that goddamned cop put me away. I'm gonna kill them both."

"I want a piece of him too," said the first warlock.

"Shut up! Both of you!" said Van Haden.

The two men flinched.

"The two of you will work together to exact your vengeance. Is that clear?"

They both immediately nodded yes.

Van Haden continued: "You will abduct the Captain and Vicki and bring them here to me. And as they're chained to my dungeon wall, you will grant them both a slow and agonizing death, as each one watches the other suffer. You can torture them to your heart's delight."

"I look forward to it," said Derrick Larson.

"How wonderfully evil!" said Clyde Burrows.

Made in the USA
Columbia, SC
07 October 2017